The
MORNING
RIDES
BEHIND US

Also by Tariq Goddard

Homage to a Firing Squad
Dynamo

The
MORNING
RIDES
BEHIND US

TARIQ GODDARD

SCEPTRE

First published in Great Britain in 2005 by Hodder and Stoughton
A division of Hodder Headline

A Sceptre Book

1 3 5 7 9 10 8 6 4 2

A CIP catalogue record for this title is
available from the British Library

ISBN 0 340 83201 0

Typeset in Monotype Sabon by
Palimpsest Book Production Limited, Polmont, Stirlingshire

Printed and bound by
Clays Ltd, St Ives plc

Hodder Headline's policy is to use papers that are natural,
renewable and recyclable products and made from wood grown
in sustainable forests. The logging and manufacturing processes
are expected to conform to the environmental regulations
of the country of origin.

Hodder and Stoughton Ltd
A division of Hodder Headline
338 Euston Road
London NW1 3BH

To Lucy

Then I will show you where the Iron Crosses grow . . .

Sgt Steiner in *Cross of Iron*

We fight rather to keep something alive than in expectation that anything will triumph.

T.S. Eliot

PROLOGUE

The New Forest, Remembrance Sunday, 1946

Moat rode his bike straight into the telegraph post and died instantly. There was no chance of any other outcome because of the type of man Moat was, raw and direct in his emotions and blind to all alternatives once his mind had been made up. Lining his bike up on the small mound of earth facing the telegraph post, Moat turned and gazed over the forest for one last time.

His lips tightened. The weather was fresher than he had expected and the light moisture in the air reminded him of waking up on the roof of his tank. It was strange that he should never have noticed before how beautiful and serene daybreak was ... well, what of it? It was too late for sightseeing now.

Through the shimmering flecks of sunlight, Moat could make out the giant chimneys of the Fox Brandy Chocolate plant, his place of employment for the past year. If he had been permitted to choose between punching the clock there one more morning, or close combat with the Herman Goring Division, the fat German's boys would have won hands down every time; but that particular battle was over now. Moat threw a mock salute at a nearby cluster of pines and threw off his jacket.

He kicked the pedal on his Triumph, closed his grip around its handles like they were the neck of his wife and felt the engine roar with power. In seconds the machine was passing over ground he had loved, moving faster than his last thoughts ever could. He died like a war pig.

1
THE FUNERAL

One week later

M rs Moat had led her life with the daring of a village hall preparing for a jumble sale, or so thought Mark Polly, the only member of T Squadron to be invited to her funeral. Moat's inglorious remains had been secretly dispatched to Valhalla a few hours earlier; the fact that he was his wife's murderer made a joint funeral undesirable for both sides of the family. Mark Polly, for his part, had always felt a lingering sympathy for the late Mrs Moat, her timidity, obliging nature and obsessive housekeeping sitting at odds with her husband's mental instability and penchant for whores. Of course, Polly knew there was more to his old comrade-in-arms than vice and anger, but given Barbara Moat's sudden end at only twenty-nine, it would be this, and not the whole truth, that the town's opinion makers would accept as their 'official' version.

Moat had rarely done himself any favours when it came to public relations, and there would be few who would now care whether a man who had strangled his wife and then killed himself, was also a good chap to talk cricket and down pints with, Polly reflected.

Nor would anyone actually want to hear how Barbara Moat preferred to lock herself in her kitchen rather than listen to her husband talk, drunk or sober, about his war experiences and fear of failure. Perhaps she had good reason to be scared of him, but fear had always been her way. It was curious that the one moment of her life that had not been governed by excessive caution was also the most significant: her decision to choose

Moat as her husband. Her remaining time with him had been a frustrated attempt to return to type.

Polly knew, though, that none of these subtleties carried any weight after an act like murder, and in any case it did not help that Moat had never had any patience with his own predicament. His need to be patient disgusted him and Moat was completely at one with those who rebuked him as an unhinged weakling incapable of carrying his own water. Polly had to admit that he did not have any answers to these rebukes, and kept his mouth shut as others denigrated the memory of his dead friend. This was in stark contrast to the rest of T Squadron who did not have any answers either but preferred to keep their mouths open and answering back – which almost certainly explained why Polly was the only one of their number to be invited to the funeral.

Moat's personal kindness, at least to his friends if not to his wife, had been legendary and the squadron had wanted to be in the church and show what Moat's life had meant to them. That public opinion had prevented them from doing so showed that, even in a community as used to death as Grumwood, there were still limits. Polly put down his hymn sheet, which he had hardly looked at, and knelt on the sharp wooden pew, its splintered base pressing against the old tweed that covered his knees.

'Our Father, which art in heaven.'

Many men had come back strangers to their wives after the war; Moat was no different in that. What *was* strange and possibly unique to the man was not the campaigns he had served in but the intensely personal way in which he had experienced them. It was obvious that World War Two had been no aberration for Moat, rather an epiphanic insight into how life worked. Perhaps he was, as his medical officer had concluded after six months of exhaustive examinations, a psychopath. After all, why had he, a whole year after the war ended, still insisted on his wife hiding their carving knives in the garden?

Moat had been a tank-man, not a knife-fighter, and it was from details like this that the town had decided that Moat's derangement was caused by something more sinister than mere combat experience.

'. . . and lead us not into temptation.'

Polly's bottom lip trembled slightly, as it did whenever he heard something he liked. It felt wildly appropriate that the prayer his civilisation was founded on should take for granted the fact that man could not resist temptation.

Polly looked around to see if anyone else had shared the same thought and his eyes settled on the olive-green beret of a small girl in an adjoining pew. Sensing his gaze, she smiled and lifted her head. There had always been something about the colour green, even before he had stepped into uniform, that had transfixed Polly; all his fixations following this vague pattern, leading him on like clouds trailing shadows.

Mark Polly was by far the gentlest, and most physically beautiful veteran of T squadron. Had convention allowed it his cropped yellow hair would have looked better worn long, and his large eyes and arrowhead cheekbones reminded the ladies of Grumwood of an angel, lost on its way to heaven. Aside from his slightly aged stoop, a feature shared by all men who had spent their war years sat in tanks, his only blemish was an oceanic pink scar splattered over the left-hand side of his face, a permanent reminder of his ascent from a boiling tank during the last hours of the Battle of Caen.

When war had broken out in 1939, there were many who doubted Mark Polly's suitability for active service, and suppressed their fears as he lined up with the rest of his friends to enlist in the Bovington Tank Regiment. There was never any doubt, in the minds of Grumwood's inhabitants, that their town contained the right amount of suicidals, glory hunters and misfits to make a decent job out of waging war on the Germans, but it was clear to even the least perceptive that Mark Polly was not this type of boy. For a start, everyone liked him. Lacking a vicious bone in his body meant that Polly was probably the only one of the town's under-twenty-ones to never have joined a fist fight or given anyone cause to look at him angrily, let alone actually hit him. Unlike many young men who evoked no strong feelings, Polly was loved by girls and boys alike, and duly learnt to love a great many of them back. His decision to volunteer for the Tank Corps, then, was not motivated by any great desire to teach Hitler a lesson, or even to prove himself brave in his own eyes, but to stay in with his pals lest they discover new experiences without him. To everyone's amazement, not least his friends', Polly had acquitted himself well under fire, keeping his nerve behind the controls of a Churchill mark II tank, and survived every major armoured engagement of the war with distinction. This good war record, combined with the sympathy his facial disfigurement aroused in the women of the town, meant that Polly enjoyed a goodwill conspicuously withheld from his other, more warlike, comrades.

In contrast to many of the men who had fought in the great land battles of World War Two, and returned to boredom, incomprehension and poverty, there was no belligerent swagger about Polly, nor any outward sign that he had given up on a country he no longer considered worth saving. This was not to say that he was any less proud or bitter than the other men he had served alongside, but whereas they wore their anger as badges of honour the changes in Polly had been subtle and slow. Most noticeably, he had lost his interest in being chased by girls, and in spending time in the company of women in general. He had also grown more withdrawn and alarmingly distant when asked even the simplest of questions and, most disconcertingly, there was now an impatient dismissiveness about him, which was most apparent in his dealings with the town's authority figures, their families and their wives.

'Let us now remember together, on this day, the life of our dear departed, Barbara Moat.'

Polly's lip curled. It was difficult to work out who he hated the most, the lying bastard of a vicar with his line in bullshit sermons, the surviving members of Moat's family feigning tears by the lectern, or Barbara Moat's bitch of a sister, who had not stopped giving him the evil eye throughout the service.

'And she enjoyed her bingo, did Barbara, yes, there's no doubt that she enjoyed her bingo . . .'

The vicar was struggling to find a unique selling point for a life he had largely ignored, and was as usual resorting to last straws in the place of opening gambits. No doubt, at the end of the funeral, most of the mourners would describe the sermon as their favourite part of the service, Polly mused bitterly.

'But that was the exact quality that most of us will always remember about Barbara, and the very thing we shouldn't be scared of talking about now that she's gone and is no longer with us, yes the very thing . . .' the vicar coughed into his hand to buy a little time '. . . yes, and the quality I refer to is the very thing that made our Barbara the woman she was. I think we all remember that Barbara always liked a little flutter and was never scared of taking a risk when the occasion called for it. Whether it was at the bingo or . . . at . . . fetes. Rides at fetes, be they the big wheel, or her very own favourite, the may pole . . .'

If Polly's hatred for Morris Much, the vicar of Grumwood, had to be measured on a scale of one to ten, it would probably register at about nine. Although picking one thing he despised about Much over any of the other aspects was an exercise that bordered on the arbitrary, Polly would have to settle on, at least for the moment, the way the university-educated barrister tried to imitate the local diction and intonation when addressing his parishioners. This would not have been so bad had Polly trusted Much's sincerity as a servant of the Church of England, or even as a man of God, but neither Polly nor anyone else did, allowing Much to interpret this as evidence of small-town prejudice.

'Fetes and bingo, games and risks, all part of life and all part of death . . .'

Much was a small fawning man of about five feet five, with large white bugger-grip sideboards and a tight cassock that clung to his body like a cocktail dress. He was a man of moderate temper, but strange desires, who only really became angry when his parishioners failed to understand his sermons. He had spent the war years attempting to seduce widows, pensioners and little girls, with varying degrees of success, and his attentions had now turned to his curate, Natalie Brookes, a borderline mental defective whom he had kidnapped on holiday in Jersey.

'So let us not be scared to evoke Barbara's memory now that she has gone, let us rather celebrate her life for what it was, a wonderful and joyous journey . . .'

Polly grimaced and tried to control the shaking he felt just under his forearms. Ever since he had come back from France this problem had worsened and it was only in the last few months that he had been able to understand its nature and source.

He could hear two voices. One had always been there, hiding but never quite going away, scared of what it should become if ever Polly spoke in its name. This was the voice of Polly's true desires. The other voice Polly knew only too well; it was the voice he heard whenever he opened his mouth, quiet enough to offer comfort and to be talked over by others. It had taken shrapnel, splintering trees and partial deafness in one ear to change this, both voices evolving from a whisper into a roar; and now that he could hear them, he wished the shellfire would start again and pound them into silence.

Polly's own improvised and highly unscientific method of ignoring his voices fell some way short of achieving this goal.

'I'm the story of two voices, one that I hear and the other that I am,' he mumbled inaudibly, his head bent to one side in the hope that no one could hear him. This improbable mantra was one he had learnt years earlier from his sister, as a spell to scare off things that did not exist. Having saved him from countless witches, wizards and evil dwarves, it was a line Polly had continued to recite in adult life as a way of combating fear. As such, it was the only way he knew of steadying the shaking without having to literally tie his arms together.

'Mark, are you all right, sweetie?' Glenda Heathen touched his arm softly, her large green eyes spinning in and out of their sockets like yoyos released from strings. 'Can you hear me, Mark?'

Her dress, a light flowery concoction stitched together from an eiderdown, rolled off her shoulders, revealing her cooking-apple breasts which heaved up and down like the anxious frowns on her face. She was, in every way, a woman of movement.

'Mark . . .'

The exaggerated blast of the organ saved Polly from explaining himself to this most understanding of friends, and Glenda, tingling with the upsurge of emotion she always felt in church, consoled herself by squeezing Polly's shaking hand and stroking his trembling leg. In front of them Morris Much pulled at his beard to signal the start of the short march to the cemetery, and with clumsy solemnity the pall-bearers lifted the coffin and began their procession down the aisle.

'What are they doing now? Are we expected to follow them?' asked Glenda Heathen unthinkingly. 'Funerals aren't one of my strong points and I wouldn't want anyone to think I was being rude . . . though God knows, I've been to enough of them these last few years,' she added.

'They'll probably put the coffin in that hole over there, the one all those awful people are traipsing towards,' replied Vivien Ross, ever aware of her role as Grumwood's most embittered war widow, 'but I shouldn't worry about that or what *they* think, if I were you – people like them have an incredible ability to absorb tragedy and carry on as before. I've seen them do it.

Mark, light my cigarette,' she ordered, as was her wont when addressing anyone of an inferior social rank.

Polly reached into his overcoat for the matches and, careful to avoid knocking Ross's cigarette holder out of her gloved hand, succeeded in his third attempt to light the Pall Mall. Ross drew her head away, as if offended by something blatantly obvious, and blew a line of smoke in the direction of the mourners. Her ailing father, Lord Ross of Breck, was once the wealthiest man in Grumwood and, despite the downturn in his fortunes, and the rise of the chocolate factory, was still the best respected. Nonetheless he was not a happy man or, for all his money, the father of a happy daughter. Despite his most strenuous efforts he had never been able to produce a son, leaving his only daughter, Vivien, as his sole heir. The loss of her husband and his beloved son-in-law, 'Lucky' Jack Sceptre, in the Battle of Caen had been an irrevocable blow for them both, though neither was open enough to admit it, preferring instead to hide behind studied flippancy and pride. The brave young tank commander had won his Victoria Cross leading a charge through deadly enemy crossfire during the closing stages of the battle. The very same engagement his batman, Mark Polly, who, positioned slightly lower in the tank and enjoying better access to the driver's hatch, had survived. A fact not lost on Polly but never mentioned or even considered by Vivien Ross who, despite several unpleasant tics, found apportioning blame a tiresome and lower-middle-class quality.

'So neither of you would mind if I just stayed over here? I'm not sure I want to see a coffin being lowered into the ground,' said Glenda, eyeing the convoy of mourners with caution. 'I mean, it's so depressing, don't you think?'

'I can't speak on behalf of the ever obliging Master Polly, but nothing in heaven or earth would induce me to stand over the grave of another dead soldier, or the grave of his wife for that matter,' Vivien snapped, flicking a line of ash at a nearby sparrow.

She glanced over at Polly who stood dumbly to attention. 'What do you say, Mark Polly?'

'I don't know really . . .' Polly paused, aware that he began his sentences like this far too often. 'I don't think her sister or any of that family care for me too much, what with me being Moat's old pal and all.'

Vivien gave out a short laugh, which reminded Polly of a tyre bursting. 'Don't care for *you*, you say! What the devil gives them the right to not care for you! There isn't a single man or woman among them who's earned the right to have an opinion on any subject I can think of.'

Vivien Ross was not a conventionally attractive woman. Her narrow face was long and runner-bean like, and her frail body, sculpted as if from sticks, could barely be detected under her father's old hunting jacket. Polly had often tried to imagine her naked – without success – and had gradually come to under-stand that, unlike so many of the local girls, Vivien Ross's beauty owed nothing to softness or incompletion. Her formidable appearance arose from a surer footing than mere prettiness, projecting a defiant and feral spikiness that few men were easily drawn to. This was not to say that Polly did not suspect her of having a vulnerable interior, just that it did not really matter to her if she did, as her lack of sensuality and cultivation of pain were qualities she had chosen, rather than ailments she had ended up with.

'Thinking again, Mark?' Vivien loosened the knot of her scarf playfully, smiling as she did so, the gesture occurring easily and therefore untypically for her. Her pale neck, so often flung back whenever she was hysterically bored, seemed to glisten in the harsh sunlight, temporarily blinding Polly, who preferred to observe Ross from a distance. Even her flint-like nose, which from afar seemed like a small hunting weapon, appeared more like a beak close up, designed to puncture and kill, rather than an organ a woman could smell flowers through.

Unlike most of the redheads Polly knew, Vivien's face was deceptively plain and unfreckled, and her hair was parted in the middle and worn straight like a schoolgirl's. Her conservative taste in clothes, in taunting contrast to her character which was anything but, exaggerated her apparent Puritanism and disdain for adornment, whilst bringing more attention to her lively face. Polly especially liked the way her mouth always opened whenever she saw him, whether she chose to speak or not, as a pike's would when waiting for food to float past its lips. He did not ask himself whether this involuntary gesture should mean anything, for like everything Polly valued, it was enough that it happened at all.

'It's no wonder the poor bastards enjoy funerals so much when you think of what they've got to look forward to tomorrow,' Polly said, perhaps keen to demonstrate his new-found cynicism in front of Ross.

'I wish you wouldn't talk that way, at least not around me, Mark; it really doesn't suit you.'

'Mark isn't a boy, you know, Vivien,' said Glenda, springing to his defence, her hand rising to her hip good-naturedly. 'I'm sure he was up against a lot worse than bad language and you putting him down for his opinions, when he was in France with the rest of the lads.'

Vivien rolled her eyes and smiled. 'I wonder where all our ex-servicemen would be without you to protect them, you benevolent witch.'

Glenda Heathen was the closest thing Vivien Ross had to a friend in Grumwood. They were born within a day of each other and, judged by the standards of the town, were considered to be too clever by half, possibly a little mad and certainly unfit for marriage, but that was where the similarities ended. Glenda Heathen had moved to Grumwood from the naval academy at Spamshingle soon after the outbreak of war. Her family, a dissolute collection of Irish tinkers, had camped in the New Forest for as long as anyone could remember, but little was known about

Glenda herself except for the fact that she had been dishonourably discharged from the Wrens for an offence that had remained obscure. Once settled in Grumwood she had spent most of the war in a small huntsman's cottage on the edge of the Ross's estate that her brother had won for her in a game of cards, keeping bees and selling honey. When not engaged in this, or in the concoction of herbal remedies and other potions, Glenda had thrown herself into volunteer work at the military hospital in Southcrawl where, according to the authorities that expelled her, she had spent the better part of her time 'understanding' soldiers in a way that did not involve the administration of medicine. For the inhabitants of Grumwood she was an exotic but suspect wildflower, wonderful for gossip and unquestionably sweet (which was more than they could say for the 'respectable' Vivien Ross) but nonetheless an outsider and therefore a threat. If this was so, Glenda was not a threat that Vivien feared greatly. Charmed by this strange and self-educated woman's love of Lewis Carroll and Edward Lear, Vivien had extended her trips to Glenda's cottage to buy honey into weekend outings, with both women taking advantage of the war to forge a friendship that otherwise might never have been. The experience of not being bored by another woman had allowed Vivien to forgive Glenda her height, emerald-green eyes and obvious attraction to men, overt sexuality being a quality Vivien found cheap in people of either sex. In spite of the wider jealousy their friendship aroused, both women felt a deep desire to flaunt it, proud that they had found one another, and that something good had come of the war.

'Mark's right about them not having anything to look forward to – I hear the poor souls have been docked a whole day's pay for attending the funeral. It's not on, is it? Your father would never do a thing like that if he still had staff, would he, Vivien? And on a Sunday too. The war ended a year ago, for heaven's sake!' Glenda smiled triumphantly; making points was not one of her strengths and it was always good to squeeze one out without immediate contradiction.

'No, Daddy wouldn't, but then he isn't the grubby little owner of a chocolate factory,' sighed Ross. 'I suppose the three of us all partake in that rare honour of not actually being employed by the bloody place. Henry Dawson would be turning in his grave if he knew what a money-loving little squirt Oliver's turned out to be.'

'You're right,' said Polly, trying to sound like he had come to the same conclusion through an independent path. 'I remember going in to buy sweets when Henry Dawson still owned the shop; the old man would throw in a few for free but Oily, even then, hated it . . . same age as me but much older.'

'What, the old man giving away broken chocolate bits? Oily couldn't have been that mean, surely?'

'It wasn't just the giving but it was that side to his dad's character he hated, the generosity and kindness, I mean. That's what got to him. I remember him telling me once I was the biggest fool on earth because I gave away my lunch one day.'

'And what did you say to that?' Ross asked, slightly annoyed at her interest.

'I said I wasn't hungry and there was no sense in me hanging on to the food for decoration.'

'What would he have done, buried it in a ditch?'

'Sold it, probably, if his actions over the past few years are anything to go by. He thought I was weak, letting advantage be taken of myself. Thought of his old man in the same way, I suspect.'

'So who was it you ended up giving your lunch to?'

'Moat.'

'We come full circle.' Ross sniffed.

'There's no doubt about it,' chipped in Glenda, 'that factory has become a bloody workhouse since Henry died; why, they wouldn't even stump up the cash for the wake, they left it to your father to do that, though why he should is anyone's guess. Moat and Barbara both worked in that factory and if it's anyone's responsibility it's the management's.'

'And the management say they're not the Welfare State and it's the family's job to provide for their own,' Mark interjected. 'There's no winning when you're playing against those bastards.'

'The family! One dry spinster and a nana that can't walk! It makes me bloody sick,' puffed Glenda, her eyes flashing with malevolent outrage. 'Ouch, I think I've got something stuck in my shoe. Here, Mark.' Glenda bent down to pull off her shoe, throwing an arm around Polly's neck for balance. His penis stiffened immediately, as it had in church when she had touched his hand, the warm vitality of her being haemorrhaging through his loins with blissful force.

'Bloody pebbles, they're all right on a beach but trouble anywhere else.'

'Glenda, I don't know what Mark will think of our company if he hears you talking like that,' Ross blushed.

'It's all right, Mark knows that us gypsies cuss, don't you, Mark? We cuss like tank-men, isn't that right?'

Polly smiled. He knew that Glenda enjoyed an erotic relationship with every man she met, whether they were delivery boys or the old men at the Legion, but despite this his bond with her was, at least in his eyes, unique. For Glenda accepted him not only for what he was but also for the thoughts he had never formulated, and for those voices of his which she had never heard. Mark's attitude towards her was one of deep gratitude mingled with intermittent but intense sexual desire, though curiously it was never her cigarette he rushed to light, but Vivien Ross's.

'They're coming back,' said Vivien.

Patches of stinging nettles began to shake and frightened moths took flight as the mourners, freed from their immediate duty, spilled over the graveyard like a disorganised army in retreat, clambering over gravestones and treading ragwort and thistles into the damp soil which separated them from the dead. Overhead a disinterested crow marked time, its wings thrashing at the surrounding space like oars trapped in a whirlpool.

'Look at them, they can't wait to get their teeth into Daddy's cake and sandwiches,' scowled Ross, 'and I bet every last one of them gloated when Labour introduced inheritance tax.'

'If they come any faster they'll scare the deer,' said Polly, a small lump developing in his throat as Moat's sister came into view. 'I'd best be off now, I've my lunch to drink with the rest of the lads.'

'I see no reason why you shouldn't come to the reception at the hall. You're perfectly welcome as far as I'm concerned.'

'And as far as I'm concerned too,' said Glenda, showing her teeth.

'I would but I've promised the rest of the boys that I'd see them down the Squirrel Skinner for our own sort of reception. I've got to go really. Sorry.'

'No, you're not. Well go, then, before you have the whole town talking,' said Ross, mostly in hope.

Polly reached out to shake her hand causing Ross to groan theatrically and offer him her fingertips. He did not have time to do the same to Glenda, who grasped him by the ears and kissed him loudly on the lips, laughing at the low-level murmuring coming from the crowd that had stopped at the cemetery gates.

'I'll see you then.'

'That's a risk we shall all have to take.'

'Bye, Mark.'

Avoiding eye contact with the cluster of busybodies that had arrived for the wake, Polly walked down through the ford that divided the church from the high street, and cut onto the dirt path that led to the Squirrel Skinner. The sky was full of white cloud now, and Polly could sense his thoughts drift out to the periphery of his known world, past his distaste for the funeral, his fear of Vivien Ross, and through to the same freezing sphere he believed Moat to reside in.

'Moat . . . ?' he addressed the cold air. A fast current of wind burst up his nose, squeezing his throat like a strangler's grip.

Polly stood still for a minute. The wind squashed past again but nothing else happened. The effort of communicating with the invisible, or at least the fact that he tried to, embarrassed and also scared him.

'Moat, you silly bastard,' he muttered over a steaming heap of pony dung, nearly tripping over a tree root as he did so. Quickly looking back, to make sure he was unobserved, Polly steadied himself, picked up his cap, and attempted to walk with some self-possession and purpose.

It would take a firm effort to pull himself back together again, and when that didn't work, eight pints of Tanglefoot would have to do, he decided, as the reassuring sight of the Squirrel Skinner came into view.

2

THE WAKE

The Colonel sneered at the other drinkers lining up along the bar. This sneer was the Colonel's basic face, the one expression all his other faces invariably returned to. His friends paid scant attention to it. For them it could be the precursor to another sneer, a full-blown rant, or the first sign of an eventual brawl. Taken whichever way, they did not care. For them it was just the Colonel's face.

'Bloody civilians and their bloody beer,' he snorted, 'bloody everywhere, they are; you'd think we're at bloody peace the way they carry on . . .' He paused for moment to see if anyone had found his joke funny. Finding that they did not he leant back in his chair and continued, 'Now what in the name of Jove was I talking about before this shower of D-Day dodgers came in?'

'Moat,' said former Corporal Terry Delaney, angrily banging the tray full of pints down onto the table.

'Moat, well of course Moat.' The Colonel ground his teeth as if he were on the verge of releasing a particularly traumatic shit. 'Moat, yes, poor bloody Moat . . . where are you now when we need you, eh? On this day of all days, where are you, son?'

It was the Colonel's habit to infer that others of the same age were far younger than him, when in actual fact, at thirty-two, he was the eldest member of the squadron by only a year. Like all the men and women who had aged quickly during the war, the Colonel seemed far older than he was, though unlike the others he had spent much of his pre-war life preparing to be sixty in the hope that this would bring him the respect he craved.

Delaney grinned wryly. If he were to draw up a list of old servicemen he needed the company of at that moment, Moat would struggle to merit inclusion. Despite regarding him as his best friend, there was no doubting the relief he felt whenever Moat left the room. It was the cessation of hostilities that had brought this feeling about, for until then Delaney and Moat were brothers united in death. Unfortunately the end of the war had come too soon for Moat, and not soon enough for Delaney, causing a mutual discomfort neither had been certain enough of to broach.

Not stopping for an answer the Colonel picked up a beer mat and thrust it in the general direction of Delaney's face. 'By God, old Moaty boy was so bad he could even stop me from looking like too much of a cunt. That boy could put the fear of God into a division of Panzer Grenadiers like no other man I ever served with,' he said, wiping the sweat from his forehead. 'I mean, the man was a foaming-at-the-mouth Kraut Killer, a right hand-to-hand blood-drinking bastard but . . . and it's a *big* bloody but, he had a heart of gold, pure bloody gold, five hundred tons of the old solid stuff, I tell you, and damn any man to hell who says otherwise.' The Colonel thumped the table and knocked back some more of his pint to empha- sise the point. It was twelve-thirty and he was already very drunk. Beside him in the corner of the Squirrel Skinner the men of T Squadron claimed as their own, sat Roy Baxter, Terry Delaney and Ralf Marsh. Like the Colonel none of these men held sobriety in too high an esteem, and were consequently looking forward to an afternoon of drinking that would leave no more than a bootprint in their memories.

'I feel done for,' groaned Baxter. 'I need to switch drinks and I need to switch 'em fast, they're mixing the bitter with pond swill in this place . . . swill, I tell you.' He glanced around the table nervously. 'Pond water, don't you think, lads?' Baxter had once enjoyed a reputation as a self-taught barrack room lawyer who had celebrated the Labour victory of the previous year by nailing a red flag to the officers' mess. Despite the expectations of his friends, peace had been no kinder to Baxter than it had been to any of the other men of T Squadron, and in the past ten months he had degenerated from a man the other soldiers had affectionately dubbed 'Trotsky', to a whingeing barroom misanthrope of middling repute.

'Where was I?' groaned the Colonel.

'Moat.'

'Christ, Moat would no sooner spare the life of a fucking Fritzy than I would . . . than I . . .' the Colonel breathed in heavily, eyeing with caution the mangy fox's head that leered over a print of the Hampshire Hunt '. . . than I would spare the life of a Fritzy,' he said, struggling to believe he could already be as drunk as he felt. 'That was the kind of man he was, you see, no quarter asked and none given, that's why it was no use expecting him to spare the life of a . . .'

'. . . his wife?'

'Get back into your sewer, Baxter.'

'. . . a pox-ridden French bastard?' Delaney interjected diplomatically.

'No, a Fritzy, you fucking fool, spare the life of a fucking Fritzy, that's who we were fighting . . . though mind you, I could grant you that one. Why not? Spare the life of some Froggy who sat out the war mending Fritzy's punctures? Why bother? We were fighting on the wrong side, if you ask me; well not the wrong side exactly, what I mean is we should have fought both the cunts, French and German alike . . .'

'Fritzy who?' asked Marsh, only an 'honorary' member of T Squadron and a man who did not mind being described as an idiot to his face.

'Aren't you listening?' cried the Colonel indignantly, perfectly aware that all those present had stopped listening to one another before the pub had even opened. 'I am trying, out here on my own and in splendid isolation, to state a case that concerns our once-alive friend Moat. Not that I'd expect you to appreciate the finer fucking points about serving with real fighting men in a first-class regiment . . .'

'Oh.' Marsh smiled and swallowed the dregs of a pint no one had laid claim to. As Marsh made no secret of his simplicity he was generally respected for it, despite the fact that many believed he pretended to be even simpler than he actually was. Unlike Baxter, Delaney or the Colonel, Marsh had avoided work at the Fox Brandy Chocolate plant on account of being deemed too stupid to master either the machines or the packing process. In the spirit of the government's campaign for full employment, Marsh, who had served in the Pioneer Corps during the war and lost his identity card when he deserted, now spent most of his week collecting empty glasses in the Squirrel Skinner, and his weekends botching gardening jobs given to him by kind old ladies. Alone amongst the men gathered around the table, Marsh enjoyed his 'work', loved his wife and was unambiguously happy that the war had ended. He had never experienced the celebrated 'esprit de corps' enjoyed by the men of T Squadron and had no particular desire to. With the exception of Polly, the others puzzled Marsh in this respect, as he was never really sure whether they still wanted to be at war or not. He was not the only one who had noticed that despite several hundred hours of talk to the contrary, none of the veterans had chosen to remain in the army or shown any desire to re-enlist.

'As I was saying,' growled the Colonel, scowling affectionately at Marsh, 'here's to the regiment and here's to Moat, by far our meanest export. Let's drink his health, boys,' he bawled, raising his glass, 'let's drink his health.' Without enthusiasm, his companions obeyed, for with the exception of the Colonel the others would rather not have remembered Moat by name. The sheer evil of his parting act was touched upon with each mention of his name, so that in not referring to Moat directly, the men could remember him in their own way, and not as the murderer he had become. The bonds of loyalty forged in battle were too strong for T Squadron to condemn their former comrade, but not so strong as to countenance approval, producing a conflict that only the Colonel was insensitive enough to gloss over.

The Colonel smiled contentedly at the 'civilian' drinkers in the pub who tried to look away, scared and embarrassed at the noise coming from the squadron's table. Though disapproving of this 'wake', so close in appearance to the celebration of a murder, no one at the bar had the courage to tell the squadron what he thought, that if Moat had killed what was to prevent the rest of the veterans from following his lead? It was a reaction the Colonel was prepared for and, despite initial reservations, was ready to enjoy. As a physically big man with a short temper, the Colonel had always known that people were frightened of him, but now that they knew that he had blown people up in a war, they had grown even more cautious, so providing the Colonel with one of few pleasures Grumwood could still afford him.

'The Colonel', of course, was not a real colonel any more than Moat had been a real blood-drinker or Churchill a real bulldog. No one could remember quite how the Colonel had gained his nickname; what they did know was that when he had tried to change it to 'the General' it had not caught on, and that his real rank was lance corporal, a position he had been promoted to, and demoted from, several times. As the Colonel never tired of boasting, he was the only 'full-timer' in T Squadron, having joined the army two years before the others, in 1937. This chronological advantage meant that the Colonel rarely tired of regaling the 'new' men with exaggerated tales of his own bravery, repeated endlessly from his and several other lesser perspectives, told with the theatrical flourish of an actor. Despite the encompassing range of the Colonel's fairy stories, there were a number of details that remained buried beneath the bulk of his anecdotal master classes, including his true pre-war status, his complete absence of pre-war combat experience and his residency at the Aldershot motor pool fixing broken tank parts, to name but a few. Even his voice, an exaggerated take on the baritone of a real colonel, was the product of self-invention, mixing the production values of cinema with those he had picked up on the parade ground, overhearing the conversations of officers and 'gentlemen'.

In fact the Colonel's story was the familiar one of a sad case who, in his first year in uniform, had been forced to marry 'a fat slut of a sergeant's daughter' whom he had knocked up outside a regimental dance in Salisbury. Their honeymoon had been a night spent in a bed and breakfast in Guildford, and the honeymoon period had been equally brief and unlamented. The Colonel's wife had already begun to stray before he had even left the camp for France, and had continued to do so quite openly with a mechanical disregard for her marriage vows and, the Colonel liked to joke, her husband's high standing in the community. Their three children, who looked too much like their mother for the Colonel to tell whether they were his or not, kept them under the same roof, but the couple had not exchanged a word since VJ Day when the Colonel had doused their house in petrol and hospitalised a car load of in-laws. The episode had left the Colonel with mixed feelings towards the opposite sex, his furious lust buried beneath a savage Puritanism that had grown more preposterous by the day, since its roots owed everything to rejection, rather than sanctimonious disgust.

'*The* important lesson to learn in life, boys, is to never, never ever, *think* about anything. Trust the Colonel and take it from one who knows.'

Baxter spluttered on his beer and spat a mouthful of it over the floor. 'Pond water, I tell you, filthy pond water . . .'

'Here, let me try.' The Colonel grabbed the glass and took a swig.

'Holy Moses, Baxter, you're right, damn you, seething pond water it is. A land fit for heroes, my arse. Here, barman, you slovenly looking shower, since when has Old Thumper been brewed in the River Stour?'

Silas Martin, landlord of the Squirrel Skinner and former middleweight wrestling Champion of Dorset, looked over at the Colonel with benevolent distaste. 'It's Old Thumper, Colonel. The same Old Thumper you boys quaff every day. Now be good lads and drink your pints in peace.'

'I've never felt patronised, never in my life,' spluttered the Colonel, 'because I'm too big a fellow to be talked down to but watch how you go, Silas, watch how you go, my lad, because I'm a man who calls his daily meals by their proper names, if you follow my meaning.'

Martin smiled at the other men and resumed his conversation. Marsh, not knowing any better tugged the Colonel's arm. 'I'm not sure I do follow your meaning, Colonel,' he said, his curly fair hair shining white in the glaring sunlight.

Delaney grinned evilly and drew a finger across his throat. This was a disingenuous gesture on his part since the Colonel's steady barrage of noise comforted and amused Delaney in equal measure. Although physically smaller than the Colonel, Delaney was, in every way, a much more serious proposition when it came to instilling fright upon a terrified third party. His body, a hard-wearing menagerie of indentations and scar tissue, seemed to throb and pull at its seams, uncomfortable in the thick skin that held it in place. Delaney's soul was made of much the same stuff; its unvarying blackness threatening to pour forth from his eyes like volcanic fluid. Those who did not know him often took his natural expression, with his face jerked forward and his whole body twitching with demented energy, as a sign that he wanted to kill them, but to the men of T Squadron this was just 'Terry's way'.

If Mark Polly had felt the stirrings of a new personality arise from his experience of war, Terry Delaney's transformation from a quiet psychotic to a confident one was well on its way to full completion by the time the landing ships had disembarked.

Where Polly was unsettled to find himself wanting to scream obscenities in church, Delaney would have happily told the whole congregation to fuck off with the same satisfaction he took in destroying a column of German tanks.

'Do I have to spell everything out to you plain and simple, Marsh? Are you not acquainted with the noble art of interpretation?'

'Looks like you're having to lead from the front again, Colonel.'

The Colonel glanced at Delaney, pleased to have someone other than Marsh involved in the conversation. 'It looks like I am, Delaney, my boy, and it looks like I shall.' The Colonel flashed a conspiratorial smile across the table, wishing that he could have some idea of whatever it was Delaney was thinking.

Working at the chocolate plant had probably hurt Delaney's pride more than it had any other man in T Squadron. Before the war Delaney had worked as a boy servant at the Rosses' manor house and despite the constant ribbing of Baxter, who considered the Rosses 'aristocratic scum', Delaney wished that he still did. The privations of war, and the taxation which followed, had used up the last of Lord Ross's fortune and now only the gardener, cook and maid were retained in their pre-war positions. To make matters more painful, Delaney's old sweetheart, Lou Polly, Mark's sister, had married Oliver 'Oily' Dawson, the manager of the chocolate plant, while Delaney was in Normandy. She was yet to offer him an explanation as to why, though no one apart from Delaney considered the situation complicated enough to merit one.

Delaney pushed his empty glass away from him, outlining a swastika in the small sea of spilt beer. He was not a man who could kill women, for unlike Moat there was a fundamental goodness in him that exceeded mere loyalty to tribe, and was made all the more perverse by his violent streak. This contrast, between the just side of his nature and the mad, attracted Lou Polly who saw in Delaney a severity that could be disarmed by love. Unfortunately for him, this was an ambition she soon outgrew, rendering the photo he carried of her an embarrassing and painful reminder of his naïvety.

Delaney had lived entirely for his affair with Lou Polly, abandoning his reticence and allowing his passion for her to grow to *Wuthering Heights* proportions, in spite of the mannered setting of bird tables and garden ponds that had formed the backdrop to their courtship. Though neither of them had realised it at the time, their mutual passion was, like water brought to the boil, destined to dissipate in so much steam, but not before Lou had promised to cut her heart out should anything happen to her 'mad Terry' in battle. Events had not worked out that way and Delaney had become the reluctant floor manager of a man he not only despised and who paid him peanuts, but who ejaculated nightly into the love of his life. Life, as the Colonel was so fond of saying, had not been fair, and to avenge himself Delaney had refused to take it seriously, grinning from one disaster to the next, wondering how long it would be before he went the way of the old woodlander, Moat.

'It's like this, boy: breakfast, lunch and supper, see? That's us, blokes like you and me. "Tea", "dinner", "drawing rooms" and "snuff", all that bull and shit, that's for pig-sticking bluebloods like the Rosses, got it? Can't make my case any clearer than that, even if I wanted to, which I don't particularly.' The Colonel laughed at his mastery of the English language and thumped the table, spilling Marsh's pint over his lap.

Marsh scratched his head. 'By God I feel giddy, how about you, lads?'

'Well on my way, Marshy. What are you brave boys drinking, the same again?' asked Delaney.

'And anything else you care to chuck into the mix, Terry . . . Moat's funeral and you'd think the other men would turn up to honour an old comrade's memory, eh?' said the Colonel, leaning back in his chair and tapping his watch with exaggerated concern.

'They're not due till two,' said Marsh with one eye on the main entrance to the pub.

'Bollocks, it must have already gone one. Baxter, what time do you make it?'

Baxter pointed to the old grandfather clock wedged between the fireplace and trophy cabinet, the time a reminder that they were all missing a day at work, an act not without its consequences.

'Jesus,' said the Colonel, genuinely alarmed for once, 'it's not even fucking five to . . .'

Mark Polly could hear the Colonel's voice booming away like distant cannonade, the sound of gunfire growing louder as he approached the pub. In front of him, the way to the back door was partly blocked by a line of badly parked motorbikes, their front wheels carelessly strewn along the banks of the footpath. These bikes had been the Colonel's brainchild, and Moat's primary enthusiasm, but for Polly they had meant extra, unpaid work. The Colonel had first acquired the idea from the Yank, a sergeant in the US Airborne 'Hell's Angels' Division. The Yank had been based with his regiment near Grumwood in the build-up to D-Day and returned after the war to marry the local girl he had successfully proposed to the night before the invasion. To his dismay, but to no one else's surprise, she had already married a South African airman, and the Yank had found himself banged up in a military prison after a four-day search for her that had turned sour. The American government had refused all responsibility for him once it was discovered that one of his parents had been born in Romsey, and since this discovery he had existed in limbo, alternating between nights out with the squadron and forlorn attempts to return home. With misfortunes like this to his name, he was perfect fodder for the Colonel, who lifted him out of the gutter and set him up in an old railway carriage outside town. Soon the carriage had become something of a clinic for the squadron and, like a good psychiatrist, the Yank listened with sympathy to their complaints, ready to assure his new friends that their problems were identical to those of his fellow servicemen returning home to the USA.

The only difference between them, the Yank claimed, was that the disgruntled American veterans had decided to fight back and reject 'the jobs' of flipping burgers at 'McCrocks' that they had waiting for them. Utilising their military training, these men had taken to the open roads on bikes pilfered from army surplus stocks and forced the civilians to treat them with the respect and deference that was every serving man's right. How much of this was true, and how much mere embellishment, remained a moot point, but the Colonel's imagination was well and truly captured and similar plans were hatched to create a veterans' motorcycle 'chapter' in Grumwood.

Despite the initial wave of enthusiasm for the idea, and the relative ease with which the squadron were able to obtain their machines, problems with the concept arose quickly. In the first place, with the notable exception of Moat and the Yank himself, who had brought a Harley Davidson Hummer over with him from France, none of the other men had any real interest in motorbikes or, more importantly, their maintenance. Even Polly, who earned his living as a mechanic, could find little passion for bringing his creaky pre-war Sunbeam Lion out of the garage, and struggled to find the petrol on those occasions when he did. As such there was something sad about the cluster of bikes that lay zigzagged against one another at the end of the footpath: Baxter's Velocette Roarer, a 1938 model but already on its last legs; Marsh's rust-coated BMW R71, traded with a German motorcycle courier for safe passage out of a POW camp; Delaney's Matchless Silver Hawk, which he had crashed four times already; and, most tragically of all, the petrol-drinking Vincent-Moto Gazzi three-wheeler, otherwise known as 'the Colonel's Pet Fuck-up', a machine that had learnt to live without hope after having been largely constructed out of scrap by the Colonel himself.

Polly shuddered. Overhead a large crow landed clumsily on the roof of the pub, struggling to maintain a foothold on the melting frost. It was a sad day when even the thought of talking to his friends scared him, but it was pointless to pretend otherwise. The first few seconds before any social encounter filled him with an irrational panic, which, if he was lucky, was usually replaced by huge relief the very second the contact had taken place. Straightening his tie Polly mumbled his mantra and, walking around the motorbikes and piles of dead brown leaves, entered the pub.

The Colonel was the first to spot him. 'Mark Polly,' the Colonel declared loudly, 'in you walk with a whore's suspender belt under your trousers hoping none of us will notice! Well there are a few of us who do, lad; we're bloody wise to you, son! Mine's a large Scotch and the rest of the boys are on the Old Thumper. And I'll have a chaser with my chaser if it's all the same to you, eh?'

Polly smiled passively and raised his thumbs in a cautious gesture of recognition. He had been of the opinion that the Colonel was mad ever since he had watched him hospitalise the crew of an American Flying Fortress for having the temerity to stand up to 'The Star-Spangled Banner', played before a showing of *Robin Hood* in Leicester Square. That was back in 1943, a full year before the Colonel had really lost the plot during the Battle of Calais and made his now infamous charge at the German gun emplacements. It was too late to argue the Colonel out of his madness, Polly thought, and there would be little point in trying to even if he could. Polly had long since decided that it would be more tactful to let things be and hope that they would not get any worse, rather than risk losing a friendship through an ill-advised intervention. Nevertheless this policy of containment had been found badly wanting in the case of Moat, and would almost certainly be exposed again should the Colonel, amongst others, continue without correction.

There was nothing in the welcoming faces of his friends that suggested life had changed in the past week, but nor could there be, for their credo had always been 'to carry on as before'. How well they were served by this advice depended on what they were following in the footsteps of, and though no one had said anything yet, Polly was sure the effects of Moat's death would be felt before the day was through. Even though he was used to the concept of impending danger, the situation the squadron was blindly drifting into held new and unfamiliar horrors from those encountered on the battlefield. Polly had heard repeatedly, in the year since they were all demobbed, that 'the new life' was just around the corner, and that a 'new Britain' was on the verge of being created by men like himself, yet every-where he looked he saw men playing out the same roles as they had before the war, their confidence dependent on theoretical conditions that remained unfulfilled. The only difference was that the political class had obviously decided that these 'returning heroes' were worth lying to, as they tried to excuse the war that they were all busily trying to forget. Perhaps the trouble was that 'the new life' could not start with so much of the old one still in place, but what epitomised 'the old life' more than Polly and the drunken veterans collected in the Squirrel Skinner? Had it not occurred to any of the old soldiers that it was *their* destiny, and not that of the money men or profiteers, that would be swept away by the 'new Britain'? As Moat had said, 'We might be the reason the politicians use for saying this country needs changing, but it doesn't mean they'll change it on our behalf.'

It seemed to Polly that, as men like him would not agree to be removed quietly, they would be forcibly dealt with like the embarrassment they had undoubtedly become. Polly felt that this was a threat he alone could perceive, and consequently one he was unlikely to share with his friends until it was too late. He reconciled himself to his ineffectuality and individual unim-portance as calmly as he had when ordered into incoming enemy fire, the gravity of the situation buried under his instinct to endure.

'Mark Polly,' sighed the girl behind the bar, 'why, the way you look, anyone would think it was your funeral you attended this morning. You're as white as a bleached sheet. You want smelling salts, I think you do.'

Polly grimaced. In spite of knowing that he was not at his best he resented the obvious pleasure the girl had taken in telling him how bad he looked and, a little absurdly, what he perceived to be her lack of sensitivity to life in general.

'Dead? Not me, I enjoy the mornings too much. I'll have—'

'Don't worry, we all heard what the big fellow ordered, so what will you be having yourself? On the house,' she added quickly, 'just like the rounds those others have been putting away like the war's about to start again. Dad's sorry about the way your friend and his wife are dead, like, and knows not a lot of others will feel the same way, so he says his regular customers like yourselves should be doing with a free slate till closing.'

Polly, quickly revising his opinion of the girl's sensitivity, glanced at Silas Martin who nodded towards the pint taps noncommittally. 'Thank you, Silas,' said Polly, not too loudly to embarrass him. 'Tanglefoot, please,' he practically whispered to the girl, his voice suddenly feeling very dry. There was a twitch in his arm and his wrist started to shake. At that very moment he could imagine, if not actually see, everyone in the bar dressed in uniform and piled on top of one another, dead. This was a scene he often saw, and it exhausted his capacity to remain still. Carefully, he squeezed his arm, squashing his body against a high chair so as to contain the spasms he was expecting. Whereas the other bars in Grumwood had separate saloon rooms adjoined to rowdier unfurnished public bars, the Squirrel Skinner was one large oval room with the bar in the centre. This lent it a chilly outdoor air, one that meant no one thought twice when seeing a man shake with fear as he waited for his drinks, a sight that could easily be confused with shivering because of the cold.

'There you go, Mark,' said the girl, who Polly now recognised as Sara Martin, daughter of Silas and the Queen of the Grumwood Winter Fete.

'Thank you, thank you very much,' said Polly, aware once again of his habit of offering thanks more times than was necessary, 'cheers.'

Moving extraordinarily slowly, so as to not trip or spill the drinks, Polly crossed the room smiling in a manner that most of the punters regarded as normal.

'Come on, Mark, you're not navigating your way across a bleeding minefield,' coughed Baxter, 'you only need to say the word for air cover . . .'

Polly lowered the heavy tray carefully onto the table, his desire to jerk his arms in the air controlled with intense concentration.

'Christ Almighty, get the silver-service routine,' said Marsh, grabbing his drink greedily.

'Get out of it, Marsh,' sniffed the Colonel, 'some of the rest of us have needs too . . . What's this?' With exaggerated pathos, the Colonel held his drink up over the table so that it caught the light. 'You cunt-eating pervert, Polly, I ordered two whiskies, not a crème de fucking menthe.'

'Be nice, Colonel,' Delaney whispered firmly.

'I'm sorry, Mark, but you know how it is, I don't want the pub thinking I'm some sort of garlic-grinding poof.'

'I must have taken the wrong glass off the bar.'

Polly felt a tap on his shoulder; a middle-aged tailor grinned sheepishly and passed him two large Scotches. He had heard of the squadron and was afraid of them.

'I think the other drink with your friend is, erm, mine,' he said.

'And a bloody good thing too,' growled the Colonel, passing the crème de menthe to the man while managing to ignore him at the same time. 'I tell you, I've had to use up more courage here than I ever had to in the bloody war. Pull up a pew, Mark.' He smiled.

Mark Polly smiled back and stared with interest at the prematurely lined face of his friend. He knew full well that Vivien Ross, a woman whose opinion he respected, disagreed with him over the Colonel, regarding him not as a strong man who did not know how to express himself, but as a weak one who would not stop talking. Polly found it futile to argue his point of view, realising that one had to be a man to fully understand the Colonel. He knew no one who better summed up those aspects of male friendship a woman was turned off by than the Colonel, for his intense appeal to one gender necessarily alienated him from the other.

This belief could be confirmed by a cursory glance at the Colonel's face. His long nose, tiny bloodshot eyes and bleached skin lent him the features of a pantomime child-catcher lost amid a rock-white landscape. His near-bald head, supported by a frown worn out of habit, was covered in folds of skin that hung from his skull like French breads baked out of cement. Only the raw warmth of his voice challenged this picture of ossification. This was not noticeable to the untrained ear and only became so when the Colonel felt brave enough to tell someone he actually liked him, or at least thought him worthwhile. At moments like this Polly could feel that the Colonel had not been born ugly, but had been beaten into his present shape. One only had to look into the Colonel's eyes to realise that his whole life had been a battle. The Colonel had endured so much war that he had never thought of looking beyond it. That was why he reminded Polly of an actor who had come to the end of a run and was now forced to accept, however despondently, that from tomorrow he would be part of the audience again. Polly was not the only one to notice that the Colonel's love for his friends – believing them to be the only things worth caring for in life – was so far-fetched as to border on the fantastical. In this, the Colonel and Moat were of one mind, with devastating consequences for any other human, animal or rival moral system they encountered on their way, for although the Colonel considered any Englishman his friend in theory, this did not translate into practice.

'. . . there's only one thing that really puts it up me, it did in the army and it still does now. You want to know what it is? Stupidity, that's what. Stupid people who are stubborn with it, people whose awareness of life stretches no further than their own simple bloody debased wants . . .'

'"Awareness of life"! Where did you read that, Baxter? One of those Austrian grot mags you've got piled away in that so-called library of yours?'

'Intelligence intimidates you, doesn't it, Colonel? What is it, might I ask, that scares you so much about growing as a human being? About admitting you're interested in things?' The Colonel curled his lip and Baxter recoiled slightly, conscious that his bookishness was not held in the high esteem it once was.

'Knock those airs off, Baxter, you're not on some bloody soap box in Hyde Park now.'

'What about you, Mark? Don't you tire of stupid people who are too ignorant to learn?'

'I'm not sure I know any, Roy,' said Polly diplomatically.

'That fence must be hurting you by now, Mark, being so damned agreeable all the time.'

'God, you like to dress things up, don't you, Baxter? All you're asking is which of us is the cunt in this conversation?'

'That's not what I meant at all, the point I was trying to make was to do with a particular attitude Mark has towards people and not bloody name calling . . .'

Polly nodded. 'I know what you mean, Roy.' He could feel his newly acquired stutter coming on. It would be best to cut it short. 'I know what you both mean. I . . . I have two sorts of attitude towards people. One of them changes just about every second of the day, and the other's the one I'm left with once I've made my mind up about someone. My friends are the people I've made my mind up about, and with everyone else what I think of them is always changing.'

'There you have it, Baxter, more sense than you've ever talked in your whole bloody life! Well said, Mark, well bloody said, my man.'

Baxter flinched. He did not like being superseded in the realm of words, and in a way he wished he could have suffered this slight from the Colonel rather than Polly. Like Polly he was also in possession of two different types of attitude towards people, but, unlike him, he found it increasingly hard to draw the line between friends and enemies, and from momentary impressions to an overall opinion of a man. Worryingly for Baxter, the two different approaches did not enjoy a complimentary relationship, causing him momentary terror, hatred and loathing towards his friends, while still, 'in his overall picture', regarding them as the most important human beings he had ever encountered. Contradictions made Baxter feel sick. It was enough for his intellect to deal with concepts let alone toy with thoughts that pulled in different directions, and the idea that what you felt towards someone could be different from what you thought of them was more than he could bear.

'So, Baxter,' said the Colonel loudly, 'here's your chance: speak, then, if it's worth the hearing.'

Helping himself to the last of the Colonel's whisky, Baxter glanced round the table and decided to take the plunge. 'Of course, I know what Mark's talking about, even if it wasn't quite what I had in mind when I asked him . . .'

'Stop wriggling.'

'If you please, Colonel. Now as I was saying, my moment-to-moment view of a man can be informed by anything, I suppose – knee-jerk fear, confusion, thinking they're a bloody fool because they drink too much . . .' there was a small laugh around the table which Baxter had hoped for '. . . but the overall view you take of a man is made up of . . . more soulful concerns.'

'That's right,' Delaney growled to everyone's surprise. 'You're right, Baxter, it's what's in the soul that really counts, that's the place friendship touches, that's where you really form your opinion when you decide what there is to a man, deep in your soul.'

Delaney seemed so certain of this that the Colonel held back from his natural inclination to interrupt with a torrent of good-natured abuse, and nodded at Baxter to go on if he wished, but a look of genuine relief had passed over Baxter's face and he lapsed into silence.

'All's well that ends well,' said the Colonel without believing it. He knew that their present position, both in the pub and in the town at large was not as secure as it might have been. It was the middle of a working day; they ought to have been at the factory, not sat in the pub. It felt doubtful that Oliver Dawson would consider the suicide of his least favourite employee sufficient reason for the unannounced disappearance of the Sunday shift. The Colonel looked round the table. There was no sense spoiling the mood over something as trifling as work or Dawson.

'He's got a point, you know,' said Marsh, confident that it was safe for him to offer a contribution at last.

'Point or no point, we'll drink ourselves sober at this rate,' said the Colonel, waving at the group of men filing through the door. 'Here they come at last, the dirty stop-outs. What we all need,' he burped loudly, 'what we all need right now is . . . is some organisation.'

'No,' smiled Baxter, free of his trance and trying not to look too pleased with himself, 'what we all need now is another round. Your shout, I think, Colonel, old boy.'

Not even Lord Ross of Breck could pretend that his Great Hall was anything other than a dismal waste of space. Certainly of all the people gathered there for Barbara Moat's wake he was the man least likely to be awed by its size or structure. From its imitation Gothic arches to the near random collection of bent-nosed gargoyles, the entire edifice suggested eighteenth-century new money spent on attempts at social advancement. The very concept of 'Grumwood Hall' was the antithesis of Lord Ross's aesthetic modesty and it had fallen into his hands as a consequence of his wife's refusal to bring up their daughter at his ancestral home in the Highlands. For a man who thrived in the open air, the Great Hall provided the ageing lord with his absolute nadir. Its greying marble columns created the impression of tree trunks on a forest floor, holding up heavily leaved branches that blocked the light from the tiny plate-glass windows high in the ceiling. In a normal room of the Great Hall's size the sunlight ought to have been dazzling, but even on a bright day candles were necessary and outside of public events Lord Ross dreaded entering the place. Not even its use during the war as a sanatorium for wounded soldiers had redeemed it in his eyes, the hall and the town indelibly tarnished by his wife's heart attack at a Women's Institute meeting held there soon after their move south.

'It's like being in the middle of the blackout, this room,' said Glenda Heathen. 'Look, even the plants think they're dead,' she added, pointing to a vase of sleeping lilies.

'It's faded grandeur,' replied Vivien Ross tartly, 'like those lives that wither on the vine in expectancy.'

'Expectancy of what, Vivien?'

'Nothing, just expectancy.'

'Well I wouldn't wither here for all the cakes in Southcrawl. I'd rather wither somewhere that felt a bit more bloody cheerful,' continued Glenda jauntily. 'I mean, look at those, it's enough to feel sorry for them even though they *are* just objects.'

'I know, they're dreadful, aren't they?' A deep leather armchair of fading maroon was pressed against the wall along-side a set of uncomfortable-looking chairs which had been stacked on top of one another in a hurry. 'Please don't think we ever use them, they're just here to be here, like most of the things in this house, just to fill the space . . .' Vivien paused, a look of agitation cascading over her brow. 'Oh who the hell are all these people anyway and why, oh why, did Daddy have to invite them all?'

'He's a very kind old man who likes to do the decent thing.'

'He's decent all right, I don't know about kind, though; men like my father would do what they thought was proper whether they wanted to or not. It's not about making people feel good, but about rule following.'

Glenda brushed the hair out of her eyes. 'Nit picker, he's a good man!'

Vivien Ross took a mouse-sized bite out of her jam sandwich and shook her head. 'Really, Glenda, there's no need for you to be so deferential. I know he's basically well intentioned, that isn't what I meant . . . Bless you!'

Glenda Heathen sneezed again, louder than before, causing the entire room to look over at her with alarm. Enid Rowling, the deceased's sister, coughed loudly and a man Glenda had never seen before offered her his handkerchief.

'Thank you, but I don't know if you'll want it back.'

The man smiled awkwardly and lifted his hand to his left ear to signify his distance from such trivialities. Glenda cleared her throat noisily and took the handkerchief from him. The air was suffocating and dry, with only a slight draught rolling in against the cobweb-covered walls. A noticeable gap was now being forged between Glenda and Vivien and the rest of the funeral party, the other mourners muttering amongst themselves suspiciously.

'Someone should have been round here with a bloody duster,' said Vivien Ross loudly. No one said anything. Above her, birds batted their wings in the rafters, mocking the silence that seemed to afflict the crowd as one. 'Oh for God's sake, I'm not a monster,' she muttered quietly, resenting whatever it was she felt in the glut of shifting eyes and turned heads. 'This is my house, this is where I *grew* up, but you wouldn't know it now, would you?' she said, turning to Glenda. 'I sometimes think I'd feel more at home living in the Tower of London . . . perhaps that'd be the best thing for this place, turning it into a museum.'

Glenda laughed. 'You'd make a first-class exhibit. Perhaps I could be one of those people who stands around making sure no one touches anything.' There was empathy in her voice. The hall was already public property, used for everything from jumble sales to school plays.

'May I interrupt you, ladies?' Oliver Dawson gave his very best smile, a smile perhaps one in twenty women might be seduced by. 'Who were you expecting, Glenn Miller? Oops, there I go again – I know there's a time and place for everything and I never can tell one from the other or which is when!' He laughed falsely, the room was talking again and his wife, Lou – née Lou Polly, was now at his side. Her smile was also false, for in her newly acquired clothes and beautiful hat, it was impossible to look her former employer and friend in the eye without a pang of guilt. In her heart she felt that they, or at least Glenda, could have stood in her place, were they to make the same deal with circumstance.

'As I was saying to these two wonderful ladies, Lou . . . what was I saying? Oh I hadn't got round to saying anything yet, but what I was going to say was something about this room, this great hall here. Norman, isn't it? A vintage Norman, would you not say? Or have I placed it a little too early? Anglo-Saxon in inspiration, perhaps – pre-conquest, in other words? Sorry if I'm going on a bit but I've just finished a book on the architecture.'

Looking up at the ceiling as if searching for inspiration, Dawson continued, 'Of course the whole matter would need to be gone into properly but I'd say the structure of this castle, if not its actual history is quite old, therefore pre-Tudor . . . quite possibly.' Slapping his chest at a job swiftly done, Dawson held out his hand to Glenda and uttered, with the same rash confidence and absence of self-knowledge that characterised everything he said, 'May I offer you my deepest commiserations. I believe you were – how should I put it? – a lot closer, if you don't take any offence to that, to my late employee Moat than the average inhabitant of this not so merry town of ours.'

'I don't know why I should be offended, Oliver, but you're wrong. I was no closer to your "late employee" than most people were.'

'My mistake, good Glenda, my mistake,' cut in Dawson, careful to speak quickly so as to avoid interruption. 'It's just that I take you as a – what's the right way of putting this? I took you as a good and unconditional friend of our brave boys in uniform.'

'Well don't,' said Vivien Ross coldly, 'don't take anything unless you ask nicely and someone else gives you permission to first.'

Oliver Dawson turned his face to one side as if slapped by an open palm, hoping to establish himself as the victim of a great confusion. 'Really, Vivien, you do say some of the strangest things! But I suppose that's the reason why we all love you.' Nudging his wife, like an older convict bullying a first-time offender, Dawson then tugged at her arm, forcing her complicity in his insinuation. It was Dawson's practice to keep her on the inside of his many jokes, barbs and calculated insults, and if Lou had wished her own say in the matter, it was forfeited the day she first sought employment at his factory.

Stood next to each other, Lou Polly and Oliver Dawson made an odd couple, not so odd as Lou feared, but far odder than Dawson was ready to accept. The incredible wealth he had accrued during the war, producing and selling biscuits to the armed forces, ensured that Lou was rarely seen in anything but the latest American and French fashions. Lou's glamour had helped release Dawson's own unfortunate sartorial ambitions and he was uniformly clad in prohibition-era gangster suits, wide-brimmed trilbys and New York spats. Whereas Lou shared her brother's wistful beauty, Dawson had ended up with the physique that befitted a life squandered through worry and accumulation. Even in heels, he was several inches shorter than Lou, though never as small as he seemed, squaring up to her in public like a merchant angry at having lost a trading opportunity. His small combustible face, widening at his leering mouth, appeared both open but squashed at the same time, making it difficult to read his true intentions. Only his body, heaped together like mounds of discarded cheese, gave the observer any comfort by way of humour, but Dawson was not a man to be caught laughing at. If Lou incited sour envy from the women of Grumwood, then Dawson suffered a less predictable response; ridicule tinged with caution and fear. Possessing the power to hire and fire most of the town, and with the ability to sink or inflate the local economy, Dawson was too important a man for anyone to cross successfully. Curiously, there was little evidence that his wealth or power, or even his wife, had made him any more than superficially happy. As a tactic Dawson had conspired to ignore the town's true opinion of him, pretending to enjoy his infamy. His real attitude towards his social exclusion, however, was a form of schizophrenia. Ever since his childhood, which inexplicably had been both loving and secure, Dawson could only relax by persecuting others, or fearing his imminent persecution. Anything else seemed profoundly unnatural and aroused his suspicions, thus perpetuating the cycle.

'A fine way to treat your guests this, Vivien.' Dawson was inspecting his glass of beer closely. 'We're not all alcoholics, you know, but some of us appreciate a bit of the harder stuff every now and then. Anything but bloody beer! What say you to that?'

By the look on her face, Lou knew that Vivien Ross was about to try something ambitious. Fearing whatever that was, and feeling uncomfortable under Vivien and Glenda's accusatory stares, Lou dropped off her husband's shoulder and looked for someone else to stand next to, her secretive face looking even more fox-like than usual. Glenda watched her slope off, Lou laughing falteringly as if to excuse herself or apologise for some act too large to name. Ever since her marriage to Dawson Lou had been unable to remain in the company of her husband and her former friends at the same time, and though Glenda would not admit it, she enjoyed the discomfort her very presence now caused Lou. Lou alone, amongst anyone Glenda had met, remained an enigma, her behaviour displaying neither confidence nor consistency. What puzzled Glenda about this was that, in conversation, she knew Lou to be capable of both.

'It's all very well complaining about our beer, Mr Dawson, but in a just world it would be *you* laying on the refreshments and the rest of us doing the complaining.'

'It would be interesting to know what logic you used to work out that particular pearl, Vivien.'

'This is a funeral wake for two of your employees and it ought therefore to be your responsibility to provide the location and refreshments.'

'Wrong,' said Dawson, thumping his fist into his palm. 'It ought to be the responsibility of the nearest surviving relatives . . .'

'Who quite obviously are not able to afford—'

'"Not able to afford"? Yes I agree, they aren't able to afford it are they, Miss Ross? But that just begs the question, don't you think? If it's a case of them not having enough money stuffed under the mattress, a fact nobody would argue with, how does it follow that it's *your* responsibility to become master of ceremonies, eh? Could it just be that you and your people enjoy playing the martyr role, eh? Anything to gain the moral high ground so you can peer down your noses at the likes of me!'

'Someone has to do the decent thing on these occasions,' said Vivien, trying to avoid Dawson's probing eyes.

'Hah! That's exactly my point, the bloody Ross family doing "the decent thing" again. Well I've never pretended to be anything I'm not, never played up to any airs or graces or made out that I'm some sort of crummy count. If you take the responsibility then don't go moaning or trying to palm it off on someone else. If the beer's flat in here, and there's no decent alcohol being served, then it's your job and not mine.' Dawson shrugged his shoulders carelessly, wise to not show the full extent of his anger. 'But it's not worth falling out over, I was merely questioning your choice of beverages after all.'

'Beverages? Who's talking about beverages, there's another eight casks of beer here if anyone wants any?' Lord Ross dressed in fading tweeds and carrying his tin pipe, stepped in between the warring couple, feigning naïvety. 'Why, Oliver, how nice to see you again, it's been a while, hasn't it? I think my fondest memories of you are still from your childhood, your father and I were good friends, you know . . .' He paused, making sure that he had Dawson's undivided attention, before continuing, 'Yes, you'll be having children of your own soon, no doubt. Funny things, children, they possess several different natures at any one time but when they grow up they usually settle on just one. Beverages, you were saying?'

'Yes, beverages,' repeated Dawson through gritted teeth, fuming that the ageing lord had slipped in two put-downs by reminding Dawson that he was once a child and by implying he was infertile. Pretending to enjoy the joust, Dawson glanced furtively around the hall, as the old man warmed up for the next attack and the rest of the room listened in silent attention.

'I'll tell you something quite interesting about alcohol, Oliver. There used to be a law right here in this county that declared that any man under fifty caught drinking would be executed but, and here's the thing, that any man over fifty could get as drunk as he cared to.'

'How strange, those were irrational times, those days,' said

Dawson, unable to help himself and more afraid of remaining silent than being made a fool of.

'Irrational? Far from it, Oliver – the young had to be fit for military service, you see, at all times. On permanent call for their country in case war broke out. But the king and parliament had no need of the over-fifties, no, they didn't have any interest in the bodies of the infirm and old, men like me. But not men like you. Those were the ones they needed sober for warfare, you see.' Lord Ross flashed his teeth, a mannerism his daughter frequently imitated. Despite his age and stoop, his features still emitted a lively sense of menace, suggesting that even if he had left the army thirty years ago, Lord Ross still considered himself to be a fighting man.

'Self evidently,' said Dawson with intense difficulty, aware that it was his failure to enlist in the army that was now the subject of this discussion, 'but there's more than one way to serve the state and fight for your country, that's what I say.'

'You may, but I'm sure there are men who served at the front line who might beg to differ,' interrupted Vivien, eager to prove that she could fight her own battles.

'Who cares what they say, they're all drunk anyway.'

'You can't really mean that, Mr Dawson, they were all men who were prepared to make the supreme sacrifice.'

'I'm sorry, your Lordship, I was merely adopting the frivolous tone of your daughter.'

'Who I'm sure was adopting the frivolous tone set by myself; enough of this, we haven't come here to argue all day over linguistics. Who would like something to eat?'

Dawson eyed Lord Ross evilly as the sprightly old man shuffled off with a plate of sausage rolls, at once harmless again as he attended to his other guests. Feeling an overwhelming urge to squeeze Lou's hand, Dawson realised she had disappeared, leaving him feeling friendless and, for once, experiencing a need for them. Out of the corner of his eye he saw that Vivien Ross gave a short laugh and turned her back to him. 'He'll be running around in small circles until he finds her . . .' he thought he heard her to say to Glenda. Continuing to feel his face grow redder, until it had become a thoroughly lewd purple, Dawson grabbed a jug of beer off a tray and drank until he satiated his hurt.

Outside, a mist had formed as the bloodshot afternoon light sank into the greys and blacks of early evening. The dogs at the hunt kennels had already started to bark for their supper; even though it was not yet four o'clock, the animals, like their owners, were surprised by the sudden arrival of another winter.

'My, oh my, is Lou Polly – oh! I mean Lou Dawson – full of surprises, look who she's talking to now,' Glenda Heathen nearly shrieked. 'It's only the "remittance man"!'

'Yes,' drawled Vivien over her cigarette smoke, 'she does seem to rather like him, doesn't she? I don't understand that girl at all, she must be the most confused person in the whole of Grumwood . . . though they do look more of a couple than she and Dawson . . .' Vivien nibbled the filter of her cigarette, cross at herself for not being able to dismiss Lou Dawson as an upstart, and for the fondness she still felt for this curious girl who had risen from maid to courtesan in the space of two years. 'Clearly she feels a duty to fall at the feet of every type of man Grumwood has to offer.'

'But the remittance man! They're nothing like each other!'

'I don't think that "remittance man" is an especially pleasant way of referring to Captain Shallow,' said Lord Ross, back with a large glass of Scotch and a plateful of sandwiches. 'Remittance may be what he's on, but his war record would suggest that it's far less than he's worth.'

Captain George Shallow had once held a commission in the Bovington Tank Regiment and led Moat, Baxter and the rest into the experiences that would define who they were for the rest of their lives. Like them, he too had fallen on hard times, but he had a far higher place to fall from and had fallen further from it. It was an open secret that he would never be sober enough to return to London high society, and would probably live out the rest of his days in an alcoholic stupor at the Falcon Hotel.

'Do you know what Mark said to me on one occasion,' said Glenda, blowing her eyes up, 'about Captain George? He said the reason they all loved him so much was . . .'

'Speak up, Glenda, I can hardly hear you.'

'. . . because they say there was hardly a day of the war when he wasn't as scared out of his wits as they were.'

'It's normal for soldiers to be frightened before battles, Glenda. They were in my day and I dare say they still will be in a hundred years from now,' said Lord Ross gravely, uncomfortable with the ease at which women drifted into subjects that were once the provenance of men.

'And you'll never guess what else I heard . . .' continued Glenda salaciously, 'that his family keep him on the £100 a month remittance—'

'That much! Oh come on, Glenda, it really can't be that much!'

'If anything it's more than that. Anyway, as I was saying, they keep him on £100, only on the strict condition that he never sets foot in London again for as long as he lives. Or tries to contact any of his brothers or sisters or anyone else he knew from his old life.'

'Well I know that can't be true because I'm realiably informed he's an only child.'

'All right then, his old friends and his fiancée; he can't drop any of them a line or else his folks will cut off his remittance.'

'So you would have us believe that poor Captain Shallow is under a form of house arrest in Grumwood, rather than enjoying a lengthy convalescence before he's able to find his feet again,' said Lord Ross, sceptically raising an eyebrow at Glenda.

'I would, your Lordship,' said Glenda, impervious to any

irony that may have entered the conversation. 'The rich in the cities aren't like the old rich out here, begging your pardon, they're like Dawson, they're all like him and completely ruthless with their own kind, or so I hear.'

'I would hardly describe Captain Shallow's parents as belonging to the metropolitan nouveaux riches, which in any case bares no comparison to Dawson, who really is something of an original.'

'I'll repeat something I did hear,' said Vivien ignoring her father, a look of involuntary amusement on her lips. 'They say that after his honourable discharge his nerves were so shot to bits that when he got home he kept thinking he was being attacked by things, hairbrushes, nail scissors, his own shadow . . .'

'I suppose that's the problem with a war like this last one and the other one before that,' said Lord Ross, wishing to add a properly masculine perspective to the conversation. 'When I went to war as a lad there were never more than a few thousand of us involved in the whole show at any one time. By that I mean this: we were a small enough number for the country to cope with once the fireworks were over. Now if only a few of our boys had gone over to France in '39 then *we* could have coped too, and when they came home shot up we could have treated each one of them like a hero and let them blow off as much steam as they liked, and those that were really in a bad way, well they could have got a nanny each if that's what it took to bring them back into the pyramid. The trouble is too many of them went over, nearly all of them in fact, and there's no way we can have them all playing up, so we just have to pretend that there was nothing to it and that they should all shrug the war off and get on with life. Which I don't think is a bad way of dealing with the problem, when one really thinks about it.'

Glenda nodded seriously. 'Umm, there is that, I grant you; that's a very good point, your Lordship. But if you ask me, he looks like someone from a book,' she said, having not really listened to a word Lord Ross had said but politely waited for her turn.

Lord Ross began to say something but stopped before making a sound; he was growing used to the limits of his waning influence and there was no point compromising his dignity by raging against the dying of the light. It felt like several hundred years since anyone had last truly felt fear around him, let alone afforded him due deference, and, like the country he loved, he was now reconciled to inevitable and gradual decline.

'Or like a man who could write a book,' said Vivien, 'the sort of writer who creates a character one really cares about, only to spend the second half of the story completely destroying the poor fellow. It's probably why he never gets up before eleven and missed the funeral; like Fitzgerald, sitting at home and boozing in bed, I suppose.'

'Are you sure? Fitzgerald was dreadfully wet, not a man of action like Shallow. Like man like book, I say,' announced her father.

'As a man, perhaps, but you're quite wrong about Fitzgerald's merits as an author; I believe his books are so superior that one can learn about life through them.' It was Vivien's reflexive response to contradict her father, but in this case she actually meant what she said as, for her, books had replaced meeting people during the war years.

'I've learnt all I want to about life, and if there's anything else to learn then I should imagine it's unpleasant,' replied Lord Ross.

'I'm sure that's a sentiment the inebriated Captain Shallow would agree with.'

'Maybe, but I shouldn't go telling him, if I were you, Vivien, it doesn't pay to make people too self-conscious about their enjoyment.'

Captain George Shallow tried once again to focus on the mouth of the girl talking to him, hoping that it would yield some clue to her identity or to the subject of the conversation. She was certainly very pretty, her long arms and flamingo legs barely distracting him from the contours of her lips buried deep under her hat, their heavily glossed surfaces twinkling like diamonds. Shallow smiled at them and then at her. His head was throbbing and he could feel his memory spill back and forth, Lou Polly's hat reminding him of a beekeeper's mask and her way of wearing it evoking images of the belles at Ascot before the war. Running his hand through his hair, so that the sweat cut through it like wax, Shallow tried to keep these associations at bay and concentrate on his immediate environment, his long calf muscles aching under the strain of ten hours of uninterrupted drinking.

'I do beg your pardon, but how do I pronounce your name?' he said, hoping for a direct and immediate way of grounding himself in the present.

Lou Dawson looked slightly confused. 'Lou-ise.'

'Ahh, as in the French diction!'

The smile returned to Lou's face; she should have realised that an officer, especially a tall, rakishly handsome officer of noble bearing, would be very particular about things like this. 'Yes, that's right, it's a French name, Louise, isn't it? But everyone around here calls me Lou, which is typical of this place, I suppose. We're always shortening everyone's names to something . . . something shorter. I think it's sad really because names are much more beautiful when they're pronounced properly.'

'Louise, if you had any conception of some of the barbarous abbreviations my men foisted upon me during the war, you would appreciate how wholeheartedly I agree with the sentiment you just expressed.'

Lou watched the captain's eyebrows rise into the arc of pained amusement she adored, and laughed politely, praying that the very lightness of her laughter would not give her love away. She had felt this way ever since she had first spotted him on

Southampton dock, and from that moment she had desired to live under his spell of sophistication, elegance and maturity for as long as he would let her. Recognising the improbability of this ambition, Lou had settled on the more modest fantasy of possessing the courage to entice Shallow to bed and feel his strong shoulders smother her in her sleep. Both of these wishes had remained unrequited, but utterly unique as they were the only secret Lou had ever proved capable of keeping.

There was a time when Lou had hoped, against all the evidence, that Terry Delaney could take her to this promised land of passionate fulfilment, and maybe even a time when she projected a similar fantasy onto Oliver Dawson, but in her heart she knew that Captain Shallow was the only man she could make this trip with, which was why it would never be made at all.

'You've a very nice name too, George, that's a lovely name, I think,' she said edging closer to him in the pretence that he may not be able to hear her.

'Do you really? How nice to meet someone who does. I think it's quite a boring name actually.'

'No, you're wrong!' Lou put her hand to her mouth; she had not eaten all day and could feel the drink going to her head. 'Really your name isn't boring at all. It's the name of the saint that killed the dragon. St George. Our patron.'

Shallow smiled. 'Louise, that's very sweet of you, but I'm rather afraid that your opinion is an isolated one, though no less valued for that.'

'What do you mean?' she asked, breathing in the mix of aftershave and smoke emanating from the scarf tied round his neck.

'Well I think my name, rather like me as a person, is more . . . more tolerated than truly loved.'

'I don't understand,' replied Lou, amazed that George Shallow could not feel how brightly he shone, especially when it was so clear for her to see, his brown eyes exciting her even as they blinked in pain.

Shallow continued to smile at her, resisting the temptation to blush slightly. It felt madly improbable that there should be anyone in Grumwood, or in the world for that matter, who could believe he was worth anything at all.

'Perhaps if you knew me a little better . . .'

'I do know you!' Lou practically shouted. 'Better than you think, I mean,' she added quickly. She could see it, even if he could not. Shallow was as much of an outcast as herself, contrary, unpredictable, wilful and miscast. He had lost his footing in the war just as surely as she had sacrificed her own when she eloped with Dawson. Both she and Shallow had become timid and faltering, playing to their weaknesses and consigned to suffer other people's strengths. Lou had only to look into Shallow's tired but searching eyes, to confirm her deep intuition that in them she had found another romantic who did not believe he was at least as attractive as she was beautiful, nor as promisingly. This was an entirely new state of affairs for her, as she was used to feeling, at the very least, a physical superiority to the men in her life. The reason Dawson had worked so hard to accumulate status and wealth was so that he could one day possess the natural authority of a soldier and the impact, if not the looks, of a film star. That Shallow could have these qualities minus the riches was of no account to Lou; she had tried riches, grown disillusioned and was ready to move on to something else.

'Maybe it's just a matter of time,' Shallow said resignedly, 'but I find that people tolerate me for as long as I amuse them . . .'

'I think you're worth far more than that.'

'. . . then eventually they grow bored of me and after that there's nothing left for them to do except chew me up and spit me out. You'll have to forgive me if it sounds as if I'm drama-tising my situation and laying it on a bit thick. Anyway, I'm talking about myself, I must apologise.'

Lou felt her breasts tingle, her mind's eye greedily imagining

Captain Shallow in her mouth. He, for his part, was now hesitating to go further, knowing that he had a tendency to speak like this but doubtful of whether it was wise to do so in front of a girl he barely knew. But the alcohol was firmly in the saddle now and, as was always the case after several drinks, he could hardly restrain himself.

'You see, I don't dread the day this happens, Louise; it can't be any worse than anything I've already seen. What's making a fool of oneself in public compared to watching a man being burnt to death in a tank? You see, I don't even fear the first signs, I merely await them.'

'What "first signs" are you talking about, I don't really understand.'

'Those,' replied Captain Shallow pointing to Vivien Ross and Glenda Heathen who were pretending not to look at them. 'It must be a strange feeling for them, being bored and embarrassed of someone they still like and not wanting to face it because there's still the ghost of some misconceived affection there . . .' Shallow drained his glass and looked at Lou to see if she was still listening. The look of attentiveness on her face was so great that he immediately berated himself for misusing such a moment with more self-doubt.

'Enough of me,' he said, conscious of playing the actor attempting sincerity for the sixth take, 'what interests you?'

'People,' said Lou without hesitation.

'Is that so?'

'But all the people I'm interested in probably aren't interested in me . . .'

'Don't count on it,' said Shallow, suddenly full of interest and aware of how beautiful this girl was. 'One never feels very confident in front of people who are interesting, especially if they're clever buggers. The truth is one never feels very interesting to oneself.'

'No, I really mean it, the people I like, who interest me, lead different lives to mine and are so different to me . . .'

'I find that people, like love, can be very patient . . . patient about differences but also with time . . . they can wait for each other, you know. It's easy to forget, but we're all still very young.' Shallow stopped himself, unsure of whether it was the drink talking and, if it was, what it was talking about.

Lou opened her mouth in the shape of a kiss, but no sound came out of it. Shallow wished there was someone there to kick him; he was ready to fall in love with yet another girl without knowing whether he even liked her, just as he had on countless occasions before with a drink in his hand. Not letting Lou reply, and hoping to get as firm a grip on himself as possible, he said in his most disinterested tone, 'I *know* we've met before, at Southampton docks when the troop ships were disembarking. You were attached, or were the sister of one of the men in my squadron, weren't you . . . or were you the girl-friend of . . . yes, Terry Delaney, I think?'

His effort at small talk was in vain. Oblivious to any with-drawal by Shallow, and still speaking in the spirit of the inti-macy they had just established, Lou said, 'Yes, there was someone, it's true, but I was very young. You can get into things like that when you're too young, can't you?'

'Of course, you're right,' replied Shallow, forgetting his resolve to remain aloof and following his instinct to confess before the consumption of more alcohol, 'it's possible to experience a great many things one isn't prepared for, most of life seems to operate on that principle. Things happen and one accepts them – not because one's strong, but because there's no choice.' Shallow paused. 'For what it's worth, you do assume correctly if you think I'm referring to love and not the war, which I am, for once. I expected the war to be terrible but love caught me off guard, as I suppose it does everyone.' His hands were trembling, he had picked another inopportune moment to crack up, for that was what he felt he was on the verge of doing.

Lou touched Shallow's cheek and gazed into his trembling eyes. 'You left someone behind too, didn't you?'

'What's all this?' barked Oliver Dawson, as he barged past Shallow and grabbed Lou by the arm, his intense jealousy for once justified and not the result of his debilitating paranoia. Every moment his wife spent away from him was rarefied torture in which he imagined her being seduced by other men, and therefore all men were rivals that had to be bludgeoned into non-being and silence, through volume alone if all else failed. 'You come home with me now, my girl,' Dawson yelled, more at Shallow than his wife, the arm-locked Lou marched along beside him.

'That "man" has the critical reactions of a gamekeeper,' said Vivien Ross, but not before Dawson had snarled at the room, 'I don't know what anyone even sees in that man, that rummy soak, that *fucking* scavenger. It'll be our daughters, I tell you, our daughters that'll pay for this when Grumwood becomes a brothel for Ivan, after those Russkies have invaded. After people like *that*,' Dawson pointed at Shallow who was wearing his usual expression of pained amusement as a form of defence, 'so-called Socialists like that,' continued Dawson, referring to Shallow's decision to vote Labour in the general election, 'he knows what I'm talking about, the day when he lets his Red chums into our country and into our women, that day, he knows the one, look at him smirk. It makes the bile come out of my mouth.'

Dawson caught a quick breath and sneered derisively. The next world war and imminent Russian invasion were spectres he enjoyed evoking when settling an argument in his favour. 'Never even done a day's work in his life, the parasite, and he wants to give our money away to the poor. What a joke.' It was usual for Dawson to weave several unconnected strands into any argument designed to make his opponent look weaker than himself, with drink increasing the width of his disapproval.

'And as for you,' Dawson continued, ignoring Barbara Moat's family who were now in tears, and pointing to Vivien, 'you can just keep your bloody opinions to yourself from now on, *Miss*

Ross. We've all heard quite enough from you, your bloody voice going on and on all the time . . .'

Vivien threw a plate across the floor, breaking Dawson's flow and creating an opening for herself: '*Enough*, that's enough. You're like something . . . something that crawled out from under a rock, an ugly crab waving it claws at anything it can. Why we even pretend you're a human being and humour you with our company, Lord alone knows . . .'

Lord Ross surveyed the room, which was split between those who were upset but enjoying the spectacle, and those who were just upset. His daughter was right, Dawson beggared belief and in the years before keeping the peace had become a priority he would have happily made short work of him. It was not that he now lacked the confidence or even the strength to do such a thing; it was just that the age he lived in would no longer countenance so direct an act. People, irrespective of their rank, manner or ability expected to be treated equally and anybody that upset this consensus was pressured to comply and complain in private, if at all. The war had undoubtedly won the argument in favour of the egalitarians but it still amazed him that he and so many others like him had passively acquiesced to a fate in which they found something new to hate every day. Nevertheless there were still some standards that could be upheld without fear of censure, in one's own home if nowhere else.

'Mr Dawson, I am going to have to ask you to leave faster than you appear to be going.'

The room fell silent as quickly as it had become noisy. Ross Senior and Dawson Junior were a fight worth watching. Vivien stepped back towards Glenda, her face caught between embarrassment and intense relief.

Dawson clutched his jaw, the prelude either to more invective or to an idea he had never thought of before, his swelling face offering few clues as to his next move. 'Have no fear, your Lordship, I derive no pleasure in standing here and being insulted by those unfit to take their proper place in the life of our community.'

'I'm not going to pretend to know what you're talking about, Dawson. I am asking you to leave, that is all.'

Dawson puckered his lips and considered launching a quick tirade at the chorus of spectators that lined the walls of the room like party-goers waiting for the next dance. No one returned his glare except Lord Ross, whose patience, Dawson feared, could no longer be relied on; the raw disdain of Ross's stare diminished Dawson's bombast, as bleach would act on a stain. Dawson had always feared and hated the Ross family, hated them so much that he was too scared to seek their approval, fearing them for what they were and for what he knew he was not. Even though his father and Lord Ross were friends, Dawson read dark intent into this, suspecting Lord Ross of condescending to and patronising his father, with the aim of keeping the Dawson family in their place. In Dawson's mind Lord Ross could only ever see him as a jumped-up shop-keeper, kindness proving this as much as disdain, for in the world as he knew it there was no stronger motivation than to conquer and control. Lord Ross could afford to be nice; he had what he wanted. Dawson could not, precisely because Lord Ross had what *he* wanted.

His plan to gradually take over Grumwood society, and displace the Ross dynasty, relied on subtlety, intrigue and money, but above all on pretence. Open confrontations like the one his wife had just instigated could hurry this displacement along, but also make victory distasteful and, if he was not careful, incomplete. Easing his grip on Lou, Dawson turned to go.

'Mr Dawson, one other thing if I may . . . I've been brought up to believe that one should never say anything about a man that one would not repeat on the day of his funeral, but as you will undoubtedly live longer than I shall, I see little reason for me to hold back in anticipation of that day.'

Dawson stood rooted to the spot, not noticing Lou wriggle

out of his grasp and rush out through the door. His inability to anticipate attacks from other people, or even believe anyone other than himself was capable of attacking, was a failure of insight Dawson could not help, his self-confidence depending heavily on his view of other people as passive. Avoiding Lord Ross's eye, Dawson turned his back to the room, careful not to betray his fear, and said, 'Well? I don't have all day.'

Lord Ross looked up at the rafters, momentarily thinking better of making a public spectacle of his feelings, but, led by deep distaste, carried on regardless; 'I've observed you for a very long time now, seen what little good there was in you sacrificed to greed and ambition, and watched your commercial interests grow along with your hold and power over people. Your first step to compensate for the worthlessness you experience as a man was to befriend this town and play the part of an endearing buffoon with business sense. That and your considerable administrative skills served you well; you performed your role to perfection. No one who aided and abetted you, and I include your father in this, could have suspected that they were suckling a monster driven solely by envy and disgust at anything fine in life. But I digress. I say I observed, rather than fought you, because I accepted that the shoddy mess of a world you were creating would belong to you and to men like you, all of you shameless in your desire to prostitute values and debase yourselves before new gods. I believe that you and your fellow architects have fairly well succeeded in this aim now, and I want no part of it. I don't respect your achievement any more than I respect you, I only sympathise with the poor unfortunates that'll have to breathe the air of the hell you'll grow fat in. You're rotten, Dawson, rotten to the core, and capable of infecting every good thing you touch. I want you to leave now and never enter this house again or ever so much as approach me . . .' Lord Ross felt his throat tighten '. . . for if you do, make no mistake, I'll strike you down and be happy to hang for it . . .' He had run out of breath. For the first time in his life Lord Ross felt angry enough to repeat himself word for word should he have to, his eyes watering from the effort of his rhetoric.

The attention of the room moved from the shaking figure of Lord Ross to Dawson, but he was gone, the reinforced plywood door still swinging on its hinges. Only his feet could be heard pounding down the corridor, their steps increasing in speed as if he were being chased.

Lord Ross bent down on his stick, overcome and embarrassed by having to speak openly and in public, his mask of detachment fallen. His daughter came to his side. 'I agree with every word you said and so does the town. They've always relied on us to do their fighting for them; it's our burden. I think the speech was probably a little over everyone's head, but I think you've won the battle for us rather conclusively.' Vivien was chattering excitedly, reminded and reassured of her father's authority. 'There's no doubt about it, Dawson broke every rule of civilised behaviour and if we had remained silent, then it'd be the back foot for us for the rest of our lives. Everyone would have revelled in our not being able to hold our own. Though for all that, I do think I had the situation in hand.'

Lord Ross stared at his daughter in disbelief but his monologue at Dawson had drained him of conviction and meaning.

'Really, Daddy, I appreciate you were trying to help and diffuse an ugly situation but I do wish—'

'Vivien, are you trying to pull my leg? Because if you are then you've picked your moment poorly.'

'All I'm saying is that when two people want to fight they should be left alone and be allowed to, people are always stepping in and stopping fights for the worst reasons, to appear nice or reasonable—'

'Or to protect their daughters,' he interrupted. 'I'm perfectly aware that you're of the opinion that when I don't agree with you over something I'm doing it on purpose, but you do talk the most awful balls. If you want to be of some use you might like to come and assist me with any bridge building that may be required . . .' Lord Ross turned his tired gaze towards the family of Barbara Moat who were helping themselves to beer and sandwiches as though nothing had happened.

'They look all right to me, Daddy; they have come through a war, you know, and have heard worse than you going into battle with that spiv Dawson.'

'They do seem remarkably calm it's true . . .'

'Lord Ross, thank you for a wonderful afternoon, but I'm afraid I'm going to have to take my leave of you now.' George Shallow stretched out his hand, missing Lord Ross's completely and thrusting his fingers into Vivien's ribs. Drunkenly he swung back to apologise, losing his balance completely and landing in Glenda Heathen's supportive arms.

'That's quite a trapeze act you have there, Captain Shallow, are you sure you need another port of call?' asked Lord Ross, his voice fading to a rasp.

'It's my duty, I'm afraid, a group of men are holding a leaving party for a chap who died the other day . . .'

'I know, I was at his wife's funeral this morning. Moat, your gunner.'

'. . . and I think they'd feel . . . well, I know they'd feel pretty sore . . . if we, I mean if I . . . I'm so sorry, do forgive me but what were we talking about Moat for? You mentioned his name and then I completely ignored you and began talking about . . .'

'A funeral party of some sort held in the Squirrel Skinner, I believe,' said Lord Ross with difficulty.

'Of course, not been sleeping well of late . . . those chaps from T Squadron, they're all very loyal, you know, and . . .'

'They may be loyal but why do they have to be so rude to one another and to anyone else who has the temerity to expect normal standards of behaviour from them?' demanded Vivien, ready to enjoy herself now that Dawson had been banished.

Shallow winced; a terrible feeling of being pinned down interrupted his drunken flow. Trying not to panic, and understanding instinctively that a special explanation was required, he answered, 'It's rather like this, if I may: those men are like the Central Asian tribes I studied up at Oxford before the war . . . just like them in so many interesting ways, in fact . . .' But how were they like them? Without knowing why, Shallow turned to Glenda for help, she was a woman who just *knew*, or so he hoped.

'You aren't off digging holes, Captain?' laughed Glenda.

'On the contrary, the captain is merely pointing to the similarities between martial societies in our own country, and those the world over.'

'Thank you, Lord Ross. Yes these men, like their Central Asian counterparts, enjoy running one another down using the vilest and most graphic imagery imaginable, as a mark of respect for their fellow warrior brothers . . .'

Vivien laughed shrilly. 'My, I must say, you've lightened my mood considerably, Captain, this is a whole side to you I would never have suspected of seeing before, the warrior anthropologist . . .'

'Like the great T.E. Lawrence, or even Wingate of Burma?' her father suggested playfully, the seriousness of the previous ten minutes having sat badly with him. Any conversation was now a chance to restore his detached nonchalance towards events and life, and his exhaustion a burden to be ignored.

Shallow breathed a sigh of relief as it appeared he had got away with it again through citing a few books and turning on the charm. 'Quite so, but I would hesitate before I compared myself to such company; you see, with my men this kind of banter is more like a sport, they revel in the irony of abusing a man they truly admire . . .'

'So they're not just bloody rude then?'

'Miss Ross, far from it, they're . . . well they're . . . I do beg your pardon but I lose my clarity when talking about men I was so close to . . .'

'Which was why you were on your way to see them no doubt, Captain?'

'Of course, that was it, wasn't it? I'd be letting them down if I didn't put in an appearance.' Shallow attempted to laugh gaily but instead pulled his expression of pained amusement. 'I'm sure you all know how it is when someone leaves for heaven without warning, and um, how hurtful it is if his old friends, well not friends exactly, he was an enlisted man after all . . .'

'Here, let me ask Elisa to fetch your coat and hat, it looks like a storm is forming.'

'Thank you, Lord Ross, ladies, it's always a pleasure, until we next meet, thank you for . . . thank you again.' Shallow walked falteringly across the hall, grinning idiotically at the bemused maid who gently led him in the right direction, Lord Ross observing sympathetically as she did so.

'Do you really think they would bat an eyelid if he didn't show up at that awful public house?' Vivien said to Glenda as Shallow finally stumbled out of the room.

'Probably,' replied Glenda staring out into the black night, before adding, 'men have a lot in common with each other.'

'I know,' said Vivien, closing her eyes and thinking of how her dead husband was unlike any other man she had ever met. 'I wonder whether it would be the right thing to do, to just poke our heads through the door, of the pub I mean. My Jack was an officer in that regiment after all and a friend of George Shallow's . . .'

'What?' said Glenda, unsure whether she had heard Vivien correctly, and amazed if she had. 'Go to the *pub*?'

'Oh nothing, I don't even know what I'm saying. Today's gone on too long, and I feel so . . .'

'Feel so what, Vivien?'

'Nothing.'

Glenda leant over and kissed Vivien on the cheek, the strength of her presence absolving Vivien of any responsibility she felt for her tired body. Silently the room watched them perform their strange dance, impressed by the spectacle and unmoved by their pain.

Polly had wondered how long it would take for his old comrades to broach the subject that had brought them to the Squirrel Skinner that afternoon; the death of Moat. There had been a number of false starts, the Colonel had provided a few vague tributes and Baxter had offered a snide remark, but the issue had yet to be tackled directly. This did not surprise Polly. The squadron had always alternated between behavioural extremes that people who led balanced lives would have found absurd. Prudish silences over subjects the men cared about were often followed by outbursts of startling frankness that would have caused a Freudian to blush. For his part Polly viewed Moat's death, and the murder of his wife, in much the same way as he had rationalised aerial bombardment during the war. Civilians were the accidental casualties in both cases, in one because you couldn't guide a shell, and in the other because a man had taken leave of his senses and gone mad, individual responsibility lost in the distinction between the two, along with judgement and blame.

'Moat,' coughed Baxter, making the name sound like 'boat', 'I suppose there's no getting around it, I'm afraid he'll go to hell for what he's done.' To his relief he had spoken too quietly for anyone to hear him. He did not repeat the point and stared instead at the dartboard, hung pointlessly over a photograph of the Queen Mother taken in her prime.

The extreme mixture of candour and inhibition exhibited by the squadron was governed by a mysterious principle that the Colonel had named 'choosing the right moment'. 'Right' not according to any dispassionate criteria to do with common sense, but based on the men's frustration at suffering typical English upbringings in which ranting had been considered poor taste, and self-analysis a dangerous indulgence. Despite this the men were careful not to break ranks and alter the tone of their discussions before they were *all* ready to, knowing that if one of them were to proceed on his own he was likely to be ignored. However once the 'right moment' had arrived, it commenced as a charge with every member of the squadron outdoing the others in anger at their former reticence. As Captain Shallow once had the misfortune to observe, amidst a minor revolt provoked by his losing a mailbag, 'There's something shocking about such practical men having so much to say for themselves.'

Polly could sense that they were on the verge of such a moment now, as the levels of drunkenness usually required for violent soul-searching had long since been reached, if not completely superseded. Most of the squadron, and many other ex-servicemen and pub regulars had packed themselves into a noisy huddle, falling into each other's laps and knocking down the stacks of old *Punch* magazines, engine parts and other unrationed items that acted as a wall between their corner booths.

'Who the hell are all these fat-necks?' slurred the Colonel. 'Look like a bunch of deserters, pilferers . . . general storeroom trash . . . bloody clerks, no mates of mine. I'd sooner watch a hog make piglets over my grave than accept a drink off any of this lot.' He made an incomplete circle with his pint glass to clarify the point, before breaking it over the table.

T Squadron were snobbish when it came to opening up new alliances and friendships, seeing themselves, just as they had during active service, as something of an elite. The Colonel had even gone through a phase of describing the squadron as 'gentlemen criminal geniuses', for reasons that were obscured by the ridicule heaped upon the description, suggesting as it did the Colonel's fantasy life. What such branding did demonstrate, however, was the way in which the men still identified with each other as a unit. Most of them had secretly resigned themselves to their ties becoming weaker once they had come home whereas in fact they had grown more pronounced.

'Most of these bastards didn't even know Moat, trust our luck to end up with the lousiest clique in the dance . . .'

'That'll be more crap then, Colonel,' said Daniel Mariner who had served in the Merchant Navy during the war and worked next to Moat on the production line at Fox Brandy. 'I gave him snouts every break for the past five months.'

'And I put the boy up whenever he and his blanket argued, which was more nights than not, I might add,' said Max Hemlock, Moat's next-door neighbour and a veteran of World War One.

The Colonel eyed them reluctantly. 'I suppose you boys are shipshape . . . in your own way. Not as if we have a full side to select from any more, though, is it? No offence meant, mind.' The Colonel tilted his head to one side and tried to wink knowingly, the gesture losing its essence in its botched execution.

The truth was that outside himself, Polly, Delaney, Baxter and Shallow, who as an officer did not count, there were only *six* other veterans who still formed part of the squadron's inner circle: Venning, a morose young man who never smiled; Chudleigh, a battered-eared pugilist with missing front teeth; Middlemist, a youth of nineteen whose pock-marked face spelt self-abuse; Stanton, like Middlemist but easier on the eye; Wren, a pop-eyed Irishman who ought to have washed more; and Cirella, otherwise known as 'the Yank', a giant of a man and not even an original member of the squadron. The one visible quality this tier of the 'inner circle' shared with one another was the way they all looked like men who had stepped off a police line-up and onto something far worse. These were the ones who were as tightly packed into the Squirrel Skinner as they had been in tanks only a year before, all of them prisoners of their recent past. The veterans that really played havoc with the Colonel's nerves were not these men or his dead comrades buried in France, but those associates who still lived in Grumwood shunning his company, having accepted their wives' authority or, more pertinently, hidden behind their women, wanting nothing more than to be left alone now that the action was over.

'Moat,' growled the Colonel lovingly, 'sweet Jesus, what was wrong with that man?' He looked over at Polly who was shaking his head.

'You see something I can't, Mark?'

'No. I can't see anything at all.'

'What're you talking about, man?'

'Moat. Without him being here, I can't even remember who he is.'

'*Was*, boy, who he *was*, he's dead now.'

'No, I know, I know that. I'm not explaining myself right. The way I mean it, what I mean, it's this: if I try I can see him smiling. Bits and pieces like that, but who he actually was, I'd need him here to remember that, if you follow.'

'Course I follow. Damn irritating habit, Mark, questioning whether a mate can follow you or not. Don't know whether I agree, though. I wouldn't have any more idea who he was if he were here, than I have now he isn't here . . . if you follow me,' the Colonel winced, 'if you catch the gist of my boom.'

'But that's exactly what I was saying. We don't really have a clue about each other, do we? But because we're here we don't need to ask the question, we just muddle along without knowing properly . . .'

'What do you mean, you saying that you don't know who I am?' The Colonel paused and raised his face to the light, his maniac eyes twinkling devilishly. 'Who am I?' he asked.

Polly looked back at the Colonel as if he required help no force on earth could provide him with. In an instant both men were laughing hard, banging the table and ordering more drinks. Over the laughter Polly could hear both of his voices offer a strange but compelling suggestion, the very curiousness of which was blurring the differences between them, making them so soft that Polly had to strain to hear their whispers . . .

'What now, Mark? Further insights? Let's have 'em, son!' bawled the Colonel.

'No, nothing like that, I just thought it would be good if Miss Ross could see us all enjoying ourselves like this.'

'You what?' the Colonel spluttered, nearly choking on his beer. 'Vivien "stone arse" Ross?'

'No. Nothing.'

'Just call them the way you see them and to hell with the rest of it, that's what Moat would say if he could hear us waste good drinking time with all this bloody talk.'

'I suppose he would,' said Polly, his stomach warm with the thought of Vivien Ross.

Next to them Baxter was holding forth on a more conventional subject, still Moat-related, that he had discussed many times before and worked to near perfection. 'It's all a matter of context, you see; when all's said and done it's all a matter of context. Who you kill or when you kill, that's all it is; context.'

Delaney laughed evilly. 'Listen to him go on.'

'I don't understand,' said a young sailor who had jumped ship earlier that week and never heard this particular debate before, 'you sound like a true nut. It says in the bible that thou shall not kill . . .'

Delaney laughed again making even Baxter feel a little uncomfortable. 'Do you know what context even means, son?'

'No,' said the sailor, 'but I know what killing means and I know it's wrong.'

'Listen, listen,' said Baxter raising the palms of his hands authoriatively, 'let's not allow this to get out of hand, for Christ's sake, we're trying to have an orderly debate here and not some kind of pub free-for-all . . .' He bit his lip as he surveyed the empty glasses that covered the table, each one challenging his belief, for reasons he could not quite understand, in the value of this discussion. 'Let's just stick to the bloody subject, eh?' he continued. 'And leave the Ten Commandments out of it for once. What I'm saying here is how come doing something in one place is right, but doing the same thing somewhere else isn't? And no funny remarks about the difference between having a tart—'

'We're being serious here,' Delaney suddenly interjected, throwing an angry glance at the table at large, 'we're being fucking serious.'

'Thanks, Delaney,' said Baxter, casting a worried look at his friend who alone among them still seemed perfectly sober. 'As he says, we're being serious. So as I was saying, it seems nice and rum to me that General Thousand Dicks Up His Arse can put us in uniforms and tell us to kill Fritz, but if one of us comes home and does the same thing then it's the hangman's noose or thirty years behind—'

'Come on, Baxter, everyone here except for Marshy knows what you're driving at, but you can't mean it, not really, when you think about it,' interrupted Polly.

Marsh looked at Polly warily. 'Takes all sorts, nothing surprises me any more,' he muttered.

'Why can't I mean it, Mark?' said Baxter, his face scrunched up in an inquisitorial frown. He had noticed, not disinterestedly, that Polly had become increasingly prone to speaking his mind today.

'Because even in France we weren't told to kill women in their sleep like Moat did, were we?'

'That's not exactly what I had in mind, Mark, my argument is more, much more general than that . . .'

'Bollocks,' snorted the Colonel, 'bollocks to whatever you're saying, Baxter. Bollocks.'

'That's another thing the civilians were protected from, the bloody foul-mouthed know-nothing "sense of humour" the likes of you still revel in, Colonel. As I was saying, the point I was attempting to make . . .'

He was interrupted by a polite cough. 'The necessity of it is that we have to kill. Which is why it is regrettable that we have to bend our moral rules in spite of their being true, and context must have something to do with that, if that's the qualification that'll keep you quiet, Baxter.' Captain George Shallow had slipped into the pub unnoticed, unbuttoned his grey coat and, through an expression of playful superiority, now asked, 'If we're all done with moral philosophy for the time being, would one of you reprobates be so kind as to give me a fag?'

It was a running joke that Shallow never bought his own and, without realising the speed at which he was moving, Baxter was on his feet offering his former commanding officer a cigarette before anyone else had time to. 'Here you are, sir – I'm sorry, I mean Mr Shallow.' Baxter flinched at his own eagerness. Despite his many enthusiastic proclamations extolling the virtues of class war, it was an open secret that he loved discussing his ideas with Shallow, and many a dull hour of the war had been transformed through their conversation.

'Have you come back from the Ross house, Mr Shallow?' asked Mark Polly.

'I have, Mark, and I'd sooner have returned from the Russian front for the atmosphere in that place. Bloody awful, from what I can remember of it.'

'Bit of the old afternoon drinking, eh Mr Shallow?' said the Colonel tapping his nose.

'Was that bastard Dawson there?' said Delaney. 'With my Lou?'

'They were there, yes.'

'That woman's made herself a whore. She's gone cheap, could just as well be a bike as be with that man Dawson,' said Delaney, 'on full-time community service.'

'She's my sister,' said Polly, a rare flicker of anger in his voice.

'Take that back, Delaney, it doesn't matter what the woman is for herself or to Dawson, for Mark she's a sister,' said the Colonel portentously, always happy to present himself in a reasonable light on those rare occasions when he wasn't in the thick of it. 'If Mark wants to call her a whore then that's his business, but it's not our place to . . .'

'I'm sorry, Mark, I meant nothing against you.'

Polly nodded and took Delaney's hand. The hard truth of the matter was that as far as his sister was concerned, he agreed with Delaney on most days, and would go further than him on bad ones. Despite remaining in regular contact with Lou, the frank and unreserved intimacy they had once enjoyed was over, and had been ever since Polly received the letter announcing her marriage to Dawson. At first their relationship had become more neutral than bitter, but the experience of returning home had changed this, forcing Polly to live with the daily consequences of Lou's decision and his new status as the brother of a pariah. Even though he tried, Polly could not hide the active sense of betrayal he now felt behind the mask of passive contempt he affected to wear. This was not so much a choice as a survival strategy, since as far as he could discern his bitter indifference had been forced on him. The only outcome he now desired was one where his personal association with Lou was forgotten, and he was free to no longer care about her.

Polly peered over at Delaney who was throwing lit matches into empty pint glasses, an eerie smile on his lips as he did so.

Delaney had not even received a letter from Lou and it was left to Polly to break the news of his sister's (and Delaney's fiancée's) romantic realignment. Unsurprisingly Delaney had taken Lou's pragmatic turn badly, falling into a wild rage that terrified the whole squadron. In floods of tears, he had hijacked a truck at gunpoint and left the front. He was found a day later in a bar in Calais (having broken every glass and window in the place) on the lap of an elderly French Red Cross volunteer who was mothering him back to health. Delaney had calmed down once the charges of desertion against him were dropped, and confined his mournful tirades and lamentations to those members of the squadron who were prepared to listen, carefully avoiding the subject when in front of Polly. On his return to England his communications with Lou were restricted to a series of heartbroken letters that she failed, or did not know how, to respond to. The last thing Delaney seemed to want was to actually meet Lou in the flesh, and he carefully took every opportunity he could to avoid such an occurrence. The past week had changed this, however, and following Moat's death Delaney had begun to shed his reserve, walking past Lou in the street and mentioning her in Polly's presence. It was an awkward situation which, given the increasingly deranged state of Delaney's ravings, had the potential, Polly feared, to become worse.

'Yes, they were both there. In fact I'm afraid we had a bit of a to-do. Rather unfortunately. I can't remember the bulk of it but the chocolate man didn't seem particularly happy with me.'

'What, between you and Dawson, Mr Shallow? He was attacking you, was he?'

Shallow nodded, pursing his lips guiltily.

'Then just give the word and we'll fucking have him, sir, cut his cunting throat.'

'Thank you, Delaney, that's very supportive of you, but can you really imagine the scene down there in hell when Moat finds he's about to be joined by Dawson? Probably no point in over-egging the omelette.' Noticing Delaney's crestfallen expression Shallow added quickly, 'But God willing, Dawson could always die of natural causes this winter. It's becoming bloody cold, don't you think?'

'With all due respect, Mr Shallow, I'd consider that a highly unlikely outcome,' said Baxter smugly. 'In fact, I'd wager my teeth are more likely to fall out than Dawson dropping dead in that centrally heated house of his, warmed by his war bonds and the love of a beautiful woman. Why, there's more chance of him wanting to do his bit in the next war than there is of him finding an earthly punishment in this life—'

'Why not?' interrupted the Colonel. 'Why can't he find his

earthly punishment in this life? Why can't we bloody give it to him, eh? What's to stop us?'

'Too right,' agreed Delaney thumping the table. 'We're meant to learn from deaths, aren't we? Dawson could just as well have killed Moat and his missus with his own hands. Tomorrow, tomorrow morning I'll be the one to go in and tell him where to stick his stinking job . . .'

'The hell you will,' shouted the Colonel, 'not when I'm still . . .'

'No. I will.'

The Colonel looked at Delaney carefully. 'Perhaps you're right, Delaney old boy, maybe it should be you. You knew Moaty best after all . . . and Lou was your girl.'

'I know, I will,' said Delaney, 'I will.'

Polly bit his finger. The trouble he foresaw was rising. Eerily there appeared to be a rare consensus around the table; Delaney was going to do something decisive and irrevocable about Dawson, and judging by the silence, no one was going to argue with him.

Shallow smiled benevolently at the Colonel and Delaney, who had started to debate the nature of the act of defiance they were to unleash on Dawson. For Shallow too many soldiers had been let down by someone during the war for any satisfaction to be derived from the running down of a pantomime villain, as every veteran had lost a Lou and for every Lou there was a Dawson. It was strange and yet heartening to realise how restored to himself Shallow felt in the company of the squadron, confident in his speech and in control of his drunkenness. If he were to be perfectly honest with himself, he was completely in his element drinking with these men.

The disquiet he felt was not, then, the fault of present company, even if his inability to concentrate on it was. Far away in the not so distant past of half an hour ago, he could see the penetrating look of Lou Polly saying to him: take me and understand me, her eyes, whatever colour they were, boring through him like pins. But as with every strong impression imparted to him by a woman, Shallow despaired at how to tear the image from his inertia and act on it.

'Sir . . .'

'For God's sake, Baxter, I wish you would stop calling me "sir", it's not as though I'm asking you to remember my Christian name.'

'It's Mr Shallow now,' said Marsh to Baxter reprovingly.

'It's the booze talking, Mr Shallow, the booze and habit, and having to spend time in the company of men like this,' Baxter stuck his finger into the Colonel's side, 'old soaks who can't stop talking about the army . . .'

'Which I'm afraid would probably include most of us, though you're right about habit, Baxter, it's a damned difficult thing to break with. Only this morning I found myself leopard-crawling across the Heath in my pyjamas, having already punched a horse and blown up the chocolate factory in the name of king and country . . .'

The table erupted with laughter out of all proportion to the remark. The other men, too far away to hear what was said, started to laugh too, the whole corner of the pub rocking back and forth in a fit of drunken self-celebration. Even the Colonel stopped arguing and whacked Baxter on the back, daring him to challenge the collective mirth with a rebuke. Only Polly felt the chill a certain kind of laughter can bring: the type that contains the germ of an idea.

'Blow up the factory, that's a plan . . .' said Delaney.

'Christ, to think we all had mothers,' laughed Shallow. 'What a rough house you all are . . . every squadron's meant to have one, but we ended up with about eight.' Shallow's self-deprecation and simple willingness to admit to a common humanity with his men had always made him popular and unique amongst officers, a quality enforced by the way he did not attempt to pretend to be any more like his men than he really was. Polly had often heard him cruelly admonish a man behind his back, and practically destroy one to his face, all in the name of morale and duty. When Shallow dressed down a subordinate there was never any trace of spite motivating the attack, only wholesome abstractions like 'wanting to do the best for yourself' or 'working for the good of the squadron'. This decency and Shallow's wish to appeal to 'one's better nature' inspired a friendly derision amongst the men, none of whom were afraid to take the rise out of their commanding officer, which did not affect their view of him as a man apart from themselves.

'Do you know what you look like, sir?' shouted the Colonel through his laughter.

'Enlighten me, Lance Corporal,' sighed Shallow.

'Like the sort of lad who's taken to the New Forest for his holidays, wears a serious expression all the time and plays on his own . . .' the table listened attentively, poised to explode into hysterics at the punchline, 'but who's a very nice lad all the same!' The Colonel double-backed with laughter and thumped his leg, the delight taken in his observation remaining a decidedly personal affair. 'And wears a jersey, a jersey in the middle of the summer!' cried the Colonel practically in tears.

Shallow glanced at the Colonel with unconcealed concern. The description was near perfect, even if the 'joke' was obscure. Buried into the Colonel's fiery bluster was an insightfulness he rarely used.

'A bang on the head as a child, Mr Shallow, that or the last whisky's finally tipped him over the edge,' said Polly.

'I'm not sure I can stand too much more of this bonhomie,' said Shallow. 'Can I get anyone another while I'm up?'

'No,' said the Colonel, snapping out of his laughing fit, 'let one of them, one of them who made money off our meat and bone buy *you* a drink.'

The Colonel pointed to the bar where Stanton and Chudleigh, two of the younger replacement members of the squadron, were scuffling with a group of older men in builders' overalls. A circle had formed around them and Silas Martin had disappeared from behind the bar, presumably to return with a blunt instrument suitable for hand-to-hand fighting.

'Who the bloody hell let those Bevin Boy scum into my boozer?' roared the Colonel. 'And at Moat's wake! This is a diabolical liberty, a deliberate provocation.'

Graham Riddle, the leader of the newcomers, pushed Stanton off his shoulder and glared at the Colonel contemptuously. 'We stopped by for a drink as is our right to . . .'

'Don't blow smoke up my arse, Riddle! You know you're not permitted in here,' the Colonel shouted, 'so unless you got permission from Moat, who isn't here to tell you to go to hell, get out of here before you make a murderer of me.'

The two men Riddle had entered with stepped carefully towards the door, leaving Riddle where he was, his fists hanging loosely at his sides like a boxer's.

'No love lost between us, eh Colonel?' he murmured, unsure of what to do next.

'None, you bugger,' the Colonel yelled back, eager to increase the speed of the confrontation, 'none whatsoever. Your move, I think.'

As a 'Bevan Boy' Riddle had been exempt from military service and had worked in the Forest of Dean as a coal miner. After VE Day he and his cronies had sought out lucrative building contracts, repairing bomb-damaged housing and constructing 'homes fit for heroes'. Like Dawson, but at the lower end of the scale, Riddle had been active in the black market, enjoying sexual favours and petrol in return for goods looted from the bombed-out houses and air-raid shelters of Southampton. With his thick sideburns, medicine-bottle figure and hairy forearms, Riddle could pose as the archetypal jolly farmer, merely making the best of a bad situation just as his forefathers had since the time of Napoleon. His manner was brazen and unapologetic, conceivably charming to a novelist or city dweller, but to veterans of the war he represented a type of man they had come to hate more than the enemy. Riddle's latest racket, at least according to the Colonel, was the slaughter of New Forest ponies for horsemeat; and evil was heaped upon injury as the meat, far from supplementing ration-hit Britain's meagre diet, was being shipped to horse connoisseurs in France.

'So what's it to be, Riddle?'

'I'm thinking. Bit brave in here with all your friends, aren't you, Colonel so-called? Wonder what you'd be like on your own?'

Unlike Dawson, who embodied every insecurity a man who did not fight possessed, Riddle carried himself with a crotch-led swagger that was openly feral, his whole self-image enveloped in excessive sexual self-confidence. Despite the fact that his conquests largely consisted of relatives, physically weaker men, animals, and sometimes unhappy women, Riddle was excessively cheerful and therefore enough of a rarity in post-war Grumwood to be welcomed, for however short a while, in most low company. There was, as Lord Ross frequently remarked, a filter-down effect at work with the reluctant social acceptance of what were essentially selfish men occurring at every level of society. Riddle and Dawson could therefore console themselves as the torchbearers of a far larger message, the words 'this county needs a man like me' never far from their lips.

Unsurprisingly the squadron, and their headquarters at the Squirrel Skinner, had resisted the trend. Within a week of returning Moat had burnt down Riddle's 'supply house' and run a fork over his chest for good measure. Riddle and his brothers' revenge had been spectacularly unsuccessful, ending with them all being flung off Southcrawl pier at two in the morning with broken arms. From then on Riddle and his cohorts had kept out of the squadron's way, making their home at the Hog In Distress, with hostilities being limited to the bare-knuckle boxing bouts every Tuesday night in the car park of the Anchor House Hotel. Even here the contests never included

Moat, Delaney or the Colonel, but usually Stanton or one of the other younger veterans, as Riddle had no wish to be killed, just as the elite of T Squadron had no desire to face the gallows. The shame in settling for this position of established inferiority had eventually spurred Riddle into action, unfortunately for him at the same time as the Colonel had decided he had shown too much leniency; Moat's death acted as a catalyst for them both.

'You're a man I've been looking for excuses not to kill, Riddle.'

'I'll slice your fucking head off if you come near me. I've got witnesses, you've started this thing, you and that . . .'

'Say his name and I'll kill you.'

'There're other ways of settling this, boys,' said Silas Martin who had returned to the bar with a pair of shotguns.

'Tomorrow's Monday,' drawled the Colonel, his voice full of sadistic pleasure, 'that's your fighting day, isn't it, you poof?'

Riddle flinched as if avoiding a blow, even though the Colonel was leaning against a beam on the other side of the room, seeing double. Behind him he could hear someone laughing. He needed to get out quickly.

'What's the matter, lost for words?'

Riddle sucked his thumb. The speed at which his anger rose and fell scared him, because, once it had abated, he was left on his own without anything to protect him from his impetuousness. Nevertheless he had not walked into the Squirrel Skinner on anger alone, rather on the cold calculation that if ever power was to shift it must occur now, in the shadow of Moat's death. By leaving the day of reckoning for a week he may have left it too late. And to back out now, desirable though it may be, was suicide in full view of the pub.

'Yes, I'll fucking fight you, I'll fight you sober or drunk if that's what I have to do,' said Riddle. His voice surprised him, his usual squeaky castrato sounding smugly assured, quiet even. Tomorrow was still a long way off. The Colonel had given him time and a lot could be arranged to balance the scales in his favour thanks to that.

'You shag, you bloody shag,' shouted Baxter, belatedly aware of Riddle's presence.

The Colonel stood glowering as Riddle double-backed out of the room leaving an impolite silence in his wake.

'To Moat and his poor wife,' shouted Marsh drunkenly, the tension between their deaths happily solved by drunkenness. The men grumbled their assent and Riddle was forgotten by all except the Colonel, who clung on to the beam muttering threats to himself. Polly got up and gently took hold of his shoulder. 'You all right, old boy?'

The Colonel turned to face Polly, his face showing the surprise of one who discovers another man in a room he thought empty. 'Mark, Mark, I tell you, you boys mean more to me than the rest of the British Army put together . . .'

'Here, sit down, come on, sit down and have some water . . . bet you haven't even eaten today?'

'Eaten? I've eaten shit, not just today but me, my whole stinking life . . .'

The Colonel flopped back in the chair breathlessly. 'Roll me a snout, Mark, there's a good lad.'

'They've smashed up our bikes; completely smashed them up,' shouted Stanton who had followed Riddle out of the pub. 'All of them, the bastards have written them off,' he cried shaking Polly's arms. 'Must have taken sledgehammers to them . . .'

'Damned hated those bikes anyway, fucking nuisance they were,' grumbled the Colonel, a little unsure of what was expected of him.

'They're all going to die anyway,' laughed Delaney, who was systematically working his way through the bar dispatching half-finished drinks. 'Makes no odds whether they've smashed the bikes or not; told you we should have buried the whole lot with Moat.'

'Bikes can be replaced but men can't,' said Marsh staring into a half-eaten pasty, the words carrying an added gravity on account of his limited intelligence.

'Looks like my timing's a bit off,' said Shallow who was looking very drunk again, having made up for lost time during his trip to the bar, 'but it's not all bad news, you know, boys – look what the good Silas has gifted us.' Ignoring Venning, who was now being sick into a jug of lavender water, Shallow dropped two bottles of gin onto the table and collapsed onto the bench next to the Colonel and Polly. 'What say you we drink these, gentlemen?'

'By Christ, only a bounder would argue with an idea like that, Mr Shallow,' said the Colonel, regaining his focus.

'I don't understand it,' said Baxter moving his chair up to join them, 'I still don't understand why Moat did it. All of us, all of us—'

'I've warned you about bull parts, Baxter . . .'

'Not a single one of us, no, not a single one didn't think he was going to die, didn't think he was already dead for that matter out there when the banging started. That's why I'm so bloody glad to still be here—'

'That's probably why then,' interrupted Shallow.

'How? I don't see.'

'You said it yourself, man. Thinking you're already dead. He wanted to kill himself because he thought he was already dead and couldn't believe that life kept on happening. Difficult to wake up every morning wondering what you're still doing alive, I should imagine, if that's the way you felt.'

Baxter nodded soberly. 'It could be something like that. Yes.'

'I'll have a bit of that,' said Delaney leering over their heads. 'That's my kind of explanation, that is, Mr Shallow,' he added, opening one of the bottles of gin.

'He was a mad bastard,' said Marsh, not to be outdone, 'he killed his wife and that's why he's dead. None of you lot ever tells a thing like it is. That's why he's dead, because he felt guilty. Probably killed her because he felt unhappy, but the reason he's dead is because he felt bad about killing her.'

'His extremes settled on the person he would be most of the time, and therefore that person was extreme . . . I mean that person he became was his extremes . . .'

'Baxter . . .'

'All right, all right, I was just thinking aloud.'

'It was a bad thing he did, a bad thing that only a very unhappy man would do,' said Polly.

'Or a bastard,' Shallow added.

The Colonel nodded sagely, hoping the matter could be laid to rest at that.

Behind them the pub was clearing out and Silas Martin and his daughter were sweeping the floor of broken glass and other drink-related debris. 'Venning, be a good 'un and ask Mr Martin to leave us be,' asked the Colonel in an uncommonly reasonable tone, his head spinning pleasantly. 'What do you think his last words were, Mark, apart from sorry to the wife, I suppose?' he asked thoughtfully.

Polly stared into his pint glass now filled with gin and shook his head. 'It only hurts when I laugh,' he said at last.

One by one the men all started to snigger, trying to conceal it at first, before giving up all hope of restraint and breaking into open laughter. 'You sound like a gaggle of poofs,' said Silas Martin. 'Poofs in my pub, good Lord, what would Moat say?'

'Too late for that bastard and his poor wife now,' said Baxter, 'their souls will already have become sunlight.'

Polly started in his chair. His ears had popped loudly, the sound of laughter sucking through them like a train racing towards certain collision. Something was different, not just with his hearing but behind it too, the loud drone of gunfire had died away and a thundering pressure had been lifted; he could not hear the voices any more, there was only his own and those of his friends. His life had moved beyond his mind, into the open air where he could reclaim it, or so it seemed.

'Dead, dead, dead, dead,' sung Marsh tunelessly, his pint spilling over his legs and onto the floor.

'You look . . . different, Polly,' said Shallow, 'thought of someone nice?'

'Time, gentlemen, time.'

Baxter stumbled up to the bar and was now addressing Venning and Stanton, both of whom were too drunk to light the cigarettes they believed they were smoking.

'You ask me what it's all about and I'll tell you,' announced Baxter, 'but you know who told me? A bloody Jerry, that's who. Surprise you, eh? Thought it might. Well he wasn't a Jerry exactly, more of a Flem, one of those Belgian Flemish collaborationist bastards handed over to us after the war. This sod, who didn't even have to fight for the Jerries in the first place but bloody volunteered to, can you believe it? Well the mad bugger had won every piece of silverware the Third Reich had to hand out, Knight's Cross, Iron Cross with Oak Leaves, the whole bloody lot . . .' Baxter paused, taking Stanton's cigarette out of his hand and lighting it himself. 'Anyway, this mad bastard loses an arm on the Russian front, gets booked into hospital but insists on returning to his unit, which they let him do. Gets injured again, this time losing a fucking eye, and the Krauts decide to use him as a travelling propaganda piece drumming up support in the Low Countries, but our friend won't have it, he wants to return to his Nazi buddies at the front, see? And in the end, the very end, they give in and let him. Is he bloody mad or what? I don't know, so I ask the nutter why he kept volunteering to go back, was he a dead-keen Nazi or just a mug on a hiding to nothing? And he says, get this, no, never much cared for the Nazis or the Krauts either for that matter, the reason I did it . . .' Baxter paused at what he thought was the right moment '. . . was because I didn't want to *fall into mediocrity*.' Baxter stuck his jaw out and raised his eyebrows, his expression anticipating a response that was unforthcoming.

The Colonel stared at him in a mixture of awe and contemptuous disbelief. 'This pissed and still with his bollocks,' he groaned.

'Pissed? Yes, I'm pissed,' admitted Marsh. 'I hate it when I get like this. You boys all go off on one and I don't know what any of you are talking about.'

'He was talking to me, you stupid bugger,' said Baxter, 'and I'm not properly pissed. I'm not even tipsy, for Christ's sake.'

'King and country, Marsh, that's what we talk about, the only thing worth talking about unless you give a fiddler's fuck for Baxter and his fucking Flems.'

'King and country?' said Marsh. 'I can't remember anyone talking about the king. Or country. Which country?'

'You need your ears washed out, boy. You don't need to talk about something to talk about something, you hear?'

'Time, lads.'

'Time? After all we've done for you and this pub? For this country? Fine way of saying thank you, can't just throw us out now, Martin . . .'

'I've been patient with you tonight, Colonel; so don't go ruining everything now. Best hurry you out fast before one of you starts crying.'

The Colonel staggered to his feet and was caught by Baxter before he could collapse into the smoke-blackened wall.

'Come on, Colonel,' said Baxter clutching his friend by the neck, 'let's get out of here before Martin turns on the mustard gas.'

The two men bundled their way across the room, leaving Polly and Shallow on their own.

'God, I'm glad I didn't die for my country,' said Polly.

'Yes,' agreed Shallow playing with his hat, 'I think that's where I'd have drawn the line too.'

'That's it,' said Martin and turned off the lights.

3
THE FACTORY

Monday morning

Dawson tried to look composed, even though there was no one else present in the room to watch him do so. He stared across his office at the glass wall that separated him from the rest of the factory, his reflection in the glass feeling symbolic of something, though of what he did not know. Everything, even his pencil leads, smelt of chocolate, steaming vats of boiling chocolate. He dropped his head into his hands and started to rub at his temples, desperate for some consistency of feeling. He felt awful; he felt less awful; he felt awful again. 'Circles,' he muttered, 'the size of these circles.'

He grunted and licked the thick crust of sugar off the side of his mug. In the background he could hear the factory engines start up nearly an hour later than they should.

'God,' he groaned quietly, his word evaporating into a puff of insight he wished he were not privy to. It was there, wedged in his stomach like a pile of undigested meat; the same remorseless, gnawing fear that he was enveloped by at the start of every working day. There was something wrong, violently wrong with the room, with the factory grey carpet, with the ostentatious Swiss cuckoo clock, with the Jacob sheep rugs that hung pointlessly on the far wall, with everything he cared to think of . . . everything was too light and too large, the furniture too big and too old, his judgement too certain and then not there at all . . . he felt awful.

'Jesus Christ,' he groaned, 'shit, oh shit.'

The worst of this morning's pain was his memory of a

conversation he had endured several years earlier with the lunatic Moat at the 1939 Bullweasel Fete, the last of its kind before the war had begun. He was just a director then, Moat not yet an employee, and their relationship stood on a different playing field from the one they would meet on six years later. This was an era when a man of Dawson's stature could still find himself drinking cider from a tub with an undesirable like Moat, both of them trapped in the democracy of a pre-war drinking culture.

Dawson sighed into his palms, reluctant to examine the memory more deeply, yet keenly aware that it had entered his head for a reason closely connected to the fall-out of the previous evening, old pain and freshly inflicted hurt enjoying a dangerously symbiotic relationship.

With automatic precision he opened the top drawer of his desk, removed a large slab of chocolate, broke it in two and stuffed one half of it into his mouth. Chewing slowly, he closed his eyes and tried to concentrate on why he had nearly killed Moat that night, and how much better he would have felt if he actually had.

Unbelievably the witnesses to the event, including Moat, had been ready to accept that it was the vast quantities of drink Dawson had ingested that were responsible for his outrageous conduct. Everyone was agreed that Dawson had behaved in a way that was essentially out of character for him since, as a notorious physical coward, he was by default a man of peace.

Dawson sat bolt upright in his chair at the formation of this recollection, the pain it carried sharper than the prick of the pencil he was digging into his hand; his ears deaf to the phone that had started to ring on his desk.

'Cider!' he muttered. 'Cider all night . . .'

Blaming the cider was not, in Dawson's case, as feeble a ploy as it would have been for another man in similar circumstances, as he had only tried cider once before. It was no secret that Dawson was a light drinker, and that when he did drink he put on such a ceremonial show that the results always ended up in memory loss or humiliation. His current hangover was typical insofar as it raised more questions than answers. Even if he wished to, Dawson would not have remembered leaving the Rosses' house the night before, or what Lord Ross had said to him beyond a feeling of being slighted, a common response to a night spent in Grumwood 'high society'.

Dawson blew his nose loudly, hoping to extinguish the lingering presence of chocolate in his nostrils, but instead drew out a clot of brown blood which he unthinkingly wiped against the leg of his desk. Deception was a device he could employ in his dealings with the world at large, but never when he was attempting to understand himself, for he was canny enough to appreciate the dangers of dishonesty without self-knowledge. He also knew full well that it was not the cider that had made him hurl Moat into the river and attempt to drown him, but jealousy. A fitful and unforeseen jealousy, punctuated by such vehement anger that Dawson had been taken by surprise at his own fury, even if his victim had not. It was what had brought this jealousy on, and not the fact that he had experienced it, that puzzled him as he sat packing the last of the chocolate into his mouth. Incredibly their argument had grown out of a conversation that had nearly convinced Dawson that Moat might not be such a deranged fool after all. Despite the awful taste of cider on his tongue, Dawson had genuinely been taken aback by Moat's erudition and readiness to discuss subjects that he would never have raised himself for fear of appearing odd. It unsettled, but also fascinated Dawson that the two men should differ so markedly in this respect, especially in the light of Moat being an 'oik' who had left school at thirteen.

When Dawson had finally asked, in a moment of uncalculated interest, what Moat considered the object of life to be, Moat had answered, 'Control without power.' Without fully understanding what Moat meant, Dawson had immediately taken the opposite view and said that he lived for 'power without control'. This was, in fact, a lie as Dawson desired both power and control, but he was interested to learn what Moat considered the difference between the two to be, and pursued the point aggressively.

He had not been prepared for Moat's answer. Instead of a line of drunken rot, that he had anticipated and been ready to dismiss, Moat had given an impassioned speech advocating a variant of backwoods' anarchism. What immediately disgusted and disturbed Dawson in equal part was the simple way Moat believed every word he was saying, with the effortless superiority of the truly naïve. Control, according to Moat, applied strictly to oneself and one's own conduct, and thus belonged to freedom and movement. Power, on the other hand, was a fetish devised by authority to hold people down in fixed spaces and occupations that were not of their own choosing. Between these two enemies there could be no peace and Dawson, in Moat's eyes, had made his pact with the devil. Without leaving Dawson any time to express incredulity, Moat had grinned archly and added that both of these concepts were flexible insofar as they could apply to anything; language, thoughts, the chocolate business and especially relationships.

Dawson was too shocked by the cohesion of Moat's response to know which part of his monstrous absurdity to attack first. Foolishly, having let Moat define the terms, he accepted their validity, and argued back that man needed power over the space he occupied, to protect it against change and interference. This was convoluted nonsense, if that, and he was relieved to be done with talk as he struggled with Moat on the river bed moments later, angrily shouting for his head.

Quite what happened between this verbal altercation, and Moat swallowing a good part of the River Stour, remained a mystery. Something had definitely snapped in Dawson, that much was obvious, and with the safety of years separating him from the incident, he tended towards an explanation that combined a cluster of factors (Lou's contention that it had been to do with his general insecurities, was an argument he was unwilling to accept).

Even though he had been so drunk that he could probably have argued Moat's part for him, Dawson was sure that it was something in Moat's face, rather than anything he said, that had set him off. This was a hypothesis supported by Moat's reaction when they hit the water. Despite Dawson alternating between grabbing him by the neck and holding him under, Moat shook with laughter, and carried on laughing no matter how hard Dawson hit him. Unsurprisingly Dawson had become even more enraged and, oblivious to the cold water lashing around him, screamed, 'Defend yourself, you bastard,' as he continued to beat Moat's laughing face mercilessly, right until the moment Moat lost consciousness and was rescued.

The incident had been attributed to mid-summer madness and, once the war had started, was never mentioned again. Now that Moat was gone there was no need for Dawson to even think about it, and yet whatever jealousy he felt towards Moat in life had not been resolved by the man's death. Recently Dawson had begun to notice that the intensity of his anger and hatred appeared to be out of proportion to an attributable cause for it, his old reasons for raging against the world startlingly ordinary when compared to the death and suffering inflicted by the war. Certainly he had never felt fully accepted by his peers, having to work his way through school helping out at his father's shop, but this was far from unique. What marked Dawson apart from other working-class children was his wish to be recognised as a personality.

As he was not an athlete, particularly funny or striking to look at, all his achievements were earned as the result of hard work rather than skill or charisma. For as long as he could remember, he had lacked an open or easy way with people, distrusting them and being distrusted in turn, a selfish and industrious siege mentality forming itself early on in life. That he had grown increasingly twisted was as obvious as his waist was wide, and to compensate for this he cultivated a disingenuous insincerity, which crippled his friendships but advanced his business interests.

Yet despite his success, he was only able to dwell on what he had not achieved, and how unfairly he had suffered for what he earned. Everywhere, it seemed to him, were people, rich or poor, being loved simply for who they were, an idea that revolted his sense of industry, for he had struggled without any natural advantage in the face of hostility and indifference, and for what? Deep down, Dawson had to accept the most unlikely of conclusions, that rather than possessing the soul of a businessman, he may have been the owner of a more poetic sensibility, sensitive, maudlin and permanently dissatisfied. Were he capable of telling anyone, the burden may have been lifted, but instead he chose to lose himself further and further in work, his poem the factory, and his audience the workforce.

Dawson shifted uncomfortably in his chair, his large backside feeling far too heavy for the wicker chair it was resting in. There was something Moat had possessed that he wanted but he did not know what it was and he had left it too late to ask. 'Let it all come to grief,' he sighed, and picked up the phone that had been ringing on and off for the past ten minutes.

'What?'

'Mr Dawson, Grundy here. They still haven't turned up.'

'What? Who? What are you talking about?'

'The absentees, Mr Dawson, they still haven't turned up for work, the same lot I was on to you about an hour ago.'

'Oh them . . . what, not even Delaney? That man's been given a position of responsibility, for God's sake! We gave him one with the precise intention of stopping things like this from happening.'

'Yes, Mr Dawson, and no, none of them, not him or any of the others have made it, the whole lot have shirked, I'm afraid. I've called in cover from wives and a couple of blokes who had the morning off but we're still short . . . I'll carry on calling around and something'll give, I hope.'

'Well keep calling, then.'

'I will, Mr Dawson, and what of the original miscreants, what would you like me to do with them when they eventually show?'

'Confiscate their pass cards and let them go, but send them up here first. Bugger around with me, would they, the shits? The ungrateful bloody shits.' Dawson literally spat. It felt as though a turning point had been reached at last, and that it was time to play his hand.

'Very good, Mr Dawson, but I think it'd perhaps be better if you let me have a word with them first, especially with Delaney . . .'

Dawson hung up and Basil Grundy found himself listening to a dead dial tone.

Grundy did not put the phone down. Instead he sat with the receiver in his hand and nodded as if in mid-conversation, scared that if he replaced the receiver immediately his staff would guess he had suffered the ignominy of Dawson hanging up on him again.

His office, similar in design to Dawson's, was portioned off from the rest of the factory by a transparent glass wall. Like Dawson he was aware of every one of his movements being observed, though unlike him Grundy did not enjoy observing others. If it had been left to him, Grundy would have preferred to work in a broom cupboard completely hidden from view, but Dawson had insisted on the 'new look' factory plan where upper management were all-seeing, and all-seen. Moving slowly to give the impression of picking a moment of his own choosing, Grundy replaced the receiver and leant back in his chair. On the other side of the glass wall little women in lab caps and paper shoes bustled past one another, all of them attuned to Grundy's predicament, if not his pretence.

Basil Grundy, a lantern-jawed man with a handlebar

moustache, had worked at the Dawson Chocolate shop during the twenties and moved on to become the town constable on his twenty-first birthday, the twelve-year-old Oliver taking his place behind the counter. Following his life's purpose 'to behave correctly in all circumstances', Grundy left his young wife and child to join the military police once war had been declared, his patriotic duty no less strong than that of the tank-men. In 1944 he had returned to England a full sergeant major and was entrusted with the supervision of billeting American troops prior to the D-Day landings. This had allowed him to live at home and enjoy his new status as a 'war hero', free to walk with his head held high through the centre of town, like the sheriff in the American West he had always fantasised of becoming. The seamless course of his life was ruined only by the untimely death of his patron, Mr Eddy Dawson, from a wasting bowel disease later that year. Eddy Dawson was Oliver's father and chairman of the Fox Brandy Chocolate plant, the monolith that had arisen from the humble sweet shop that Grundy had once served his apprenticeship in. The feverish Eddy had connived to use his deathbed as a device to wring out a solemn vow from Grundy; one in retrospect the ex-apprentice wished he had not given. Playing on Grundy's respect for him, and his appreciation of status, Eddy Dawson had begged him to enter the chocolate plant as head foreman and a junior partner, thus providing a responsible set of hands to steady his untrustworthy son's carelessness. Grundy had been caught off guard, and was genuinely elated by the old man's display of confidence in him, reinforcing as it did the quiet notion of his own destiny he had come to believe in during the war years. Unlike the men of T Squadron, who in Grundy's opinion were a pack of moonlight flits, he alone represented the decent hard-working majority of the town, the ones that read papers and made sure the milk was delivered on time. This was why he had dedicated the bulk of his life to keeping the peace and promoting industry, he reasoned. Now that the war had ended and the onus had moved to the home front, it was even more important for men like him to hold the centre together and stand up and be counted, mediating between time-wasting Bolsheviks like Delaney and Baxter on the one hand, and tactless entrepreneurs dizzy with their own success like Oliver Dawson on the other. Grundy had accepted the dying man's offer with open arms and a grateful heart, mindful of both his duty and a raised salary.

Within weeks of accepting the offer and beginning work, Grundy had realised that he was a man hopelessly out of his depth. Oliver Dawson had proved to be a very different man from his father, the product of a darker and more slippery psyche. Far from controlling the situation Grundy struggled hard just to keep up with it, reacting to but never pre-empting Dawson's next move. By the end of his first year Grundy, by his own reckoning, was working as a glorified dogsbody and troubleshooter for the capricious playboy of the New Forest, no longer even a puppet in his own right let alone a man.

Far from making him a figure of fun, his misfortune had made him a figure of sympathy, a development his immense pride had blinded him to as he struggled to maintain cohesion and output, while Dawson planned ever more ambitious takeovers and expansions. This meant that Grundy, though overlooked and undermined, still had a role to play, and so he retained his station through a combination of ongoing useful-ness and Dawson's sadistic pleasure in watching a man of 'prin-ciple' squirm under his command. Grundy had come to realise that his situation, far from being unique, was typical of Dawson's relationship with his employees, 'cat and mouse' being Dawson's favourite game.

Grundy was pulled out of his daze by a loud rapping on the near-soundproof partition. Staring through the walls of his glass cage were the yellow rat-like eyes of Enid Rowling, the surviving sister of Barbara Moat and an inefficient machine-handler with a taste for self-righteous gossip.

'Ahh, Enid,' he practically shouted, 'come in. My mid-morning tea: how very kind. Always the small things to start with, I say. And from there we can work our way up.'

'Mid-morning nothing, Mr Grundy. I'd say you've your hands full without lifting a cup of tea, if you'll beg my pardon,' said Enid, pulling her way in through the door as if in a hurry. 'I'd say you'll need both hands today to deal with what's coming to yer.'

Grundy, who was as desensitised as anyone could be to Rowling's nonsensical ravings, politely ignored her, and continued to address her as he would any normal human being. 'Very brave of you to come in this morning, Enid, following on from losing Barbara and all that fuss at the wake yesterday. You could be forgiven for spending the morning in your bed, there are many who would.'

'Bed is for idlers and dirty French philanderers. Besides if I stay in bed the master docks me another day's wages, and I ain't missing those for no one not even Barbara, who's not here to help *me* now, mind.'

Grundy smiled uncomfortably; it was safe to say that if Barbara had been timid Enid was anything but. 'Well as I say, very brave of you to hold up so well in the face of so much . . . hardship and misfortune. We all have to bear it, but it doesn't make it any easier . . .' He paused, noticing how much more regal his tone was with Enid when compared to his conversations with Dawson.

'Brave is what you'll need to be for what I have to report, Mr Grundy. Very brave.'

'Report what, have you something in particular to tell me?'

'Them shirkers!' hissed Enid malevolently. 'I've seen one of 'em!'

'Which one, where?'

'The worst of 'em, Mr Grundy. Terry Delaney!'

'What, Delaney, here?'

Enid nodded, her face beaming with the satisfaction of a school sneak. 'Here all right.'

'Well don't just stand there nodding; tell me where the devil the man is! It's important that I find him before Mr Dawson does, for his own sake, mind.'

Enid broke into a fit of phlegmy laughter reminding Grundy of a hag whose rightful place was the ducking chair, a method of coercion unfortunately denied to him. 'I'll tell you where he is all right, I'll tell yer. He's sitting outside laughing at you and the master, that's what he's doing, the leery little scoundrel!'

'Outside where?'

'The factory, of course; he's been out there these past two hours, sitting beside the big water tank . . .'

'What, he's there now?'

'. . . leaning against the tank, sunning himself and drinking and smoking for all the world to see.'

'Ye gods, drinking alcohol by the water tank, you say? I don't believe it, he's gone completely mad.'

'That's what I've always said, Mr Grundy; that boy's touched, he is.'

'If he's been out there for two hours why's it taken this long for anyone to report it?'

Enid shrugged blankly, pleased to have delivered her bad news for the day.

'My God, I don't believe it. Monday morning, for the love of God. I'll go and deal with this myself. Drinking, for God's sake. That boy's got a screw loose, I tell you he has.'

Smiling quite sweetly now, Enid sipped the tea she had brought in for Grundy and watched him rush out of his office, his face an endearing mix of fear and bluster.

Grundy found Delaney exactly where Enid said he would be, doing exactly what she said he would be doing, dressed in buttoned-down shirtsleeves and Oxford slacks, his lab coat buried under a pile of empty bottles and cigarette butts.

'Maybe I should go out to Australia, it's a new world there, I hear,' were his first words.

'They should have sent you to Australia a long time ago, son,' whispered Grundy unable to believe his eyes. 'By God and Christ, boy, there had better be a good reason for this,' he muttered as he narrowly avoided treading in a splattering of sick he had just become aware of, 'there had better be some *bloody good* explanation, there really better had.'

If Delaney was at all conscious of Grundy's presence he did nothing to show it. His remark had seemed addressed to himself, and not to the apoplectic foreman. Instead of responding to Grundy's breathless rasping, Delaney began to tie up his shoelace, his face showing no sign of haste or strain.

'You can sit there with your legs crossed all day, if you like,' said Grundy crossing his arms patiently, 'sit there like the kingpin of the leaderless resistance, drinking your bottle like the big man you are . . . thinking all the while that you're a bit more *bloody* special than the rest of us, right? But let me tell you this, no one's got the better of Basil Grundy yet and I'm damned if I'll let a shithouse gnat like you be the first, you understand that, Delaney? You'd better understand that, lad . . . understand it for your own good. Right, since you don't seem much in the mood for talking I'll do your talking for you and try to drum some sense into that hard head of yours, try to acquaint you with a few of life's truths, lad.'

Delaney finished tying his shoelace, resumed his reclining position against the water tank and began to roll a cigarette, a barely suppressed smirk on his lips.

'It's the three R-H-Ts, boy, ever heard of them? "Rank, Hierarchy and Tradition" three times over. That mean anything to you, son, or am I just talking to the four winds? Delaney, oh Delaney, good morning, sunshine, is there anyone in there?'

The sun was blindingly bright and cold and Delaney had to squint with his arm raised over his eyes to see into Grundy's face, the towering arc of the foreman's body hanging over him like a marauding Stuka. 'R-H-T, boy, ring any bells? Eh? Bells, Delaney, bells, you know, the ones that go ding bloody dong

. . . and to think you once used those horrible arms of yours for saluting.' Delaney clicked his tongue; he did not like it when Grundy, only twelve years his senior, referred to him as 'boy'.

'I don't give a fuck for what you're talking about, Grundy, so why don't you fuck off back to Dawson and clean his dentures.'

Grundy felt his knees go weak with indignation. 'Delaney, you aren't an accident waiting to happen, you are an accident that has already happened, a disgrace to the country you served and the uniform you served her in. My, you've fallen, lad, fallen real low. Boy,' he continued, still unable to believe his ears or eyes, 'I'm worried *for* you . . . you are the original reason some good man coined the term "for reasons best known to himself", he was thinking of you, Delaney, a no-good stockade-bound bastard like yourself, by God he was.' Grundy caught his breath. He had always been of the opinion that the best way to handle 'the problem soldiers', as he called them, was to revert back to military-style discipline by putting on his old sergeant major's hat and talking to the lads in a language they would understand. This robust approach had proved remarkably successful with elderly civilians and women who had been nowhere near the army, but had achieved nothing with hard cases like Delaney or Baxter who were more irritated than cowed by Grundy's parade-ground tirades. Even Grundy himself, who certainly believed in what he was saying, had started to lose confidence in the effectiveness of this approach and in his own role as a man who could be relied upon to get things done. Maybe it was time to try a different angle of attack, he thought, as he watched Delaney swig the last dregs of his bottle of gin and toss it over his shoulder.

'All right, lad, I'll give you this one, it doesn't look as though either of us is going to make much headway, not if we carry on like we are anyway. Doesn't seem as though we've got the common ground for a proper discussion; how's about us trying to map some out, eh? What you say to that, lad?'

Delaney lifted open the top of his sack and pulled out an unmarked flask, his expression distant but not, Grundy thought, wholly unresponsive.

'Aye, it's a mad world all right,' Grundy said reflectively, 'losing a pal can't be easy, we both know that, and it doesn't make it easier once you thought you'd got through the hard part and returned home in one piece. We both know that too . . . must have been a tough day for you boys, I admit I might have overlooked that, your squadron being so close. Where are the others now anyway, Baxter, Venning, the Colonel . . . you haven't all decided to pack your old kitbags to Australia?'

Delaney unscrewed the cap off the flask, held it to his lips and took a giant swig, emptying it in one go.

'Don't feel like talking, eh? I can understand that, don't much care for it myself but I seem to be doing it all the time these days . . .' Grundy paused, doubtful of what tack to pursue. 'You know, Delaney, you know what my old man used to say when the sun was out like this? He'd say, "On beautiful days like this, lad . . ." No, that wasn't it, what he said was shorter. What was it? Let me think now; oh aye, it was, "Beautiful days are beautiful days to work on", in, I mean, days to work in. Anyway, what he meant, what I'm trying to say to you, Delaney—'

Grundy stopped. Delaney was staring up at him in a way that could not be construed as friendly. Talking quickly, so as to escape his discomfort, Grundy continued, 'Look, I'm not standing here on me thumbs for nothing, lad, I'm trying to give you a second chance, and a third and fourth one at that, so don't go biting the hand that feeds, we're all just trying to get along here . . .'

Delaney hacked at his throat loudly and spat out a globule of dark black phlegm, the mucus landing inches away from Grundy's leg.

'You're in a bad way, son, it's plain obvious to see. Talk to someone before you kill yourself,' Grundy garbled, his palms and back becoming damp with sweat.

In a movement executed too quickly for Grundy to anticipate, Delaney was on his feet and leaning into the foreman, face to face. 'It's the chocolate, Grundy, that fucking chocolate; when it heats up it gives me a headache . . . I prefer it out here.'

'It'll be winter soon, lad, you'll be grateful for the heat,' said Grundy stumbling backwards, his earlier anger and disbelief entirely dissipated.

'No, you're not listening to me. The only reason I'm here is to go back into that factory and tell Dawson what I think of his job.' Delaney's voice was shaking.

Dawson stared in horror down the gangway connecting his office to the rest of the factory. Coming towards his tier at an unnervingly fast speed was Terry Delaney, stripped of his lab coat and brandishing a bottle of Scotch at his side like a pistol. Struggling to keep up with the pace, and wincing like a grand master of failure was Basil Grundy, the workforce on either side of the shop floor parting before the two men like the Red Sea. Dawson felt as if he was standing directly on the impact area of a natural disaster, one that he had not only predicted but had been foolish enough to specifically request. Quickly Dawson reminded himself that he held the power and that there was nothing to be scared of so long as he remembered this. Closing his eyes, he tried to conjure up some image of strength he could identify with but in his panic all he could think of was soldiers, and he shuddered as he remembered that a military past was probably the only creditable thing Delaney had over him.

Delaney was at the door now and with a turn of the wrist and the force of his foot he kicked it open, his black pupils bearing in on Dawson's wobbling body with inquisitorial menace.

'Open your eyes and put on your glasses, damn you, I'm not here to kill you,' Delaney practically shouted.

Fumbling quickly with his glasses case, and happy that his fear had been confused for his much-mocked (and hastily invented to avoid conscription) short-sightedness, Dawson puffed out his chest and replied with as much composure as he could: 'The bloody cheek of you, Delaney, you've already done enough to get five men fired as it is. Knocking on the door of a senior manager's office is not optional in this factory, it's in the rules. I ought to tell you to get out and come in again—'

'Fuck the factory.'

'I'm sorry, Mr Dawson, but you did ask to see him . . .'

'That'll be all, Grundy,' said Dawson, his voice assuming a less trembling pitch, though his legs were still shaking like jellies. 'I know what *I* asked for; I just hope that our Mr Terence Delaney here knows what he's asking for too.'

Delaney started to say something but settled for grinding his teeth, the rigours of binge-drinking and the rush to Dawson's office catching up with him.

Dawson watched the panting Delaney cautiously, relieved that the man seemed to be too out of breath to say anything else for the moment. This was, he again reminded himself, his factory and not Delaney's or any of the other 'workers' whose lives owed everything to his 'largesse' and little to their own half-hearted attempts at making a living. More pertinently, Grumwood was not Russia; Grumwood was *his* and *he* was Grumwood, the bloody king of the place should it even need stating. He wiped the sweat off his top lip, as he had wiped the sweat he shed understanding war bonds and American loans while the rest of the toiling fools were spending their evenings drunk or at the pictures . . . this was more like it, Dawson thought, experiencing the self-restoration that only seconds ago fear had denied him.

It was obvious why he had been forced to collect and keep the likes of Delaney and Baxter where he could see them, since for all his apprehensions it was important that these men had a daily and absolute reminder of who was Boss.

If anything, the disciplinary operation he was about to embark on was necessitated by more than just the compulsion to master a threat, he reasoned as he watched the sneering and quite obviously drunk figure of Terry Delaney shift his balance from foot to foot.

It was important that these misfits were under his surveillance not just because he hated them, but also because he feared them, a powerful consideration that he could never overlook or make too much of. He hated them so intensely that he wished they were all lined up in front of him with Delaney, if only so he could give voice to his hatred and be rid of it for a moment. And who was this Delaney anyway? A loser, who had never once noticed him at school, bid him good morning or recognised his latent genius in ascendancy. How could such an insignificant human type be behind the exaggerated sense of inferiority that threatened to pull Dawson apart?

To his surprise Dawson found himself resisting the strong urge to mouth words of hate, make hateful shapes with his hands and shake his head if he was already rebutting the Squadron's puny attempts to defend themselves against his raging obsession.

'I hate the way you can't see what a hateful piece of work you are, Delaney,' he heard himself say as Grundy closed the door behind him, leaving the two men alone with the eyes of the factory floor as their mute witnesses.

Delaney, if it were possible for him to in his present state, looked slightly stunned. This was not a side to Dawson he had heard before, the spontaneity of the remark almost, but not quite, engendering his respect.

Dawson, again to his surprise found that he had no idea of how to follow on from this unplanned statement, thus allowing Delaney to resume his threatening pose and murderous smile.

'What can I say, Dawson, Mr Dawson, I mean – the feeling's what you'd call very mutual,' he intoned with an ease that made

Dawson's flesh creep. 'That's the trouble these days, isn't it? Workers hate management, management hate workers and none of us know what's to be done about it. Me? I'd send us home so you could run your poxy factory on your tod.'

Dawson snapped the pencil he had been wanting to snap in half and snarled, 'You, you fucking oik, you bloody louse you. I don't know why I was ever persuaded to employ you in the first place.'

And yet he knew exactly why. His attitude to men like Delaney was remarkably in keeping with his attitude to those factory girls he had slept with before Lou (and which could even include Lou for all he knew). Satisfaction and pleasure, though important, were always secondary to leaving his mark and *spoiling* them in some way, just as he now wanted to mark and ruin Delaney and make him more like himself; truly hurt. Frighteningly Dawson could remember the source of this urge, at once embarrassing and dangerous so vulnerable did its recollection render him. He had once, albeit privately, harboured hopes of being appreciated and possibly even liked by those who relied on and worked for him, a thought that had always made him feel curiously sorry for himself and one he sought to destroy through his mastery of other people's lives . . .

'So, Delaney,' he said, his anger and fear satiated by a presentiment of the mass sacking he was planning, 'what else have you got to say for yourself?'

Down on the factory floor Enid, half demented with excitement, poked her bony finger into Basil Grundy's ribs and asked, 'What do you figure to those two shags up there in the big beef's office?' The 'f' in beef slithered off her lips like a hiss.

Grundy eyed her warily, knowing her question, if that was what it was, to be not so much an enquiry as the precursor to her own analysis of events.

'And don't go telling me to be mindin' me own business either, with the whole factory and you gawping at them too,' she added, cutting off Grundy's standard response to her natural curiosity. 'We've all been expecting it, so what say you to it, Grundy?'

Grundy took a deep breath, raised his jaw to the ceiling and pretended to adjust his necktie, his manner suggesting a man in search of loftier conversational heights. He was not the only man in the factory who wished that Moat had killed Enid, and not her sister Barbara, that fateful morning.

'You stop pretending you're above tit and tat and give me an answer like I asked.'

'Very well, Enid. I must confess that it's not my style to discuss boardroom matters with staff but since you're so insistent—'

'Get on with it, man.'

'We have a saying in the army that goes something like this,' Grundy lifted his jaw even higher and assumed the stance of an after-dinner speaker; '"It is one thing for a man to fall, but it is another for a man to fall with *panache*."'

Enid stared at him uncomprehendingly.

'And I'd say that our Terence is currently finding out what it is like to experience the latter, to fall with *panache*,' Grundy ended, pleased that he'd used the milder version of this maxim on account of Enid's gender. 'Or to put it another way,' he continued, unsure whether he had made his point, 'there's a narrow line between falling over, and falling over with panache – a variation on the first saying, if you like.' He was again pleased that he'd remembered to substitute 'falling over' for 'fucking up', an expression he prided himself upon never using in female company. 'And I'd say our Terence—'

'He's a right cunt, ain't he?' Enid interrupted. 'Eh, that one, a right one he is, Terry Delaney. And the boss too, a right greasy one Oily Dawson is an' all.'

'If you must have it that way, Enid,' said Grundy who, to his surprise, had not gone red or even blushed.

'Aye, a right scrunter an' no mistake, greedy bastard he is

too. Makes even his woman's greed look modest next to his.'

'If you must have it that way, and since you must,' Grundy continued, relaxing his shoulders as if relieved of an obsolete loyalty to a troubling burden, 'you should let me add that we'll still be working for the bigger of those two unmentionables come eight o'clock tomorrow morning.'

'First sensible thing I ever heard come out of your mouth, Grundy,' said Enid, her words slow enough to be intelligible to him at last.

'I want us to be set straight for what we're owed. Fix that and I'll be off,' said Delaney.

'I beg your pardon! "What we're owed"? What the devil do you mean by that, man?' Dawson had anticipated an avalanche of abuse that would befit a convict on his way to the gallows, but Delaney's passionless claim for what appeared to be some form of compensation package had truly thrown him. '"Owed"! Have you completely taken leave of your senses! You're having a laugh, aren't you? Tell me you are.'

Delaney, as unfazed as Dawson was startled, replied, 'For the day of Moat and his poor murdered wife's funeral, what you owe us for that day. That's what I'm asking for. Nothing else, mind you, just that.'

Dawson broke another pencil, unable to believe his ears but frighteningly close to Delaney's intended meaning now. 'Are you attempting to tell me that you want the pay you were docked for missing a day of work?'

'Attending a funeral, Dawson, the burial of a dead man.'

Dawson slammed his fist down onto the table so hard he felt a knuckle give way, his face a picture of wounded outrage. 'You, you dirty peasant, I . . . I hardly know where to begin with you,' he yelled, nearly choking on his words. 'In the first place you didn't attend any bloody funeral, you just sat in the pub with your scum accomplices and filled your face full of liquor like the damned drunk you are—'

'We were paying our respects to the dead,' said Delaney with a straight face, 'just like those at the funeral you attended were.'

'You think you were what? Let me get this straight, you are asking me to pay you and the rest of those three-time losers a day's wages?'

'No.'

'No?'

'No, I'm telling you that every man and woman employed by you in this place should receive the day's wages that were docked.'

'By God . . .' Dawson let himself sink into his chair, his vehemence replaced by an immobilising form of incomprehension.

'After all, Mr Dawson, I wouldn't have thought you, the "directors" or "shareholders" struck off a day of your own pay for doing the God-fearing thing.'

'You're mad, absolutely bloody mad, you want institutionalising, that's what you want, bloody institutionalising.'

A look of satisfaction blew calmly over Delaney's face, his expression the same as an ancient saint finally attaining a state of grace. Dawson shuddered in his chair, the room all of a sudden feeling caught in the tail of an icy draught. There was worry draining in his eyes, their nervous activity resembling that of an exposed confidence artist trapped in a tent with an angry crowd. He reached out for his telephone but the receiver evaded his grasp, the cord feeling twice as long as its official factory length.

'I feel sick,' he said, 'you're making me feel sick, Delaney, sick in my guts. This could be an emergency for all I know. Open a window, damn you. I can't breathe. It's not good for a man to go back and forth with anger this bad.'

Delaney did as he was told, his swinging arm free of any obvious sign of urgency.

'Open it wide, I tell you, I can't breathe in here,' said Dawson pulling off his tie and unbuttoning his collar. 'Come on, all the way.'

This was a type of panic that only a fundamentally stupid man could experience, Delaney thought, as he watched Dawson fidget in his chair like the spoilt charge of an absentee duchess. His behaviour lacked the solemn dignity of an honest soul who was truly hurt, and expressed only the momentary displacement of a rogue caught in a situation his imagination lacked the wit to predict the outcome of.

Dawson shook his head dumbly, searching in vain for a recognisable point of entry from which his pre-rehearsed lines and put-downs could be employed to remaster the situation, confusion making him lose the fine thread of his vanishing anger.

'Delaney, I made . . . I made a mistake with you, you're not just a foul slacker, or even a bloody madman, though you are that as well, you're a . . . a bloody Bolshevist, a follower of Trotsky with no respect for the natural order. You dare come in here and dictate terms with me . . . with me!' He half-heartedly slammed his fist on the table again, further inflaming his tender knuckle. 'Why, if I listened to you . . . to your seditious, there's no other word for it, seditious request, I may as well hand the factory over to you while I was at it. Because that's where all this would end, isn't it, Delaney? You're not just some cadging oik, you're a damned Bolshevik with a programme to oust me, and don't tell me otherwise . . . you maggot.'

Delaney rubbed his eyes, the bright sunlight which had entered the room from behind Dawson's desk burning against them like flares. 'Yes, you might have it there,' he said, his hand half covering his face.

'Cur! You won't even deny it!' Dawson croaked, the strain evident in his voice as he waved a clammy fist at Delaney accusingly. 'You stand here, in my . . . in my *office*, for the love of God, and you lack even the animal sense to deny it!' Dawson shook his chair to emphasise his point, his frustration at allowing the confrontation to last so long matched by his ignorance of how to bring it to a close.

'Not so much a "programme" or whatever you call it, Mr Dawson, nothing so active, more of an eye on your overall picture.' Sleeplessness was making Delaney less sharp and slightly indistinct, a feeling he was enjoying.

'Overall what did you say?'

'Picture, Mr Dawson, the frame all this is happening in now.'

'The *frame*, what bloody frame are you talking about? You mean this factory, don't you? Me and my factory, my bloody life, because I tell you, man, I have no overall picture other than this factory you're standing in now.'

'If that's true then I don't think it too prudent to spend so much on a house you might be turned out of.'

An image of his father flashed before Dawson's eyes along with a supernatural presentiment of all he had gained and all he risked losing. 'Turned out of here? By who? That's it – now you listen to me, Delaney, you listen like you . . . like you've never listened to anything before because all this . . . nonsense,' Dawson bit his lip, he had been looking for something stronger, 'all this fucking nonsense must end, will end, right here in this room, you understand me? Right this minute.'

Delaney swayed slightly on his feet and shuffled back a few steps. 'You don't mind if I sit down, do you, Dawson? I feel fucking knackered too.'

'You!' Dawson glared at Delaney, aware, despite another wave of fresh anger, that their local conflict was being played out above the factory floor, the tiny thimble-like heads of the workers reflecting off the wall of the glass office like marbles scattered on a mirror. 'All right, Delaney, sit down if you must but while you're doing so listen, don't hear, *listen*.'

Delaney scratched his head in a way that made Dawson feel that the distinction had been considered but not properly understood.

'And stop that bumpkin routine while you're at it! There ain't going to be much for you to smile at when I'm through.'

Dawson raised his fist to throw it down again but thought better of it. 'And forget the sort of grandfatherly rot Grundy's probably tried to placate you with, I'm ready to talk real hard facts, the kind that are true whether you care to recognise them or not, you understand that, Delaney, yes? Because I've heard what you want now: you want me out and this place for yourself. Well it's time I declared my hand too, understand?'

Slumped in Dawson's favourite oxhide armchair Delaney, who looked like he had never understood anything at all, lit a cigarette, happily disregarding Dawson's 'allergy' to cigarette smoke.

Ignoring him, Dawson continued, 'This'll hurt you but I've seen what protecting you from the truth has achieved. I've tried to be your ally but instead you've forced me into becoming your enemy. Right, where were we? Yes, facts. Fact number one: the one fact there's absolutely no bloody getting away from. How to even tell you this . . . ? All right, I'd like to say that in the past year your conduct at "work", if I can dignify what you do here with that term, has been just awful, but to be honest we both know it's been far worse than that, don't we?'

To Dawson's amazement Delaney nodded at this rhetorical flourish, waving his cigarette in time to Dawson's words as if he were listening to an agreeable tune.

'Playing it like that, eh? Fine. And we both know the reason for this "failure to perform" is because you hate me, don't you? And the reason you hate me is because I'm the master of your sweetheart and the master of this town and your master, am I not?'

Delaney inhaled deeply on his cigarette reducing its length by nearly half.

'I'd say that that's fact number one because you see, Delaney, life is an experience when you learn from it and a mistake if you don't. I'm sure that you're not such a bloody fool as to not see the difference between the two. Me standing here talking to you with the respect of the town behind me —'

'Who are you trying to convince, Dawson, with all this?' cut in Delaney, his tone showing the first signs of an anger to equal Dawson's.

'– and you sitting there with nothing,' carried on Dawson, 'having learnt nothing, wanting to return to the past or to some imaginary state of affairs where you would be in my place and me in yours. Which brings me on to my second point.' Dawson wiped the spittle that had gathered at the corner of his lips onto his sleeve, the words coming easily to him now. 'You and I, and this'll surprise you, aren't so very different, in fact we're quite alike in one crucial way – got you there, haven't I?'

Delaney crossed his legs and flicked his cigarette across the room to the glass wall, which it bounced off like a missile. His eyes, were Dawson watching them, betrayed enormous self-control.

'You see, all I'm doing is playing the same game as you are, only at a higher level, and winning at it, that's all.' Dawson paused and ran the back of his hairy hand across his mouth which, in his enthusiasm, was showering saliva liberally over his desk. 'And it's because I'm winning, a fact that everything and everybody in this bloody town testifies to, it's because of that that I'm able to call the shots and tell you what to do. It's because we both have our places, me knowing mine but you, it seems, not knowing yours . . .'

Delaney laughed. 'Knowing your place? Come off it, Dawson! Is there ever such a thing as really knowing your place?'

'How old are you, eh? What've you been doing while the rest of us were discovering the facts of life?' said Dawson leaning his head close to Delaney's.

Despite the freshly lit cigarette in his hand, Delaney drew his hand to his nose in anticipation of Dawson raising his voice again, the smell of chocolate, coffee and undigested meat being more than he could bear. He grinned inwardly, wondering what Lou must make of it every morning.

'Of course there is such a thing as really knowing your place, you idiot, how do you think the bleedin' trains run on time? The driver doesn't walk into the controller's office like you seem to think you can walk into mine, he gets into his bloody engine and does his job,' Dawson explained, his voice raw with overuse. 'Look, let me put it in language you'll understand; you wouldn't like it if a floozy you'd taken out talked out of turn to you or showed you up? You'd tell her to hold her peace and mind her place. Well that's just like me and you . . . that's what explains the differences in our position and our behaviour, you a man of violence, and me a man of the world.'

'A what of the world? I thought you said we were the same.'

'You're not listening, are you! I didn't say the *same*, I said "alike", and the two are as different as chalk and cheese. So don't get any funny ideas about us being the same just because we want the same things.'

'Then what's the difference again? You're losing me, Dawson.'

'The difference? The difference is that unlike you, Delaney, I have no bloody reason to resort to violence or disobedience to get what I want; you, however, have no other means at your disposal. That's the bloody difference, you plank.'

'Very interesting that, wish I'd thought of it.'

'Exactly what I'd expect from you, sarcasm as usual; you're just proving my point.'

'It would've been good knowing this before, could've saved us some time.'

'Delaney, I'd be lying if I said this was just a difference between the powerful and powerless; it's much more than that, it's the difference between those that deserve power and those that do not . . .' Dawson had moved back through indignation to philosophical self-justification, the frame of mind he felt most himself in. 'We're not only different people, we're the representatives of two totally different types of human life, caste groups as the wogs would have it. Maybe we needed to go the long way around for that to become as clear to you as it is to me. And as for your ludicrous request for pay, well, you know we work every second Sunday of the month, you and the rest of those cheeky oiks on the floor know that, yet you still chose to stay away. Therefore I refuse to pay you a damned penny. Simple as that.'

Delaney brought himself to his feet and picked his bottle of whisky up off the floor. He had always prided himself on seeing through the petty trials and tribulations of life, to *what exactly* he did not know, but in Dawson's case he was fairly sure any insight of his was on firm ground, so he said, 'You know what, Dawson? You're a frightened man, a very frightened man. You always have been but you're even more that way now. It marks everything you do. That's why you attract other frightened people, like my Lou.'

'Frighten people? Of course I frighten people.'

'I said—'

'Oh come on, Delaney, don't be so naïve! Where would I be without the ability to frighten people! The battle for "hearts and minds" makes no sense to me now, what do I want with those? They're the property of a host of bucket-lickers anyway; the only thing that matters to me is control.'

'Power without control,' muttered Delaney.

'What did you say?'

'Nothing; just a saying of Moat's,' said Delaney turning to go.

Dawson stood up clumsily, the agitated twitch on his brow suggesting he felt cheated or had at least expected something more from his exhausting victory. 'So, Delaney, it seems we've come to the end of another chapter, a conclusion at last, wouldn't you agree . . . I'm talking to you, man,' he called out, the growing hoarseness in his throat marring his harsh intonation.

Delaney turned the top half of his body round indifferently and raised his eyes to the ceiling, the bottle in his hand lending him the appearance of the last man standing at a party. 'Still more of yours to come?'

'I don't recall giving you permission to leave. You're in my employment until I say you aren't. But it does seem that for once you've read my mind correctly.' Dawson squared his back so that his shoulders were nearly level with Delaney's neck. 'It seems to me that the conundrum we find ourselves in can be described thus,' he said, his inability to let the situation rest indicative of his irritation at still not knowing how Delaney's mind worked, 'life is obviously too short for us to remain enemies but it's also too short to try to become friends so I'm going to have to let you go, you and all the others, you've simply left me with no choice but to evoke the final solution.'

Delaney scratched the back of his neck with his index finger. 'Well at least you're done now.'

'No, *you're* done now.'

'Such is life,' Delaney smiled, his voice devoid of any sarcasm.

'You're going just like that, are you?' coughed Dawson breathlessly, ill at ease at having to point out the obvious, yet reluctant to end proceedings without a definitive last word. 'No apologies, just your tail knocked between your legs and off you go. Pathetic is what I call it, absolutely pathetic.' He sniffed unconvincingly. He could feel his trousers sticking to his underwear and his underwear to his skin; with some effort he tried to laugh and succeeded in making a short snorting noise, which he hoped Delaney would pick up on.

'Off you go, little man, off you go,' he chuckled, making little walking movements with his fingers, his laughter carrying across the room for reasons of reassurance rather than humour, 'and one more thing before you do, Delaney . . .'

'What now?'

Dawson leered over his desk as menacingly as he knew how and thrust his crotch into the open desk drawer, causing it to close with a small bang. 'Do you know anything of the pleasure of having sex with two different types of women within an hour of each other?'

'No,' said Delaney, 'not that I can think of; not unless you're talking of whores.'

Untroubled by Dawson's last throw of the dice, he closed the door firmly behind him without slamming it shut.

'Well I do,' replied Dawson, almost in a whisper to the empty room.

Grundy waited a full minute before allowing himself into Dawson's office. Normally he would have waited until Dawson had called him in, but he walked straight up to Dawson's desk and, in a tone he knew would provoke his boss's wrath, asked, 'I take it that the . . . business with Delaney has been settled to your satisfaction, Mr Dawson?'

Dawson lifted his head slowly off the clenched fist it had been resting on, more sleepwalker than leader of men. 'Who asked you in here?'

'Just checking that everything was all right with you, Mr Dawson. The Delaney matter specifically. There's still no report of the others, by the way, Stanton, Chudleigh, Baxter, Middlemist, Venning—'

'Shut up, for Christ's sake, I know the name of my own staff, don't I? I may dream of the day when this factory can be run by robots but we're not there yet. In the meantime I'll have to make do with morons with names like those. Anyway, not those particular names, I've sacked the bloody lot of them, for good.'

'If you say you have you have, Mr Dawson,' Grundy said, hesitating before adding, 'but that could involve, at the very least of it, a lot of paperwork. A lot of paperwork for each man, with regulations being what they are since Bevan got his hands on trade. You'll need my help with it, I expect?'

'I don't see why,' Dawson scowled, 'how hard can it be to throw some files into a waste-paper basket? What I really need is the help of a good policeman.'

Grundy blushed. His son was the town constable, happily married and living by the pier in Southcrawl, his appearance in Grumwood no more than a twice-a-week affair. This had granted Dawson the free hand he wanted, enabling him to run the town on his own terms, a situation that had suited him right up until the moment he saw Delaney marching into his office that morning. It was obvious that the very thought that there might be trouble he could not control had not occurred to Dawson before, and now that it had it was the fault of Grundy.

'Well I'm no policeman, Mr Dawson, and if you want my boy back in town you only need ask him, he's a good lad with a family, but not scared of his job or responsibilities . . . so if that's all I'll take my leave.'

'Here . . . here wait a minute,' there was something in Grundy's tone that made Dawson want to be nice to the man; he could not tell exactly what it was but he guessed that it was his uncharacteristic briskness. There was nothing that made Dawson more charming than the feeling that one of his toadies was ready to turn against him, and needed placating. He had lost enough staff for one day and it would not do to have too many enemies at any one time.

'They shouldn't be too hard a lot to replace, should they, Grundy? What would you say, given your experience in these matters? Ought to be more where they came from, it's not as if it's skilled labour we're dealing with after all,' he said, smiling with difficulty. 'Machines are bound to take over in the end anyway . . .'

'Are you really sure you want to be rid of them *all*, Mr Dawson?' said Grundy, swallowing the bait. 'I admit I'm not one hundred per cent sure of the exact figure you had in mind, regarding the men I mean, but it does seem as though you're talking about quite a lot of them, not all of whom are bad lads, I might add, if you'll pardon me speaking frankly, of course.'

'Go on, go on,' said Dawson waving his hand regally.

'Then why not just sack the real hotheads, Mr Dawson?

Delaney, of course, we could all tell you gave him a rightful seeing-to, Baxter and the Colonel as well, but in the case of the younger ones, well, I don't really see the sense in letting them all go . . . they've just fallen in with bad company, young men do that. But give them a reason to feel genuinely aggrieved and they'll carry on like coal miners, all moral superiority, certainty and contempt brewing up into a *righteous* hatred of us . . .'

'They're all rotten to the core,' snapped Dawson, irritated at having given Grundy enough slack to hold forth, 'you don't seem to realise the size of the problem we're dealing with; there's no sense in just pissing about with the ringleaders, they *all* need taking out, every one of them, out of the equation. Even a blind man can sense when bad apples have spoilt the whole batch. And anyway, stop being so hysterical, you seem to forget who has the whip hand here.'

'There's an old army expression about babies and bathwater . . .'

'Use your loaf for once and stop being pious. I have to do what I have to do to protect us and the whole bloody social order from *them* –' Dawson jabbed a stubby finger in the direction of the factory floor, '– even Delaney admitted that much to me. He bloody knew he was in the wrong and told me he was when he left. He said that he knew this mess was their doing, not mine.'

'Then he's a brighter lad than I gave him credit for,' said Grundy cautiously. 'Still feels a little on the harsh side though, Mr Dawson, punishing the naïve along with the knowing.' He stroked his moustache thoughtfully. 'Replacing them won't be the only problem we come up against, though . . .'

'What else are you thinking of?' spat Dawson, his mood returning to the properly confrontational again.

'Well, like I said, I don't know how many men you're planning on letting go exactly but if it's as many as I think you had in mind . . .'

'What are you driving at, Grundy? Cut to the quick.'

'The small matter of how their friends and workmates will react to our decision.'

'I told you I'm getting rid of them all, they won't have any friends left here to bloody mourn them. This is 1946, Grundy, not the year of the Tolpuddle Martyrs or the Peasants' Revolt.'

'That still leaves the problem of how the rest of the factory will see it, Mr Dawson; mass sackings can leave everyone, good and bad alike, looking over their shoulders. You remember how the lot at the armaments factory in Aldershot behaved when production—'

'They'll take it lying down and shutting up just like they take everything else. Don't look at me like that! You know I'm right because you know them for what they are and you know them for what they're not too. They're the mass, the same bunch of nobodies that willingly took the jobs in the first place and would let their wives be violated before they gave them up,' barked Dawson, impatient with a subject that seemed so simple before he had allowed the discussion to start. 'If only you'd been firm and shown some toughness in the first place, or if my father had, years ago . . . but neither of you had enough balls. Look where it's led us to, to the bloody dogs.'

Grundy picked up a broken pencil and fiddled with it awkwardly, frightened that he had pushed Dawson too far, his boss's awesome levels of energy easily dwarfing his own at arguing skills.

'Look around you, Grundy,' Dawson continued, 'these should be our glory days, production's never been faster and demand never higher. The country's growing rich again and we at Fox Brandy ought to be right there in the thick of it. That's where you'd hoped we'd be, eh? But look at what we're stuck with instead, a full-blown mutiny on our hands with me having to act as policeman and you a bleeding nanny.'

'I see what you mean, sir . . .' Grundy stopped himself. He hated calling Dawson 'sir' but it was an army habit he reverted to when deferring to authority. 'I see entirely what you mean, Mr Dawson, but I do think you are exaggerating things somewhat,' he added with rare, but quiet passion. 'In current circumstances you have every right to . . . well I don't know what I'm trying to say exactly . . .'

'Don't know? What don't you know, man? What is there to not know?'

'Let me put it this way,' Grundy stretched the words out for all they were worth, 'one of the things you learn about life when you get to my age, Mr Dawson, is that happiness and unhappiness, they exist side by side and often at the same time as each other . . .'

'Good God, Grundy! I had you down as slow but you're exceeding yourself! What the devil are you talking about, or for!'

'My point, sir, is—'

'Save it! And I don't mean for later but for ever!' Dawson walked round his desk and stood by the glass window overlooking the factory floor. 'We've had too much talk for one day, it's time to get things done. Homespun philosophies have their place but I didn't build this factory up on 'em, that's why we don't have unions here and why we don't suffer like they do up north with strikes and suchlike. What's needed now, as I've said countless times already today, is to cut the cancer out before it infects the body, and to do it fast. Then we'll have this factory up to the levels my father could only dream of.'

'Don't be too hard on Mr Grundy, Mr Dawson,' said a third voice, 'it's the second thing he's said today that isn't shit. Never heard him say anything that wasn't shit before today.'

'Enid?' Dawson stared aghast at his employee who was calmly leaning against the open door, her hag-like presence suggesting the beginning of an insurrection or, worse, a strike.

'Sorry not to knock first, Mr Dawson, but the door was wide open and you were talkin' as is your way.'

'What . . .' Downstairs, in the far right of his vision, Dawson noticed a line of workers moving towards the arch of the main exit, the hurried thud of their feet making his unsettled stomach feel like a windmill. 'What, what's going on down there? Where are those workers going?' he asked, pointing to a second cluster of men and women leaving their machines.

'You can calm right down, Mr Dawson, I've big good news for you – the Jaguar motor car you ordered and were telling all about, it's been delivered today, bloke's only driven it into the forecourt, everyone's on their way to have a look. You can't blame them. I mean, it's not every day you see one of those driving machines.'

Dawson shook his head with relief and slid off his sweat-heavy spectacles. 'Thank, thank bloody Christ for that.' He laughed, his world having moved from restoration to collapse and back to splendid restoration again. 'Don't just stand there, then,' he boomed jovially, a new sports car always able to draw out the best in his erratic nature. 'Let's have a look at it. In fact, why don't we have ourselves a ride in the beast!'

'Wonderful idea, Mr Dawson,' Grundy exclaimed, enjoying the spirit of sudden lightness that had engulfed the room and all three in it.

Enid clapped her tiny hands dementedly and rushed out of the room squealing, 'The motor car, the motor car, the boss is going to take me for a ride in it!'

'A capital idea, Mr Dawson, a capital idea, and if you don't mind me saying, just what the situation required,' said Grundy raising an eyebrow archly.

'Exactly,' chuckled Dawson, flattered that Grundy had acknowledged his ability to manipulate events to his advantage. 'Give 'em a bright new Jag and all thoughts of workers' solidarity can go hang, that's the truth about the good people of Grumwood . . . should you be so stupid as to believe they were in *need* of *truth*,' he smirked.

Confidently he tapped his nose and took Grundy by the shoulder, their physical contact sealing Grundy's part in the conspiracy, their earlier altercation consigned to the ash heap of healthy misunderstandings.

'Hah hah, that's a good one, Mr Dawson, a good one that is,' chortled Grundy, comfortable again in his role as court sycophant, the militancy of the previous moment the fault of another man he no longer acknowledged. 'Yes, I've yet to meet one of these so-called socialist fellows who wouldn't swap his principles for an MG Midget,' he bellowed unselfconsciously, his master's sentiment still fresh enough to warrant slavish repetition.

'The new car, beggars belief! To think I've been looking forward to that for weeks . . . I don't know how it could have slipped my mind . . .' mused Dawson as he clicked his tongue and cantered onto the gangway. 'It's incredible how you can lose sight of the important things in life when you're neck deep in trivial rubbish.'

'Wood from the trees, Mr Dawson, wood from the trees, yes, we all lose a little bit of perspective from time to time. Wouldn't be human if we didn't,' Grundy replied somewhat unnecessarily, comfortable that his relationship with Dawson was back to its old footing, but with slightly more mutual respect than before, he could not help but notice.

'What a day, what a day we've already had!' sighed Dawson, finally at peace with his surroundings.

'Yes, Mr Dawson,' smiled Grundy, surprised that Dawson had used 'we' in an inclusive way for once. If this was a fresh beginning, then it hinted at new and exciting possibilities, perhaps even an eventual shift in power if one were to consider his boss's recently exposed frailties. 'Team work, Mr Dawson, team work, that's what gets us through days like these . . .' Grundy pondered philosophically. He had always felt that Dawson could neither survive nor cope without him, but now he was absolutely positive of it. 'Yes, it was interesting exchanging ideas and strategies with you back there, Mr Dawson.'

'Look down there at that!' Dawson grabbed Grundy's wrist and pointed to a shaft of sunlight that fell over a sliver of oil shimmering on a chocolate vat. On a normal morning it was his habit to treat moments of transcendental beauty such as this as a puzzling annoyance, but today Dawson said, 'Fancy that, Grundy, sunshine on chocolate; who'd have guessed it, eh? Looks quite pretty. Unlikely that.'

'I suppose it does, Mr Dawson,' said Grundy, thinking of how fast the Jaguar would go in the hands of some person more properly deserving of it.

From his spot, hidden between the pipes in the upper gallery, Terry Delaney watched on unimpressed. It was fast turning into one of those mornings when he would have appreciated the company of a sniper's rifle. To see people become so excited over the arrival of a car had at first depressed, and then angered him. He had seen enough of cars in the war, and had even been moved to drive a few, knowing that he would never actually own one of the things. As far as he was concerned they carried people around from place to place and were faster than using one's legs, but that was it; horses served much the same purpose and no one apart from little girls made a song and dance about them.

Delaney could feel his stomach tighten as he observed Dawson descend the steps and land on the shop floor with a jaunty thump, much like a politician leaving home the morning after an election victory. Those workers still on the production line gave their boss a small cheer as he brushed past them to inspect his new toy. Shaking his head in silent disbelief, Delaney tried to pick out the faces of the individual workers and relate their behaviour to the people he knew and worked alongside. Their smiling faces told him nothing. It was incredible how completely the world had changed.

He could date this realisation back to his first trip to the Fox Brandy factory a year earlier, an unfortunate experience that had bound him irrevocably to the man he hated most in the world, Oliver Dawson. He had arrived at the gates of the plant certain that no matter what he was offered, was promised or said, he would not accept a job there. Delaney's first surprise of the day came almost at once when Dawson had greeted him personally and acted as his chaperone on a lengthy tour of the factory, the second surprise being the changed physical appearance of Dawson himself. Far from the sulking and scrawny individual, given to fits of temper behind the backs of more prepossessing individuals whom Delaney half remembered, Dawson had filled out into the very caricature of a cigar-smoking capitalist, lacking only the top hat. Without wasting time on formalities, Dawson had embraced Delaney in the French style and welcomed him into the factory with the fanfare and warmth of a circus ringmaster.

This powerful, but misleading impression of camaraderie was reinforced by the manner in which Dawson had immediately drawn Delaney into his confidence, addressed him as an equal and talked to him as one friend might do to another. In hindsight it was easy to see that Dawson's conversational technique was the end product of several rehearsals, his frank intimacy little more than an imitation of the real quality, and both, like his newly cultivated taste in clothes, were small parts of a far larger act Dawson had embarked on. Delaney, unlike many 'interviewees', had suspected as much at the time, but, without a good reason or means of exposing Dawson, had had no choice but to take his 'goodwill' at face value. Dawson had helped himself in this by not hiding from Delaney, correctly guessing that the easiest way to neutralise any possible resistance was through honesty, or at least the appearance of it.

'I'll come straight to the point,' he had said, his voice firm and considered, 'I don't want there to be any hard feelings between us over Lou. I'm not worried there will be, mind you, I know you to be man enough to not care about little things like who's shacked up with who, but I think it's only right to

say something now, just so that *you* know I'm not bothered by
it either. Whatever went on between you two happened before
I came on the scene and I'm not one to hold grudges, everyone's
entitled to a past. A lot of things didn't last the war and there
was no use in thinking relationships would be an exception
anyway; they're probably the least valuable of the things that
didn't last when compared to important buildings, fortunes and
governments but still . . . they didn't last. Right, well, now that
we have that out of the way . . .' and that had been the end of
the matter. It seemed of no consequence that Delaney could
think of little that mattered *more* than relationships and if it
had not been for his relationship with Lou he probably would
not have thought the war worth fighting in the first place. He
might have also added that matters could just as well work the
other way and that a lot of things that would survive the peace
may not deserve to, namely Dawson's relationship with the
woman he still loved.

Despite spending what felt like several lives wondering what
he would finally say to Dawson when he confronted him,
Delaney had been ashamed to discover that his response to
Dawson's speech was one of mute assent. His hours of brooding
and waiting had amounted to nothing. When put on the spot
Delaney had taken a sharp intake of breath and said precisely
nothing. Had he been more articulate, and equipped with a
sharper memory, he might have repeated a sentiment he had
overheard Vivien Ross express several times; 'I think we're
returning to a situation similar to the one we suffered back in
the thirties before the war began. Fundamentally weak relationships between men and women are thriving again. During
the war that wasn't so, they were tested and fell apart. But now
hypocrisy is back in the saddle, and falsity will endure.' But
being inarticulate, and terribly poor with his timing, Delaney
had missed his opportunity, shrugged his shoulders and allowed
Dawson to change the subject to chocolate-bean production.

From that point on, Delaney conceded, he had surrendered

his advantage, and was no more or less to Dawson than any of the other minions he employed. If this were not enough, Dawson's offer of a relatively senior post and 'generous' working hours and wages (at least compared to those workers who had not fought in the war – 'nothing's too good for our heroes, Delaney, nothing's too good') had pushed Delaney off any of the remaining moral high ground he needed to be on to pursue a fight.

To his amazement, and without any knowing collusion in the matter, he realised that Dawson had successfully bought him off with a package of concessions that he was largely indifferent to, if not entirely unfit for. What made Dawson's tactical triumph all the more absurd to Delaney was its suddenness, combined with the fact that he had never properly noticed Dawson before the war, considering him at most a small noise that need not be taken too seriously. At best he had thought him a low-level grafter, but certainly never a man he would associate with women, or that women were drawn to, and definitely not a man he could envisage being married to his beloved Lou. Dawson's exhaustive tour of the factory on that first morning had broken this lazy assumption, the very innocuousness of Dawson's former self brought up to date and compensated for by his self-glorifying anecdotage and endless line in boasts. He had watched with tired eyes as Dawson dipped his hand into a tub of chocolate and licked his sticky fingers clean. 'See this, Delaney? See this brown gloop, this is basically the product of nigger sweat, not real chocolate; we don't make the *real* stuff here, there'd be no point, people wouldn't be able to tell the difference, see? *Real* chocolate's what they get up in Fortnum's and tastes all bitter and horrible, comes from Africa, I think. What the *British* public wants is dyed sugar and caramel lumps, the sort of thing auntie likes, as we say on the tin. Some bloke once said that if you give the public what you think they want you end up underestimating them, or something like that, but that's a cartload of crap, Delaney, and you'd best believe it. Like I say, it all comes down to the chocolate test, that is, if they were bright enough to tell the difference between the gloop and the real thing in the first place, they'd *still* prefer my product.' It had probably been the only truly honest sentiment to come out of Dawson's mouth that day but, as Delaney would learn, when it came to expressing his contempt for ordinary people Dawson could always be relied upon to be honest. Within minutes of this project-defining speech Delaney had watched Dawson sack a junior foreman on a trumped-up charge of allowing birds to nest in the roof of the building – 'we're making chocolate, not bloody pigeon crap' – the real reason being that the man's wife had stupidly called Lou a whore to her face, the retaliatory action taken by Dawson on his wife's behalf and not at her behest. 'But she is a *hoor*, isn't she?' Delaney had heard the factory floor whisper, as Dawson passed sentence on the unfortunate chocolate packer. This was an ugly sentiment that Delaney unhappily subscribed to, angry that it was true and angrier still that he acknowledged it to be so. If it hurt to hear this slander in the mouths of others it stung even more to experience the truth of it in his heart, for no matter how hard or long he thought about it, Lou's behaviour and choice of partner remained inexplicable to him. Where it may have seemed obvious to his friends that Lou should wish to keep as much distance between her new life and old as possible, Delaney, still confusing her beauty with moral purity, was baffled by being written out of her life altogether. His fall to non-being made no sense to him as he was sure that her goodness had not been a product of his imagination, and nor had it, but Delaney had not reckoned on her fear of 'being left behind by life'; 'life' had never been a concept he had sought to compete with.

His foolish belief that he was a realist, rather than a rural idealist, and his damaging pride meant that he had played into Dawson's, and ultimately Lou's, hands, by avoiding them whenever he could and acting out the role of an old man past caring, despite being two years short of his thirtieth birthday. There was still so much he did not understand, and questions he wanted to ask, not just of Lou and Dawson but of everyone who regarded his fate as bad luck, but nonetheless normal. Eventually resistance had grown too painful and Delaney had begun to accept reality as it was, just like the good realist he had forced himself to become, until he at last stopped being a soldier and became just another one 'of the blokes that fought in the war'.

'You're going to enjoy working here, Delaney,' Dawson had said. 'Take a look at the skirt around this place, most of 'em shag like men, ugly men at that, but God do they shag, not that I partake in that sort of thing myself, of course, but you should have seen them go during the war. Well it's time for you to take *your* turn now.' These words had had the unlikely effect of making Delaney feel mildly prudish, but he had made an effort to smile, a moment too late to convince Dawson, who sneered, 'So you don't think I'm a comedian, Delaney? It doesn't matter; enough people around here do, as you'll find out in good time, when you realise that the chocolates aren't the only thing with soft centres in this place. Oi, Grundy! Get your stone arse over here and meet our Terence, the big war hero . . .' Dawson's tone had already started to turn bitter before Delaney had put pen to paper on his contract, the effort of perpetuating a front nearing exhaustion as he gained what he wanted: 'I'm making a special case for you, Delaney, but that doesn't mean you can expect any favours from me once things get going. You may be a cut above the rest of the muck here, I grant you, but unlike my father I judge men on performance, and not on their bloody humanity.'

It was after hearing these words that Delaney finally gave up any remaining hope of knowing Lou again. Class, social standing and the natural rights of man had been matters she was most sensitive to, not due to any snobbery on her part but from an excess of social conscience that, as a servant, she found difficult to act on. Lou, unlike Delaney who was insensitive to status and questions of inferiority, had considered it the height of bad manners to ever mention 'rank', or make anyone more aware than they had to be of their income and place in society. She often carried this near fanatical belief to the point of absurdity and ignored perfectly obvious differences between people, preferring instead to treat everyone with the courtesy she was obliged to show the Rosses, her employers. Kindness earned Delaney's respect and forced him to reconsider his opinion of Lou's otherwise prissy code.

The question of what had become of these morals, and the strength with which she could stand up for them, now that she was Mrs Dawson of Fox Brandy, remained unanswered, but because more pressing with every word of Dawson's that was designed to bolster his own self-importance, and remind others of the absence of theirs. Not only Delaney, but every living cast-off of Lou's former life agreed that it would have been hard, even if she had cared to try, to find an individual, be him barroom bully or concentration camp guard, more antithetical to her pre-war beliefs than Oliver Dawson. Despite tending towards moderation in Lou's company, Dawson still said things, spoke to people and acted in a way that would have been unimaginable to Delaney, even though during their time together Lou had often chastised him for being a harsh and careless man. Where this left Dawson in her eyes, Delaney did not care to guess, but having overcome his disbelief at Lou's preference for Dawson over him in the first place, Delaney now struggled to find a way of explaining what could possibly *attract* her to the man.

Was he, Delaney wondered, not duty bound to report 'the truth' to Lou about the man she had married and tell her what Dawson was really like, or was this just another manifestation of his helplessness and self-pity? Hearing Dawson describe his staff as 'muck', and watching him yell at yet another subordinate, had convinced Delaney at last that there was no truth about her husband with which Lou was not already acquainted. He had merely deluded himself into thinking so, in order to continue loving her. Once robbed of this long-standing illusion, Delaney had forgone all hope of intimate reconciliation with her and accepted further unpalatable truths. Dawson's bestiality was no drain on his appeal, but a central aspect of what had drawn Lou to the man, either in the hope of rescuing him or saving herself from unnecessary martyrdom. Rather than bestowing her good qualities upon Dawson, and opening his heart to life, she had merely inherited his bad qualities and compromised what was left in a marriage of convenience.

Delaney had no doubt that Lou would not see matters this way and, if asked, would insist that she found Dawson's brutishness sweet, his foul sulks endearing, his selfishness a legacy of his own fear, and his dishonesty and loathing of people the fault of a hostile environment. Lou was nothing if not an expert self-justifier, and for all the complexities of their triangle, it was the Colonel who had summed up the situation most succinctly when he had said, 'Face it, Terence, the no-good scrubber has upgraded. You don't have anything she wants.' This was, by now, highly speculative theorising as Delaney had no intention of ever speaking to Lou again on this subject or any other, yet nothing in the past year had proved it wrong. His acceptance that he had lost her had destroyed what was left of his morale and left him wide open to Dawson's offer of work.

Trying to see his position as others would, Delaney had attempted to address the facts of his situation and ignore, for once, his actual feelings. He was alone, back from years of thankless service and in the prime of his life. Delaney could remember the years of unemployment his father had suffered, as numerous as the Great War campaign medals kept in a frame above the fireplace, and this memory steeled him against settling for a similar destiny. His pride had already made a fool of him once and it would be fatal to allow it to do so again. Reluctantly, and in full knowledge of the shame he would subsequently have to live with, he accepted Dawson's shilling and signed on. The rest of the men of T Squadron, with the exception of Polly, had taken no persuading to do exactly the same thing and by the end of the week they were employees of Oliver Dawson. Delaney had been the first to concede that they had got what they deserved, but maintained they had done nothing to deserve the choice they had been given. The one superiority that he had stubbornly clung to was his glorious past as a tank-man, but even that had counted for nothing in the end, leaving him with no option.

But now it was time to take direct action.

Carefully Delaney slid his legs out of his hiding place and lowered them to the aisle below. Looking from side to side to ensure he was unobserved, he walked softly down the fire escape steps to the level of Dawson's office. He was quite clear about what he must do, his memories of the recent past burning out the alcoholic fog that had blunted his mind earlier that morning. He was going to take what he was owed, what they were all owed and no more. To help himself to more would be an act of theft and make him no better than a criminal. It would not do to overlook the importance of occupying the moral high ground in this affair, and his actions must be above any taint of personal opportunism. Obviously it was impossible to take *exactly* what they were all owed without blowing Dawson's safe, which was out of the question, and as Delaney had no mathematical brain on him it was hard to calculate what that sum was. Whatever the figure may run to in pounds – and had their conversation gone the way Delaney had intended he would have found out – it was well in excess of any unit of ten he could count on his fingers and far more than could be found in the petty-cash box. If Dawson could not pay back his debt in the currency in which he had incurred it then other, less conventional, methods would have to be adopted.

Dawson's office door was as he had left it, unlocked, and

from the loud tooting of the car horn and the roars from the staff outside Delaney was confident there would be enough time to do what he had to do, uninterrupted. Looking over the room he eyed the plethora of items scattered like confetti over the various cabinets, tables and drawers. Opening the large rope sack he had walked in with, Delaney started to fill it, unmethodically choosing a calendar and then an armful of model planes. Clocks, an enormous calculating machine, a typewriter, pencils, rubbers and rulers followed; everything Delaney could lay his hands on, until he was satisfied that he had bagged enough 'stuff' to equal the cash Dawson owed them in wages. Briefly he considered urinating over Dawson's desk to finish the job off properly, but hesitated at the crassness of such symbolism. If it did not look like he had appropriated enough booty when he got home, he could always come back later and take the lamps off the new car. Dawson had, whether he had known it or not, begun a war, and Delaney, having had some experience of these things, was ready to claim first blood, liberated at last by the bold simplicity of his hatred.

4

LODGINGS

Shallow woke up wondering what he was. A clue to his status as a thinking thing lay next to him in the fully clothed form of Mark Polly. Warm rays of sunlight fell on Polly's slightly open mouth, his sleeping face a tribute to the slow pace of life in rural Britain, thought Shallow, mindful that he had no idea what they were doing in bed together.

Polly's twitching hands lay outstretched before him like grateful recipients of a miracle, the rest of his tangled body wrapped up in the sheets. Shallow, for once, was relieved that he no longer woke up with erections, the scholar in him detecting something faintly Greek about the scene. Over on the reading chair he could hear the Colonel, slumped in a peaceless sleep, swatting imaginary flies and swearing at the ghost of an ex-wife, his cheerless presence no more explicable than that of Polly's. Shallow closed his eyes and spared a nostalgic thought for the days when he was still able to wake up and wonder who he was, rather than what he was, his degeneration not nearly as amusing to him as he suspected it was to others.

Without wanting to break out of the soothing rhythms of his trance completely, Shallow tried to lift his face off the pillow, discovering that he could do so with disconcerting ease. Hesitantly he rocked his head from side to side, waiting in vain for the anticipated pain that would force him back down into a cowering foetal position. No pain came, and he began to shake his head and arms a little faster to no harmful effect; the sun was out and there was no denying how good he felt. This, and the complete absence of any signs of a hangover, or even heartburn in his chest, could mean only one thing: he was still pissed.

He whispered the word in a slurred voice he did not recognise as his own. Holding a trembling finger to his brow, Shallow tried to concentrate on the last thing he could remember clearly before he had got *very* drunk . . .

In fact, being *very* drunk the night before was one of the few things he could remember clearly; the irony of being *so* drunk that he could actually remember getting into such a state not lost on him. Sadly for Shallow, there was nothing particularly new about this, the only novel feature of the situation being the sensation of weightlessness in his stomach, a feeling that reminded him of looking forward to birthday parties when he was young. It was unfortunate that the only difference between the liberating aspect of this feeling, and the oppressiveness he usually felt in the mornings, was that he could barely wait to go out and get drunk again, rather than just resign himself to it as he normally did.

Over the course of his life Shallow had moved through a shy and lonely childhood, to the confidence of an alcohol-fuelled adolescence and army career, and back to an introspective and lonely manhood. Drink had been the key to his inner self, and the oil on the lock when all was lost.

The last occasion on which he could actually remember drink setting him free was the day he had come to on the floor of a Maltese restaurant in Paddington, only to discover that Germany had started World War Two. Usually a memory spanning a gap of several years was guaranteed to bring Shallow down to earth, the passage of time and wasted time being synonymous parts of the same curse. But any natural apprehension was heavily outweighed this morning by the lingering presence of alcohol, and he felt emboldened enough by his rude health to allow his thoughts the rare opportunity to remember.

The war had belonged, like all news heard over the wireless, to a parallel universe that Shallow only occasionally felt the need to be diverted by, far removed as it was from the real world of South Kensington and the Newmarket racecourse. Once or twice an event from the other world, the Spanish Civil War or the Munich Agreement to name two, would threaten to penetrate the bubble Shallow and his set inhabited, but any encroachment was always minor and its effects never more than superficial and temporary. On the morning of 3 September 1939, Shallow's greatest fear, as he lay half listening to the Prime Minister's broadcast, was whether he had offended Gee Carstairs' sister the night before, having 'insured' her breasts for a fiver each, and her front bottom for a shilling. As usual nothing had provoked this jape, there had been no game or conversation that had led up to the subject, Shallow had merely aired his figures out of the blue for laughs, and as usual people had laughed, though not too hard, he hoped, as he had had 'a thing' for Gee's sister and she would be due back at Cheltenham before October.

Gradually, as one news bulletin followed another, it began to dawn on Shallow that what he was listening to might, in some oblique way, have an eventual bearing on him, and that his world and that of the news broadcasts were finally destined to meet, if not merge in outright collision.

Four days later, after a binge worthy of a medieval protectorate, Shallow marched into the Earl's Court recruitment office with Gee Carstairs and a drinking crew of complete strangers, announcing to all those present that he was ready 'to smash Hitler's bloody mug in because it's about time someone did'. The whole place had roared with patriotic approval and yet another drinking bout had begun there and then, the eager volunteers proclaiming to all four winds that any Englishman who would not join them would miss out on the cakewalk to Berlin, and hold his manhood cheaply for evermore. In their euphoria they did not notice that they were out of step with the general mood both on the Earl's Court Road and in the country at large, the older men looking on indulgently and the calculating men already looking away at something else. Three days later Shallow was in uniform, and waiting for a commission in his father's old cavalry regiment, his sense of purpose growing in proportion to every admiring glance his uniform attracted. The word was that they would be charging into battle on iron horses and not the oat-eating kind; that there would be no trenches this time around or wet winters in France, just the cut and thrust of a war of movement. Shallow, though not averse to being thrown off a horse, had never learnt to ride one, and was delighted by news which offered the promise of finding his time and place in the world at last, a wasted decade of boozing finally behind him. It was in this confident frame of mind, and with Prudence Carstairs' blessings, that Shallow disembarked in Calais and prepared to take his place amongst a new breed of warrior, ready to ride into the mechanical dawn of total war. What this entailed was six years of consequential folly that would lead him through the fall of France, the battleground of El Alamein, the Normandy landings and finally to Grumwood, the Squirrel Skinner and a bed shared with Mark Polly.

'Not all bad, then,' mumbled Shallow to his pillow. He could remember his father boasting of his exploits in the Boer War but being at a loss to find his front door keys, and Shallow felt no different when attempting to remember the night before, his distant history undermining his grasp of the recent past. He scratched his forehead; there was a girl in there somewhere, and probably an argument or two ... Lou Polly and Oliver Dawson rang a bell, but what did either of them have to do with him?

Shallow smiled wanly, aware that he was taking this problem, if a problem it was, too seriously. In truth, he did not care very deeply about the night before or the one before that, at least not yet, not while he was still drunk and meditative. The easiest way of keeping any attacks of pride, dignity or guilt at bay was to ensure that he remained drunk all day, which would not be too difficult a task providing no one got in his way. There may have been a point in his life when he would have found this conclusion depressing, but that period had long since been surpassed by a drunken wisdom. Learning to cope with forgetting large swathes of his life had come in two distinct stages for Shallow, the passage through which was not without difficulty, but necessary if he were to take his drinking on to the Olympian level that awaited him.

The first stage was primarily defensive; Shallow would boldly pretend he could remember everything about the 'night before', irrespective of whether he could account for a single one of his actions or not. This deception, necessitated by the terror inherent in wondering whether he had become another man under the influence of drink, was a vital one for Shallow in the teething years of his alcoholism. The admission that he could turn into a Mr Hyde when drunk would have forced him to concede that he had lost sovereignty over his life and, worse still, compelled him to accept criticism from those sober enough to provide it. To avoid this humiliating penance, Shallow required a defensive strategy that demanded much low cunning on his part, amounting to no less than a permanent vigil the day, if not the week, after any notable binge. Shallow would claim to have absolute and easy familiarity with any subject a friend brought up with him, just in case they had already discussed it the night before during his memory lapse. The trick of always pretending to know what everyone was talking about or referring to, far from making Shallow an irritating know-all, earned him a reputation as an understanding and empathetic conversationalist.

It would have been difficult, should anyone have actually wanted to catch him out, to do so as nearly all his drunken escapades occurred in an emotional fog that defied factual post-mortems, but as Shallow was *so* drunk at the time he never remembered this, thus condemning himself to continue in his deceptions. This was the background to his entry into the second stage of his pre-war epiphany, during which it was no longer even necessary to plead sobriety, as the difference between his behaviour when drunk and when sober had become so small as to render any distinction meaningless. When he found himself apologising for his 'unacceptable conduct' friends would give him a puzzled grin and reply that his behaviour had been no different to how it normally was, bar the odd slurred word or dropped glass. And so it transpired that despite the intense blackouts and guilt, Shallow's drunken conduct was little more than a whimsical, if slightly affected, exaggeration of his daily self. It did not occur to him that if this was so, if the final result was no more than a pastiche of what his world would have been without alcohol, there was little point in devoting his life to his reckless habit. The simple fact of the matter was that drinking and drunkenness had become too easy for him, and he was too good at both, and hopeless at everything else, to stop. It was impossible for him to know, with any certainty, at what point after this realisation his drinking for pleasure had been replaced by drinking for England, but he suspected that the date of the Battle of Caen was as good as any to confirm what he already knew. Life, especially for a functioning alcoholic, was an opportunity to drink, rather than a space in which other less destructive pursuits could be attended to. This did not mean that Shallow was the type of soldier who found his nerves tested in battle and sought drink as an obvious refuge. Battle, like the whole war for Shallow, had merely been the continuation of self-destructiveness by other means because, unlike many of the other men who fought, he had already known what he was; a drunk.

This was as far as his thoughts could take him, for they all led back to the war but could go no further, his memory as long and sad as those monuments erected in every town and village to immortalise the sacrifice of those who went to it.

Shallow picked a packet of cigarettes from under his pillow and stared at them, marvelling at how he could have known they were there. Crediting a telepathic connection between his brain and nicotine, Shallow lit one and surveyed the room for more clues as to how he and Polly had become last-minute bedfellows. The array of tin mugs still filled with gin, brandy and floating cigarette ends, were evidence that they had bravely drunk on to the very end. Nothing too untoward about that, thought Shallow, mildly relieved at there being no darker explanation for why he and Polly had shared body warmth, but dismayed at having been so desperate for company as to actually need another man with him right up to the point of collapse. If this was so then it was possible that he really *was* worse.

His eyes emitted a small wash of tears, the result of the cigarette smoke blown back in from the window above the bed. Shallow always opened it before going to sleep should he wake up in the middle of the night and wish to throw himself from it. Narrowing his eyes to stop the water, he began to sip at his cigarette and blow rings of smoke into the draught, the predictable sadness of another lost morning nearly upon him.

'Morning, Mr Shallow,' said Mark Polly, his voice as attendant and friendly as a scout's. 'We were a long way gone last night, weren't we? God, I was, I can hardly remember a thing about it.' He laughed, his fresh intonation betraying nothing of the previous evening's excess, and even his oath lacking the bitter resonance of the other tank-men's appeals to the Lord. 'Um, what are you doing, sir?'

'Trying to see the world as it is. All at once, without the weight of past associations. But you needn't mind me,' said Shallow, straightening into a sitting position and coughing melodramatically, 'I'm nearly finished and you've probably helped restore my good mood by waking up anyway.'

'Hope the "seeing the world" thing has gone well for you, sir.'

'Not too badly, I'm not likely to be burdened by the weight of expectation . . .'

'No, I'm not feeling so good myself,' said Polly, pleased that he did not appear to be in any trouble. 'I hope that I didn't wake you by snoring.'

'That's what I like about you, Mark Polly my boy,' shouted the Colonel from the foot of the bed, a half-drunk mug of gin in his hand. 'You're man enough to admit to being *nice*, and not many men are, we try and hide it lest some sneaky sod take the piss. Cheers.' The Colonel drained the mug and looked at Shallow's cigarette hungrily. 'Hope you don't mind . . .'

'Be my guest, but try to blow the smoke out of the window, the landlady doesn't like the smell on the furniture, and, smoker that I am, nor do I.'

'That'll explain why this room's so bloody cold then, never sleep with 'em open myself, windows that is, catch myself a bloody chill or worse; you should take care you don't end up with one, Mr Shallow, what with all this bloody airing. Still, very shit or bust, and we like that, don't we, Mark?'

'There are worse things I can think of than catching a cold.'

'Aye, aye, good point, Mr Shallow; they didn't waste their time with you at that bloody college of yours, did they, that's for sure. Mind if I borrow a match, good man? No, I hope you didn't object to our overnight stopover, sir, I know you told us to bugger off once we finished the last of our gin, but you probably won't remember saying that now and didn't really mean it anyways, you sort of only said it in a jokey way . . .'

'Yes, I would have almost certainly been joking.'

'. . . and Mark and me couldn't exactly walk home, and some leery cunt had smashed our wheels, if I remember rightly. So I hope there aren't any hard feelings at us taking this small liberty . . .'

'Not at all, none in the slightest.'

'I said Mark could share the bed with you, what with me being such a big frightening man and all, no point in you being scared out of your wits when you came to.' The Colonel laughed heartily, pausing to look around the room for the first time since waking up. 'Mmm, no doubt about it, an interesting little place this, the Falcon Hotel Annexe, eh? Must admit I've never been in here before, good little gaff, though, lots of natural light. Must come in handy when you want to read the paper.'

'Yes . . . it does.'

'Not very big, though.'

'No, but I don't often receive guests so you are both a welcome change. The landlady doesn't allow me more than one visitor at a time, actually.'

'Bloody good of you to not mind us here then, a proper officer you are, reminds me of the time when we were all stacked on top of each other in the tanks, stacked like sardines, we were. There were no airs and graces back in those days . . .'

'And what days they were, Thatcher,' it was Shallow's practice to call the Colonel by his real name, 'what days they were!'

'That's the stuff, Captain!' agreed the Colonel gesturing out of the window with his cigarette. 'Rhododendrons, tulips, ground elder, all flowers, soldier class, officer class, we're all bloody drinkers! And come nightfall there isn't a single one of us that doesn't appreciate a good kip in a warm bed, general and private alike. Not one of us you'd call polished let alone smooth.'

Polly winked at Shallow; the gin was already having an effect on the Colonel.

'Here's to the grand leveller, I say, whether it be booze, fillies or taking a sharp one in the guts. The problem today, if you ask me, is that we spend too much time harping on about our differences, how one sod drinks from a different kettle of fish to the next. Well I say shit and balls to that; it's the similarities we should be looking to, how we all have hair and bloody hands to lift gravel with. Best stress what we all have in common with each other, ain't that right?' continued the Colonel, his cold breath the colour of freezing mud. 'By God, it's good for the soul waking up with friends, if you'll pardon my familiarity, Mr Shallow, because that's what we all class you as now;

I mean, if I were to meet most of our blokes for the first time again I don't know whether I'd take the trouble of getting all that close to them, but in the case of you two I can tell you it'd be worth the bother, no doubt about it.'

'What have you both got planned for today?' asked Shallow, changing the subject.

'Work, I'm afraid,' said Polly looking slightly worried at being reminded of a world outside the room. 'I hope I'm not late, the garage opens early on Mondays . . . does anyone know what time it is?'

'Work!' snorted the Colonel. 'The devil take work, I say, there're other things to do today, or any other day besides blasted work . . .' He paused. 'I've got a feeling we went over this last night . . . Delaney, wasn't it? Said he was going in to fix Dawson today?'

'I hope for his sake he's either forgotten or recanted.'

'Mr Shallow, let me tell you something about my place of "work",' replied the Colonel, avoiding the question, 'it is a bleedin' shithole that could depress even the Bob Hopes of this world . . .'

'All the same they'll still be expecting you this morning.'

'. . . an absolute catastrophe of a place run by a man with a girl's finger for a cock, an adding machine for a brain and a fish for a heart.'

'Fish, have you already mentioned fish today? But yes, I gather that Oliver Dawson is not especially popular with the workforce. I think I met the fellow again last night actually.'

'You can say that again, Mr Shallow, "not especially popular". Ha! That's one way of bloody putting it, I suppose.' The Colonel clutched at his head, the vague throbbing at his temples fast escalating into a heavy pounding. 'Why, the only thing that bothers me about this damned hangover here is the fact that Dawson doesn't have it yet; that's how much I hate the swine, that much.'

'Hate, that's strong stuff, Thatcher, you don't want to be walking about with that.'

'Ha! Don't fret about me, Mr Shallow, it does me good to hate, keeps me going, doesn't it, Mark?'

Polly, who was combing his hair in the mirror, smiled absent-mindedly and nodded. Under the mirror was a copy of *Good Housekeeping*, the magazine open on a page titled 'Home must be the greatest rehabilitation centre of them all'. Polly noticed that a paragraph had been torn from the main page, under-lined and highlighted. It read: '*What You Can Do For A Returning Veteran* After TWO or THREE weeks he should be finished with talking, with nightmares and oppressive remem-bering. If he still goes over the same stories, reveals the same emotions and otherwise draws attention to himself, you had best consult your family doctor. This condition is neurotic.' Polly put down the comb and hid the article under a page detailing the recipe for Chelsea buns.

'Is there anything that keeps you going, Mr Shallow, some-thing a little more genteel than my "hate"? Apart from the obvious, of course,' said the Colonel, indicating the empty bottle of gin on the chest of drawers.

'You've put me on the spot there, haven't you?' said Shallow without any trace of discomfort in his voice. 'Let me see, what keeps me going . . . yes, loss, I think, loss keeps me going.'

'No, don't follow that at all, straight over my head, think you're going to have to give us a bit of assistance with that one, Mr Shallow.'

'I find loss helps me, Thatcher, because it's irrevocable, that means it's happened and there's nothing I can do about it, and that, improbably enough, forces me to do something produc-tive with it, because I know it's here for good.'

'Wise words, Mr Shallow,' said the Colonel who, at the first sign of a possible mental challenge, had stopped listening for the day, 'wise words indeed.'

'Do what with it, your loss, Mr Shallow?' asked Polly.

'Drink,' replied Shallow.

'A good idea,' said the Colonel. 'Now what's the likelihood

of that landlady of yours having some booze tucked away for poor wayfarers such as us . . .'

Shallow left the Colonel with a box of cigarettes and Polly holding a note excusing his lateness for work in the hand-writing of Lord Ross, a favour Polly had not asked for but had nevertheless appreciated. In all, it had taken Shallow ten minutes to refuse offers to drink, wash, shave and smuggle both men out of the front door without being seen and remember to leave his slippers and dressing gown in the house, a modest improve-ment on his usual routine.

Out on the lane stretches of frost lay along the telegraph lines and the branches of every tree, the winter sunlight burning the cold off Shallow's face; its rays shimmered on frozen puddles and the bonnet of a passing car. Streaks of pale yellow cloud hung over the town post office like punctured chain mail, poised as if to drop, the echo of an owl call contributing to the seasonal confusion. Shallow, of course, was not aware of any of this, the natural world having long since evolved into a vast and indistinguishable backdrop to those more pressing matters that involved the self. Nothing, not even an assortment of burning vehicles and shelled-out tanks, could have reached Shallow in his haste to move from one drinking place to another, his eyes fixed as though tied like battered kites to the strides of his Jermyn Street suedes.

It was not until he reached the ford that led to the town's high street that Shallow stopped to check his watch, half suspecting that time might have tricked him by going forward an hour as he slept. The church clock read 11.30, the watch on his wrist 12.00, and the sundial on the roof of the town hall 12.30. Whatever the actual time was, Shallow estimated that he was at least half an hour ahead of himself and, in his enthu-siasm, an hour too early for his daily 'arrangement' at the Candlelight Club, a converted library happy to take advantage of the prohibitive licensing laws. The worst thing that could happen to him if he tried to kill an hour wandering round town was to meet some person who may, thinking him the amiable fool he was when drunk, try to talk him into a conversation he was completely incapable of having. Moving as though fearful for his life, Shallow cut to the churchyard, looking furtively for a bench out of sight of the main road. Avoiding the path that led to the front gates, Shallow made his way past the graves of the Great War dead, and on through the section reserved for those who fell in the next conflict, his stomach tightening at the sight of familiar names.

Standing above the humble row of headstones marking the resting places of ordinary servicemen was the black marble pillar dedicated to the memory of his late best friend 'Lucky' Jack Sceptre, paid for by his father-in-law, Lord Ross. No body had ever been retrieved from the boiling cauldron of metal Vivien's husband had perished in. Although Shallow had attended the unveiling service, he had never really paid much attention to the memorial, considering it a slightly excessive manifestation of the family's grief. The world would be full of such memorials, had every grieving family the money to pay for one, and Shallow had felt it unfair that, brave as he was, Jack should be singled out for special treatment. Thinking in this bloodless and theoretical way had helped Shallow forget that, unlike everybody else killed in the war, Jack Sceptre had been his best friend. Faced with the reality of their relationship Shallow had considered it safer, and certainly more dignified, to hide behind duty and treat Jack's sacrifice as the rule, rather than as an exception, and had thus only ever talked about his late friend in the most general and impersonal terms. Today he felt differently, exposed before the admission of his own loss and stripped of those remaining affectations of taste and correct behaviour that Harrow had bequeathed him. Ignoring or just plain unaware of the suspicious gaze of the church warden, Shallow walked up to the pillar and read aloud the inscription 'We must be free or die who spoke the tongue that Shakespeare spoke', heard his voice break with emotion and turned away, Jack's words, 'I can think of nothing better than going to a certain death with you fellows,' stinging his teary eyes.

'Lucky' (a most unsuitable nickname for the man even in life) Jack Sceptre was a different species of soldier to any Shallow had encountered before. A member of the pre-war Grumwood hunt, and a true gentleman who retained the attitude of a cavalier well after mechanisation, Jack Sceptre embodied the popular conception of a blue-eyed British hero, the loss of both his brothers in the Battle of Britain either confirming or belying his moniker depending on one's attitude to survivors. By 1944 there were very few of his kind left, and Jack was already something of an anachronism in the regiment, his silk scarf and velvet waistcoat objects of awe and amusement to the grammar school technicians who filled the officers' mess. Shallow had warmed to Jack immediately and taken to imitating his clipped manner of speech, casual attitude towards physical annihilation and esoteric sense of dress without so much as a second thought. Indeed, all the junior officers, after their initial reservations, had done the same thing, presenting visitors from other regiments with a sight more in tune with a music hall (mustard-coloured duffel coats, monocles and deerstalker caps) than the front line. Shallow had more cause to be grateful than most when Jack, his immediate superior, had appointed him his second-in-command and given him his own troop to lead. From that point on, to the end of the fighting, Shallow's style of command, like Jack's, had been an exercise in unhurried and easy nonchalance, the whole war no more than a dreadful irritation that had somehow got in the way of dinner. Whatever Jack, or Shallow for that matter, may have felt beneath this studied exterior was a secret that would be taken to the grave. Having never confided in each other in life, there would, in Jack's words, 'be no second act in death', leaving Shallow to ponder whether his friend had been anything like as terrified as he was, or a true hero to the end.

The morning of Jack's untimely death had been spent listening to a particularly dispiriting briefing. In the minds of the nervous young troop commanders it seemed to offer multiple possibilities of death – from above in the form of supporting air cover, from below in the shape of minefields, and from either side thanks to flak from enemy artillery. The grim drift of the plan was for the entire regiment to follow a rolling barrage through a narrow gap in the German lines, the opposition having already been 'softened' by the American airforce which was notorious for their inability to hit their intended targets. 'Remember, chaps,' Major 'Beano' Bob Ballock had said, 'they wouldn't have asked me, and I wouldn't be asking you if you weren't the best, got it? And that's what you have been punished for! That's why we've been given the job! And make no mistake about it, Jerry knows it too, which is why we can expect him to fling the kitchen sink and any other leftovers come 0800 hours, so no long faces, gentlemen, fortune favours the brave!'

No one, not even the experienced officers, had been comforted by what they had heard, but a brave face of professional resignation had been kept up for the sake of the new men, whose taut nerves and contracting stomachs could almost be heard in the silence that followed the major's talk. Ten minutes later the attack had been cancelled. 'Thank God for that, bloody suicide mission if ever I heard one,' the major had announced to a tent full of relieved faces. This may have been the wrong thing to say, as an hour later the attack was on again with one small amendment: it would start as soon as the tanks were ready to move. Jack and Shallow had fallen about laughing at the amendment, and had laughed even harder as they raised their hands and volunteered to lead the charge. 'What have we let ourselves in for now!' Jack had laughed, then they both slowly realised what they *had* actually let themselves in for. Much of Shallow's war, he reflected now, had been spent like this, the values of his childhood and schooling merrily leading him into dangers he lacked the imagination to conceive the full horror of, or the experience to properly understand.

'Mr Shallow, is that you, Mr Shallow?' called Morris Much hopefully. The vicar of Grumwood had already suffered a dreadful start to the day, his curate making a scene over having to bring him breakfast in bed, and the verger threatening to resign over his refusal to meet the deadline of the blackmail payment relating to the molestation of a wartime evacuee. The sight of a dashing, if jaded, war hero in his churchyard seemed to be a free gift handed to him by providence. 'Mr Shallow, what a pleasant surprise,' he practically yelled, the object of his attention sealed in a world far away from the one they were currently standing in.

Shallow's memory of the morning of the 'Goodwood Meeting', as they had dubbed the attack, was dominated by noise, uprooted trees and fields full of dead cattle. The thick clouds of brick dust, whose heat he could still feel, had risen dramatically from the ruins of Caen, obscuring the rising sun, and blown about his cramped turret like sand in a beach hut. Squinting through his goggles, Shallow could hardly tell his neighbours' vehicles apart from the enemy's Tigers parked on the ridge above, the fall-out from the bombardment transforming the chocolate-box countryside into a derelict building site. Slowly, as the smoke cleared, colours and shapes began to reassert themselves and for a moment a ghastly peacefulness, frightening precisely because of the false hope it offered, settled over the field of battle. Beyond it lay open country and the ruined suburbs of Caen, but immediately before them was the 'corridor' they were to advance down, its narrow entry stretching out like Tennyson's 'Valley of Death', their revving tanks a modern-day Light Brigade.

Jack's was the first voice bellowing down the wireless intercom: '*Gentlemen, the morning rides behind us! Go, go, go!*'

The engine of Shallow's cumbersome American-built Sherman jerked into life with a deep mechanical burp, very nearly propelling the vehicle into Jack's tail, the only tank to do so; the others had appeared to move all of a piece, as they were meant to, or not at all.

'*This isn't a tractor convention, Shallow One, mind where you're going. And the rest of you who are still sat on your arses, bloody hurry up and get started.*'

Trying to forget his fear and think as carefully as he was able, Shallow watched the Tigers on the ridge lower their guns, unable to really believe that they had conspired to attack these monsters but equally reluctant to obey his fear and turn. In the absence of a decision, the tank seemed to make its own mind up and continued on its course, its occupants wishing, not for the first time, that they had joined the infantry.

'*I'm feeling awfully exposed, aren't you? Over.*'

'*Get off the bloody air, Jarvis, you're giving me the willies.*'

The seconds passed slowly as the tanks rumbled on, the silence of the field under the clatter of their tracks reminding Shallow of a flotilla of noisy motorboats far out to sea. In spite of the devastation of the surrounding area the Germans, though eerily still, looked very much alive, their positions as concentric and compact as the aerial photographs had shown them to be prior to the attack.

'*My, they're beauties, aren't they?*'

'*It's like the Somme; Jerry builds pits to hide in, we shell him, he hides, we come to get him, he fucking wallops us.*'

'*What are they waiting for?*'

The shelling began all at once and covered everywhere, its sudden fury waking the attackers from their daydream. Their textbook formation was immediately forgotten as each tank turned left and right in a frenzied attempt to avoid being hit, every driver hopeful that these contortions would have some bearing on whether his tank would last the day or not. Shallow, knowing better, realised that he was in the hands of chance and ordered Baxter not to swerve but to continue in a straight line, shouting at Delaney to hold his fire until the tank had stopped and he was sure of a hit. Baxter would later cite this as evidence of Shallow's daredevil bravery when recommending him for the Military Cross.

'*Jack Five, Jack Five, you're absolutely miles ahead. Slow down, slow down, over.*'

'*Never mind me, open up on Jerry. Range one, zero, zero, zero. Give him every round you've got, over.*'

'*A okay off.*'

'*E okay off.*'

'*T wanting to know if I can come back tomorrow, urgent business to attend to in Piccadilly Circus.*'

'*Get off the bloody air, there's a war on, don't you know.*'

Shallow's recollection of what he was supposed to have done next was not clear, and he still had difficulty in equating his actions with other people's reports of what they consisted of. This was the strange fifteen-minute period in which he knew he had acted bravely, though could not really remember *acting* in any way at all, his responses as normal as possible, given that he was in a situation no sane world would have found tolerable.

All order and attempts at cohesion had been forgotten, with every crew concerned primarily with thoughts of their own survival; that was his strongest memory, that and the journey back to their own lines being even more fraught with danger than the way ahead. Shallow gave himself over to the memory completely, the vicar's chattering barely touching him.

Every gun in the squadron had been blazing away, his turret a dark parody of a busy kitchen with both Baxter and Delaney shouting inaudibly at him through the petrol fumes and smoke. It seemed a miracle that they had not already been hit, the field full of patches of flame where seconds earlier a tank had been, their own shells sizzling impotently off the sides of the Tigers as fast as their cases could fly out of the six-pounder. Despite the repetitive thud of outgoing fire, Shallow could hear the screams of trapped crews quartered by armour-piercing shots, the crackle of their exploding magazine racks providing a near musical accompaniment to their last cries for help. With intense concentration he had bracketed out this 'background', focusing only on his immediate objective, a habit he would remain true to in Grumwood long after the battle was over.

'*It's a sheer bloody massacre, sir, you've got to do something.*'

'*Keep your cool, Baxter, and Delaney, stop firing, what the hell do you think you're going to hit?*'

'*Do something, sir! We're fucking for it if you don't!*'

'*Shut up and drive, Baxter.*'

It was clear to Shallow, in his isolated state of serenity, that the attack (reflected in the wireless intercom the tanks were communicating through) had moved from its abstract to industrial phase. All that remained for him to do was to push the Germans off their commanding ground, hold on to it, and wait to die, or else be reinforced. Absurdly he found himself pleased that battle, unlike his pre-war life, was never more complicated than it needed to be, with a simple set of options for every problem encountered and very little time to regret choosing the wrong one.

'*Baxter, nobody said you could go sideways, this isn't soccer. Bloody well get us back into the battle.*'

'*That's the stuff, over!*'

'*Get off the air.*'

'*You got him! Hit him again!*'

'*Those are trees.*'

'*Ignore the guns either side of us, remember our job's to get to the end and break through.*'

'*Procedure, gentlemen; this isn't a sewing circle, over.*'

'*Could someone acknowledge my original message? Over.*'

'*Bollocks, bastard sniper's just hit my driver Gill, best little driver in the corps, over.*'

'*Wish someone would hit my driver Baxter, the whingeing bugger, over.*'

'*Stop bringing fire on me, we're both Surrey, over.*'

Far from being obliterated by the allied barrage, the Germans had flirted with the British armour and drawn them into the narrow corridor for a classically executed ambush. It often struck Shallow at moments like this, that for all their ideological and sartorial backwardness, or perhaps because of it, the Germans *were* better at war than the British. It was a suspicion he dearly wished he would live long enough to debate in the officers' mess should the ridge ever be cleared of the enemy, a prospect that was growing increasingly unlikely with every incoming explosion.

'*Keep going, chaps, keep going and we'll all be home and dry in the end!*'

'*Jesus, Jesus, Chopper's head's clean off, we're about to boil up!*'

'*For Christ's sake, Stanton, remember radio procedure when on air!*'

Shallow's appraisal of the situation placed him in something of a lonely elite, with the rest of the squadron continuing to advance stubbornly down the corridor oblivious to their ghastly losses and the mounting congestion. Not for the first time since he had joined the corps, Shallow appeared to be operating on an entirely different wavelength from his fellow officers and, as he was not used to being right, his complete certainty over what to do next would have worried him were it not for more immediate dangers.

'*Fuck this for a game of soldiers. Baxter, turn the bloody tank around. We're going to try something else.*'

It was time to gamble. Ordering Baxter to pull out of the attack and advance face to face with the German armour that ran parallel to them, losing any advantage of movement or surprise, Shallow calmly instructed Delaney to take careful aim and make it count or else death was the next step. The alternative was to continue with the charge, an ugly option as the coordinated fire from the German battery, methodically rolling up and down the corridor, meant eventual if not immediate extinction, with only the sheer number of targets providing the survivors with any hope of reaching the German lines. Bizarrely, and in keeping with the character of the man, it was this idea of reaching the lines which had appealed to Jack Sceptre, his tank sprinting ahead of the others in apparent excitement at its prospects of coming first in the race.

'*Where the bloody hell are the rest of you? Looking everywhere for you fellows and the only thing I can see is Germans, over.*'

'*Sorry, sir, didn't you hear the original message from B? Every one of 'em canned. Most of A bailed out too, over.*'

'*Hope they've got a bloody good excuse, over.*'

'*Sorry to report but those aren't stones they're throwing at us, over.*'

'*E Squadron someway short of a full team, we're pulling out to resume play in the morning, advise you to do the same, over.*'

'*Bollocks, tomorrow's for silver medallists, we're British, over.*'

'*Bravo D, the rest of you buggers are a shower of appeasers! Never heard such treasonous talk in my life, don't want to hear that sort of depressing balls over the air! Where's Shallow? Over.*'

'*Was up your rear end until a minute ago looking for a safe place to hide, had a change of heart, am now abandoning the meeting to do some repair work on those bloody Tigers, over.*'

'*Good thinking, don't forget to blow them a kiss from me, out.*'

It was to be Shallow's last communication with Jack Sceptre, who for a few minutes could still be heard by the entire regiment, his own gunner and driver excepted, both men tragically adjusted to the wrong frequency and unable to hear Jack above the noise of their own engine.

'My God, Jack, you're bounding way ahead of the pack, slow down, you can't take them all on your own, over.'

Shallow meanwhile, controlling his voice with exaggerated calm, so that he sounded like the film star he reminded his men of, instructed Delaney, in his own time, to lift the gun by a fraction of an inch and fire. The German Tiger, whose gunner had competed with Delaney and come second, was blown into tiny shards, just as the British tanks had been when they were hit. Delaney grinned at the burning mess. It was the first German tank the squadron had accounted for that day.

'See, they die too . . . now move the gun round, same height but four yards to the right, no great hurry, but try not to get sidetracked.'

All three men were amazed that the glorified tractor that had been their home for the past month, maligned, cursed and ridiculed as it was, had now revealed itself to be a bringer of death, equal to its German tormentors and more agile at close range. Following Shallow's instructions, Delaney aimed, Baxter stalled the engine, Delaney fired, and more Germans died.

'See, easy now that we've switched places and taken our turn . . . reload.'

The enemy, thrown by the lone tank's audacity, hesitated before falling into the same chaotic pattern they had inflicted on the British moments earlier, their tanks reversing over their infantry in panic and clumsily blundering into Shallow's line of fire. Shallow, feeling every inch the shooting-gallery impresario, carried on issuing his instructions, startled at the speed at which his words were converted into destructive acts, and how this connection between his voice and death was no more than what his men expected of him. There was, he realised, a grim and elemental part of his being that had been waiting all his life for war, a passion he would never have been aware of had it not been for this battle.

'Fuck it, fuck it, we've never had it so good!'

'Baxter, concentrate! I want you to continue in the direction you're going in and stop exactly when I tell you to, let's not let them off the hook now.'

'We're going to run out of shells, sir.'

Shallow sensed that their stroke of luck was no mere fluke but the turning point of the battle, the moment when Richard III was knocked off his horse and Harold was hit in the eye with an arrow, the masterstroke that precipitated victory. And it had been such a pleasure to take part in, Delaney grinning with satisfaction, Baxter gently encouraging him with oaths, little about any of them, or Shallow, revealing the existential gravity of their position.

Jack Sceptre, meanwhile, had not been so lucky. His brave dash to the end of the corridor had been a solo mission unaided by those few tanks that could still move, Shallow's dramatic assistance having come too late. Mark Polly, Jack's driver, had spent the advance pretending that he was driving a goods van to Grumwood, and was therefore unaware of how isolated they were from the rest of the squadron. The gunner, Jim Templeton, was dead, killed seconds earlier by a stray tracer bullet, his warm body slumped by Jack's feet, its heat giving his commander the impression he was still alive.

'Just a few yards from Jerry's position now . . . machinery must have let us down . . . can't seem to get a shot off, about to be blown to glory, no choice but to ram him . . .'

Jack's tank had gone careering into the German field guns like an errant dodgem car, its tracks rolling over the front line before imploding into flames as it collided with a lorry full of ammunition. Polly, leaping straight out of the driver's hatch with a sliver of burning oil on his cheek and singed eyelashes, bounded past the astonished German gunners relatively unscathed. Behind him Jack Sceptre dropped out of his turret and staggered into a German foxhole, his face reduced to two wet holes dribbling tears, the rest of his body bearing a close resemblance to burnt fruit. Those German soldiers that had been ready to shoot the figure watched aghast, the spectacle of his injuries freakish even by the standards of the battle-hardened Wehrmacht. Reluctantly, an officer ventured over to the hole, the safety catch on his Luger released in anticipation of what he would find. But the dying man did not do what was expected of him. As if reminded of some ghastly dereliction of duty, the figure that had been Jack Sceptre crawled back out of his dying place and stumbled up to his burning turret, moved through the flames and closed himself into the tank, inculcating his dying life in the contraption that had taken it.

From his vantage point on the ridge Shallow saw none of this, believing his spirited counter-attack to be the beginning of a turnaround. In keeping with the British tradition of sympathising with the loser, it was Jack Sceptre who was posthumously awarded the Victoria Cross, and Shallow who ended up with a Military Cross as a conciliatory nod towards his initiative.

Shallow, hoping that his part in history was temporarily secured, had ordered Baxter to switch the engine off and allow the remaining German tanks to leave the field. The aftermath that he surveyed from his local victory was like no other he had seen in its destructive one-sidedness. The rubber tracks of the wrecked tanks were like giant whips, as their burnt-out hulks lay scattered over the meadow: a herd of slaughtered dragons. The screams of the battle had been replaced by a low and monotonous groaning, causing Shallow's hands to shake with empathy, a magnanimous gesture tempered by the fact that he, unlike many of those he felt for, still had hands to shake. Everywhere the wounded were struggling to their feet, their injuries offering the worst of them the promise of an early trip home.

'*Where have you been hit?*'

'*Face, stomach, legs, arms and hands ... and I think they may have scorched my moustache too, how about you, old boy?*'

'Altogether a wee bit on the burnt side myself, and you, Hooper?'

'Like a rack of well-done roast beef that you'd ask them to take back and do properly.'

'Aren't you the lucky one! I reckon my new nickname's going to be bloody Hallowe'en Jack!'

'I'm stuck I'm stuck . . .'

'Stay put, Mike! Help is on its way.'

'I'm stuck.'

'We're getting someone over to you as quickly as we can.'

'Someone kill me, kill me, I can't be like this, it's not me, I have a wife . . .'

Shallow, conscious that duty no longer compelled him to be sat in a tank, climbed out of his turret so that he could see more, and perhaps be of some use to the wounded. No sooner had he done so, than he felt an enormous blow land against his shoulder. He came to moments later, still on his feet a few yards from his tank, the realisation that he had been hit by a stray lump of shrapnel from an anti-personnel mine dawning on him, the exactness of this thought quite at odds with the rest of his muddled perceptions.

'Never thought I could be hit so hard by anything and not fall over,' he heard himself say.

'You did fall over; you lay on that grassy verge and screamed your bloody head off, man,' said a voice with a strong Welsh accent.

'Did that really happen?'

'Yes, you lay there crying about how you never wanted to fight, and about all the bloody birds you bagged before the war.'

'Oh I am sorry, I don't remember doing that at all . . .'

'Don't worry about it, boyo,' said an injured Welsh major whom Shallow had never seen before; 'it happens to the best of us, I'd get that shoulder seen to, if I were you.'

Shallow permitted himself a rare moment of self-congratulation as he joined the other walking wounded waiting for the ambulance. The pain in his shoulder had hardly made him bad-tempered at all, and the realisation that he had acted like most people's idea of a hero excited him . . . it was only the thought of how Jack had, or had not, got on that undermined his spirits just as it would continue to do two years later, as he stood alone in a cemetery in Grumwood.

'Do forgive me but one must jump at the chance to make contact with intelligent life when one is lucky enough to find it,' panted Morris Much breathlessly, his overcoat flapping witch-like in the breeze. 'You looked deep in conversation, I mean deep in thought, how could you be "deep in conversation" when you're standing on your own! No, deep in thought, that's what you appeared to be, a man deep in thought. I hope my little intrusion hasn't interrupted any important thoughts . . .' Much rolled the 's', capturing Shallow's attention as he hoped, but falling somewhere short of the connection he had intended to achieve, his use of 'thought' exposing his unfamiliarity with the concept the word sought to represent.

'No, no important thoughts,' replied Shallow, 'only relief at finding out that my thought wasn't a new idea, just a crappy old one that I don't need to bother about.'

'Why relief, Mr Shallow?' asked Much, more interested in the physical existence of Shallow than in anything he was likely to say. 'All thoughts have value, do they not?'

'Vicar, if you had any idea how much time I've wasted confusing self-pitying tripe for profundity you wouldn't chide me on this point.'

'No, I don't suppose I would,' said Much smiling at his tolerance of Shallow's use of 'tripe' and 'crappy'. 'You know, if there is ever any . . . *matter* you need to talk about, or thing that's troubling you, well, I am here for that kind of thing, you know.'

'No, I don't think there will be,' replied Shallow honestly, 'but thank you all the same.'

Morris Much watched Shallow trudge down the grey stone path and out of the graveyard, a vast and uncharacteristic pity descending on him, the object of it unclear. Carelessly he pulled a lump of ivy off the monument he was standing next to, wrapped it round his hand and sighed, the world a tremendous irrelevancy when compared to his compassion for it.

5

HEARTLANDS

It had taken Vivien Ross seven months and sixteen days to move out of the marital chamber she had shared with her late husband, 'Lucky' Jack Sceptre, and into the narrow room she had slept in as a child. This was the same amount of time that it had taken Vivien to finally realise that her husband was dead, or at least, if not dead, then never coming back to her. It had been impossible for her to accept the finality of his death, preferring instead to view his end as one option amongst several and not a reality composed of irrefutable facts.

In one crucial respect this was an attitude validated by experience, rather than by hope or simple desperation. When Vivien dreamt she still found Jack waiting for her just the other side of sleep, his smiling presence reassuringly normal. The two of them could once again enjoy the conversations they would have were he still alive, on which trees needed pulling up or which hedges to prune, Vivien only occasionally whispering to Jack that she missed him, as she would have if he had been out to work all day. The happy banality of these meetings created an atmosphere of timelessness so that Vivien was never further than a night's sleep away from Jack, mercifully removed from the full extent of her unhappiness thanks to her rejection of the news that had caused it.

Vivien's otherworldly distance from a world governed by calendars and clocks suited her father's variety of grief, which took the form of doing nothing all day except think about the past, and occasionally come out of himself at meal times or for the odd round of golf. For Lord Ross the privacy and remoteness of his memories and their near secretive nature helped make them more intense, thus freeing him of the need for human company. Months passed, and in the end it was the remnants of their once robust pride, and their unwillingness to be pitied as washed-up eccentrics, that had forced the Rosses back into the daily life of the town they had abandoned. In doing so both of them had successfully avoided the thing they feared the most: acknowledging to the other that Jack was actually dead.

The closest either of them had come to doing so was Lord Ross's decision to erect a memorial to Jack in the village grave-yard, but as the purpose of this object was 'to keep Jack's spirit alive', Vivien had little trouble reconciling the lump of stone with Jack's continued existence as a disembodied entity. The only inconsistency that blemished the single-mindedness of her stance was a hope that embarrassed her sense of propriety. At night, Vivien prayed that if she could somehow prove worthy of her enormous loss and endure it, life would eventually reward her fidelity with another man. The tacit acknowledgement of Jack's death contained within this prayer was hidden beneath much piety, as was the self-righteousness that enabled her to look down on all those widows who shed their tears and then remarried. Pain had become a crucial component of Vivien Ross's life and letting go of it would be akin to losing an organ.

It was in this mood of tolerable gloom, that Vivien gazed at the pathetic smallness of her room and felt the pleasurable tinge of self-pity that always accompanied any consideration of her own life. The arrangement of the bed, desk and chair in a tidy line, was similar to the decor found in the dormitory of a girls' boarding school. Only the absence of dolls and other playthings hinted at the true age of the occupant.

Vivien picked the heavy atlas off her bedside table and gazed at the worn cover, before putting it down unopened. It would stay where it was for no other reason than it filled a space that would otherwise be empty, like the furniture that lay stacked in the Great Hall. Every detail of the room was the same as it had been when her father had decorated and furnished it for her, the pine chair standing in exactly the same spot as it had when Lord Ross first left it there, next to the first editions of *Kim* and *Our Island Story* propped by her bed. The balance between what Vivien had accepted as a child, and the extent to which she had imposed her own personality on her room, lay firmly on the side of her father's judgement. It was his perception of what his growing daughter would need in life that made her few possessions endearing without being truly sweet. Looking at the beliefs that had defined these purchases, Vivien could not help but feel sadness for the person she was, more than for the person she had become. Hard work, proper behaviour and firm resolve may have helped her survive life but none of these qualities had allowed her to enjoy it. She had spent ten times as many nights trapped in this mausoleum than with her beloved Jack.

Vivien drew her hands up to her face and covered her eyes, a thin wash of tears sliding between her wedding ring and finger.

'Oh heck,' she said, amused slightly at her choice of words, 'I don't even *sound* twenty-nine.'

Most mornings were like this, a brief nod towards her unhappiness followed by a long dialogue with her memory ending in a tear or two. That so many years of her life were still ahead of her hardly mattered, for she no longer felt in any real need of them, the keenest of her emotions still rueing the days she had wasted with Jack, as he tried to prise her from the shell she so stubbornly remained in.

Despite the two years of marriage being the happiest of Vivien's life there was no sense in pretending they had been completely idyllic. The memory of the tears shed attempting to prepare a cake for Jack's leaving party, and its subsequent taste, were still too fresh for Vivien to forget. She recalled in irritation that she had been a difficult and haughty woman (and with what end in mind? It was difficult to remember . . .), but Jack had suffered her bad tempers and moods cheerfully as she ceded control of her life, letting love in at last with good humour and some grace. In truth, it had been a relief for her to finally allow the pressure she had put herself under at the start of their relationship to give way to a happiness taken in real things and people, the stilted world of her expectations crumbling in the open air of proper companionship.

Unfortunately for Vivien, her growth had been too slow for history, and by the time Jack had coaxed the woman out of her, war had arrived, leaving it too late for them to enter the next stage of their lives together as a mother and father. Ironically Vivien had welcomed the war as a useful break from the intensity of her new-found happiness, the reasoning behind this encapsulating the sort of woman she was at the time.

Moving to the window, Vivien ran her fingertips over the cold bridge of her nose, their firm ends offering an antidote to the hot flushes she had been experiencing recently, the outbreak of which coincided with sightings of Mark Polly, much to her baffled annoyance. Despite her self-discipline and cool vigilance, involuntary physical states and sharp emotions often took Vivien by surprise, their sudden presence an oblique warning of what an unguarded life might entail. Like anything that threatened Vivien's unhappy equilibrium, these strange fluctuations were commented on and mocked (by Glenda), but neither probed nor examined, their destructive potential plainly obvious to her. Such feelings were, as her father said, 'best left alone', yet Vivien could not help but notice that Lord Ross had not left things alone with Dawson the night before, and nor did she feel her usual need to today. Clearly, so much had been passed over in silence that Vivien no longer knew which buried desires or thoughts she sought protection from, or why she even considered her life worth protecting.

The sound downstairs of the help cleaning up after the unfortunate farce of the day before had blended with the wind thudding against the dilapidated windows of her room, a reminder that unlike many mornings, this was one in which Vivien had planned to do something. Before that, routine required her to check on her father who usually spent these hours increasing his chance of a heart attack over a copy of *The Times*, his only contact with the world outside Grumwood.

Despite the enormous size of the hall, Lord Ross and Vivien's rooms were next to one another, and therefore, since the two servants no longer lived on site, the only part of the building that was properly inhabited. The practical arguments for moving to a smaller house were so obvious that even Lord Ross must have already known that they were rendering any discussion of the matter pointless. Like her father Vivien was reconciled to dying in the house, but whereas Lord Ross wanted to end his days there with all his heart, Vivien was so used to her unhappiness that the thought of choosing to do otherwise had simply not occurred to her.

Vivien knocked twice on her father's door, and receiving no answer entered the room to find Lord Ross staring out at the garden reflectively. His habit on hearing Vivien enter was to read aloud from the paper and wait for his daughter to make a sardonic comment on the day's news. For some reason this had not happened today, so Vivien coughed loudly to announce her arrival, which her father still seemed oblivious to.

'Hello, everything in order, I hope . . .'

'No, not really, no not all,' he replied quick as a flash, belying Vivien's belief that he was not aware of her being there, 'not feeling myself at all this morning. Gin, eh? Used to be the drink for down at the heel washerwomen or maniac Chinamen, but yesterday every bloody bugger was asking for it, everybody, even the damned vicar. Didn't you notice? Still, all things considered – oh excuse me,' Lord Ross burped militarily, 'yes, when all other options are considered, it is still a marginally better drink than "chilled white wine", the tipple of our French allies. I wouldn't be surprised if that's what that bounder Dawson likes to drink, chilled white wine and canapés . . . I can just see it.'

A quarter-full bottle of gin lay at the foot of Lord Ross's chair and it was quite clear that it, and not tea, had been his drink of choice that morning. The room smelt of animals and tobacco, despite there having been no dogs in the house since Jack left, prompting Vivien to make a note to check for dead mice once her father had been driven back to bed.

'Oh you're not still thinking about *Dawson*, are you, Daddy? It's just that you dealt with his show rather conclusively last night; you really did put him in his place in front of everybody. I'd rather hoped that might be the end of the matter.'

'Who else in this damned town could afford to, Vivien? I don't consider myself a man of action any more, far from it, but just look at our fellow churchgoers. Every man jack of 'em at the mercy of a cad who wouldn't know a tin of caviar from a pot of marmalade. Where's the self-respect of a place like this gone to? I tell you that man's cost us. Costs us dear.'

'Self-respect takes too much from a poor man, as you've always liked to say, most of them just want to be left alone by life . . .'

'To make a bit of money, yes, I know, and I know we must be understanding of those who don't enjoy our natural advantages, etcetera etcetera, but when are *they* understanding of us, I ask you? Now don't get me wrong, daughter, I appreciate the fact that complaining is just as dull as agreeing in its way, but ever since the war killed off conversation . . .'

'With every person in this town moaning about rationing or being sandbagged in the blackout whenever they visited London . . . Really, Daddy, you know you're starting to sound every bit as silly as I do when I go on so.'

Lord Ross squinted and lifted an arm off his chair. 'Going on? Nobody's going on . . . such a silly thing to say. I am merely attempting to have a conversation with you; is it so wrong to want to do that? You complain that I never talk to you but now that I open my mouth you ask me to stop. Where's the sense in that, Vivien? You're not being logical.' He swallowed quietly and dropped his arm onto his lap. 'Have you not noticed how any argument between two men in this town is settled by one asking the other how much money he makes . . .'

'Imperfect, I'm sure, but preferable to chariot racing, fisticuffs or the proverbial duel. Come on, you've got yourself pretty tight and you've yourself to thank for it. Help me pick up your gubbins and get you back to bed,' said Vivien, employing a familiar tone that did not come easily to her.

'Duelling? Are you being deliberately flippant? What are you talking about duelling for? Why always this pressure to try to be so *amusing* about everything all the time? Always looking for the stupidity in something before you really listen to it. If I want to sound like a crashing bore then please allow me to. Now I was speaking of the real opium of the people, money of course . . . or worse, the true cry of the egalitarian mob, "His Lordship has more than I do, so I can't be blamed for killing his deer or making myself at home on his land." My God, if I was a thinking man it would make me wonder, the total and merciful anticlimax of actually achieving anything with one's life . . . I wonder if death isn't made up of the same stuff.'

'Daddy, you're ranting.'

Lord Ross had sat up in his chair, the mauve flush in his cheeks the most obvious sign that he was now too drunk to stop talking. Without taking his eyes off Vivien, he thrust his hand under his chair and groped about for the mug he had been drinking from.

'It's there on your left, if you must have it. I don't like it when you start behaving like this, you never used to when I was younger . . . I don't know why you think it's necessary to begin now, especially in front of me. You forget that I already know you, and know you're not really like this.'

'Be quiet and you might learn something about how our enemies think, Vivien – I think that's where I'd got to . . . it's not for my own health that I'm . . . now you've made me lose my thread, what was I saying?'

'If you really do think it necessary to go on talking rot, then you were blathering away about how "our" enemies settle or finish their arguments, all of it absolute rubbish in any case,' said Vivien folding her arms impatiently.

'Of course,' replied her father, the wild look in his eyes almost too large for them. 'Which brings us not so neatly back to the unfortunate case of Dawson, every path always leading back to that man as you may have noticed . . .'

'If you insist, though I can't understand for the life of me why you have to keep bringing him up, it's not as if we can really learn anything about ourselves from his shoddy life.'

'Be quiet and you might learn something about the way our friend Dawson likes to end an argument . . .'

'Stop telling me to be quiet! You're literally repeating yourself and as I've already tried to tell you, I don't care in the slightest about him or his arguments.'

Lord Ross held up his fist theatrically. 'He uses precisely the same means as he does when he starts an argument, and it all goes a bit like this, "I make more money than you so I can relieve myself wherever I bloody well like, be it on your belongings or over your souls!"'

'Oh really! Bring in the toilet and souls in the same sentence and you end up sounding just as he does. I wish you could hear yourself when you're this bad, I have trouble recognising you.'

'Each of us adopts the characteristics of his enemy if he has to spend long enough under his whip,' said Lord Ross screwing his face up biblically.

Vivien shook her head. 'And as you brought him up sharp last night, and made a damned fool of him in front of everyone in this town, I see absolutely no reason why we're still talking about the pig . . . he'd revel in it if he could hear us. There, you're making me repeat myself now, I feel so frustrated with you for being so awful and ruining my good impression of you.'

'Don't try so hard to be funny, and if that's not what you're trying to do then stop sounding like a prig, and in any case, I did no such thing,' sighed Lord Ross agitatedly. 'Made a fool of him? I wish I had. All I did was defend the sanctity of this house against his aggression; I could hardly do less.'

Vivien, controlling her temper with difficulty, replied, 'Quite,' and moved to open a window. Her father's evolution from the dignified stoic of the night before to the frantic drunk of the present moment was too seamless to be dismissed as an old man's eccentricity. His fluctuating moods and drunken mornings, as frequent as one a week, indicated more than the encroaching senility that Vivien had at first tried to pass these lapses off as. A change was occurring in both their lives and Vivien did not know, as yet, to what port of call it was heading or what it would ask of them once it had got there.

'What was it that bearded buffer Tennyson said to Victoria? That if God made the country and man the city, then the devil must have built the country town . . . I've more than half a mind to go and tell the whole of Grumwood that.'

'You could, but then everyone would probably think you were mad, which, despite your best efforts, they don't at the moment. Things could be worse, you see. Now I really think it's time you went back to bed, yesterday was more beastly than usual and you're still affected by it.'

Lord Ross rose from his chair and for a happy second Vivien took this as a sign of assent. Instead he picked up his pipe and continued in the superior tone he used when drunk on an empty stomach, 'She was Jewish, I think, Dawson's mother. Expressed it in a nice way, though.'

'What?'

'Expressed her Jew-hood in a nice way, Dawson's mother, that is if she really was a Jewess, which she might not have been.'

'Wait a moment, Daddy, what do you mean by "expressed it in a nice way", or "Jew-hood" for that matter?'

'Her Jewish nature, she put it across well . . .'

'Just as you can express your Christian essence well or in a bloody nasty way too,' added Vivien quickly, mindful of the cattle trucks that had moved East without comment during the war years. 'You seem determined to make me nostalgic for the months in which we didn't exchange a word.'

Her father looked at her uncomprehendingly, thrown by whyever it was she had thought her last remark necessary. 'Well, as I was saying, have you ever noticed how a thoroughly bad lot, and I think we both know to whom I refer, have no redeeming features, none at all,' he waved a hand, 'how each fault compliments and leads on to the next, which is why it's so easy to dislike a bad lot, because they're not like us, not fully human in the proper sense.'

'What, do you mean the Jewish people?' asked Vivien aghast.

'No, of course not, you silly girl, who's talking about the Jewish people? I mean Dawson and that thing on his arm who used to work in our kitchens.'

'Our bedrooms actually, she was a maid,' corrected Vivien, relieved.

'Bedrooms, kitchens, no matter, the pretty little thing who can now be found on his arm receiving his piece of silver . . . that's the bad lot I'm talking about, still on the subject of Dawson, see? A man you'd have down as a canal rat even if you met him as a toddler and who I find about as funny as a baby's open grave.'

'I don't think she's all that pretty, and I wish you wouldn't go on about things you dislike . . . not least because you've got me thinking about that jumped-up little strumpet.'

Lord Ross closed his eyes as he always did when listening to things he did not like to acknowledge the existence of. 'Dislike! Things I dislike! Did I even mention dislike? I'm talking of a force much older and evolved than mere "dislike" . . . Hate, girl. That's what I speak of! Hate in the high old way.'

'Well hate, then, I wish you wouldn't talk about it even if you feel a bit of it. It's as if you're making it even more true by valuing it so highly.'

'I feel more than a *bit* of it, Vivien, much more than a bloody bit of it; I feel it in its purist and most absolute form. I feel it every time I remember my son-in-law, *your husband, for God's sake*, every time I remember him and think of the country he died for. And the *vultures*, the vultures we've left it to.'

'But not hate, then . . . not if you're remembering Jack.'

'Yes! Hate! Why not hate? Tell me, why is it that we all believe in the existence of hate, right up to the point when it's our turn to feel it, and then we deny it and pretend it's actually something more palatable like hurt or anger? I mean listen to them, Vivien! Listen to what the anodyne herd actually say, "Oh I don't personally hate *anyone* and never have." Ha! Well good for you, Mrs Mob Rule, because I say that I do! I say that the word must exist for a reason and there must be some other poor human being who hates too . . . allow me that.'

'You're confusing a cold disregard for someone, or a dismissive form of contempt for something common and vulgar, the kind of thing the Germans had a line in. You're making a bit of a fool out of yourself actually.'

'Why? Because I'm talking about the real article in all its glory? The sort of thing those cowboys at the Squirrel Skinner have in their eyes every time you give one of 'em a glance! Next to that any "humane" feeling is a farce.'

'I don't see why hate has to make love a farce, why can't love expose hate as a farce, there's at least as much of it about.'

'Because hate, my dear, is more real than love is, just ask the men Jack used to command, they'll tell you.'

'What does any of this balderdash have to do with them?' said Vivien, sensing that her father was terribly close to what he wanted to say.

'It has everything to do with them! Aren't they the reason the war was fought? And what a bloody war, eh? A contradictory beast fought for empire but also for freedom, starting with the old rules and ending with new ones. That's the reason the rabble in town hate, and it's for the same reason that I do:

they're bloody confused! They're so conservative at heart people actually call them Communists, but they're like me, men who have arrived in minds and bodies they don't recognise, plonked down in a world it's impossible to make any sense of.'

'Would that explain why you're making so little sense? Look, Daddy, once you got back from the army, you always said the world had gone to hell and that you struggled to understand it, and that was nearly forty years ago.'

'I may not have been able to understand it but at least I liked it! The old world worked and I don't believe this one ever will. Have you forgotten how good things used to be, Vivien? Tricks were so dandy that we ended up transporting our way of life to people who thanked us for our troubles. Everyone was happier, especially the poor who weren't tortured by unrealisable dreams as they are now, they knew they weren't as good as us and they didn't mind because we looked after them, I mean, their children used to run alongside trains and wave, for God's sake.'

'Are you sure you aren't thinking of India, Daddy? And be careful with your voice, it's getting very hoarse.'

'The past, Vivien, the damned past, it's like a poem recited before me in front of all of this, this *present* effluvia,' Lord Ross shouted, thrusting his stick in the air, his object not so much the ceiling as the year it was situated in, 'but all this rubbish talks too loudly for me to hear the poem's words. And the past speaks too quietly, Vivien . . . I can barely hear it any more . . .' Vivien reached out to touch her father's arm. 'No, I'm all right,' he said, breaking free of what he mistook to be an embrace, 'just growing old and leaving too many wretched and unusual epitaphs. But for you, Vivien, there's still so much time left, so much time to be free.'

'I beg your pardon?'

'Marry! Marry again! Leave this place and be happy!'

'Have you gone mad? What are you talking about?'

'You know exactly what I'm talking about, Vivien, damn

your pride! I might not be able to run or climb trees but I still have my eyes! Those eyes have watched you become so lonely that you've forgotten the rules of conversation. The only way you still communicate is through a type of guesswork based on other people's responses to your bitter sarcasm. What's happened to your femininity, my dear?'

'Dear God, what need do I have of that!'

'You'll go nowhere in life by belittling what you once held to be of value, whether it be your old character or your old room. You've mourned too much and learnt nothing from Jack's death—'

'Oh do be quiet! I've learnt the true lessons of companionship since his death, not some flowery Victorian view of "love". I know now that for something to be beautiful, it doesn't need to last for ever or even lead to anything else. It's enough that it existed.'

Her father snorted, the sound ruder than he had intended it to be. 'Come on, Vivien, that's the line you've been trotting out ever since the telegram. I dare say it's true. But it's no more than a brave reflection on a painful event, not a model on which to base the rest of your life.'

Vivien felt her wrists twitch with rage. She wanted to throw something at her father. 'I don't know what you expect of me when you rag me like a servant . . . I can just about stand a lecture on hate, but why be such a beast as to bring Jack up? And all these other *personal* things that are none of your business anyway. You're the bitter one, Daddy, a bitter old man who's got out on the wrong side of bed with gin in his hot-water bottle. Today you decide to knock down our taboos because it suits you because you're drunk. Well bully for you, because I've heard as much as I need to.'

Vivien glared at Lord Ross, conscious that the timing of her insult was somewhat awry. Her father appeared to have talked himself into comparative sobriety.

'For heaven's sake, Vivien, look at you, a typical British

woman who can only make reference to her feelings when she's upset. I call spades "spades" so why can't I call Jack "Jack". I can accept that I may be no better than you when it comes to bitterness, but I don't mind being that way whereas, beneath your mask, I know you do. Join life again before it's too late, I implore you, or else become one of those widows who finds other women to go to garden shows with.'

'So what would you have me do then? Place an advert in the *Hampshire Chronicle* or perhaps throw myself at the next man I see like those common tarts in town do? While I'm at it, why don't I just whistle into the yachting club at Southcrawl and become the mistress of some syphilitic admiral! What do you think I am? You never married after Mummy died and I have my standards too.'

'Standards! Matters have degenerated even further than I thought! To listen to you, Vivien, without having fathered you, would be to hear a woman twice your age speak. When you talk of standards what you really mean is a fear of life. Don't you know that these high standards of yours will lead you straight to spinsterhood and a room full of cats? That is, if you really do have high standards, and aren't just scared that no man wants you.'

Vivien looked as if she was about to answer her father with a blow to the head. Instead her bottom lip trembled and she let out a short gasp that may have been accompanied by a tear. 'I don't know why you have to be so cruel to me, Daddy, I've always been good, not like the others . . .'

Lord Ross, reminded by his daughter's pain that he was not drunk any more, went red and lifted his hand towards her. 'I'm sorry, Vivien, I've gone too far. I want you to have a different life from my own. Not make the same mistakes I have.' He hesitated. 'Every woman needs a man to be happy and I can't take the place of one for you. Isn't there anyone who could replace Jack? He doesn't have to be a lord or a holder of a VC, just a good man who loves you.'

Vivien felt a light falling-away feeling in her buttocks. To her horror she knew that there was one. Clutching her father's hand she sobbed uncontrollably, not desolate but a little girl caught out.

Mark Polly lifted his head out from the old Ford he had spent the last half hour under. 'I can't stand that noise any more, Arthur, turn it off whatever it is. It's driving me bloody mad. And that bloody smell too.'

'What noise, Mark?' answered his apprentice, Arthur Duke. Apart from the belches of brown smoke drifting from the chocolate plant, smelling more of burning creosote than anything edible, the air over the town was empty and silent.

'That damned generator, or drilling thing or whatever it is that's crunching away like bloody landing craft on a pebble beach. And something smells rotten too, like it should have been buried by now.'

Arthur Duke looked around the garage, it was usually a pretty noisy place, but with the boss away and only the van to work on a strange and still atmosphere prevailed, creepy but not loud. Nevertheless Mark could sometimes be a strange one.

'No crunching, Mark, none that I can hear. Might be that hangover of yours; told you, you could go home, not much to do today that I can't do myself. Can't smell anything either. Not except the chocolate.'

Polly glanced at Arthur suspiciously, wary that the boy had not the wit for a trick this subtle. 'You really can't hear it then, this *errringhinghhh*, no? Blasting away like thunder.'

'I thought you said it was drilling?'

'Well drilling, then, it's all the same.'

'Not a bit of it, Mark. You ought to go home, you're tired. The smell of petrol will make you sick after all that beer you had, boy.'

'Less of the boy, you cheeky bugger ... Christ, it's loud.'

'Where do you think it's coming from, Mark?'

'From everywhere, can't you hear? You must be having me on if you can't.'

'I told you, Mark, I can't.'

The likelihood that the sound was not real lay in inverse proportion to how loud Polly believed it was, which at present meant that it was the most ear-splitting din he had ever been subjected to. If past experience was anything to go by, then both of his voices had united to form a single deafening drone in protest at their dismissal the night before. Polly's hope lay in his having beaten them once before; their sound effects no more than a throwback to demons he had already overcome.

Polly frowned. 'Don't sound so loud now. The smell's gone too.'

The problem for Polly was that what grew out of his head could not be switched off from the outside as simply as a plug pulled from a wall. Instead he faced an ongoing vigil, the noise stopping as soon as he realised he had the power to stop it, but this responsibility to his own sanity frightened him. If most people simply listened to what they heard according to the laws of a physical universe, then Polly realised that he *was* what he heard, the 'inside' and 'outside' of his mind an indistinguishable bloody mess. Unlike his pre-war fear of the supernatural, that Lou had helped him laugh at, there was no doubt that these post-combat voices had been real, but were finally beginning to fade. The answer that this could in some way be attributable to the death of Moat was attractive, but Polly felt that if he were to be truly rid of them, he would have to talk to someone. It pained him too much to think of Lou in this role, and, despite her haughtiness, he was seized by an image of Vivien Ross, not listening to him but undressed.

'One of us needs his ears checking then, Mark . . . Mark?'

'All right, Arthur, wait till you get to my age and then you see if you don't hear mad bollocks too.'

Arthur shook his head, smiled at the oddness of a man he did not fully understand, and took Polly's place under the van.

Lou Dawson peered surreptitiously into the garage and watched her brother wearing a bemused expression, the one he wore when making fun of his madness in front of other people. Not wishing to be observed, she moved round the entrance and walked on as fast as she could. It had been a long time since they had last spoken, and even longer since they had last spoken of anything of consequence. It was their past closeness that made their separation so painful, but Lou did not see any immediate, or even distant chance of this changing, the passing time making any reconciliation more remote.

Lou had once wanted to see people, or at least be seen by them, but recently she had taken to avoiding them whenever possible. It was the greatest, and by far the quickest turnaround of her short life and was caused by intense social embarrassment. It seemed inexplicable that only months earlier the very thought of stepping out in tailored clothes next to her new husband, the most talked-about man in town, had flattered and excited her. When confident, it was in Lou's nature to be loud and vivacious, and in private with Dawson she was still capable of being both, their arguments even-sided affairs. In public, however, these qualities had been replaced by a timidity quite at odds with anything that had gone before, creating an enigma that surrounded her to her detriment. To reply to her critics in her old and fiery way would have been possible had she felt indignant or wronged, but Lou experienced neither, considering herself to be the villain of the piece.

For the first few months Lou had continued to feel wonderfully proud of Dawson and, more bafflingly in hindsight, their 'relationship'. Unlike her affair with Delaney, Lou's sudden marriage to Dawson felt like a union far greater than one founded on love or mere attraction, symbolising a shift in her life's aims and expectations. If people wanted to think that she had swapped the smell of flowers for the smell of lucre, let them; she would discover far more of the world with Dawson than on her own or with Delaney. Whereas her brother was perennially beset with reservations, Lou had the gift of smothering hers, to usher in change.

Unsurprisingly Dawson, whose eyes were opened to a world larger than work, felt much the same way, his thoughts turning towards children and a bloodline fortified by beauty, a quality he had never reckoned on before. Not even the brooding presence of Lou's brother, far away in France, could spoil the liberating effect of this brief and happy moment in their lives. Lou had never truly been taken care of before, Delaney having been neither her chaperone nor her suitor, but her equal in poverty and experience. In Dawson she had discovered the opportunity to take advantage of her beauty, set aside the drudgery of her routine, and have some fun, as so many of her counterparts were doing with German soldiers in occupied France.

Being the subject of so much attention, and catapulted into the centre of town life, suited Lou, who abandoned her previous reservations as being the stuck-up piety and sour grapes of a have-not. Both she and Dawson delighted in discussing the way they thought the town viewed them (positively, they thought, for the most part), Dawson happy at last to find a Queen to his King, and Lou discovering how much fun life could be in the absence of inhibiting principles. These were days uninterrupted by worry; the one sour note was struck by the slowness of others to change to new realities, their dourness and conservatism a constant, albeit minor, irritation. Every once in a while Lou would think about her brother or relatives, but try as she could, it was hard to take very seriously the thought of them suffering in the rosy autumn of 1945. Elsewhere bombs had dropped on Hiroshima and Nagasaki, and a million Germans had fled from their homes, the whole of Europe torn apart by war, famine and pestilence. Had Lou known, she later rationalised, she was sure she would have cared, but the moment was there to be lived through first and nothing could be more important than that. Come Christmas Dawson had bought Lou her first car, learning to drive it a happy afterthought they would attend to later, and she had given him a magnificent trilby hat, paid for with her taste and his money. No one else had been invited to their Christmas feast, as the Dawsons had become the very model of a modern self-contained unit. Unknown to Lou, there had been few Christmas presents elsewhere in Grumwood that winter; the struggle for life having replaced life itself for the vast mass of their underfed neighbours. She had barely noticed her brother return from France, and would have had to remember her former self to be able to, something she was determined to avoid at all costs.

By the New Year the Dawsons' desire for attention had become a kind of game in which they sought to shock the town by upstaging themselves with every outing, so that a trip to the post office necessitated the use of the Bentley or at least a new pair of shoes. The playfulness Dawson exhibited during these japes surprised and moved Lou just as her capacity for tasteless exhibitionism had touched him. Since neither of them had any need for anybody except in the capacity of an audience, it had taken until the summer before they realised that no one had any need of them either, the novelty of their act having long worn thin. Lou had gone from flaunting 'it' (a favourite expression of her husband's) to being ashamed of it, the poverty of the majority slowly dawning on her like first light after a hangover. And so it was that Lou versed herself in the new arts of darting behind lamp posts, walking with her eyes glued to her feet and staring into any space that did not have eyes to stare back at her. The party was over and guilt and shame had taken the place of song and dance. Although Dawson had noticed this change in his wife, not being able to understand it had prevented him from taking it too seriously, and without realising it his attention had returned to his business at the expense of his bride.

Despite her old cares, sympathies and insecurities returning to her, Lou found that the arrival of these traits made little practical difference to her life. The trouble was that having changed once, no one was willing to let her change back again. Most mornings were spent with long trips into town on meaningless errands, the hairdresser's, ladies' club and church hall all strictly out of bounds, alleys and back streets her new habitat. On those few occasions when she dared show her face in a crowded shop, the respectable women stared as if she was the worst type of profiteer, and the tarts sneered at her as they would at one of their own who 'had got ideas above her station and got lucky'. As for her old friends and brother, the less she thought of them the better, as she was certain she knew what they would say. This lack of energy sapped her of the anger needed to defend her corner, her outbursts of emotion occurring in front of Dawson, the man the town mistakenly thought she was in thrall to, or at least scared of.

Ironically her lack of identification with the town she had once loved gave her something in common with T Squadron, who in this respect were her fellow sufferers, but there was too much pain around for anyone to share their neighbour's burden, especially when that neighbour was married to Oliver Dawson. The most important thing was to keep her head down and stay on the move, hours and hours could pass this way and the sooner they did the better, for she had a new difficulty: as of yesterday she was in love again and this time it was for its own sake.

It was not the sort of day, if ever there was one, when Lou wanted to see the gaunt figure of her ex-fiancé, Terry Delaney, striding towards her. But this was exactly who she saw now, a large bag of what could have been swag tucked under his arm in the time-honoured style of the rural burglar.

Normally their meetings barely qualified as such, with Delaney crossing to the other side of the road in a hurry, or glaring at her before taking cover behind a tree. Painful as this was, Lou could not say that this arrangement did not suit her, and it was disconcerting to find that Delaney did not appear to be bound by his usual inhibitions today.

'Fuck me till I die screaming, I'm face to face with the woman herself,' said Delaney in a way that was not meant, and could not be construed as funny. They were not off to a good start.

Lou winced and looked about for help before remembering that there was no one who would consider acting the gentleman on her behalf. As Dawson had frequently warned her that when in town she would have to look after herself.

'That's a nice dress you're wearing. Did he buy it for you?' said Delaney, his cheerful face in contrast to the venomous intent of his words.

Lou wanted to say something sensible or calming, but all she could think of was the terrifying look in Delaney's eyes, his beady black pupils twinkling just as they always had when he was too angry to go completely mad. Hurriedly Lou tried to recall the look she wore the moment she last lost her temper with him but it was too far away from her now, lost in a haze of pampered nights and easy days.

'I've come back from the factory, seems like I've got to that point with him where arguments, he says, don't make our friendship any stronger. What you think of that, Lou? Me out on my tod now, jobless, would you believe.'

Erroneously Lou thought it would be opportune to react to this news sympathetically and said, 'Terry, what will you do? Let me speak to Oliver . . . you only see one side of him, he's not all bad.'

Scared of Delaney as she might be, Lou was not so alienated from her strengths as to forget the way she could draw a man in to her, right up to the point where he felt completely understood, if not aroused or fully loved. It was a quality many of the town's wives were unhappily aware of, because as insincere as Lou's motives often were, in person they always felt true. And yet there was a limit to them. In the case of Terry Delaney her empathetic skills had once been *so* true, that they could never be *ordinarily* so again, and any attempt to evoke them was a miscalculation with instantaneous results.

'You hypocritical bitch, what do you care what I, or any poor man does? I've my pride and I'll be damned if I join the brotherhood of idiots you feel sorry for this week!'

'I know you've your pride, Terry, more than anyone—'

'Shut up! You're only kind to a man when you're forgiving him, aren't you, Lou? Excusing him his past or carrying the weight of his shit! Don't you roll your eyes at me, girl! Go and comfort someone else, you do-gooder tart.'

'Terry!' Delaney was hopelessly out of date in his accusations, as it had been a long time since Lou had felt sorry for anyone else, or helped the town poor with their ration cards. It was ironic that he chose to scold the girl she had been years earlier, the girl who had been proud of her social conscience, rather than address who she had become.

'Save it; save it for someone else. This town isn't short of demons for you to provide a shoulder to cry on. Christ, listen to you, *"let me speak to Oliver"*. Let me speak to Oliver bollocks. I'm damned if I'll make you feel needed again.'

If Delaney had planned to make Lou cry he was well on his way to achieving a complete breakthrough.

'And to think you used to collect people like wounded birds and, mug that I was, I thought you were a saint for that, a fucking saint, Saint Lou, I thought.' He shook his head knowingly. 'But it wasn't quite like that, was it, because all along you just needed fodder to feel superior to, bitch.' Delaney spat, two years of unbridled hatred rising to the surface. 'Deny it then, tell me I'm wrong.' Madly, he found that he wanted her to.

From beneath her tears Lou could see it was too complicated to explain anything, let alone everything, to Delaney, but sadly nothing less than this would do. Pulling out her handkerchief, she blew her nose noisily in the hope that she would strike such a pathetic figure that Delaney might leave her alone.

'Lost for words, eh? Can't say it surprises me. When the chips were down you never could come through, could you?'

Maddeningly Lou did not know how to respond to Delaney, since even if she had *known* how much he hated her, the strength of his grievance would have still come as a shock. He did not seem to realise that she had never meant to hurt him, only to help herself. Perhaps this was the punishment owed for hiding from the consequences of her choices, and evading the human debris that lay in their wake. It was impossible to explain to Delaney – a man she had once tenderly caressed in her arms – that her feelings for Dawson *were* genuine but of a kind that Delaney would never understand. The indulgent satisfaction taken in Dawson's endearing posturing, and her protectiveness of his vulnerabilities, were all so different from whatever it was Delaney had brought out in her. And in attempting to bring Delaney up to date by admitting that she loved neither him nor Dawson but longed for another, insanely true as it might be, would virtually guarantee her status as town bicycle and end in her being tarred and feathered. If there had been a point when it would have been useful to reassure Delaney that her love for him had once been real, but also unformed and untested, that time was long gone.

It was all so complicated, Lou thought, as she stood open-mouthed and in tears, a hopeful crowd of children gathering behind her to watch the grown-ups argue and shout.

'Don't look so scared, Lou; I'm still the same Terry. Look at you, looking at me like you've been pulled out of the taxidermist's window . . . I'm not going to strike you. Christ, you're as bad as your husband . . .' There was a momentary softening in Delaney's tone. Though a borderline psychotic, Delaney was no bully, and felt frustration rather than empowerment whenever people were scared of him. Making his point, unlikely as it seemed, was more important to him than throwing his weight around, a trait he disapproved of in his friends, but was incapable of seeing in himself. 'Pale as a sheet, you are, like something out of the taxidermist . . .'

'What's a taxidermist?'

'The man who stuffs foxes.'

'You think I'm a whore, don't you, Terry?'

Delaney was about to reply in the affirmative but some memory learnt in battle forced him to hesitate.

'You won't hurt me more than you have with your talk, by telling me I am.'

Delaney put down his bag, full of the goods stolen from Dawson's office, and ran his hand over a small but deep cut down to the bone of his thumb. In his experience, there was no such thing as victory, and it was unwise of him to believe this confrontation could end in one now. Their unwelcome, if not wholly unexpected, meeting was not turning out as he had intended it to, the actual event bearing little resemblance to his many rehearsals of it. By deluding himself into thinking he no longer cared about Lou, Delaney had overcooked his imaginary diatribes against her, which had been part of his mind's daily routine for the past two years.

The second problem, Delaney realised as he looked at Lou's perfectly formed face, was that she was not quite the monster she had become in her absence. Lou was still beautiful, more beautiful than before, and she had lost the dismissive 'got to get on with my life' look she had worn on their previous post-war encounters. It was also evident that they had more in common than Delaney would have credited, with no amount of jewellery or visits to the hairdresser able to conceal the loneliness of Lou's predicament. It was obvious that though Delaney still possessed the power to hurt her, which pleasantly surprised him, he did not have the power to make her love him, which was what he had secretly hoped for, however improbably. His advantage over her was entirely negative, as it was with most people he scared; so many of them and none brave enough to tell him why.

'You poor cow.'

'What?'

Delaney shook his head resignedly. The vigorous ruthlessness he had attributed to Lou had fallen away. It was time to bring matters to a close. 'You've never had the guts to fall in love with an equal, Lou, that was your trouble. The lucky man may not have been me but it'll be no one now. You're not a whore; you still have . . . something, Lou. But you're through here, like I am.'

'I did love you, Terry . . .'

'It's easy to say you love someone when you don't any more.'

'But I got over you, I had to.'

'Don't give me that. Anyone you can "get over" isn't worth getting over. Might be the truth about me, though.' Delaney grinned, the sun in his face. 'Perhaps I'm not that special, but you knew what I was. I didn't deserve what you did to me. You should have left me alone and not made me love you.'

'Jesus, Terry, what do you want me to say, "Don't make me sick of you, Terence, and leave our old love in peace"? Or admit that I left you a little before you were ready to leave me? You've never even asked me for my say.'

'You've never offered, but go on, have your piece if you want. It won't make any difference now.'

Lou's eyes flashed. 'I will then. You've no bloody idea what it was like when you all went away and left us on our own, no idea what I had to go through stuck in that house with no one to help me. How deadly boring it was too, hauling out cast-iron and oak bedsteads just to straighten out the sheets every morning. Beds no one slept in, Terry; me alone in those dark rooms I was scared of.'

'Rooms we'd have been grateful for in France,' interjected Delaney, more out of habit than from any desire to correct. Lou's candour was having the strange effect of making him care less about her, their association suddenly feeling as old as it really was. It had taken Delaney a long time to recognise that Lou's behaviour might not have been exceptional, and his own betrayal far from unique. To listen to Lou complain about the humdrum circumstances of her defection brought home to him a truth as incontestable as it was banal; Lou had been an ordinary woman in a war that had killed a number of ordinary men. The rest, as Dawson was so fond of saying, was history.

'But they weren't in France, they were here and I was alone. And the enormous cupboards, moving them out just to dust corners, and then having to haul the monsters back again. And once the soldiers came to be billeted it was even worse being a single girl, if you could believe that,' Lou thrust out a hip, her tears largely cleared away, 'and not just the comments but the work, more *work*, emptying out soapy basins, like reservoirs they were, and lifting, always lifting jugs and kettles and at arm's length to avoid doing myself an injury, and doing this up and down stairs and corridors, well you've seen the place . . . can you blame me for leaving . . . for taking Dawson up?'

To Lou's astonishment the rage had left Delaney's eyes and was in her voice; she had been shouting with the same intensity as the rest of the street had been listening.

'Do you understand, Terry, do you?'

'I . . .' Delaney groaned, seemingly tired at the effort with which he had loved her. 'Of course.'

Lou brushed the small tracks of salt, which had replaced the tears, off her face. To her surprise she felt energised, a host of words ready to fall from her mouth, their arrival more comforting than the loving embrace of her husband, which was what she usually sought when she was hurt. Owning up to her selfishness had liberated her, but she sensed the danger of being carried away with this new freedom.

'You haven't heard the half of it, Terry.'

What she wished to impart to Delaney was the *thinking* that had led her to Dawson, but explaining it meant taking a philosophical diversion that she felt neither of them was ready for.

There was not a single person whom Lou had known, who had not enjoyed something special about themselves when they were young, no matter how small, a quality that had nothing to do with their character, but which poured out through their laughter and speech. She wanted to tell Delaney this, and explain that losing this uniqueness and remaining the same person was what was hard. Lou knew this from experience because she had tried to protect her spark, or whatever it was that made her stand out, and failed. Curiously the same could not be said of Delaney, who was as wired as ever; but would anyone, Lou wondered, have wanted to remain as he was anyway?

But how she could address this *fading* she felt, as she moved further from the broken promises and second chances that defined her, without confusing Delaney or, worse, beginning their argument anew, she did not know.

'Do you understand me any better, Terry, do you want me to go on?'

Delaney yawned. It had been a long day and he was not angry any more.

'I don't know,' he said, 'they've had a good show, we should pass a hat round.' He pointed at the crowd that included a good third of the town's unemployed, vying with each other for a clearer view of the warring couple.

'What do you want from me then?'

'I'm damned if I can remember!' Delaney nearly laughed. 'Seems like I had so much to get off my chest that I can't recall it, maybe because it doesn't warrant the saying. I felt it at the time, mind, felt it even more before you started talking, but I've passed through it.'

'Like that, eh?' Lou snapped her fingers. 'No more nasty wind left in Terry's stomach for him to blow off with?'

'Good luck, Lou,' said Delaney, his heart free of rancour but less special for its loss, not just for now, he sensed, but for a long time after.

Lou allowed her hands to fall off her hips and smiled wanly, the sun reflecting off her red mackintosh like a flower opening in winter. 'You are a one, Terry, a right fucking one,' she said and raised two fingers to the crowd, their attention no longer on her but on a man falling from a window into the street.

The interior decor of the Candlelight Club was an accident Shallow refused to take personally, though not all of its members shared his epicurean detachment on this matter.

'Look at that arrangement of puke over the wallpaper, it's enough to make you look at Soviet Russia with envy,' announced Les Mills, 'you'd have a hard time believing an Englishman "designed" it, eh? I'm amazed the bugger was able to eat enough of the right stuff to spill his guts out in that colour, what with bacon, sugar, margarine, jam, syrup and treacle all still rationed. And to think the war ended a year ago . . .' Mills wiped the gin-induced moisture from his crispy moustache. It was half past midday and he was not uncommonly drunk for that hour, alcohol playing only a slightly smaller part in his life than it did in the life of his friend, George Shallow.

'You country dwellers can take it! You should see how it is in the cities. Worse than the thirties, believe me,' interjected a voice from a nearby table.

'The cities! What bloody cities are you on about, man?'

'Codstock. Where my ship docked only this morning. I'm sorry, I'm being rude, may I please introduce myself? Captain Rory Burke of HMS *Keown* at your service,' said the man.

'No, you may not introduce yourself, you cheeky shag! Codstock, a city? It's not even a proper fucking port.'

'Sit down, Les,' murmured Shallow, not because he felt that Captain Keown would take exception to Mills's behaviour, but to obtain a better view of the commotion that had started on the street outside.

'In a minute, George, in a minute. There are unanswered questions to be asked here. How the devil did you reach here from Codstock anyway, for starters? It's absolutely miles away, and what the devil's wrong with your eyes for you to keep blinking like a madman?'

'I'm partially blind, I'm afraid to report . . .'

'Ought I to apologise?' Mills turned to Shallow.

'Nonsense, laddie,' said the captain in an accent that was changing with every word, 'you weren't to know.'

'Where did it happen?'

'The wops' fault in a roundabout way, if you must know, which you must, I suppose. They captured me when our ship went down, coming back from Crete in '41, though, interestingly enough, it wasn't actually their fault now I think of it, my going blind, that is . . . I was only an officer's mate then, so they threw me into the hold with a gang of Spanish Republicans, God knows how they'd got hold of them but they were a tough lot, boyo . . .' The captain stopped and looked as though he were about to remember a key detail, before shaking his head and tutting. 'Anyway what it amounted to was that these devious Catalan wretches made up a ghastly hooch distilled from prunes, raisins and sugar—'

'We used to drink pure meths before the bombing raids, you know . . . but do continue, I sense we're coming to the object of our little tale.'

'And I drank a litre of the stuff and literally went blind. I'm just getting my sight back as it happens. I wonder if you could help me, actually; as you'll appreciate, I find driving difficult at the best of times and . . .'

But Mills had lost interest in his new companion. Throwing himself down on the tattered armchair opposite Shallow, still blocking his friend's view of the street, he grunted, 'It's like the song says, "bad times are just around the corner", which is enough to make me shit boulders, because if these aren't the bad times then I don't care to know what are.'

'That's right,' called the captain from over the top of the chair, determined to continue in his mission to befriend Mills, 'you can't so much as drive a car without the police stopping you to check for stolen pork, why only this morning . . .'

'But what do they expect when the people are reduced to eating black bread!' grumbled Mills, who had never eaten black bread and did not have any intention of ever doing so. 'Even the Government of the Socialist Republic of Great Britain is promising a "grim and rough" 1947, well how much more grim and rough can it get? I doubt most of us will see it through the winter with all this fuel rationing.'

Shallow shook his glass sympathetically. The Candlelight Club, though too far down at heel to be considered even moderately salubrious, was still a long way from the grim and rough world Mills was describing. Were it not for the gaudy purple curtains and lampshades, the lingering smell of baked stoat's uterus and clouds of dust, Shallow would have thought it a rather snug refuge for the utterly desperate, a social type of which Grumwood was not short.

'We'd have been better off losing the war, at least that way the occupying powers would have been obliged to feed us.'

Over at the small bar, no bigger than a chest of drawers turned on its side, two men dressed in muck-brown tweed were swapping ration cards for nylon stockings. Unfortunately for them their transaction had been spotted by Les Mills. 'What was it the President of the Board of Trade said?' he asked them loudly. '"I shall do my best to prevent people who have been defending this country from being fleeced by those who stayed at home." Ha! Go easy on the extraction of the piss, gentlemen, there won't be enough left for the rest of us! The Department of the Board of Trade, bah! It makes you wonder. *They* may not be able to see what's going on but I certainly can. They say there're at least 18,000 deserters, posing as country squires, still at large in this country and good luck to the buggers, I say, because if they think they'll find any sustenance in this painfully inadequate land of ours . . .'

'I don't know, things aren't so bad, Les; they've been worse,

I mean. At least we aren't waltzing about Europe killing one another any more,' said Shallow, regretting this remark as abruptly as it left his mouth. Mills, like Oliver Dawson in this respect if not in any other, was a firm believer in the imminence of World War Three.

'Riots in Liverpool and Aldershot,' continued Mills, 'and in detention barracks all over the country, and they still want to send poor sods over to the Middle East in those giant urinals they call troop ships . . . and what for? A gaggle of ungrateful Arabs who expect us to stop the Jews, of all people, from killing *them*! What the hell has any of it got to do with us? We've already had our bloody war, haven't we? And what was that you said about the absence of killing on mainland Europe? Well that won't last for long, I can tell you . . .'

To listen to Les Mills speak on any subject apart from medicine, mused Shallow silently, would not lead one to conclude that the crashing bore of the Candlelight Club was also the town doctor, a parish councillor, a war hero, and the unhappy owner of the Keys to the City of Southcrawl, 'twinned with Le Havre'. That Mills was all of these things, and the recipient of several more responsibilities besides, was a secret he guarded possessively, his Candlelight Club persona the role he felt most comfortable in.

'Hear, hear!' cried Captain Keown, his glass falling out of his hand as he tried to clap. 'Couldn't put any of that better myself. Now about that carload of pork I might have mentioned . . .'

'Cheers, old boy, and stuff the pork, I prefer turkey, if you catch my drift,' said Mills as he glanced with interest at the attractive woman in red heels shouting at the thin man in the street.

'Now there's no need to be rude about my pork, men have died bringing that stuff out of Malta . . .'

Shallow and Mills had gravitated towards each other pragmatically, being roughly of the same age, the same class, and damaged by similar wartime experiences. It was for these very same reasons that they had later become firm friends. Their midday meetings at the Candlelight were part of a routine they both cherished, their half bottle of gin a welcome diversion from the tedium of Mills's surgery, and from the ongoing solo binge that constituted Shallow's life.

Mills glanced at his watch. 'I think there's still time for another, for me I mean, you can stay here all bloody day . . .'

'Lucky man that I am.' Shallow smiled.

'Yes, of course. You wouldn't actually want to stay here all day if you could, would you? Not unless you were to get very, very drunk, and be accosted by bollock brains like the good admiral over there. Tempting, isn't it? And not just for men of our fine moral calibre. I gave that bounder from your old squadron, Stanton I think his name is, five days off work so he could go down the labour exchange to better his prospects and what does the bugger do? Go straight down the pub. You defy them to surprise you but they never do, do they? They must take their lead from us, I'm afraid.'

'Indefensible. Still, Stanton had a bad war. Bad life too if the men are to be believed; you must have known that, you both being local to this place.'

'What, you mean somebody actually had a good war? Always looking for the best in people, aren't you?'

'I'm not sure about that . . .'

'I don't know about you, Shallow. If a stranger took a look at you they'd think you had all the vanity and ostentatiousness of a second-rate talent, no doubt harking back to the King's Road spiv you once were . . .'

Shallow stared down at his tattered Austin Reed slacks and wondered what Mills could be talking about, his clothes all dating back to before the war, before realising that this was probably his friend's point. He, like Mills, was topping up on the night before and in no mood to correlate meanings to words this early in the day.

'But you have the kind eyes of a first-rate talent, though I must say you do live a long way behind them ... I mean, sticking up for a lazy shag like Stanton who would have undoubtedly had a bad life irrespective of where and when he was born.' Mills put down his glass and looked greedily at the bottle out of which its contents had come. 'Do you know, I think I should quite like this room were it not for all the bloody red and purple carpets. Reminds me of some ghastly gypsy caravan with cement for wheels. Not that the owners would hear of a change, not even when I was practically their only client.'

'When was that, Les?'

'The first time I was injured out? Late '44 if I remember rightly, after the Americans had left for D-Day, when these injuries,' he ran his hand along his torso and leg, 'were still *fresh.*'

'You've yet to tell me the tale of how you acquired those. If it's not in too bad taste to ask after all this time.'

'So you've picked that route-one approach off the mob who fill up my surgery, have you?'

'Have I?'

'Of course you have. Well I'm sorry if my reticence has got your hopes up but the reason I've never said anything about the burns is because there isn't a terribly interesting story to tell. You see, I didn't do anything brave to get burnt, it was more of a case of the fire coming to find me. In hindsight the whole thing feels quite embarrassing if you must know,' sniffed Mills.

Shallow leant over the table and poked Mills in the chest. 'Les, if hindsight means being sat here in this dump with me, then don't listen to what it has to say, because it'll only be bull. I've spent most of the morning thinking fairly uselessly about myself, so it'd be a relief to have the record changed, even if it means listening to more of you.'

'I don't think you know what you're letting yourself in for, George.'

'Come off it, you like the sound of your own voice enough when pontificating on our national decline, I don't see why you can't turn it to more personal subjects.'

Mills checked his watch again, his eyes struggling to see the time amidst the mauve gloom that hung over the room like fog.

'Not much to report really, George. I was, as you know, an unwilling pilot for our illustrious Bomber Command, flying two missions a day. We were sent out on a shaky do in bloody bad weather, clear weather in other words, to some munitions factory near Hanover, I think. The whole thing was meant to be a piece of cake but we knew better of course; you probably came up against similar things in the tank corps. Anyway, we got to where we were meant to be going and the next thing I know my kite's had it . . .'

'What, completely out of nowhere?'

'Pretty much. One minute we're admiring the view and the next thing we know the sky's full of inoffensive puffs of smoke that you'd never guess was flak. You brown jobs on the ground might have thought you had it bad, but it was a literal walk in the park compared to the banging we got in the air. White winds of flaming flame, old boy, blazing through the plane like a blow-torch on rust. It can't be stopped once you're hit, you just watch it charging through and narrowing your options to zero . . .'

'Why didn't you get out of the bloody way?'

'It's too beautiful to look at and it all happens too quickly. Besides, where is there to run to? Like I say, there aren't an awful lot of options. Next thing you know the fire's working on your skin, which is when you find out how thin your skin actually is, and after that you hear yourself scream, which is about the only way you know whether you're still alive or not . . .'

'A bit like being boiled up in a tank?'

'I don't want to take anything away from that experience, old boy, but being Air Force I am going to insist that we had it a little worse. "Alive" is the wrong word for a man on fire in mid-air, "not extinct" would be the more appropriate term,

not living as we are at this moment, if you can call this living.'
Mills pointed at Captain Keown who was now fast asleep in
his chair, a thick trickle of saliva progressing down his chin.
'More, just aware, aware of the terrible pain you're in, screaming
all sorts of gibberish . . .'

'What sort of thing?'

'Oh you want examples, all right then, how's this: "I'm on
fire, I can't fucking see, someone please help me",' shouted
Mills. 'The universal language of war, you get the picture,' he
added resuming his normal tone.

'How the hell did you get out of it?'

'I'm not sure,' said Mills. 'On one side there was the light,
bright white blinding light, probably just the sky, not heaven
anyway, though there's no harm hedging your bets. That and
the memory of the girl you left behind or whatever it is that'll
get you through it. And on the other side there's the fire. But
if that's the only side you're prepared to believe in then you'd
throw yourself out of the cockpit. So you turn to the light and
close your eyes. You see, it's far easier to sit there and think
it's happening to someone else, which is what it *does* feel like
were it not for the awful pain . . .'

'But how did you get out of it, practically, I mean?'

'Oh that? It was the rear gunner who put the bastard fire
out in the end. Plucky little fellow by the name of Hughes.'

Shallow did something with his hands. 'I'm rather happy I
don't have a similar story to tell you about getting out of a
burning tank.'

'I'm sure you have others.'

'Fortunately I was never hit, though I was at Jack's grave
this morning.'

'Jack, of course, I was there when they unveiled that memorial. Sad business.'

'But I suppose it must have been a similar sort of experience, give or take four thousand feet . . .'

Shallow lied. He had, in fact, been hit twice in a tank while in North Africa, losing two crews and jumping out of the turret on both occasions. Though he had behaved like anyone would have in the same situation, Shallow had considered his escapes the moral equivalent of a captain deserting his sinking ship, and had privately judged his actions as cowardly. This conviction had inspired his heroics at the Battle of Caen, but the possibility of it happening again still haunted him every time he sat in a car or boarded a bus, the interiors of both reminding him of burning armour.

'I can't complain, George. Like I say, it's a rather boring story, I was burnt nearly everywhere apart from my face, I kept my hands over that . . . be a while before you catch me sunbathing, though. No point forcing the issue.'

Shallow raised an eyebrow in appreciation of his friend's understatement and downed the last of his gin. The story had not had the effect of making him forget his woes. All it had done was to stiffen his resolve to become very drunk again.

'Failure of imagination, George, that's all any of it was, a complete failure to imagine that war would be as awful as it was simply because we lacked the brains to do so. Anyway, I'd better be off. I've sick people to see.'

'Oh, already . . .'

'Not if you try to persuade me to stay.'

'Please stay, Les.'

'All right then, just for one more.'

Mills emptied the last of the bottle into his tumbler, the shaking in his wrist an early warning of what was to come. 'Why don't you do something with your life, George? I know I've asked you the same question a hundred times before, but since you never give me a satisfactory answer you can hardly blame me for asking again. I know your nerves are shot up but you're still infinitely better off, in just about every respect I can think of, than half the poor sods I hand out sick notes to.'

'What could I do here, Les? Farm? Fish? Work in the chocolate factory?'

'But "here" isn't the world.'

'And what good would I be in London or anywhere else? At least the air's fresh in Grumwood.'

'Underachievement, it kills a man you know, George.'

Shallow groaned. He had heard this several times before, usually as part of the prelude to Mills telling him he was a jolly good fellow, but one in need of help.

'You're a jolly good fellow, George, but you need help, we all do, none of us can funk along without it, no man makes it alone. Success, as we liked to say in the RAF, is a team effort. Why not study philosophy? There'd be a lot of interesting chaps for you to pass the time with at university, I think.'

Mills felt a slight tightening in the back of his throat, the type that always hurt when he was on the verge of drinking too much. He checked his watch, but he could not see the hands properly any more. He really had overdone it this morning. Opposite him, Shallow was busy answering a question Mills could not remember asking him. It was embarrassing that out of the two it was always he who lost control first, when it was he who had responsibilities, as his third wife so often reminded him. Clutching his wrist, Mills pulled himself up in his chair and concentrated on Shallow's words.

'I don't know what good that would do, Les. My philosophical ideas are only interesting when related to human situations, not philosophical ones.'

'Why don't you try writing a novel, then?'

'I should tell you to fuck off for that!'

'I'm serious, why not?' said Mills, confident of making sense of this new idea. 'A sort of Hemingway caper, but set right here in the New Forest, it'd be about us; you could call it *The War Pigs* or perhaps *Homage to a Firing Squad*, or is that a bit pretentious? Yes, I rather think it is, been done before, hasn't it?'

'Aren't we overlooking the importance of talent?'

'Bollocks, if you're not a writer then I don't know who is.

I'm getting excited just thinking about it. You've got the lot, boy, alienated from your immediate environment, if not the time you live in . . .' Mills half shouted, his lucidity stronger than his eyesight or balance.

'How could *that* help?'

'George, George, George, I'd have thought a man like you of all people could see that in every work of genius we recognise our own rejected thoughts; they come back to us with a certain alienated majesty in the works of a true artist. A man like you could be the interlocutor . . .'

'I'm not any good at *anything*, Les, let alone writing. That's the long and short of it, I'm afraid.'

'Rubbish, you're always coming out with profundities. And stop complaining, you never stop doing it and it never suits you.'

Shallow took a deep breath. 'A deep grasp of shallow things doesn't make me a philosopher or novelist or even fit company for the pub. I wouldn't rate anything that's come through my brain. I'm not fishing for sympathy, just that I mean it when I say that I've never been much use at anything except perhaps in the army for a bit.'

'For God's sake, you're a decorated officer, man.'

'Come off it, Les, we were both in the services long enough to know that any old plum could become a decorated officer after a few years' service.'

'You must have been good at games at school?' Mills blinked, his view of Shallow's face expanding to double vision. 'You're making me lose my footing, old boy, why be so stubborn about being useless? Everyone was good at something when they were young, even if was the sack race. I was a dab hand at the old egg and spoon, myself; trick was to keep the thumb on the egg.'

Shallow laughed caustically. 'Look, Les, I used to come here on holiday with my parents as a child, I was an only child and my parents tried as hard as they could to keep me company and impart something useful but it was a losing battle. All I was good at were useless things like hitting windows with stones. Or making stupid noises with my tongue, clicking it on the inside of my mouth, like this,' and Shallow made the noise, like a gun being cocked. 'I feel sorry for my parents in a way, they were decent people but typical of the time. We'd sit at the table in a cold but loving silence listening to the clock tick. It made me shy, shy because I was warm but didn't know what to do about it. Booze was a blessing, something I could specialise in, and my teens were spent as a different person, up for anything and full of the joys of drink. The army, well that you know about, and now this,' Shallow pointed to his bottle, 'full circle, back on holiday in the New Forest.'

Mills stared at Shallow with a head full of admiration and not a little curiosity. He remembered the time they had discussed death, and how it could be better than things that happened to one in life, and why this had established, in his mind, a wonderful basis for their friendship. Or was it *another* wonderful basis for their friendship? There were so many . . . Mills blinked again, he did not know why any of this was occurring to him now. Carefully he tapped his head to try to bring it back to whatever it should have been thinking about, but he felt too drowsy to concentrate. 'Hot in here today, isn't it, George?' he said, undoing the knot in his tie. 'Bloody hot for this time of year. You know, I think I missed breakfast this morning. Not good for me, drinking on an empty stomach. Always comes to tears, especially on hot days like this. It *is* rather warm, don't you think?'

'Not especially, shouldn't be with all that fuel rationing you were banging on about.' Shallow licked a finger and held it up in the air. 'In fact, it's freezing.'

'Good for you, Jimmy, because I'm boiling up, can hardly think,' said Mills in a poor Scottish accent he often resorted to when drunk. 'Be burnt to a wee crispy lest some clansman open yonder window . . .' he mumbled, pointing at his shoes.

'Are you all right, Les?' asked Shallow, a slight note of concern entering his voice. 'Here, perhaps I should ring ahead to the surgery. You don't look too well.'

Mills tried to nod but instead shook his head, its contents feeling more comfortable being shaken from side to side, than nodded up and down. 'Jesus,' he said, 'can you see the time on my watch, George? I can't seem to figure the hands out.'

Shallow grabbed Mills's wrist. 'I think it's stopped.'

'Ha! Now that would explain a few things,' chuckled Mills, 'boy, oh boy, would that explain a few things.' There was no fudging it; Mills really did feel as if he had drunk too much today, too much to convince any patient that he was a proper doctor, low as the expectations of his surgery were.

'Intensity without depth, overachievement in friendship and underachievement in life, that's us, isn't it, us and the men we led into battle?' Mills said, steadying himself to his feet with the help of the table.

'Quite right,' agreed Shallow, grateful that the conversation had widened to include them both, and that his friend's initiative was not so dulled as to preclude movement.

'But there's no point getting sentimental about it, about the kind of people we are. I can tolerate sentimentality in songs or films but never in love or friendships.'

'Why ever not, Les? I thought you were quite proud of the quality.'

'Because only unhappy people resort to sentimentality, folk who aren't content with the way their lives have developed, George. People who use maxims to explain life's pain away.'

'Isn't that practically a dictionary definition of us?'

'Whether people are sentimental or not will depend on whether they're happy or sad at the present moment,' said Mills, maintaining his balancing act with the help of a lamp. 'Life is moving along too fast and throwing up too many new heroes for *our* antics to be long remembered, at least by anyone but the most backward, or by those who have achieved the least . . . arseholes, in other words.'

'Us, in other words.'

'Us? No, not us, anyone but us, for God's sake! Ours is a different type of tragedy altogether,' declared Mills knowingly, 'they'll say our tragedy was that we had to play at being a pair of arseholes in order to be more popular, when all along we were just too thick to realise they all loved us for who "we really were".'

'But that's not really true, is it, Les?'

'Of course it's not really true, George! Because the real tragedy is that we sussed them out years ago and knew they really *wouldn't* have preferred us to be ourselves, only that they needed to think they would have. But we knew better, we knew them for the hypocrites they were, and the fools they required us to be, the bloody cunts.'

'Losing focus a bit there, I think, Les.'

'Losing what?' Mills groped upwards as a mountain goat would, his face scrunched up like tissue paper. 'There, on my feet again, back on track again,' he said, stumbling towards the window which he immediately fell against. 'Just get this thing open so we can all breathe.'

'Mind your hands on that glass, remember as a doctor you're your own last line of defence,' warned Shallow.

'What you need, George, is a good woman to take care of you,' said Mills, sticking his head out of the window and resisting the urge to be sick on the crowd below; the air around him felt so weightless and light, as he fell head first through it.

'It's the doctor! Look, it's the doctor! It's Dr Mills!' One by one the crowd, still reeling from the street enjoyment of the Terry Delaney–Lou Polly argument, gathered round the bleeding and inert body of Dr Les Mills.

'Christ, is he dead?'

'Turn him over on his back so we can see!'

'He's had a tumour, can't you tell? There's blood coming out of his mouth!'

'All of you get out of the way and make some bloody space, sharpish,' called Shallow, emerging from the dim entrance of the Candlelight Club. 'You there, run to the surgery and fetch Dr Thompson, tell her that Dr Mills has taken a tumble and is in need of some on-the-spot attention.'

Shallow knelt down and felt Mills's pulse; it was perfectly sound and his breathing was regular. 'Can one of you fetch me some water, in a vase or something with enough of the stuff to throw over his face?'

'What's happened to him, sir?' asked a town urchin who Shallow recognised as his former batman and regimental pugilist, Derek Chudleigh. 'He hasn't broken his neck, has he? He don't look too bright.'

Patiently Shallow pointed up at the first-floor window Mills had fallen from, barely higher than the top of the front door it sat above. 'Chudleigh, how many men in your experience have died from falls of that height?'

'It's a mad world, Mr Shallow, a mad world in which stranger things have happened.' Chudleigh grinned, the gaps in his teeth as black as the gates of Hades, thought Shallow, his head dizzy with the mob's expectation of death or serious injury. 'I thought I told you all to give the doctor some space, the last thing he needs is to come to with a lot of strange faces breathing over him.'

'We ain't strange faces, he's our doctor.'

'You know perfectly well what I mean, now move over.'

Obediently the crowd shuffled backwards, Shallow's authority accepted unquestioningly by even the most inquisitive. More in sorrow than in pleasure, Shallow realised that for all his faults he was still an officer and gentleman in their eyes, his professional alcoholic's sixth sense allowing him to snap in and out of sobriety as the occasion demanded.

'It don't seem right just leaving him like that.'

'Then make yourself useful and fetch a blanket while we wait,' said Chudleigh in a voice Shallow recognised as an impersonation of his own, the two of them playing at a military response to the crisis. 'We don't want any more drama than what we already have.'

'What was he doing falling out of windows in the first place, that's what I want to know?' cried a woman whom Mills had barred from his surgery on account of her hypochondria. 'A man don't just go falling out of windows, not unless he's been pushed.' She glared darkly at Shallow.

'Can you smell the booze on him?' muttered another, next to her.

Sensing trouble, Shallow decided to strangle the potential inquisition at its inception. 'Listen, you, if it's any of your business, which you seem to think it is, Dr Mills has spent the entire night delivering babies, rushing from one emergency to the next ... babies that would have doubtless been in pretty bad shape were it not for his intervention,' there was a murmur of approval that bordered on reverence, suggesting that Shallow had been believed, if not entirely cleared of attempted murder, 'and he was therefore dead on his feet or, more precisely, asleep on his feet, a state that many of you who were in the forces will remember,' Chudleigh nodded sagely, 'and a state I often still find him in after a hard night's work. One which he is too generous to reveal to any of you, his patients, for want of giving you cause to fear for his health,' Shallow addressed the crowd solemnly, ready for any potential detractors, 'hence his fall from the window while trying to wake himself up with the sole purpose of being alert enough to deal with your complaints ...' The murmur had become a hushed sense of awe. 'He may not be the world's most sensitive man,' continued Shallow, 'but you all know him to be a bloody good doctor. Now can one of you help me pick him up?'

'Steady on, old boy,' said Mills, opening his mouth but no other part of his body so as to give the impression of a speaking corpse. 'Who said I was the one with the gift of oratory? That would have made a fine funeral speech, but let's face it, if any of it had been true what would I be doing hanging around with an old soak like you?'

An old man guffawed loudly. 'Always been the way,' he croaked, 'gentlemen and doctors, always the worst bastards.'

'Quite right, quite right, my good fellow,' agreed Mills, opening his eyes but still lying flat out on his back, 'quite right. My God, something's hurting but I'm not quite sure what it is. My pride, perhaps?'

'Make a good pub anecdote, Doctor,' said Chudleigh teasingly, surer of his ground now that the threat of death had been lifted from the scene. 'You overworking yourself, make a good story of it, your fall.'

'Are you suggesting that I'm the sort of man who reduces his life to a set of anecdotes, you scoundrel?' asked Mills from his place on the ground. 'I can assure you I do far more than that, I positively prepare my life for anecdotes, and what don't fit gets left out!'

The men in the crowd had begun to laugh, their wives either laughing uncomfortably and shaking their heads or shaking their heads and not laughing at all. Inaudibly, Shallow breathed a small sigh of relief. It would not be his, or Mills's scalp that the town would collect that day.

'God, George! I haven't had as much fun since the Luftwaffe dropped "A Last Appeal to Reason" by Adolf Hitler after the fall of France!'

'And we all said we don't care, because we can all get on better by ourselves without them French!' sniffed Chudleigh approvingly.

'Yes, it must have simplified things for the Germans too, but that's us British, eh? The worse it gets the harder we laugh; sangfroid, dear boy, sangfroid, I . . . I . . . oh my God, is that my sauce I see before me?' Mills said and passed out as though on cue. A black jet of blood was spilling over his brow, its texture neo-alcoholic in composition.

'Looks like a damn drink that does, rum, the doctor's bleeding rum!' gasped Chudleigh.

'Strange . . . I could have sworn he was on gin,' said Shallow, 'still, as I keep telling you, there really is no cause for concern . . .'

'He's dead!'

'Nonsense, he's no more dead than I am.'

The sinister aspect of the presence of blood was offset by a sudden burst of snoring as Mills turned over on his side and curled up into a little ball, quite obviously asleep and at peace with the world.

Shallow bent down again and touched Mills's neck in imitation of a figure in a medical pamphlet he had once flicked through. 'He's all right, the damage is only superficial; as I've already said he's only tired, that's all he is.'

'A right madhouse we live in, what with doctors choosing the streets for forty winks! And former officers consorting with villains!' snorted a particularly vicious woman who had been standing guard over Mills's body.

'This isn't the first time it's happened. Oh no, last week my Frank caught the doctor stealing eggs off the milk float with this "captain" here . . .'

'I hear they're all like that at their medical schools, mad and wild like beasts . . . and who's ever heard of a leopard changing its spots?' answered the first woman. 'If you ask me there's something just not right about this whole scene.'

'No one did ask you. Now all of you, shut up. Chudleigh?'

'Sir?'

'You take over here.'

Far away from the commotion, and the dull swathe of eyes watching him, Shallow sensed someone waiting, observing him for who he himself might yet be, rather than for his part in the 'Mills show'. Acting on an impulse as certain as the one that led him to duck a sniper's bullet two years before, Shallow stood up and pushed his way through the crowd, making no attempt to excuse his departure.

Standing on the opposite side of the street, gazing at him

through her hands, was Lou Dawson, her look full of confused and childish longing. In her shiny coat and heels she seemed spectacularly ill-attired for one who did not wish to be noticed, and Shallow, ignorant of her true intentions, assumed that it was attention at large, rather than his own, that she sought. But Lou's vamp-like posture, rocking gently from foot to foot, disguised the rapture she felt swept open and drowned by, its rush provoked by the sight of a man she barely had the confidence to speak to.

If Lou's eyes bordered on the loving, Shallow's were simply apologetic, the need to say sorry so acute that it bordered on near terror. Having abandoned the crowd who expected certain standards of behaviour, if not actual leadership, from him, Shallow was now as giddily drunk as he would have been had Mills not taken a dive out of the window. This at least, went some way towards explaining why he was striding towards a woman whom he had doubtless embarrassed himself in front of the night before.

The mystery of what *had* actually happened then, matched by an abiding feeling so clothed in shame that it made it difficult for Shallow to think of anything else, obscured any romantic motive on his part. As far as he was concerned his purposes were practical and proper to a man of his class and background. The path to the other side of the street was no more than a mission to absolve his conscience of whatever it was that lay behind his dreadful half memory. Though, in his haste, Shallow forgot that he was not meant to mind humiliation, as Lou's gaze reinvigorated his lost faculty to care.

'I must apologise for the last time we met, last night I mean. I was very drunk so please forgive me for anything I did or said. It's no excuse I know, but it's never my purpose to hurt or offend ... I imagine I made a complete fucking fool of myself, if you'll pardon the use of such a coarse expression.'

'It should be me who's apologising to you.'

'Really? Why's that?'

'Of course it should be me,' said Lou faster than she would have done had she been talking to anyone else. 'It was my husband who started it. You were good not to whack him for what he said to you.'

'Really?' Shallow said again, unable to believe what he was hearing.

'Really.' Lou smiled, her eyes fluttering like net curtains in a storm. 'I'm so, so sorry about him. He gets so jealous when we go out together that he can't help himself. You've nothing to be sorry for, Captain Shallow, it was all his fault.'

Rainbows were not as colourful as the relief Shallow felt on hearing these words. He was free to enjoy the day, if not the rest of his life, for if a moment as splendid as this was capable of being repeated, he had badly misjudged the future. In place of wariness or hostility, or the manipulation of guilt the sober use to punish the drunk, he had found the promise of another world, one full of the most astonishing kindness. Not only that but a ticklish sexuality hung in the air between him and Lou, teasingly offering him far more than he had actually been given. This strange closeness, born of carnality, revealed an insight into Lou's character far deeper than any conversation could, forcing Shallow to wonder how many of his own secrets were being given up to Lou in the same way. That mutual attraction should assume such intense heights, so quickly, struck Shallow as absurd, his pragmatism in revolt against the near divinity of Lou's smile.

Yet if this revelation were not true, and no more than an alcoholically induced mirage, it was still happening in broad daylight on the high street, and for the moment Shallow could think of nothing else that mattered more.

'Your husband . . .' said Shallow, the act of speaking providing an immediate and necessary grounding, 'you have a husband, of course . . . several people have, but I think I remember yours particularly. I mean, I knew who he was but I'd never met him before last night. Christ, what the hell am I trying to say . . .'

'He was standing close to your face shouting at you. Like he does with me.'

'Did he? To be perfectly honest, I . . .' Shallow felt his shoulders tremble, why would he be anything less than perfectly honest with a woman who knew him for what he was? 'I do remember the shouting, there was a lot of that, wasn't there? But I can't recall a great deal of what was said . . . even though I remember who was doing most of the talking. It *is* your husband I'm thinking of? He of the thick murderous fingers, the noisy fellow, am I right?' To his surprise, and despite having said nothing of consequence, Shallow was losing his tired and ironic tone, and was on the verge of sounding positively chipper. 'You see, Mrs Dawson—'

'Please call me Lou. It doesn't sound right you calling me anything else.'

'You're right about that . . . Lou. Well look, Lou, when you get into the sort of state I do, you forget things that have actually happened and hold on to details that would seem absurd to anyone else. That's what I do when I can't remember the proper sequence of events. The details are like picture cards that act as a sort of map for me; without them I'd have to rely on other people completely. So in the case of your husband, what stood out for me were those butcher fingers he kept waving about; no, I said he had murderous fingers, didn't I?'

'I think you did, but why *murderous* fingers? Not that I'm trying to defend him, you know.'

Shallow smiled at her curiosity, indicating a genuine interest in the way his mind worked that he hardly shared. 'Probably because he said he wanted to kill me, a detail you can hardly blame me for blanking out and putting into my own peculiar code. Unconscious repression, I think it's called. Am I making any sense to you or just talking dreadful rot?'

Shallow had no idea whether he was being funny or tedious until he heard Lou laugh. 'They are short and thick, his fingers.

That's the way he's built, though. I find it quite . . . sweet, I suppose. Not that anyone else thinks he is. You've probably realised he doesn't like being that way, it's why he throws his weight around so much, to make people scared of him. Most of the time it works.'

'Did we really argue that badly then?' Shallow frowned. 'I do remember him being angry with me, I think, or maybe it was the whole room, or maybe I made it up . . . but what could we have argued about? I don't even know the man.'

Lou pursed her lips and inched closer to Shallow in the hope that her presence would provide the answer to this most obvious of questions.

'Did I insult him by mistake?'

'No, I told you, you did nothing wrong. It was awful. I was so embarrassed I wished I was the one who was drunk.'

'Then it must have been a very one-sided battle because I've no recollection of doing anything to start a fight or even defending myself once one started. I hope I didn't hide behind anyone's coat tails . . .'

'No, you were wonderful, wonderful and above it all,' gushed Lou, turning the points of her breasts into Shallow's chest. 'You could see that it wasn't worth a bit of your time, so you let Oliver dig his own hole.'

'That makes "my time" sound more important than it really is.'

'You were doing plenty of that last night . . .'

'Doing what?' said Shallow, the sudden change in his tone suggesting that he might not be so far away from terror as he thought.

'Running yourself down for no good reason.'

'I've got to stop doing that then.' Shallow laughed with relief. 'It must be damned boring for you to listen to even if it is true.'

'I hadn't thought of it like that. But you're not boring and it isn't true.' She smiled. Where others saw a drunk, Lou saw a brave man struggling with things he could not talk about, the lines across his head a sign of gravity and his sunken face requiring hope to light up again.

To prove that Lou was right, and that her interest in him was well founded, Shallow opened his mouth to release a string of prepared witticisms that he hoped would be adequate to the moment, all of them borrowed from his pre-war repertoire. Not a word, however, passed through his mouth. The silence between him and Lou Dawson was too beautiful to fill or pollute. Instead he reciprocated her smile and touched her shoulder. To his surprise she turned on the spot, bending like a dancing partner, and leant into him. Together, as if acting on a pre-arranged agreement, they locked arms and walked down the street, through the patch of scrub that separated the town from the country, and out onto the floodland that had never been built upon. For Lou and Shallow the lives they had ended up with were surpassed in these few moments by a new and constitutive reality appearing before them, their old worlds fading with each step.

Lou whispered something into Shallow's ear that he did not hear properly, and laughed. Shallow realised that she was now holding his hand and that if he touched her cheek she would stand on her toes and kiss him. He did so and, as he guessed, so she did.

The barren common which lay ahead of them, populated only by thickets of bracken, New Forest ponies and highland cattle, could fairly be described as Grumwood's only 'view', the rest of the town held in by thick woodland. Without consciously intending to, they had both stopped kissing, for how long they did not know, and were gazing into the distant storm clouds gathering over the Isle of Wight.

'I hate looking at this nowadays,' said Lou as if addressing the landscape itself.

'Why's that?' asked Shallow, his voice deeper than before, assured even.

'I don't know. No, I do, but it's difficult to explain to someone who doesn't come from here.'

'I know.'

'How can you?'

'Because this landscape has too many associations for you that you wouldn't expect me to appreciate.'

'What?'

'I mean it reminds you of too many things that you don't wish to be reminded of.'

'How did you know?'

'Pretty as you are, you aren't the only one who's felt that way.'

'You feel that way about this place too?' asked Lou, her questioning lips contracting into the shape of a neatly symmetrical O.

'No, not here; in fact I feel the opposite of that here – here I'm in my own world that begins again every day when I wake. London's the place I'm talking about, that's where my ghosts are.'

'You don't want to go back there, do you?'

'Perhaps . . .' Shallow glanced at Lou, her pouting mouth offering the promise of a London he could go back to on the condition she went with him. 'Perhaps I may go back one day. But there are parts of the city I like more than others. Some of it makes me feel like everything's hopeless—' He did not mind saying anything now, the suddenness of their intimacy the guarantee of its truth.

'I know, and there's no other world apart from the terrible one you're used to where nothing happens . . .' Lou stopped talking, hardly aware of what she was saying but prescient enough to realise that she had interrupted the man she loved. 'What were you saying about London, the parts that got you down?'

'Not down so much, but certainly parts that made me think of life as something pointless. Madly enough, one of the most beautiful spots when I come to think of it, Tower Bridge. Do you know where that is?'

Lou shook her head.

Inwardly Shallow warded off the temptation to ask how it was possible to reach Lou's age and possess such an incomplete knowledge of the geography of her own country, but instead continued, 'The first time I became aware of this . . . this sort of life-denying repulsion really, was New Year's Eve about ten years ago. I was knocking about with a bad crowd, not my usual set of friends, and had spent most of the evening wondering what I was doing with them.'

'I know *that* feeling,' Lou cooed sympathetically, 'that happened to me all the time.'

'Anyway, I was having a terrible time of it, feeling like a fake for acting up with these idiots, and to top it all off we ended up getting turfed out of a party near Trafalgar Square and having to cross the river at the stroke of midnight. And I remember staring into the water reciting awful poetry that was complete bosh that I reserved for audiences as easily pleased as the lot I was with, and saying all the other things that were expected of me and doing my best to impress these entirely worthless people, and just thinking; is this all there is?'

'I know, it's horrible, isn't it?'

'And it wasn't just the people or the view, which normally I loved, that stank but the whole of life and everything in it and whenever I walked past that spot it was as though I was encountering the same view of life again, the true one that lay behind any of the good bits that I might have kidded myself into believing were "real" since then.' Shallow looked at Lou who was lovingly adrift in the sound of his every word. Briefly it occurred to him that he might be the straight man in an enormous wind-up but the desperate sincerity of another human being starved of emotional contact persuaded him that for once, irony was not king of the day. 'I've tried to explain it before but have never been able to. Not properly and not without ending up saying something else. If I made it sound too simple people would suppose they understood me but if I tried to tell them how I truly felt they'd think me mad. Which didn't stop me from trying to tell them, but it must have made an awful impression . . . trying to say things that were so different from the things the person they thought I was would say. There was no way people knew of taking it . . .'

Lou was stroking Shallow's hand carefully, her eyes past questioning the impact of her love for him, and already planning a future in which they could rescue each other.

'I'm being long-winded . . .'

'No, I started it when I said I didn't like it here any more,' said Lou, outraged that her new hero should be blamed for his own eloquence. 'I came here all the time when I worked at the Rosses' house. The big view made me feel free, like life was free, that the sky didn't end anywhere . . . and that it meant life didn't finish where houses stopped and the forest began but went on to lots of places I had never seen before, still haven't seen,' Lou lowered her voice, 'but places I could be free in all the time. It's not the same now, or maybe it never was. Looking at this now makes me feel like I was telling myself stories that I needed to believe in. Because if all of this was just what it was then it wouldn't have been worth it, I wanted it to be something more, something else . . .'

Resisting the urge to parade his superior learning by quoting Nietzsche – 'truth is an error without which a certain species cannot live' – and thus souring the moment, Shallow said as simply as possible, 'I know. It's the same with me.'

'This doesn't even feel nostalgic, only sad for coming here and being that age and thinking all those things.'

'You're right, associations about a place aren't just what happened to you there, but what you thought was true about life, or even the truth about life, when you were there.' Shallow squeezed his fingers against the bridge of Lou's nose and she moaned quietly. 'I think there's something to be said for creating new associations, happy ones that are more powerful than the old. Every view should be leading towards somewhere good or special, a city you want to travel to, a voyage you want to make, real or imaginary it doesn't matter. The point of a view is to reassure, that's what I'm trying to say.'

Lou murmured gentle acquiescence, pushing her hand under Shallow's coat and opening her cold palm on his chest. 'It's excitement that reassures me, that's why I used to like it here. It was always a cross between danger and there being nothing to do . . . I think it was my fault, though. The way I've let things go. Life was still good but I let it down. I haven't been brave enough, have I?' Lou asked as she clutched Shallow's torso, her raised leg balanced in his hand. 'I haven't been brave enough,' she repeated, pushing her legs through his arms as though climbing into a carriage.

Drawing his breath, Shallow stared over her shoulders into the fading sky. Overhead, the first dark clouds had eclipsed the sun, turning the light into the colour of an underwater photograph, the clearing suddenly feeling several miles below the level of the sea.

'You're a brave man, though,' Lou whispered, turning her tongue over his shaving cuts, 'I know you are.'

The smell of burnt gorse and the damp of oncoming rain filled Shallow's nostrils along with the womanly stench of Lou's perfume. 'You look like one of the girls from the films, the one who the best scripts were written for,' he said to his partial disbelief; although this statement was undoubtedly true, it was not the sort of thing Shallow would normally say to a woman inches away from his face. Slowly he lowered her back down.

'What did you think of me when you first saw me?' Lou sounded half drunken; despite Shallow's prodigious intake of alcohol, his behaviour was the more inhibited of the two. 'Did you notice me when you disembarked at Southampton dock?'

Shallow hesitated. He could not remember seeing Lou for the first time then, or on any other occasion. Like everyone else she had appeared in his life without being announced, his awareness of her occurring well after her first entrance, or so he supposed. 'You shouldn't worry about what people think of you . . . these sort of occasions are always overrated, Christmas, birthdays, first meetings . . .'

'You mean you didn't notice me.'

'I don't believe in love at first sight, more like at second or fourth. You need a few moments at least to get a feel for one another. That first moment stuff does happen but it's not always at the first moment, if you see what I mean. I've felt that way ever since crying on my birthdays as a little boy, these things aren't that important . . . it's only unhappy people that make us believe that they are.'

Lou pulled away a little, not angry but to show she was capable of disagreement. 'Maybe that's because you don't think well of yourself, why you keep running yourself down.' As she said this her cheeks flushed, allowing Shallow an early insight into what she could be like when she was difficult. 'Of course occasions are important, they wouldn't be occasions otherwise. You don't feel proud enough of yourself to live up to them.'

Shallow muffled a laugh; it was apparent that it had not taken Lou very long to become an expert on him and thus have the right to hold an opinion on his life.

'I want to help you,' she said.

'Are you sure? At the moment you're still safe.'

'How am I safe? How long in a town of this size will I be safe?'

'You're safe because I'm a weak joke with dire consequences. Consequences mitigated by the fact that they only properly apply to me. I'm sorry if that sounds like another over-the-top self-dramatisation, but there you are. I'm only telling you the truth.'

'Is that what you truly think?'

'No, I think if you're serious about what you say then these consequences will apply to you too.'

'How do you know I don't want them to, sir?' said Lou,

dropping her hand firmly inside Shallow's trousers, her fingers kneading his balls like ripe fruit.

'That's a delicious thing to say, Lou . . .'

'I'm here for you.'

Shallow's world-weariness was falling away, a tired and over-worked affectation that he could sense he wanted no more of. In its place he wanted life, and life with Lou Dawson, her thick kissing lips sinking like cushions under the dry and firm taut-ness of his own.

'Have you ever wanted things to end quickly so they'd end well?' she said, catching her breath. 'Do you know what I thought when I first saw you? I thought it doesn't matter how rich or how beautiful you are, you'll always find someone who doesn't want you. Someone you can never get to the other end of. I think you're like that, and that's why I love you and didn't think you'd want me. There's peace in you. Deep in you.'

Ignoring, or just unaware of Lou's use of 'love', Shallow replied, 'I'm no more than what I am, whatever that is. If I have peace in me it's by not pretending to be any more than what I am.' Shallow stared down at Lou in a way that could not be construed as pretending to be any more than who he was. 'I told you, none of us are important. We're all alike . . .'

'That's rubbish, such rubbish that I don't know why you even bothered saying it. "We're all alike" – rubbish we are! I've never met anyone like you: never. The way you talk about feel-ings, and the way when you're happy or angry you give the real reason why you are and not just an excuse. Do you know how few people are like that? Do you? And the way you remember being young and admit to being scared and don't suck up to people just because of who they are . . . do you know how few people there are like that? And even when you breathe it sounds like you're talking to me . . .'

For the first time since they had embarked on their exodus from Grumwood, Lou looked uncomfortable. In her heart she knew she would never be able to return to her former life, far less be at peace with it.

'I had better go,' she said, letting go of Shallow's hand, her departure too sudden for him to wonder whether 'good luck' would have been more appropriate than 'goodbye'.

'Cinderella,' he said, her shiny red coat flapping behind her as she broke into a run.

The Colonel arched his shoulders and faced the dilemma he always squared down when skipping work: to visit his father and then go to the pub, or to go to the pub and forget about his father. On this occasion, it was the more compassionate side of his nature that won the day, and with barely a thought for his next pint of Top Brass, the Colonel retrod the path that led him back to childhood and, so many believed, his original damnation.

The Colonel's father still lived in 'The Pit', a collection of pre-World War One buildings and corrugated iron shacks on the outskirts of town. Some new construction work had begun with the aim of creating 'homes fit for heroes', but the local council had considered any heroes in the Pit unfit for houses, and consequently very little about the place had changed, its name as apt as it ever was. (A name which, as the Colonel's father liked to say, was still better than 'The Hole', the slum that stretched out between Southcrawl and Little Hamlock.)

Despite the obvious deprivations of the area, the Colonel had fervently bought into the myths of his nation, believing that a little suffering hardened the soul, and as the only child of a mother who had died giving birth, he was pleased to say that he had experienced his fair share of it. A life without suffering was not so much incomplete as completely incomprehensible to him, pain forming a part of the Colonel's being every bit as important as his hands or feet. It was, were he to reflect on it, the only constant companion in his life, as present in his enjoyments as in his agonies. It was 'foundations' as warped as these that had persuaded Dr Les Mills to conclude that the Colonel and Moat both suffered from a history of mental illness that predated their call to arms, the crucial difference being that whereas Mills believed that Moat constituted a danger only to himself and possibly his wife, the Colonel, without any shadow of doubt, was a potential danger to anyone he came into contact with.

Displaying a rare timidity, the Colonel opened the large iron gate that separated the Pit from the rest of town and stepped inside. This was the scene of many a raiding party he had led out as a small boy, the warlike fierceness of the Pit children as legendary as that of their elder brothers, who in 1916 were in France fighting the real war.

The Colonel puffed out his chest as he recalled the memory of his pre-military 'military record'. Not once had the more affluent and refined children of the town successfully stormed the Pit and beaten the Colonel's gang on their home turf, a fact that he was still rather pathetically proud of. This glowing reminiscence was undermined by a rumbling in his stomach that he recognised as worry and not, on this occasion, his stomach ulcer. Without a drink in his hand to throw at the problem, the Colonel took the painful step of turning his mind to separating this particular worry from the general stream of pain his thoughts were always accompanied by. He did not have to go far in his search; there was something wrong with his parting from Mark Polly and it had probably been this that had niggled him in his wanderings round town for the previous two hours.

Their final exchange, before Polly had left to go to work, had contained elements that, in a more severe context, would have led the Colonel to reproach his friend if not actually thump him, but, caught by surprise and still relatively sober, the Colonel had lacked the opportunity to fall back on either of these options. He knew that, in part, their uncomfortable farewell could be explained by Polly having a job he enjoyed, a privilege the Colonel could not claim to share, and consequently was fiercely jealous of. Jealousy was a wasteful emotion that did not sit well with the Colonel, and he was loath to acknowledge it, especially towards a friend. Instead of arguing his case Polly had kept quiet, causing the Colonel to ask, 'What's up with you, Mark?'

'Oh you know . . . you're not an easy man to say no to. Sometimes when it gets like this, I mean.'

'"Like this"? Don't beat about the bush, boy, let's have it straight.'

'To tell you the truth you scare me a bit when you get . . . well, like this, Colonel, not that I'm frightened of you but . . .'

'Frighten you? You're having me on!'

'No, you do. A bit. It's hard to know how you'll react, not all the time but sometimes.'

'I'm sorry, Mark, I'd never realised that was part of the game plan. You know me, boy, I'm a heavy rope in hard wind and always have been, can't help it . . .'

But it had troubled him, hinting at a whole world where the fact that he frightened his friends was taken for granted, where his friends indulged him just as he used to indulge Moat, and where, most frighteningly of all, he was not thought of as 'normal'. Fortunately for the Colonel, he did not believe in thinking or analysing 'stuff' too much. As he was so fond of saying, thinking in hindsight was how people 'missed the point and disappeared up their arseholes'; any activity requiring patience or self-control an anathema to his brittle nature. To realise what a problem was, was to be over it; and with his stomach settled the Colonel continued on his way, his vexation happily dealt with.

'Afternoon, Colonel! Mind giving me some of your money?' called a child the Colonel vaguely recognised.

'You mind your mealy mouth, son,' snarled the Colonel, the juvenile equivalent of his former self failing to arouse his sympathy.

'Daddy, it's me!' said the child. 'Ma says you should be paying your way.'

'Tell your ma to go to hell, boy,' yelled the Colonel over his shoulder. 'I've enough dung to carry without taking on the worries of the world or those of any old bike looking to stitch me up with the oldest trick in the book!'

'But, Dad . . .'

'I'm not your pa and I'm telling you your ma's a whore so on your way before you see my nasty side.'

The child, who was in fact the Colonel's wife's son, though not his own, gazed at his stepfather's back understandingly, mindful of the complexity of adult life. The Colonel, without looking back, raised two fingers in the air, his gesture neither comic nor crude enough for the boy to confuse it for anything other than what it was intended to mean.

Despite the Pit being situated in an ugly treeless stretch of country, the Colonel could detect the faint smell of chrysanthemums in the air, reminding him of a happier time he could not quite identify, and yet nonetheless could remember vividly. As was so frequently the case, any feeling or memory that did not fit the hardened personality he had carved out for himself was discarded, so that untutored and raw feeling often caught him by surprise, as did thoughts and dreams, for his conscious mind had grown too narrow to accommodate anything but the most base of beliefs.

'What are you all looking at,' he growled angrily, 'never seen a man go about his business before?' Even though the Colonel had timed his trip to coincide with the middle of a working day, women and men lurked idly by their front doors, oblivious to the cold and too frightened of him to offer any type of greeting, or respond to his lack of one. 'Idlers and tinkers, soft cocks and busybodies,' he rasped. 'Perfect place to bury a dead body, nothing here but brutes and dumb animals.'

Grabbing a broken branch, and flicking it about like a riding crop, the Colonel picked up the pace, his walk unconsciously turning into a parody of a sergeant major on parade, whistling the marching song of the Grenadier Guards loudly as he went. Had they been braver the inhabitants of the Pit may have laughed, but instead contented themselves by looking on in disbelieving silence, the Colonel's temper well known to them all.

At the foot of the Pit, far enough past the other buildings to suggest more than just a physical distance, stood the house the Colonel had grown up in, the path to it marked by a wheelless Ford van, several times repainted and mounted on bricks. An old dog, a stray that belonged to the community, finished relieving itself against the van, and hobbled up to the Colonel in the hope of some food or affection. It received neither; rare for a man of his background, the Colonel had no love of animals, especially ones that got in his way, as this one was in the process of doing.

The dog yelped at the blow, before settling on the side of the path, waiting, the Colonel speculated, for the tumour that he hoped would kill it. 'Too many damned dogs in this town, too many by half,' he spat, the fear he always felt as he visited his father coursing through his body.

'Same place, never changes,' he whispered, the sound of his voice comforting him, though not as much as he hoped it would. Scattered round the front of the house were a bath, a bedstead, rolls of wire, wheels, perambulators, handle-less bicycles and an old Union Jack draped over a parrot cage. Unperturbed by the debris, the Colonel carefully examined each item, making a mental calculation of what was worthless and what could fetch a price. To his evident pleasure, heaped in irregular piles by the side door, like equipment dumped by an army fleeing the battlefield, lay strips of iron and tin, most of it rusted and spread across what was once a garden. This was his father's business, his office and his workshop, and, most importantly of all, his legacy.

In spite of the appalling mess, the old whitewashed walls

emphasising the dirt that had gathered, there was a homely and lived-in feel to the house, evident from the puffs of smoke rising from its chimney. This was because the Colonel's father no longer lived there. For the past two years he had occupied the cellar, renting the rest of the house to a couple from London who were at first astonished, and then awed by their new landlord's choice of accommodation.

The narrow steps down to the cellar, situated at the edge of the dilapidated greenhouse, were covered in brown slime and smelt of moist crumbling brickwork, an aroma the Colonel loved nearly as much as that of a freshly lit bonfire. Even by his standards, though, the cellar made an unlikely home, the dampness so acute that he could feel it slip under his flesh and work its way out through his skin into the clothing worn to protect him from the cold, his bones wet within.

'Pa?' he called into the gloom. The room was lit by a single small bulb hanging from the ceiling and by daylight coming through two narrow ground-level 'windows'. 'It's me.'

At the foot of the steps were piles of potatoes and mouldy bread, inseparable from the wet sacks they were packed in, and sat on top of them like a king, smoking his pipe, was his father, Seth Thatcher.

'How're you, Dad?'

'Same. You?'

'Bit worse for wear.'

'Be because you're a cunt, boy. Same reason it's always bit worse for you.'

His father was a meaner, smaller, more knowing and less bumptious version of the Colonel, with a starved face and deceptively easy manner, willing to set the highest stakes for the smallest incident and ready to follow through. 'That's why.'

The Colonel grunted half-heartedly, knowing better than to contradict this 'joke'.

Dressed in a faded demob suit like his son, Seth's appearance was clean-shaven and tidy and thus quite at odds with his dwellings, his personage being the only clean thing in the cellar with the exception of a small photograph taken of the Colonel as a boy on a donkey. In contrast, the Colonel, unshaven and reeking badly of beer and sandwiches, was the one who gave the impression of living underground.

'Been home yet?'

'Home?'

'The one you made with that woman.'

'Not likely! Packed out months ago.'

His father laughed at this and emptied his pipe over the floor. 'Just dust left in it. You're like me, a practical unpractical man, you know that?'

'Like a man who says he ain't, so he can get out of work?'

'No, you fool, a practical unpractical man ain't a liar, which is what that is. He's practical unpractical; that is, a fellow who tries to live a practical life at great cost to himself, but can't because he's a fool but does so anyway, see?'

Unlike the Colonel, who could at times appear human, there was no hint of vulnerability in his father's viper-green eyes and emotionless drawl.

'Now don't go looking at me like an American who's just been stupid enough to ask me what I think of Churchill, you soft bollocks. Say you can look after yourself? Don't make me laugh, you were calling me to tickle you at twelve and still wipe your arse at sixteen,' his father scoffed, the mucus in his dry throat rattling as if he was gargling marbles. 'Look after yourself, you say. You might think you do but here's one old pa who knows different. I know so.'

'I didn't mean it like that,' said the Colonel. 'I didn't mean anything.'

'That's true enough. Here, fill me another pipe. I've a cigar in that drawer, some sausage meat and a bottle of port from upstairs. You have it.'

At moments like this the Colonel felt so close to the old man that he would have liked to stand up and thank him, but as usual he remembered himself, the thought of doing something so insane not even worth contemplating.

'What've you been up to?' the Colonel's voice was trembling slightly, completely unrecognisable from the one heard in the pub, factory or elsewhere. Unconsciously he was imitating his father's curbed and clipped style of speech, one his own bombastic diction was most unsuited to. As such, none of his words sat comfortably with themselves, rushed, half-formed or incomplete, his conversational strengths muted in this strange half-lit world.

His father lit his pipe and sucked in heavily, ignoring the Colonel's question for so long that the Colonel nearly repeated it, before replying at last, 'Been making a chicken coop, don't ask why, only thing I eat these days is Spam.' He spoke quietly in an irregular accent bequeathed to him by a life in the army, the words 'don't' pronounced dan't, and 'spam' span. 'Probably finish it this afternoon. Providing it don't rain.'

'You can work down here?'

'Not enough light, my eyes are no good, specially when I need sleep.'

'How are they upstairs?'

'Don't know. They've stopped bothering me now they know I've no use for cakes or sympathy.'

'Bastards.'

'No, good people. Just so I've no use for 'em don't make 'em bastards, son. No different from what we are, just a darn sight richer and brought up different. Often see 'em wandering around half dressed. Kind, though, you can tell they're that. One of 'em was an officer in the last war; think the other was his bag carrier. Fruits they may be, but they are what they are, and straighter than most folk in this town.'

'Least you can eat fruit.'

'Don't tell jokes, son, share 'em. You know the most noble and holy thing in a man is his sense of humour.'

'Aye, but one man's meat is another's poison.'

'The three Bs lad, bull, bollocks and balls. You never could make me laugh, not on purpose. Now don't come the old soldier with that look, you; you'd freeze the balls off a brass owl with that stare, lad. Lighten up.'

'Bit cold in here, that's all. You need to be careful not to catch a chill. Hard to feel like joking in this damp.'

'I'll worry about it when it happens and when it happens I won't be here to worry about it.'

'By the by, I may never have made you laugh, but there's a lot of folk in town that consider me something of a funny man.'

His father cackled evilly. 'I dare say there are. Oh you're funny all right, that's you, my boy, a funny man but soft bollocks.'

The Colonel pulled the cork out of the bottle of port; experience warned him that he might be in need of it.

'Like the time you told me with a straight face that your motto, your motto, for God's love, was "Commandos die hard" and you weren't even a commando, haha! Or when your mates said that you tried, no one knew why, to paint a desert rat on the side of your tank, ended up looking like a bloody great shit splash! And you weren't even a Desert Rat! That's my boy!' His father slapped his leg and shook his head, his old body shaking with mirth.

The Colonel took a long draw at the bottle, losing all sensation of taste as he pumped it down his throat. This type of parlour game was a one-sided sport with his father as the fox and he the hare, always the hare. At least, the Colonel thought as he wiped the head of the bottle on his sleeve, his father had never discovered his nickname, since from that real murder might ensue.

'The lord knows who you think you are, boy, not a humble fellow like your old man, that's for sure. Sit there and look all quiet but I know you well, boy, for the bully and braggart you are. Always have. And it'll never change.'

Ignoring this rather unflattering thumb-nail sketch the Colonel said, 'Something I was going to ask you . . .'

'Advice, you say? No doubt you need it. And you're too much the bull to take it anywhere else; well then, let's have it at the double.'

'The factory, I think I'm out of a job, not sacked but I want to leave. Not only me but the rest of the lads too . . . we're in the shit.'

'Lads, ha! For God's sake, you're fully grown men, not that you'd credit it. The shit, eh? I dare say it'll be your own fault.'

'Bugger me, no! It's that jumped up tinker, Dawson; he won't settle, he wants our hides, he always has. God knows what makes people like that but he's a real dark one.'

'That why you're not at work then? Not going to make him change his mind by carrying on like you're the wolf and he's the lamb. He didn't make his money taking lectures from the likes of you, son.'

'The bastard never gave me a chance! You know him for the low sort he is, a man who'd let others do his fighting for him, who'd happily guard the Dorset coast while others shed their blood.'

'Save that talk for the boozer, you're with me now. You did no more than what you had to, it don't make you a hero.'

'But he didn't even do that and now look at him and look at me! Where's the bloody justice there? I tell you, it's passed the point of no return . . .'

'Point of no return? Pah! You're just drunk, boy. That and your sense of drama.'

'Can't you see it?' said the Colonel, raising his voice. 'I know it, *feel* it, it's us or him and I'll strike the next man who tells me what to do.'

His father whistled slowly. 'You've always had a temper, got that from your mother. Call the shots as you find them, nothing else a man can do. All this will be yours one day,' his father gestured round the cellar. 'You don't need no damned sweetie-arsed factory to work at, never have. Let 'em hang. Didn't know what you were trying to do there in the first place.'

'By God, you're right,' said the Colonel thumping his fists together.

'I don't know about God, where he is or what he's up to but my belief is that he's a hard man. Take it from me, you weren't put on this earth to work, son, neither of us were.' His father looked at him thoughtfully. 'Give me that bottle while there's still something in it and put the kettle on, I'll need you sober to help with my ferrets. Potter's got something in her eye and I'll want you to hold her while I take a look.'

An hour later the Colonel left, failing, as he always did, to tell his father that he loved him more than anyone else in the world and that they would meet in heaven when they died.

6

GLORY

'This was,' said Vivien Ross later that day, 'a very bad idea.' To her obvious discomfort, Glenda Heathen did not contradict her. In the past, giving voice to something she did not want to be true, and having it denied by a sympathetic friend, had been the way Vivien sought assurance. Glenda appeared to have forgotten this convention.

'I really can't think how I ever agreed to it. Not in hindsight anyway.'

'You never did agree to it, sweetie. You thought of it, it was your idea.'

'Oh don't,' Vivien bit her lip, 'but how did I even get to hear about it? Are you sure you didn't tell me?'

'Yes, I'm quite sure I didn't. You read about it in a book of ghost stories. And then you found Jack's letter. It's not the sort of thing I'd have suggested. I don't feel comfortable prying into that . . . sort of thing. It's creepy.' Glenda gave her shoulders a little shake to emphasise her point.

'And that's exactly what convinced me, if you'll remember. That if *you* didn't feel comfortable with it then there must be something to it . . . though I only wish I'd listened . . .'

'To me?'

'Yes, to you. And then waited. Now I suppose it's too late.'

'Of course it is, but you shouldn't worry about things you have no control over, I wouldn't be surprised if it turns out to be a harmless load of old rubbish, fun even.'

'Oh I don't doubt that, it's not that I actually think it'd work, just that it'll be yet another way in which I heap more unnecessary humiliation on us through my naivety . . .'

'Come *on*,' Glenda rolled the 'n' as if it had been trapped in her mouth for some time, 'I bet you you'll find it funny. You'd be mad not to.'

'But I am mad. It's true, isn't it, I really did go mad and everyone was too polite, or busy talking about it, to tell me that I had. How else could I have agreed to something like this?'

'Arranged, Viv, you arranged it with their help and now you've outgrown the urge. It won't do you any good pretending that you're a passenger carried along by other people.'

'Don't remind me . . . Oh it's all right for you.'

'I'll be here with you. Look, behaving all worried is daft, we're both in for something a bit peculiar, I admit that, but they're probably scared stiff too, so let's play along and see what happens . . . we might even learn something!'

'I suppose you're right, it could be quite amusing . . . Oh no, it won't be.' Vivien clasped her hands over her face and cursed her stupidity; for one who was so often accused of being a cold fish she had managed to manoeuvre herself into a hot spot worthy of the most wilful teenager. The irony being that she had arranged the day's activity with the aim of securing peace of mind, though the reality, she feared, would offer nothing of the sort. 'It's not only that it's embarrassing, we're probably committing sacrilege.'

'I hadn't even thought of that, Viv, but then again, that must have been the sort of thing that put the vicar off when you raised the idea, don't you think?'

'Don't remind me . . .'

The genesis of the plan had occurred to Vivien over a year ago, its inspiration the product of an unanticipated mistake. Morris Much, with whom she had so often quarrelled, had refused to include a soldier's prayer that Jack had asked to be read at his funeral, should he die. The vicar's reason was the ambivalent attitude towards celestial faith displayed in the text, arguing that if Vivien wanted the prayer read aloud, she would have to choose a different graveyard for Jack's monument to be unveiled in, something he knew her father would not agree to. After much bad feeling and recrimination Vivien acquiesced, having no high opinion of the prayer in any case. The prayer itself, despite the vicar's objections was not intrinsically controversial, and if not exactly religious, was still broadly English in spirit:

Endow us with the courage of uncertainty. Accept an unruly but contrite heart. And in the frailty of disbelief we cannot overcome let us seek the remedy from within ourselves, and offer mercy that the world cannot give.

It was on the other side of the prayer that Vivien had found the true cause of the vicar's objections. Written there, in Jack's unmistakable hand, was a short note on 'spiritualism' and 'the other side of death'. She could scarcely conceal her relief since his note seemed to confirm the evidence of her own dreams, in which he spoke to her, still alive and mindful of her need for him. What made his message so precious to Vivien was that it was the only parting note he had left behind, on his last visit home. As Jack was confident he would not die (which, Vivien had to admit, was a factor that weighed against the note's sincerity) there had been nothing in the way of a will or testament, so that this small communication assumed all the importance of a dying wish and last conversation. In his note (addressed to her in name) Jack had asked that should anything happen to him, and were she not able to come to terms with her loss (how well he knew her!) she should contact the Irishman in his squadron, a private by the name of Wren, who claimed that his ancestors had the gift of speaking to the dead. In this way they could exchange any outstanding news and say goodbye properly.

The problems with this bold plan had begun almost immediately. To her horror, Vivien discovered that Wren was the foul-smelling man she had taken for a tinker (having once prevented him from gravelling the drive for an exorbitant price and without her permission), who was often seen splitting up fights in the Squirrel Skinner in exchange for pints and bags of pork scratchings. Moreover, like other members of the squadron he was a regular at the local magistrates' court and in continual trouble with the police. Jack would have had to try very hard to invent a man who appeared less like Vivien's idea of one who could commune, on decent or sober terms, with the dead. For several weeks she feared that she might be the victim of a practical joke, devised by Jack because he thought he would be alive to share and enjoy it with her. Time and again she returned to the note to spot clues of his real intentions in the hope that somehow, through repeated reading, the words would eventually yield the truth. Despite her fear of confusing what she wanted to believe with the facts, the plainness of the note's language along with her knowledge of Jack's quirky and understated nature convinced Vivien that she should surrender to her intuition and obey his request. Glenda too, though wary of the idea, had agreed that Vivien was not just indulging in self-delusion, remarking on the practical tone of Jack's specific instructions.

Thus emboldened by her friend's opinion, Vivien had reluctantly approached the vicar to ask him to act as the 'official' representative of the church at their séance and thus preside over Grumwood's first meeting of spiritualists, an unfortunate precaution she had thought necessary. Appalled at the suggestion, and welcoming a rare opportunity to parade his moral credentials (his curate having announced her pregnancy that very day), Much threw Vivien out, suggesting that she should consult a psychiatrist before coming to him with such desperate and ungodly schemes.

Not deterred, and never a fan of the vicar's brand of Christianity in the first place, Vivien had struck out alone, making discreet enquiries about the authenticity of Wren's credentials and beginning a correspondence with the far-off

Irish village he hailed from, in an attempt to verify his heritage. As she hoped, Wren's sister confirmed that their father had had this 'gift' and that it was said to have passed down through the male side of their family, though whether it had skipped a generation in her brother's case she did not know. Several ex-squadron members, who could be trusted on account of their disapproval of Wren and his cohorts, agreed that during the war Jack and Wren had often discussed such matters, lending credence to the claim that they were more than just officer and batman. From then on the plan entered its practical phase and negotiations were taken over by Glenda and Baxter, Wren having been traced without any difficulty to the railway car he shared with Cirella, 'the Yank'.

The problem for Vivien was that these intrigues were the product of a very different state of mind from the one she currently found herself in. Whereas there may have been a time when this project had been crucial to keep her going, that time was now passing, even if she had found nothing to fill the void it had left behind. Were it not for her extraordinary loneliness, these plans would never have got as far as they had, for the year spent between dreaming them up and the present had allowed her enough time to see how absurd they were. Now that she knew Jack would not come back, the séance, far from being a holy and sacred event, was rendered no more than an obsession emptied of meaning. It hurt her to realise this, but it would have hurt even more to continue with her delusions. All that remained for her to do was to complete the séance with as much reserve as possible, and continue with the rest of her life.

'God, here they are!' giggled Glenda. 'Go on, open the door quickly, you don't want your father hearing the bell and coming to see what's going on!'

'There's no danger of that, I caught him drinking again this morning.' Vivien glanced out from behind the curtain. 'No, but look, you open the door, it's important that I retain some sort of . . . dignified distance. I don't want them to think that they can take advantage of me. Take advantage of my position, I mean, no, my *trust*. It's hardly as though I can go to the police, is it? I mean if the whole thing turns out to be a dreadful con.'

'Oh it won't be that,' said Glenda, excitedly, 'at worst silly, at best . . . magical!'

'All right then, I'd better open the door,' said Vivien, laughing more out of nervousness than anticipation. 'Let's see what we've let ourselves in for.'

Baxter, as Glenda had correctly predicted, was feeling no more comfortable than Vivien, though the emotions of his companion Wren were far harder for the two women to fathom. Both men were badly hung over. Baxter, concerned at how this might look, had already brushed his teeth five times that morning. Wren had contented himself with picking a plant out of the Rosses' flowerbed, and sticking it in his top pocket.

'Right, Wren,' said Baxter to his shorter companion, who was dressed in an olive-green boiler suit, 'if these ladies want to waste their time and money on your soothsaying, so be it, I don't believe in any of that airy-fairy stuff myself, I'm a rationalist and materialistic atheist, but so much as embarrass me once, I don't care how, and I'll kick your arse out of the door sharpish, do you follow? No funny business.'

'Have no fear of that, Baxter, you old worrier,' replied Wren, scraping his boots over the cobblestone path leading to the front door. 'No idea how you could think such a dreadful thing of me! Caution's a useful beast but you're full of too much of it, I say. Can't think of what you'd be on about.'

Baxter clenched his face. 'Just to smell you to start with; I've no objection to a bloke living his life as he pleases, it's the right of each of us, but you could at least have had a bath. If only to find out what one was like.' Baxter was certainly right that even in the outdoors the smell of Wren could be unfavourably compared to that of freshly laid compost and smouldering vegetable waste. 'You always were a stinker. Peace hasn't made you no better.'

'Don't have the opportunity to have a bath where I'm holed up; we don't all have your advantages in life, Baxter.'

'I didn't say it had to be a bath. You should've poured hot water over your head, jumped in a lake, or done *something* to make it look like you'd made an effort. Take my word for it, you could grow spuds behind those ears of yours. And . . .' Baxter unclenched his face in order to continue, in spite of his disgust, 'I thought I told you to wear your best clothes. Those togs make you look like a bloody clown.'

Wren feigned an expression of injured innocence. 'You may not like the grease but it keeps me warm and dry in winter; we're not all so lucky as to sleep in houses. Catch a death if I made contact with water in this weather. And what gives you the right to be so angry with me? I thought you said no one minded if you jumped work for the day. I'll split the fiver both ways, which is mighty generous as I'm the one doing all the work and you were just the fixer.'

Baxter nodded, aware of his duty to the world's poor, but Wren's high-pitched Limerick accent and failure to ever wear a tie always brought out the authoritarian in him. 'Look, Wren, I'm not out to give you a deliberate hard time, I just don't want us shown up – £5 is a lot for what you're bringing to the table and their kind don't take kindly to being mugged by an Irishman.'

Wren scowled, this time genuinely. 'Grateful as I might be for you acting as my agent in this matter, Baxter, I'd take care to remind you that I'm no side-show freak, my gift is as true as the Shannon's clear and you'd do well to pay heed to it. There're only so many of your hurtful comments I'll take, man.'

Baxter glanced at the twitching curtain. 'All right, all right, keep your hair on, all I meant to say was no farting or swearing in front of the ladies, remember these are proper toffs of a sort. So cut out the familiarity, and when you start . . . your thing, try to remember yourself. Talking to the dead is no excuse for forgetting your Ps and fucking Qs.' Baxter squirmed slightly as he said this. Despite his politics, or perhaps because of them, every meeting with a supposed class enemy, especially when she was a woman was drowned in deference. Try as he could, the urge to debase himself was impossible to resist, his upbringing by a man who bought new shoes to vote Tory preventing him from doing otherwise, for unlike Delaney and the Colonel, Baxter's rebellion was entirely intellectual and not in the least bit instinctive.

Wren looked at him condescendingly. 'I'll do as I have to. But don't you worry, the dead are a lot more clean-mouthed than the likes of you, Baxter.'

Baxter looked relieved rather than talked down to, his sense of national superiority too engrained to think Wren capable of patronising him. Although he had never found it in his heart to actually like Wren, a curious and superstitious individual who smelt of onions, he had still come to accept him in the way soldiers learn to respect those who may be called upon to save their lives.

'Right then, zero hour,' said Baxter by way of finishing the conversation, 'let's get the job started.' Gingerly he approached the front door and looked for the least intrusive way of announcing their arrival, caught between using the doorbell or banging the knocker.

Before he could decide, the door was pulled open with an abruptness that caught him by surprise. Standing before him was Vivien Ross, clothed in a close-fitting floral-print dress quite unlike anything Baxter had seen her in before. Surmising that it had been cut and fitted for her by the one it was originally intended for, Glenda Heathen, and fairly struck by its sex appeal, Baxter had not had time to sincerely compliment her on it before she said, 'Please tell me, Mr Baxter, tell me that he is not the one.'

Wren pulled off his cap and doffed it in a way that even a simpleton would realise was 'a piss take' (the phrase Baxter hissed under his breath as he watched him do this). 'Pleased to meet you again, Miss Ross, most pleased,' Wren said, grinning idiotically, the Irish in his voice turned up for reasons broadly connected to showmanship, 'and as with each of our meetings it's no less of a pleasure than the last. As to whether I'm the "one" or not, well you know I am, even if you may never have had the pleasure of seeing me close up, before.'

Ignoring Wren, and directly addressing Baxter, Vivien said, with a great effort to control her temper, 'Mr Baxter, you don't— Ouch!' She felt Glenda poke her in the back, but continued, 'You don't mean to tell me that that . . . *goblin* is the medium?' The light humour of her conversation with Glenda had departed, and in its place was the bossy snobbery she always protected herself with when sensing humiliation.

'Goblin. That's not a very nice thing to say about Wren, Miss Ross; he may not look like the rest of us but I assure you he's very highly respected in . . . in what he does. And besides, he's . . . salt of the earth.'

'What? You mean he's not properly evolved?'

'No, Miss Ross, I . . . I say that he has qualities that those of us who are more developed can . . . lose sight of sometimes.' Baxter glanced at his hands nervously; clearly he had not understated the effect a face-to-face meeting with Wren would have on Ross.

'Because of our relative distance from the earth and the salt it contains?'

Baxter, his face reddening for the want of an answer, nudged Wren for help.

'Come now, Baxter, Miss Ross only jests. Why, we've met, met in a manner of speaking, that is, several times before . . .'

'Not at such close quarters, Mr Wren, and I wish you wouldn't use phrases like "manner of speaking", it doesn't impress me in the slightest, if it's your intention to.'

Glenda Heathen strode forward, her duty to break the ice clear to all. 'Why don't you both come in and set up your things, if you need to do that, do you? No, you probably don't, it's not like painting or decorating, is it? Come in anyway and tell us what form the ceremony will take. This is exciting, isn't it? Do you do it all the time, Mr Wren? Or do you only take special calls like this one?'

'Only when I'm called to, Miss Heathen, only when called to.'

Glenda was the only person present who could conceivably be described as excited, the others all lost in their personal worries or worlds. Churlishly, Vivien Ross made way for Wren, who immediately began to display exaggerated awe at pieces of antique furniture, while behind him Baxter made a great performance of wiping his feet clean on a Persian carpet he had confused for a mat.

'A lovely house, Miss Ross, as good as its great grounds, may I say, and would that be an original wormwood grandfather clock?'

'Don't mind him, Miss Ross, he's not used to houses,' joked Baxter feebly, 'all his lot come from caves, from what I hear.'

'Caves!' Glenda laughed. 'What's it like to come from a cave, Mr Wren? Do you sleep upside down?'

'Up, down and all around, Miss Heathen, but mostly in a carriage by the old Watercress Line, there's something of a community of us old soldiers there at the present.'

Vivien scowled at Glenda who did not notice her friend's annoyance at her fraternisation. 'I think you'd be better off in a cave than in a dusty old railway carriage. I hear there's one free in Wookey Hole, if you don't mind sharing it with a witch.'

Wren chuckled good-naturedly, baring his luminous teeth lupinely. 'It's whether the witch would have me!'

'Where would you like to do this?' asked Vivien curtly. 'And Mr Baxter, kindly instruct Mr Wren to put that down, it cost a lot of money and would be impossible to replace.'

'Wren!' said Baxter slapping his companion in the chest, a painted King Charles spaniel falling from his grasp. 'Don't go touching things that have nothing to do with our business here!'

'And please ask him to remove the tin thimble he's already buried in his pocket and put it back where he found it. It may not look like much to him, but it's been in our family for generations.'

Without any trace of embarrassment Wren did as he was told, amused by this contradictory woman. 'You shouldn't mind my light fingers, ma'm, no you shouldn't, for they have no bearing on my . . . how should I say, deeper gifts.' He laughed, raising an eyebrow archly.

'Mr Wren, I can assure you that my objections to yourself are all-encompassing, excluding only those parts that are useful to me, and that part which my husband held highly, though why that could be I'm at a loss to say.'

At the mention of Jack, Wren was once again all mock deference, virtually dropping onto one knee. 'Ah, Captain Jack Sceptre, an officer and gentleman, Miss Ross, a truly fine leader of men.'

'I'm sure you'll be able to tell him yourself in few moments, Mr Wren,' said Vivien sagely, 'once the experiment is under way.'

'No experiment, Miss Ross, a proven science. Like your two-times table you learnt as a wee colleen.'

'So I'm to understand that you've done this before, then?'

'I can verify he has,' interjected Baxter, trying to keep his gaze off Glenda's smiling eyes. 'That was what first brought our Wren here to your late husband's attention. The captain was very interested in Wren's hobbies. He was very open-minded in that way; I say that because a lot of us weren't.'

'Apparently Mr Wren contacted the souls of the recently departed on the battlefield,' said Glenda, the idea of the dwarf-like man possessing supernatural powers amusing her, 'right at the spots where they'd died.'

'They contacted *me*,' corrected Wren.

'I can just imagine the scene,' sighed Vivien. 'Well no one's died in *this* spot so you'll probably have to try particularly hard.'

'It were no pretty sight,' added Wren, 'speaking to those poor slaughtered souls. And to think it was me they chose to talk to.'

'I think we've established that, Wren,' said Baxter.

'I believe Mr Wren is trying to say that his gifts were not allocated to him in order to satisfy our physical credulity. He may not look like a spiritualist but that doesn't mean he isn't one. Am I right, Mr Wren?'

'Eh?' Wren appeared momentarily wrong-footed.

'Miss Heathen means that you look too funny to have special powers, but that might be because only funny-looking people have them,' clarified Baxter unnecessarily.

'The only thing he looks like he's had allocated to him is fleas,' sniffed Vivien. 'Ye gods, can't we begin?'

'Would either of you like anything to drink before we start?' asked Glenda to her friend's growing irritation. 'Tea or coffee?'

'Bring out the brandy and have done with it,' said Vivien, waving her hand in the direction of the drawing-room drinks cabinet. 'I'm sure we'll need a bottle each before this day's through.'

'Very kind and very perceptive of you, Miss Ross. It is a good idea for everyone to partake of a little spirits before making contact with *the* spirits, if you'll pardon my little pun.'

'Not really,' said Vivien dryly. 'So what are we supposed to do to start? Fall about the floor with our arms in the air?'

'Don't you put a glass in the middle of a table?' called Glenda from the drawing room. 'Shall we do it in here?'

'No, I'm sure the kitchen will do, if that's all right with Mr Wren?'

'The spirit world ain't as fussy as us, Miss Ross.'

'Good, because you've brought a funny smell in with you and I don't want it being rubbed off on the furniture.'

'So are we going to do that weird thing with the glass? You know the one, where it moves about the table every time we ask a question or tell a lie?'

'No, Miss Heathen; that is one method, but not the one I favour, it's rather Anglo-Teutonic for my tastes, truth be told.'

'You what?' spluttered Baxter.

'Jack *was* an Anglo-Saxon, Mr Wren,' said Vivien.

For the first time since he entered the house, Wren dropped his protective grin, and addressed Vivien in what possibly could have been his actual speaking voice: 'Please, Miss Ross, if we are not to waste each other's time you must do exactly as I say. Your husband trusted the ancient methods of the Woads, or Celts as you know them, and you must do the same. You see, without your help we'll be in the old proverbial. You're the most important one in all this, so humour me and cooperate. And cooperation in this case means belief, Miss Ross, belief.'

Wren was so serious as he said this that it was hard for Vivien not to laugh in his face, the intensity of his words in ludicrous contrast to the stubby frame and rounded mouth from which they came. It was this easiness to laugh that stopped her from doing so, she, like the others, recognising a straightness of purpose in Wren, which, though inviting mockery, would not tolerate it.

'So what, if you don't mind the endless repetition of this question, would you have us do to start, Mr Wren?'

'The kitchen table will be good, and sorry, Miss Heathen, but the only thing we'll need these glasses for is to drink brandy from,' said Wren, taking the bottle and a glass with him as he led the party down the corridor and into the kitchen. 'I've used glass before and things can get awful messy. Only thing more dangerous is actually asking the spirit world a question. That can lead to anything.'

Anxiously Vivien grabbed his arm. 'Mr Wren, as I understand it you've never once laid foot in this house before and have, to my knowledge, no access to its architectural plans.

Can you then please tell me how you know the way to the kitchen?'

Wren stopped, just short of pushing open the kitchen door. 'Can't say I know the answer to that,' he said smiling, a puzzled look on his face, 'only matters that I know how, though, don't you think?'

Vivien swallowed hard and bent her head a little to the left, an expression she often used to demonstrate reluctant assent.

'You said that using glasses gets messy, Mr Wren, how do you mean "messy",' asked Glenda. 'Nothing's going to spontaneously combust, is it? I've heard that sometimes happens with those boards you use to find out who loves whom with.'

'Well, Miss Heathen, I've seen some mad things. Glasses thrown against walls, broken glass all over the floor, and then they, the evil ones if you're unlucky enough to get them, they always encourage objects to fly about the place too, door knobs, carriage clocks, you name it. Like I say, it can get messy, far better to use hands. You know where you are with those. And as for boards, forget about 'em. Strictly for schoolgirls and students of the art.'

For the past few seconds Baxter had appeared completely stunned, now he found his voice again; 'Hang on a minute, Wren. Hands? What do you mean *hands*? Not my hands?'

'That'll be right, Baxter. Hands. We sit in a circle, close our eyes, hold hands and think of Captain Sceptre, and nothing else. So you leave the rest to me. You all just think of the captain, his essence if possible but if you can't think in essences then your memories of him will do.'

'You mean I have to join in with this too, Wren?'

'Of course, Baxter, you didn't think I'd invited you along just to hold my old boy, now did you?'

'Christ! I'm not cut out for this sort of caper, Wren . . .'

'How will you know we're all thinking of Jack?' asked Glenda mischievously. 'Are you a mind-reader as well as a clairvoyant?'

'Because if you don't think of him, he won't come to me,

and if he won't come to me then Miss Ross won't hear what
he has to say. And then we'll all have wasted our time.'

'My, Mr Wren, you have left us with an awful responsibility.'

'I have, because I've no choice but to. And no talking to each
other either; I hardly need say that that'll ruin concentration.
Yours and mine together.'

'You want everyone to think about Jack?' said Vivien, her
voice strung with unease.

'Is that a problem for you, Miss Ross? I thought that you
might find that part easiest of all.'

'I'm afraid you were right on the first count. It is a problem.
Look here, Mr Wren, I'll level with you; it seems obvious that
you possess some level of mind-reading skills, and that if we're
all to sit in a circle, as you suggest, it seems conceivable to me
that you'll be able to read our thoughts. It's equally clear that
you're quite skilled at other, more mysterious "work" and, as
you say, have a gift for it, though how you came about it is
anybody's guess.'

'From the gods, Miss Ross, from them through my father.'

'Yes, and through his before him, I'm sure. What I find
fascinating is how practical your gift is, low-level even.
Reading my mind and finding your way to the kitchen are
cases in point and, I must congratulate you, expertly executed
with just the right balance between discovery and knowing
what you were doing all along. It's a rare gift, I grant you,
one that I'll admit I've never come across before, but probably no less rational to its practitioners than hypnosis or
psychiatry.'

'What are you trying to say, Miss Ross? That I'm a fraud?'

'This, Mr Wren: I have your card marked. Translating what
we know into thoughts, what we think into words and what
we can speak into your own mouth, is all well and good, but
to actually pretend, as you doubtlessly will, that it's my dead
husband talking to you from beyond the grave is in bad taste,
to put it mildly. It's a dishonest thing to do, Mr Wren, that I

could find hurtful if I wished, and under these circumstances I won't be party to it.'

Glenda rolled a lock of hair around her finger; the distinction between conjuror and spiritualist was not one she thought Vivien would have objected to.

Far from being offended, Wren sat smiling at her, an awful and knowing look in his eyes. 'Are you sure that's the real reason you're so upset, Miss Ross, or is there something else you haven't been telling us? It's all right, I don't blame you for it, but you can't impress the spirit world with your clever talk, they help me see through your excuses like you say you see through me.'

Vivien went bright red. The information was there at the forefront of her mind, waiting for Wren to read it – the conversation with Glenda a few weeks before in which Glenda had revealed a curtness that stunned her. 'You know, Viv,' Glenda had said, 'you have to snap out of it, people can go on and on living insanely because there's no one there to tell them to stop doing it. It's my job to tell you that you're throwing yourself away. You can't carry on like you are; if you're not careful you'll be old and bitter before your time.' The words reflected something of Glenda's self-made pragmatism, but put Vivien on the defensive.

'But don't you miss him too, Glenda? Jack was your friend, and he was always talking about you.'

'Of course, but how much can I miss someone I wasn't married to? You miss a man in proportion to the role he played in your life, and love him as we all did, Jack didn't play a very large role in mine. That's the whole thing about dying! When you hear that someone has died you never really believe it, not when all you have is someone else's word for it. It's the experience of living without them and finding out the parts of your life they can't share with you that brings it home. And that's why no one else can miss him as much as you, Viv, and it's hopeless to think we could. He only had one wife and it was you!'

'Glenda, you can't fool me so easily. What are you holding back? Is it because he started to cuddle you after he drank all those sherries at Max's?'

'Don't be so crazy, all men can get like that.'

'What then? Is there something?'

'Only that you should realise that our loved ones are different things to different people. Around us Jack was the life and soul, but to the town he was a bit two-dimensional; when he was with them he was completely with them and then he was totally off somewhere else . . .'

These words had upset Vivien to her core, the truth that Jack was not a symbol of greatness, but imperfect, making her even more protective of his memory, and aware of the solitariness of her and her father's ongoing vigil. Faced with the thought of three others, Glenda in particular, joining her to evoke his spirit, aroused a bizarre jealousy in Vivien that Wren was only too aware of.

The smile had not left Wren's face as he said, 'It's true, isn't it? Why not unburden yourself, Miss Ross, and enjoy the freedom of not having to be right for once?'

Checking Wren's eyes for signs of smugness or superiority, and finding nothing of the sort, only the unthreatening warmth of a man who had nothing to fear from such qualities, Vivien held out her brandy glass and said, 'Go on, Mr Wren, I'll have a drink and take the reprimand in that order, please.'

'I'll leave the reprimanding to the local constabulary, Miss Ross. I know what you're thinking, and you're right in your way, though if you don't object to us trying for your sake, it won't matter. None of us were as close to Captain Sceptre as you but if we all play our part and think of him as well as we each knew him, to different degrees as that may be, then there'll be nothing to worry about. This isn't about who knew him best or first, and it isn't a race. We all need to help each other to help you.'

Baxter felt his jaw drop, he had never heard Wren address

anyone, let alone his social betters, in this way before. 'I think I'll have a spot of brandy myself, if that's all right . . .'

Glenda clicked her heels and clapped her hands as if discovering the rules of a wonderful new game. 'Here's your table, Mr Wren. It's time for the expert to take over.'

'Right,' said Wren in a close approximation to a pantomime Irish voice, one he subtly slipped into when not discussing 'his gift', 'well I suggest we each have a couple of drams of this,' he raised the bottle, 'and begin.'

Glenda nudged Vivien, narrowing her eyes shrewdly. 'Remember what we talked about the other day, Viv, what I said about trusting your feelings, and not your way of explaining them to other people,' she whispered, 'that thing you do when you want to make yourself conversationally clear, before you properly understand what you're talking about yourself. It could help here to drop that. I think we're at this man's mercy! He seems to know everything so let him do the explaining for us.'

Vivien nodded, only half hearing her friend's well-meaning advice. To her amazement they were both about to take this seriously.

Baxter coughed uncomfortably. 'So you want us to hold hands, then? You ladies don't mind, I hope. I wouldn't normally presume.'

'Not at all.' Glenda winked, the warmth of her hand sending a charge of energy into Baxter's flimsy grip. 'Whatever Mr Wren thinks is necessary for the success of our enterprise.'

'Why shouldn't they want to hold your hand, Baxter?' said Wren, his eyes moving round all four corners of the room as if checking for something. 'After all, who can turn down a nice person? Now I'm going to have to ask you all to be quiet.'

'Do I need to be quiet too or do you want me to perhaps ask Jack a question?'

'No, no, all you need to remember, Miss Ross, is that a woman haunted by a fixed idea is insane, and I'm here to cure you of your idea. Everything that will flow from the other side, or "that place" as we call it, will rely on your energy and on my mouth as you so aptly put it earlier. So don't be worried at giving yours a rest.'

Vivien let this impertinence pass, the balance of power had shifted; they were in Wren's kitchen now and the man who smelt of squirrels was in control. 'Well I shall try not to confuse hope for the truth, this time around,' muttered Vivien, her last words feeling rather childish in the circumstances, as Wren silenced her with a cautionary scowl.

For a moment they all sat in silence, the manic twittering of birds gathered on a nearby holly bush filling the room reassuringly. Far from feeling the ridiculousness of their situation, all four of the spiritualists seemed grateful for the break in their lives that the séance had afforded them, even Wren, on whom the onus of responsibility lay. The illusion of calm was broken by the unmistakable sound of Wren breaking wind. With great effort Baxter and Glenda suppressed the urge to laugh out aloud, though to their surprise Vivien remained motionless, her eyes closed in a perfect picture of concentration.

Another minute passed, the birds stopped their song, and premature thoughts of how long it would take the spirit world to answer their call filled the mind of Baxter and, to a lesser extent, Glenda. The grandfather clock in the hall struck two, Father Time seemingly ignorant of their concerns, and the braying of a donkey echoed around the floodplain. Baxter swallowed a cough, the situation already too bizarre for him to feel anything like the embarrassed terror that he would have normally experienced in this kind of fix.

Then, without warning, Wren began to shake his arms, causing a chain reaction of shakes round the table, the movement occurring too quickly for the others to see how it had started. Hacking at his throat loudly and barking indecipherable parade-ground commands at the top of his voice, Wren then screamed, 'Arms left, chest in, stomach out, eyes right! Come on, you miserable little weasels, I'm watching you!'

Baxter, scared of what Glenda or Vivien's reaction to this outburst might be, had more than half a mind to tell Wren to shut up, but this urge was next to nothing compared to his horror at what came next.

Without missing a beat, Wren's military orders mutated into a note-imperfect rendition of 'What Shall We Do With the Drunken Sailor', sung in the voice of a Scottish pansy, Wren clicking his tongue dementedly at the end of each verse and snapping his fingers under Glenda's nose.

Throughout this Vivien sat motionless, a deathmask expression solidly emblazoned across her face, as Glenda, no less bizarrely, tapped her foot in time to Wren's outbursts, reminding Baxter of a head girl determined to make a good show of it.

Afraid that he may be the only one missing out on the revelations of the spirit world, and of hitting one of the ladies by mistake, Baxter held back from kicking Wren under the table, the singing breaking up into a hotchpotch of various accents and half-clipped conversations Wren was pursuing with himself. The worry for Baxter was that Wren, far from 'putting it on' as he had expected him to, was sincerely and deliriously in the grip of some larger mental problem he had not had the wit to fathom before.

A loud gasp was followed by silence, as Wren let his head drop onto the table with a thud. Glenda opened an eye, closed it and opened the other in a type of wink, her eyebrows raised in amused points. Baxter blew out a sigh of relief from both corners of his mouth, while Vivien remained the only one of them still in 'that place'. Despite being no closer to having made contact with Jack, there was a quiet acceptance that Wren had certainly done his best to move from one world into the next, the paucity of results shaded by his immense efforts.

'Do you think he's done?' whispered Glenda.

'I'd be very surprised if he is,' replied Baxter sadly.

Steadily, with his chin pressed down to his chest, Wren started up again, quietly at first, his words mainly elfin gibberish. Unperturbed by there being no one to communicate with, Wren continued in this vein, not quite meaninglessly but not in a way any sane person could have regarded as constructive, his baby talk giving way to bouts of gargling and the occasional snarl. Gradually one voice, clear and distinct, began to gain dominance over Wren's other noises. To Baxter's discomfort, even in full knowledge of Wren's extensive gifts of mimicry, this voice was not one he had ever heard before in his repertoire. More importantly, unlike any of the other voices that had gained 'possession' of him, this one was unmistakably human, and English. Speaking like a spoilt and plummy undergraduate, with the authority of one who thinks he's conducting a private conversation with no risk of being overheard, Wren announced with a mild lisp, 'If you really want to go back to the start of it all, my dear friends, then you must go back to my mother, always nattering on and attending to practical things. She never really understood me, you see. And that's what made me angry.'

Vivien froze; the voice was remarkably like what Jack's might have been as an adolescent, and without thinking she reached out for her glass of brandy and drained it, leaving Wren's hand trembling on the table.

Baxter was also aware of some shift that heralded, he feared, the first signs of Wren overplaying his hand. Vivien Ross may have been ready to tolerate fiddlers and fools at her table, but Baxter deduced that she would not put up with Wren getting too clever by half, something that impersonating the accent of her ex-husband would undoubtedly qualify as. Firmly, and without drawing Vivien or Glenda's attention, Baxter tried to kick Wren out of his chair, missing his target and knocking a table leg. The table shuddered a little, reinforcing the impression of a ghostly presence filling the room, Baxter's second kick causing even greater embarrassment as he felt his shoe come off and fly into Glenda's lap.

'So,' continued Wren, leaning back in his chair with the ease of a professional raconteur, 'we get to the part where she and I, my mother, lest you forget, hit absolute synthesis: a coming together of opposites, for those of you not familiar with Hegel. Not that she knew what it was like to *be* me, we'd have to wait for you before that happened, Viv; but because she adored me, she'd pretend to know what I was talking about. This usually coincided with me ceasing to care whether she really did know me or not, and our normal relations, which really were quite loving, would resume again. You might ask why I stopped caring about whether she was being sincere in her desire to understand me, and I think I could reply on her behalf that even though I could have been speaking Greek as far as she was concerned, anything that came out of her son was bound to be worthwhile. Call me conceited and I'd say you were right. I was an indulged bastard in those days; it was the army that straightened me out. You'd agree if you'd seen what I was like before, unless you're the type who likes pretentious bores or, worse, one of those people who believe that no one ever really changes . . . such a tiresome attitude. Sorry to sound so angry, but there's something about being brewed up in a tank that makes one re-evaluate one's life.'

Glenda's face had turned grey, Vivien's white and Baxter's green. They were listening to the voice of Jack Sceptre and there was nothing any of them could do to stop him.

'She is in here, isn't she, my loved one?' he shouted. 'Bloody bad manners to keep ignoring a chap who's talking to you.' Thrusting his arm across the table the man who was Wren grabbed Vivien's hand tightly. 'Ask her how much of herself she's prepared to forsake to remain true to the truth. It's a question she'd understand, she was the one who said that truth is more important than love. Remember that? Never easy loving one who believes the truth is what she wants, eh Viv?'

Wren's face lurched forward as he spoke these words, their passage from his mouth as involuntary as the dribble that showered forth from its corners. Helplessly Vivien tried to release her hand from Wren's maniacal grip, his very touch enough to prompt thoughts of throwing up, and not just the contents of her stomach but plenty of her other parts too, beginning with her mind.

'Damn you, woman, I'm trying to help! Don't you want me to help? There are plenty of others who'd be only too glad!'

The voice Wren was using was far too autonomous in its spite and scope for it to be a cunning trick invented by the Irishman for the sake of his audience. Whatever it was that was using Wren to project its dark message bore no relation to any living thing encountered in daylight, its cruel hiss reminding Vivien of the half-remembered nightmares of her youth.

'How long do you think you can carry ideas around without them affecting you or defining you, Viv? You should see some of the stuff in my head, old girl. Oh why did you have to wake me up? It all rises to the surface in the end, but I must admit, I admire your efforts at attempting to remain the same person despite it all. Remaining true to your laughing Jack and not marrying one of those hard-faced men who did well out of the war. Oh you're true blue, Viv, true blue.'

Vivien felt her head turn; it was too grotesque to listen or watch any more, her immediate bearings and gravitational centre lost in a wave of revulsion. 'Please . . .' she whispered, but it was no use, she was no longer the woman she was before all this began, the whole of her former life mocked by her failure to stand up to whatever it was in the chair beside her.

Pulling away from the table and staggering to his feet, Wren grabbed a towering spider plant and brought it crashing down to the floor.

'Do you want me to punch his lights out?' shouted Baxter unhelpfully, his patience utterly exhausted.

Wren leered at his former comrade-in-arms and threw his right arm out in a Nazi salute. 'All of us,' he yelled, 'have the war to thank for everything. And not just us, but our sons and our grandsons' sons!' As he spoke, his contorted face swung from side to side, his free hand physically trying to pull his mouth apart to release what was welling up inside. Falling over, he cried out in utter pain, 'Tell her *the truth* and leave me, you evil bastard!'

There was a quiet whimper from the floor, and then in normal speaking tones they all heard Jack Sceptre say, 'I love you, girl, but for God's sake let me go.'

'Wren, you fucking fool!' shouted Baxter, jumping to his feet. 'You've really gone and done it now!'

Wren, who was slumped in a sobbing heap under the table, rolled onto his front and covered his ears. 'Don't give me that, you bastard, you—'

Baxter felt Glenda's near hypnotic touch pull gently at his shirt. 'Now,' she smiled, 'even the dead are entitled to their opinion, Mr Baxter.'

'But he . . .' Baxter pointed down at Wren and realised that he did not know what he wanted to say.

Glenda turned her face to his and let the sun blaze across it. They both looked at each other for an indeterminate time, Baxter all of a sudden very glad to be where he was, Wren's séance a useful pretext for this view of pure beauty.

'I don't think any of us have seen anything like it,' Vivien Ross said over the table, 'and I don't know whether I ever want to again, I rather suspect not, but I do not think that's a reason for not checking on whether Mr Wren, as I'm sure we can all rely on him being again, is in need of our help or not, Mr Baxter.'

Baxter had never known what it was to be dazzled by eloquence before, but forgetting Glenda for the moment, he gazed at Vivien, his look full of admiration for anyone who could speak, or even continue as before, after what had so recently passed.

'Right,' he said, 'you're right . . . but I'm sorry, sorry on his behalf for all of that trousers he was spouting—'

'There's no need to be,' Vivien cut him short, 'I think we've all learnt something, my lesson perhaps the most obvious of all.'

This was not what Baxter had expected to hear, so, moving quickly before Vivien recovered from her state of grace (or was it shock?) and their luck ran out, he hauled Wren up off the floor by his collar, and squeezed his nose.

'Wakey, wakey, Merlin,' he hissed into the crumpled-up Irishman's ear, 'we're back in the land of the living again.'

'What the hell happened?' mumbled Wren, his head rolling between his shoulders as though it had no connection with his neck.

'You went bloody mad, sunny Jim, that's what happened.'

'Ah,' said Wren, his gait transforming from that of a dishevelled mouse pulled from a teapot, to the card-shark woken from a deep and drunken sleep Baxter had observed so many times before.

'You went absolutely bloody mad, worse than what I've seen you even when you're pissed. You're lucky the police weren't called.'

'Ah,' he said again, catching Vivien Ross's sympathetic eye.

'So you've got your bearings again, have you?' asked Baxter in a sarcastic voice, doing his best to play along with Wren's routine.

'Yes, old friend, I know where I am now,' said Wren, 'but by Jesus does my head hurt. How long was I out for?'

'"Out" is hardly the word any of us would use, Mr Wren,' said Vivien, 'you were actually quite lively. You were only on the floor for a few seconds, and even then you weren't "out" but crying, in the main. Which, going on the basis of your "possession", I don't blame you for at all.'

'Then there's no need to explain anything,' said Wren, pushing Baxter away, 'you already know more of my work than I do myself.'

'Yes,' said Vivien, 'I think that's probably true.'

Wren bowed slightly. 'And then I thank you for your wisdom and patience. My methods are raw, and not for everyone's consumption.' He glanced at Baxter and snarled so quickly that no one apart from his target had time to notice, before adding, 'You have shown yourself to be a woman worthy of a great man, Miss Ross, and a great woman in her own right, may I say.'

Glenda watched Vivien closely, for if there was to be a moment in which her friend's old behavioural patterns were likely to reassert themselves, then it was now.

'Thank you, Mr Wren,' said Vivien, her placid tone suggesting that neither flattery nor humbug had made any discernible difference to her belief in what she had just seen and heard, its truth utterly independent of Wren's post-séance embellishments. 'I hope £10 will be adequate payment for your time and . . . exertions.'

Baxter looked as though he had been jumped by a box of frogs. 'Ten pounds, Miss Ross, for that! But . . . but he wasn't even clear, just blinking mad!'

'Mad it may have been to your philistine ears, Baxter, but mad it was not to those more enlightened than yourself. For all that, I am sorry, ladies, sorry that it was not all it could have been or all I'd have liked it to be, and had we more time we may have attempted more voyages and, who's to say, made them glorious,' Wren intoned, sounding rather more like a plumber worried about leaving a job half finished, than the spirit walker of a few moments earlier. 'The trouble is that a séance is like hearing a clock go tick-tock, when all you want to hear is the ticks, so you force yourself to hear tick, when the clock is actually going tock. And what you end up with is hearing strange noises that sound like neither.'

'I beg your pardon?' asked Vivien politely. 'But even by the standards of the past half hour that was rather unclear.'

'What I mean to say is that you can try to impose what you want on truth, Miss Ross, because you won't end up hearing your own impositions, you'll hear strange half-realised distortions, and that's the sound of truth refuting you. It's like that with the spirits, you see, which is why you may be still asking yourself what in God's name happened . . .'

'No, I'm not really. I thought, despite what Mr Baxter said, that it was all rather clear.'

It was Wren's turn to look surprised. 'Well if that doesn't knock me sideways. It took me a while to realise that there's a difference between the way I see things and the way the world does, which is why I like to keep an eye on both versions, but doesn't that just top it all, a lady like your good self seeing things like I do. It's a surprise, Miss Ross, a happy surprise.'

'I'm feeling full of those, Mr Wren,' said Vivien, surprising them all by then announcing, 'I think it's high time we finished this bottle of brandy and made for the public house.'

As usual, Marsh had the distinct feeling that he had been missing out. His morning had been spent in the usual way, putting up fences and hammering in posts, with a short break for lunch, before helping the mildly infirm Miss Collins erect her new greenhouse. The most taxing problem of the day had concerned putting her ladder back in her tool shed; it had been easy enough to remove but impossible to fit back into the space he had taken it from. In the end he had sheepishly admitted defeat and left it against her back wall, slinking off without saying goodbye so as to avoid facing her. In the meantime, though, his friends had boldly forged ahead with what Marsh liked to call 'life proper'. First he heard the news trickle down concerning the 'strike' at the chocolate factory, followed by Dr Mills's fall and then, were this not enough, Lou Polly's stand-up row with Delaney in the high street. Given that all of these incidents involved people with whom he was on close speaking terms, Marsh believed that he would at least be privy to some 'inside' information, his hopes rising spectacularly when he bumped into Delaney and Captain Shallow chatting together outside the chemist and they were joined within minutes by the Colonel carrying one of his father's chickens under his arm. Obediently Marsh had followed the small group to the Squirrel Skinner and waited for the first-hand reports to come flying in, but instead a strange and long-winded conversation had arrived in its place. Doubtless the good stuff would appear in fits and snatches but, in the meantime, the other gentlemen at the bar talked largely to please themselves, a pattern Marsh had become depressingly used to.

'It's as I say,' said the Colonel banging his hand down on the bar, 'England ain't England when it ain't run for the benefit of Englishmen. Oliver Cromwell could have told you that, God rest his soul.' The first pint of Old Thumper had gone down predictably well, banishing his noonday demons and reinvigorating his sense of the fitness of things so that, in short, Eric Thatcher was once more the Colonel. Of his visit to his father he preferred to say little.

'I never said otherwise,' replied Marsh shyly, regretting a careless remark made about French cooking that the Colonel had jumped on furiously, 'I only said that it was nice to try things they have out there that we don't have here, like those flaky breads things they used to hand out to us when we marched through towns.'

'France! For Christ's sake! France! Could someone please tell me what we thought we were bloody doing saving their skins for the second time in twenty years, when all we got was mass graves for our troubles the first time round?' thundered the Colonel. '"Flaky bread things", they should have been giving us golden apples!'

'They're not the most grateful people in the world, I'll give you that,' said Shallow, his mind clearly focused on other, less political matters, 'but it's a mistake to expect thanks for every good deed, I suppose.'

'Couldn't have put it better myself, Mr Shallow—'

'I heard it's quite nice there, down in the south . . .' interrupted

Nora Martin, the landlord's youngest daughter, unwisely. 'Didn't you think so, Mr Thatcher?'

'France! The south, the north, what difference does it make?' yelled the Colonel. 'I thought the place was a complete and utter hole, so bad in fact that I didn't think it was worth letting on that that's what I thought. It's probably why I got on so well out there, see, I knew I was an Englishman; that made adapting easier, made it a question of acting and holding your nose until you got home.'

'Yes, understanding your own natural superiority does make being around foreigners easier,' offered Shallow. 'Personally I always found the Italians the worst, booby-trapping bottles of Chianti in the desert and then rushing up to surrender like butter wouldn't melt in their mouths . . .'

'Don't remind me, Mr Shallow,' howled the Colonel, wiping his mouth clean of beer. 'And the sad thing is, from what I hear they're all over London now, and before long it'll be the same here. Imagine a cesspool working on the same scale as Niagara Falls, because that's what we'll get when the wops arrive with all their diseases.'

'What wops?' asked Marsh.

'The ones that are coming here,' said Delaney, an ironic grin spilling over his lips, 'the ones that are ten men thick right here at this bar.'

'Yes,' drawled Shallow, 'I dare say the first thing the crafty buggers will do is reintroduce trams just so there's another way for me to be killed when drunk.'

'I liked the trams,' said Marsh.

'Marsh, are you the moron you so often purport to be, or are you only threatening us with that quality, knowing yourself to be deep down an ironist to rival the great Mr Coward?' posed the Colonel in his best received English. 'For I am trying to make a point about race in this once great nation of ours, and I could do so better without your interruptions.' He winked at the others, puffing out his chest, never so much himself than at moments like these. 'Because if we don't stop the Eyeties, the Maltese and God knows who else streaming in here like cat food . . .'

'Cat food?' Marsh blinked.

'Then we'll be robbed blind like charity shops without locks!' concluded the Colonel illogically, jabbing at Marsh's neck with his finger.

'What, you personally? Robbed like a lockless charity shop?' asked Delaney. 'What have you got that's worth robbing? And what have the Maltese done to you except win the Cross of St George, or the Eyeties, who fought like women anyway; you're talking trousers, Colonel. Buttonless slacks.'

'Terence! You miss the entire force of my point. I'm no hater of other races, be they Ice Cream Sellers or East End Crooks, but I believe that everyone's out for what they can get, with that cunt in trousers, Dawson, being my case in point. Everyone out for a quick buck, but if I go looking for one in their country . . .'

'Whose country?'

'Any country, they'd rob me of my suitcase and everything I own not because I'm a white man but because they want my stuff. Same reason why I don't want them in my country poncing off my rights and eating into this great Welfare State of ours that we seem to hear so much of, but still don't have. You see, I don't want them to have a piece of it not because they're niggers or wogs, but because what they want a piece of is *my money, my country and mine*. And if they come they'll be about as popular here as we were over there in Bombay, Rome, Lahore or wherever.'

'That's bollocks, Colonel,' grunted Delaney. 'What do you think we were doing over there in the first place, civilising them? Bollocks, we were robbing them blind. You could be Dawson or any other bugger who enjoys the whip hand, mouthing off like Hitler.'

'You can't say that! I hate Hitler!'

Sensing a gap in conversation Marsh readied himself to ask Delaney about his confrontation with Dawson when Shallow, who appeared to have been drifting in and out of their conversational orbit, intervened. 'The trouble with all of this, Thatcher, is that you may be right, in a small way, and for a limited period of time, but what then? Soon we'll be faced with a different set of problems. I mean, if we keep what we have for ourselves we risk allowing the whole world to go backwards, so that we may get to keep what we have, but we'll stop "them" from wanting it.'

'But that's exactly what we should want to happen! I don't want them to have it!'

'No! No, because what we have is a universally good thing. By depriving "them" of the chance to make their countries more like ours we'll drive them back into their past, into what they were before we found and civilised them, whatever the bloody hell that was, and then we'll have a new war against Mullahs, Rajas, Witch Doctors and Sheiks to deal with. They'll spurn us and fight us.'

'And I'd like to think our descendants will handle themselves well in it!' muttered the Colonel emotionally, this rare reference to what may have been his children, or children's children surprising them all. 'And keep those jealous barbarian hordes in their place.'

'That isn't what the man's saying, Colonel, he's saying that we've taken what we want from the world, and left what we can't afford, and if we don't open up . . .'

'I've always suspected you of being a bit Welsh, Delaney.'

'I *am* a bit Welsh,' Delaney replied, a slow throbbing in his temples suggesting a possible escalation in their sharp exchange of views, 'I am a bit Welsh, so what of it, you fat bigoted bastard?'

The Colonel grabbed Delaney by the neck and shook him joyfully. 'But that's not what's important, what actually matters is that we're all British, Terence, *British*, not niggers, or wogs,

Krauts or bloody fuzzy wuzzies, but white British arseholes who drink beer! Fat white bigoted bastards who drink beer!'

'I'm not an arsehole,' objected Marsh, 'or a fat bastard.'

'You're sounding like a bloody fool,' said Delaney pushing the Colonel off him, 'like one of those French D-Day dodgers who wore victory hats and shaved the hair off the women once it was safe to.'

'So sticking up for my country makes me a bloody fool, does it? I'm British and I hate people who aren't British, what's so difficult to understand about that?' said the Colonel, ready to not be nice now that his peaceful overture had been rejected.

'There's understandable prejudice and the un-understand-able kind and you're veering towards the latter stuff, Thatcher,' said Shallow.

'Don't understand the difference between the two, Mr Shallow; I think you're getting yourself a little bit confused.'

'You can prefer our way of doing things, and wish the world was a bit more like us, or just hate people because they've black faces and no freckles, an attitude worthy of the camp opera-tors at Belsen, Thatcher, a group of unholy jokers I'm sure you wouldn't want to be too closely associated with.'

'To hell with *those* murdering bastards and all those like 'em,' roared the Colonel. 'My argument's with the defilers of my country, not honest sons like you both! Now less of this serious stuff, what are we all drinking?'

'Travel changes nothing,' sighed Shallow. 'A half of gin.'

'Don't you think you blokes, excepting you, Mr Shallow, of course, ought to tell me what's been going on today . . . all this trouble at the factory. Must mean something?' said Marsh, his hand lifted in the air like a child asking questions in class.

'Marshy, Marshy, Marshy,' groaned the Colonel amiably, 'if Drake could wait until he finished his bowls you could at least let me finish my pint.'

'I have.' Marsh cupped his hand to his ear. 'Can you hear that noise outside? Sounds like a bloody battle's started.'

'I'll have another pint,' snapped the Colonel to Miss Martin, 'to add to whatever beverages these gentlemen are having.'

'You know you'll have to pay for your drinks today, Dad says . . .' But the barmaid's timid qualification had come too late for the Colonel, as he hailed Polly, Venning, Stanton and the Yank, to his corner of the bar, ordering drinks at the top of his voice for them all.

Polly had not gone home after leaving the garage. Instead he had walked to the transport cafe at the station and watched the trains arriving and leaving. His capacity to think without interruption, and towards no obvious conclusion, had never troubled him, for thought without object offered the consolation of nothing to contrast it with, and it was long into mid-afternoon before he remembered himself. If he were capable of tracing back the meandering course of his mood he would have found love for some nameless woman, well known to him but beyond his grasp, at the centre of it, but it did not occur to him to do this. Rather, he had allowed himself to be distracted by the hum and chatter of conversation, drifting out from the guardhouse, where talk had replaced the need to consult an evening paper or arrive home on time.

Depending on whether or not the conductors were to be believed, there were reports that the tradesmen had heard workers from the factory say that change was afoot, and that there would be 'trouble at the works'. From here information had become decidedly interpretational, breaking down on class lines. Dawson was either, if you were a shopkeeper, doing a lap of honour round town in a new car, 'swanking' in the glory of having sacked half his staff, or, if you were prepared to listen to the mob, ready to be turned out of the factory and robbed by a gang of wreckers led by Delaney. The small ripple instigated by Moat's death was growing in size, and from the worried faces of the middle-class professionals checking their watches in the waiting room, Polly sensed something approaching insurrection in the air. Although there were no palaces to be stormed or kings ready to take flight, history seemed to have caught up with Grumwood, encouraging Polly to make his way to the Yank's train carriage. Here he found the air charged by a mood of militancy, as his former comrades lit bonfires and symbolically hacked away at patches of nettles, the most enthusiastic stopping just short of pulling up a row of newly planted trees. Despite there being no previous agreement for all those men of the regiment who worked at Dawson's factory to skip work that day, it appeared that none, apart from Delaney, had turned up, and that even this had been too much for their boss. All the workers, including several who had grown apart from the hardcore, considered Delaney's act of defiance in standing up to Dawson a victory worth sharing, and a fitting tribute to Moat, though whether it had been meant that way or not remained unclear. From Polly's weak knowledge of history, the atmosphere of the gathering pointed towards a minor riot, if not a Peasants' Revolt, rather than the calculated takeover of power by an organised revolutionary cadre. The mass, and spontaneously agreed-upon decision to march to the Squirrel Skinner, rather than seize control of the telephone exchange, had confirmed his suspicion, as had the non-strategic damage done to a post box, and the tearing down of the Town Council's notice board.

Those few shops still open had battened down their shutters, children had been brought in from the streets and a phone call had been made to the police in Southcrawl. Polly realised that afternoon that the life of a country town is made up of very few faces, the same middle-class professionals ubiquitous in their dominance of committees, boards and associations; but on this occasion the hidden town, those that made up the numbers in the pubs, the Pit and farmyards, joined the factory workers and decided to speak for themselves, choosing to unite in the mindless destruction of poorly constructed property. To his misfortune, but, at a deeper level, pleasure, the vicar had cycled into the middle of this melee, had been divested of his transport and clothing, and thrown into the river, his dog collar wrapped around the Yank's hand like a knuckleduster as the mob entered the pub triumphantly.

'I can't believe it!' Marsh laughed on hearing of the 'one-day revolt', as it was to become known. 'Not one bugger turning up for work! And now you lot lording it in the middle of town! It's bloody chaos, it is!'

Some of the men entering the pub, who had turned up to work and would turn up again tomorrow, lowered their heads or laughed bluffly, all too aware that now was not the time to spoil folk myths in progress.

'Christ, isn't that something?' Marsh beamed. 'I wish I could have been there! Why, if it was me I'd be telling everyone,' he said, thumping Delaney on the back admiringly, 'letting everyone know that I'd started the whole thing by telling Dawson to fuck himself!'

'Nothing to tell, Marshy, I said what was what and sort of left it at that.'

'False modesty, dear boy, false modesty,' shouted the Colonel, already too drunk to gauge the size of the trouble they were in, but pleased to raise the subject in front of a decent-sized crowd. 'No use hiding your light under a bushel, you're a hero, man! The hero of the bloody day, ought to have congratulated you earlier, knew you'd go and do it, it's why I told you to,' he said, clearing his throat. It was not that the Colonel had felt envy when he first heard of Delaney's heroics, just that he was utterly lacking in perspective and proportion, believing his pronouncements on nation and race to be as interesting as anything Delaney could have done, until told different.

'Too right he's a bloody hero!' shouted Baxter, marching ahead of Vivien Ross and Glenda Heathen, who were sheltering some way behind him in the doorway. 'Gave him everything but the kitchen sink, didn't you! Marvellous!'

'The kitchen sink? Jesus!' said Marsh. 'The kitchen sink, fancy.'

'Hooray!' enthused Baxter. 'The revolution starts in my back yard and I'm not even there to grab the red flag off the washing line! I'm proud of you, Terry, right proud of you! The days of taking the word of a factory owner over that of a hired hand are numbered.'

'Oh I don't know.' Shallow smiled languidly. 'Like most wars I reckon this one will rumble on and on.'

'Nothing to do with me,' said Delaney, pointing a thumb at the band of men behind the Yank, 'mine was a solo mission. Seems like the riot's the work of these lads.'

'There'll be no riots in my pub,' growled Silas Martin across the bar.

'Don't worry,' winked the Colonel, 'I've got the situation in hand.'

'You'd better have, Colonel, because if you ain't the Lenin of this little jolly, then I'm more than prepared to accept it's Hitler. 'Oi, you!' Martin shouted at Stanton. 'You leave that sword on the wall, you hear?'

'Sorry,' the boy replied sheepishly.

'So what's all this I here about you starting revolutions, Terence?' asked Martin, pouring Delaney a half pint of Scotch. 'Didn't think that sort of thing was quite your bag.'

Delaney shrugged. 'Told Dawson what I thought of him and said we wanted our wages for the day of the funeral, he disagreed, we fought, I'm sacked.'

'I like that, a man of principle!' remarked the Colonel solemnly. 'Do you hear that, lads, Dawson offered Terence a pay rise if he was only willing to sell us out, and Terry said to him . . . he said, "Dawson take your damned pay rise, soak it in champagne and choke on it, you time-serving pimp"!'

'Never heard you talk like that before,' said Martin raising an eyebrow.

'Never have talked like that before.' Delaney grinned, his

admission drowned out by the howls of jubilation as the sack of swag from Dawson's office was discovered, and its contents poured over the floor.

'Where've you been, then?' Delaney asked Baxter. 'I heard you disappeared somewhere with that,' he said, staring at Wren, who had floundered into the bar and sat down on the lap of a stranger, very much the worse for the wear.

Baxter shook his head. 'One of these days I'll tell you, Terry, and you won't believe me.'

'Been like my day, then,' said Delaney, 'one of those when you think you're remembering it all wrong.'

There was a small cough from behind them. 'Mr Delaney, I wonder whether I may buy you a drink, by way of thanking you for putting Mr Dawson's ugly nose so far out of joint.'

Delaney regarded Vivien Ross carefully before smiling in assent; since leaving her father's service he had never heard her address a remark directly to him, but in the strange atmosphere of the afternoon, this unimaginable offer caused barely a murmur, her appearance in the Squirrel Skinner no more remarkable than it would have been in church.

'Don't know if I really need any more to drink, Miss Ross, but I suppose it'd be mad to turn down an offer I don't get every day.'

'Miss Ross was, ahem, kind enough to invite me and Wren for drinks this afternoon,' said Baxter, feeling as if some explanation was required.

'Wren?' asked Delaney. 'You and *Wren* at the Ross house?'

'To help gravel our drive,' laughed Vivien, a rare strain of colour in her cheeks, 'gravelling and drinks!'

'Sounds a most progressive regime you're running there, Miss Ross!' said the Colonel, before turning to Mark Polly. 'And what's old useless here done today but tinker with a few clapped-out motors! You've some catching up to do, son.'

Polly had been unable to hear or concentrate on anything from the moment he had seen Vivien Ross walk into the pub.

As usual his thoughts yielded nothing tangible, only a heightened and discomforting awareness of her being, and of her being beautiful. 'I'll catch up,' said Polly in a voice most people would have reserved for declarations of love.

Vivien could not have been more embarrassed had she been caught pointing a toe at the ceiling while pulling at her stockings. Shorn of the icy superiority that insulated her from the gaze of men, she half expected the room to erupt in laughter at her. It did not, but Polly had gone as crimson as she felt her face to be.

Quietly Polly asked, 'Would you prefer to sit round the other side, Miss Ross? It's rather noisy in here.'

'But I'm sure there's safety in numbers.' She smiled, Polly's tenderness at once calming and encouraging her. 'So you haven't played a very active part in the day's proceedings, Mark?'

Polly hesitated, grabbed by a natural reticence to answer questions quickly, which Vivien confused for distrustfulness.

'You needn't mind telling me, I'm not on the side of the enemy today,' she said.

'Not as such, Miss Ross, but I didn't . . . start anything today, I don't work at the factory or live with the others by the train lines.' Polly paused, and added, 'I did wake up with Captain Shallow, though.'

To his surprise Vivien registered no more shock than the squadron had when she had offered to buy Delaney a drink, the world all of sudden a place in which things like this seemed quite normal.

'Sharing bedding with your men; there must be something about that in regulations,' she said, addressing Shallow who looked ready to fall off his stool. 'You must have been feeling very, very friendly.'

'I'd trust my men with my life . . .' he began.

'I'm sure you would, but it's the smaller stuff I'd have thought you'd have had to worry about.'

'Worry?' asked Shallow, the pleasing appearance of Glenda

Heathen distracting his attention. 'It's hard to credit it,' he slurred, 'I've got to thirty-three and realise . . .'

'Yes?'

'That Christ must have felt pretty young when he died.'

'God!' Glenda laughed. 'Here come the shooting stars again!'

'Bullfarm,' growled the Colonel.

'I beg your pardon?' said Glenda.

'You heard me – bullfarm,' repeated the Colonel, 'rhetorical, testicular bullfarm.'

'A knock is better than a punch,' said Glenda, trying to make light of the Colonel's desire to give offence.

'And so is that, trying to damn me with faint insults.'

'Oh don't tell me, *Mr* Thatcher, don't say that I ought to have known what I was letting myself in for if I came in here?'

The Colonel glared at Glenda but did not make any effort to reply to her, the absence of a justified line of attack obvious even to him. Glenda stared back, reluctant to give the Colonel the satisfaction of seeing her breaking off eye contact. Like most people, Glenda did not like the Colonel, not since he had drunkenly announced to the factory floor that she deserved to be raped. Perhaps it was his status as a serial cuckold or the indifferent cut of his genitalia or both, but no one made the Colonel feel less wanted than Glenda, her very being in the world a challenge to his own.

Glenda, who in normal circumstances would have felt nothing stronger than mild antipathy towards the Colonel, detected a harsh strain of sexual Puritanism in the man, to compensate for which he fell back on cruelty. Glenda's impertinent questions and jaunty air were an invasion of his privacy and an affront to his pride. In his mechanical descriptions of sex, and boastfulness, she detected insecurity, and in her lightness and gaiety he saw a decadent sensualist. Unsurprisingly their few meetings had invariably ended with the trading of insults, the Colonel's discomfort around Glenda so plain and extreme that few of his friends had the courage to comment on it. On this occasion, however, it was the Colonel's insensitivity that encouraged Polly to say, 'What do you want to upset more people for, Colonel, we've got our hands full with enemies as it is.'

'I don't think Mr Thatcher deserves the compliment of rational opposition, Mark,' added Vivien quickly, her patrician eyes shining purposefully. 'He is the sort of man who prefers a single bed to the extra space provided by a double, so as to not be reminded of his marital status. Perhaps that's why he enjoys bullying people so much.'

'Bullying people!' snorted the Colonel. 'Have you ever heard such rubbish, lads; me, bully people? I look after them, for Christ's sake.'

'It's quite possible that you feel threatened by Miss Heathen's superior manners and insight, but that's no reason to be unkind to her . . .'

The Colonel snarled like an aggravated dog on the verge of slipping his leash. 'Insight! Ha! You ladies aren't the only ones to be blessed with the holy gift of insight! The Colonel ain't blind, and there's things I'd say if I weren't so polite, not that any of you lot would credit me with restraint.'

'And what does he see?' asked Glenda, dropping her lip in a mockery of real expectation.

The Colonel squinted, momentarily resembling his father, the malevolence in him advancing before the bluster. 'Right, let's see how you like a taste of your own medicine. Have *you* ever noticed how folk carrying on with each other don't mind letting other people see them drool like puppies, without wanting them to know exactly what they're getting up to! But they want to be watched all the same because they're so bloody proud of their feelings!'

'You're meaning to be impertinent, that much I can surmise . . .'

'Bah,' said the Colonel and looked deliberately from Mark to Vivien and then back to Mark again. 'You work it out!'

*

On the opposite side of the room the Yank yelled out a suggestion; 'Any of you guys fancy picking up some scrunt?'

Looking aghast, the Colonel, who had briefly wondered whether insinuating that there was a relationship between Ross and Mark Polly might constitute going too far in some people's eyes, shouted back, 'There're ladies present, you horrible colonial scalp-hunter, show some respect for their sensibilities if not ours.'

The Yank had taken full advantage of the wartime fad for multiple partners and led a somewhat Bohemian existence in his train carriage that the Colonel could not help but frown on. As such, and once the initial promise of their relationship had run aground, he had never got to know the Yank any better than he had, nor wanted to, the two men the leaders of their separate little cliques.

'Hey,' said the Yank, looking hurt, 'go ahead and bad mouth me but who're you going to turn to when it comes to fixing those bikes? Mark says they're irreparable, I'm the only guy here with the know-how—'

'Let me stop you right there, because as far as I'm concerned those hulks were always more trouble than they were worth, good riddance to them and let them rust. If I want your help with anything it'll be dragging mine over to my old man's for scrap.' The Colonel chuckled, his enjoyment barely affected by the exodus of Polly, Glenda, Shallow, Baxter and Vivien Ross to a nearby table, only Delaney remaining his companion at the bar. 'Lasting power and integrity, two qualities that will see us through life, eh Terry?'

Delaney nodded slowly and turned his glass around in his hand. 'I hope they will, Colonel, because there'll be no jobs for us now. We'll be marked men.'

'Nonsense. Dawson can't cope without us! All this will have done is improve our bargaining hand with him.'

'You don't believe that?'

'You bet I do! We've shown our teeth, and we'll be treated

with some respect at last. He needs us to man that factory; you wait for a few weeks and then you'll see him come back with his hand held out and his tail between his legs. You've got to take the long view with these things, Terry, or else you'll be lost in the detail like the rest of these poor bloody fools.'

Before Delaney had time to reply they were interrupted by a noisy newcomer, who they recognised as little Enid from the factory, her insults plainly audible, and there being no mistaking as to whom they were addressed: 'There you are, you dirty striking bastards! Are you boys going to be in for the chop when the master gets hold of you tomorrow! Thinking dirty unclean hooligans like yourselves could get away with it, well Enid knew you couldn't!'

Grappling onto a chair, Enid, the factory gossip, laughed out loud at the ferocity of her remarks and pointed a bony finger towards the Colonel and Delaney. 'You two being the worst two bastards! You should have heard the master fume! He won't have it! No, he won't! Not from the likes of you, those were his very words they were.'

'Enid, what are you doing out before midnight? Does the devil know you're failing to keep up appointments?'

'Oh you're a cocky one, aren't you, Colonel! Well you won't be so cocky breaking up rocks on Dartmoor! Piss and wind don't carry so well out in the cold air.'

Delaney held back a laugh that he was afraid would have sounded too good-natured. 'Help me put this one up in the ducking chair, Colonel, so we can see once and for all whether she sinks or swims.'

'Go on and laugh, Delaney, laugh, you bastard. You can call me a witch but at least I'd do an honest day's work for the coven! What manner of creature might you be to laugh at me?'

'Isn't that a coincidence, Enid, my dear, because that reminds me of a question I've been waiting a long time to ask you,' said the Colonel, picking up a walking stick from the bar, 'and since you're standing up there on that chair I reckon I'll be able to go one better.'

'You leave me alone, you brute,' shrieked Enid, her voice breaking an octave lower than usual.

Thrusting the walking stick under the hem of Enid's thick cloth skirts, the Colonel pulled upwards, revealing, as he did so, two shrivelled testicles and the ghost of a penis.

Like a magician, the Colonel raised both eyebrows and bowed theatrically. 'There you have them, just as I always thought!'

'You filthy worm!' shouted Enid over the storm of derisive laughter released by the exposure of 'her' secret. 'Curse you!'

'And for my next trick I'll demonstrate that Dawson is not a man but an unwanted smell in trousers,' guffawed the Colonel, pulling Delaney close up as he whispered, 'I've been sitting on that one for a while; it was the doctor who told me of Enid's little secret when "she" complained about "her" piles!'

'Amazed you held back for so long.'

'Timing, Terence, timing.'

'You've had it, the whole lot of you have had it!' Enid howled, clambering off the chair and picking up a butter knife threateningly. 'All had it!'

'Is it like this in here every night?' asked Vivien Ross.

'And you'll be for it too!' shouted Enid at the table. 'Consorting with low lifes like these, you should be ashamed! You stuck-up bitches!'

'No one's "had it",' said Baxter in answer to Enid as much as to Vivien, 'those days are long gone, not only here but all over, come and gone, they are. The time of you and your "master" are done with.'

'I had no idea you felt so strongly, Mr Baxter,' smirked Vivien who was feeling as intoxicated as she could remember, a pleasurable popping in the back of her head accompanying every word. 'We'd have done more to make you feel at home had we known earlier, broken a door down or smashed a window or two. I can't help but feel that our "times" are somehow mutually exclusive of each other, wouldn't you say? And where, while we're at it and before proper class-war hostilities start, does this leave me and Glenda or, for that matter, Captain Shallow, who I understand is a Labour man?'

Baxter looked embarrassed. 'You'd better ask him, that is to say the Captain can answer for himself. We've no quarrel with good men like him, never have, I mean, I don't know whether he's a proper socialist . . .'

'Nor do I,' said Shallow, flicking ash into his gin, 'I've no idea whether I'm a proper anything. The pub's my sphere of influence really; I like to think I know what I'm doing in here. As for outside, well, that's another problem. Unlike you, Baxter, my beliefs don't truly add up to any sort of pattern; I'm amazed that anybody's do, to be honest, but mine simply don't cohere. They more or less fall like scattered showers, first here then there, never coming down on one side or the other but not forming one of their own either . . . frustrating when I think of it because . . . because I can't imagine it any other way.'

'What you need to do, sir, is to get to grips with some ideology . . .'

'Leave him alone,' said Glenda, lighting her cigarette off the one falling from Shallow's outstretched hand. 'We keep hearing about extremes these days and it all seems to come from self-important men with nothing else to do but tell other people what's good for them. I agree with the Captain . . .'

'You do?' Shallow looked surprised.

'Of course, all you're really saying is that your thoughts come to you before your answers do. That's all an extreme is, it's a mind that is already made up. Like that oaf, the Colonel, with all his jingoism or you with your ideology, Mr Baxter, you both misunderstand the proper nature of life. At its centre is something that is always left untouched by every kind of ideology you can think of. Of course you'll all claim that your systems go to the very heart of life, and explain its core, but

they all stop just short of it, however well they describe everything else.'

'Exactly,' said the Colonel, thumping his drink down on the
table, 'as I've already said, we're British and that's all that
matters . . .'

Brushing the Colonel off her shoulder, Glenda eased out of
her seat, smiled at the others still sat at the table, and wandered
over to the bar. Stood there was Venning, a sullen young man
she had never seen laugh, and Stanton, who could have passed
for a younger Mark Polly had it not been for the patch over
his right eye. These were hollow youths who had lied about
their age and followed the older men to war before their eigh-
teenth birthdays, too young to remember life before the war
and too tired to make a useful contribution once it was over.
Returning home with campaign medals had been particularly
useless for them as they lacked the ordinary social skills to take
advantage of them. Though they were adept at loading guns
under fire, they were completely inept in the company of women
and other civilians, having left for France before their first village
dances. Neither their broad shoulders nor their undernourished
faces had succeeded in making them attractive to girls of their
own age who were scared of them, an effect exacerbated by
the way in which they had both copied the manners of the
older members of the squadron and shunned civil society.

Noticing Glenda through his one good eye, and in a hurry
to think of what to do with his hands, Stanton twisted round
in a semicircle, knocking over a pint in the process and putting
his cigarette out on Venning's back.

'Don't worry,' said Glenda, coming over to him; 'I can get
you another one.'

As he watched Glenda open her purse, and inhaled her warm
feminine scent, so unlike the leather, tobacco and alcohol he
was used to, Stanton tried to find the voice to reject her offer
but lacked the air in his throat through which to project it.
Venning, whose world had also been turned inside out by this

intrusion, held his head down firmly over his pint, watching it lest it fall over too.

'You know what they say about men who are physically clumsy?' said Glenda. 'It means that they could have done something that requires real grace in life, like dance, which is why they get all the small things wrong. Because they've never discovered their real natures.'

Venning had gone the colour of a strained turnip, and Stanton, who was conscious of every defect he thought he may have possessed, glanced anxiously down the bar to see if there was any sign of a rescue he was not sure he wanted.

'Do you two not talk to girls?' asked Glenda, drawing them both closer to her by lowering her voice. 'I can see that you don't, you probably think they're silly, don't you?'

Before he knew what he was doing, Stanton had thrust a packet of cigarettes into Glenda's hand. 'Take one,' he gasped, 'I've loads more at home.'

'So you can speak,' she said, 'I was beginning to wonder whether you understood English.'

If her words were meant to gently sting the boys into action they had their desired effect. Venning, no more in control of his actions than Stanton had been, stood up and offered Glenda his stool. Soon both of them were talking at the tops of their voices, recounting everything that had ever happened to them, with a careless disregard for chronology, accuracy and propriety, encouraged by Glenda who sat between them, laughing as loudly as they spoke, a leg resting against each of their laps.

'She has quite a gift for communication, doesn't she?' said Vivien to Mark Polly, who had fetched what would prove to be their last drink of the night.

Instead of replying Polly fiddled with his beer mat agreeably, his mouth half open but his words unformed.

'Oh go on, say something, you're free to agree or disagree . . .'

'She makes people like her,' conceded Polly, his large eyes blinking in the smoke, 'she does it easily.'

'I know that.' Vivien laughed.

'A good trick if you can pull it off, making people like you,' Polly replied, sure that he had nothing further to say on the subject, but not wanting to risk a single moment of silence, so badly did he want their conversation to continue. 'She . . .'

Vivien was looking at him as though she were happy enough for him to merely be there, their talk quite immaterial to her longing for a male presence in her life. 'She what, Mark?'

Next to them the Colonel was filling Shallow's glass from his own, a heated discussion concerning a progressive tax on gypsies in the offing. Baxter had left the table and was lecturing Marsh on socialism in one country. There was no possibility of anything Polly said being overheard and this freedom, so like the freedom to say whatever one liked, stopped Polly from saying anything. His fingers tingled and he could feel the loss of sensation in the lower part of his chest, a heavy anti-gravitational pull dragging him further into himself than he wished to be drawn. The truth was that he had run up against the acceptable limits of what he could possibly say to a woman of a different social class to whom he wanted to make love . . .

'What, Mark?' repeated Vivien, the aroma of burnt chestnuts from the fire lingering in her brick-red hair.

'I think it makes you look younger,' he blurted out.

'My hair?'

'Yes, how did you know?'

'Never mind that, in what way does it make me look younger?'

'With it down like that,' Polly gushed, unsure of what had possessed him to make so stupid and uncalled-for a remark, 'it makes me see what you looked like when you were younger, before you decided on who you were going to be.'

'You mean before I became the dreaded Vivien Ross?'

'No, no, before you became hard, I mean you had to be hard to help you through the difficult times, but your hair down makes you fresh in that way we all had . . . of being.'

Vivien experienced a strange fluttering sensation, like rain water on her heart. 'Mark, did you just make a favourable comment about my physical appearance and offer, if I heard you rightly, a technical opinion on it?'

'I guess I must have . . .' Polly did not get as far as he would have liked, perhaps fortunately, as he had no idea how far he would like to have gone, for at that moment the pub was silenced by a loud banging on the bar.

'Colonel, so-called Colonel,' screamed Graham Riddle, the humiliated woodsman of the night before, his voice an off-putting mix of self-importance and rage, 'you may have forgotten our little rendezvous. But, unfortunately for you, I have not. Do you hear me, *I have not.*'

The Colonel looked up at Riddle bemused, strained his eyes as if he could not see him properly, chuckled to himself and resumed his conversation with Shallow as if nothing had happened.

Red with embarrassment, Riddle kicked over the table nearest to the door and grabbed a poker off the fireplace, brandishing it in the air like a pike. 'There's the small matter of a man who you thought you could humiliate, Colonel, the small matter of that man's pride to be avenged.'

'It must be a very small matter,' quipped Shallow, 'because my friend seems to have forgotten all about it.'

'You stay out of this, you toffee-nosed fop,' insisted Riddle. 'It'll be my right to drink in this pub and anywhere else I like once I've beaten the hell out of this . . . prat,' he scoffed, the insult falling hopelessly short of the anger that propelled it. 'So let's have it, Colonel, bare-knuckled in the car park.'

The Colonel shook his head in a show of sympathy for his abuser, the cause of their quarrel the night before and its outcome too far away from him to raise his ire. Waving his hands in the air, as though he were about to surrender, the Colonel sighed. 'You've got to learn to stand on your own feet, Riddle, Piddle or whatever your bloody name is, because the

Colonel isn't always going to be there to hold your hand. You've got to learn to move on and get past measuring yourself against me all the time. There're other bad men out there and new adventures to be had. And anyway, you know you'll always lose, get upset, fail to fuck a girl and end up finding solace in your barn. It's time to grow a beard and move on, man.'

'So you're scared to face me man to man, are you?'

The Colonel snorted good-naturedly. 'Look, I'll let you have smashing up our bikes, to be honest they were a drain on our resources, not only that but I'll let you have coming in here again and waving that thing over your head like Mr bloody Toad, in fact, I won't even bring up the fact that you stink of fucking fish but, for God's sake, Piddle, get out of here while the going's good, or else I'll really lose my temper and make you cry.'

Without taking his eyes off the Colonel, Riddle aimed the poker at his enemy and squeaked, 'As sure as night follows day you are scared, man. Scared of a real man half your size. Outside with you, for I'm done with this parlour talk of yours, *Colonel*.'

'You surprise me, Riddle, I'd have thought you'd have gone from yellow to brown by now . . .'

'Careful,' whispered Shallow, holding the Colonel back by the arm, 'he must have something up his sleeve to be so cocky. It's rehearsed. I don't like it.'

'Never you mind,' said the Colonel out of the side of his mouth. 'I'll have him as soon as look at him.'

'But he knows that too, he's too sneaky for my liking.'

'Bah!' the Colonel said waving his hand, the thought of administering a good beating releasing blood into his brain. 'The car park it is, and as many rounds as it takes for you to understand the sacred concept of humility, Riddle, you two-foot-one charade.'

Not waiting for the crowd to empty out of the pub before him, Riddle strode through the lounge bar and out through the kitchen door, the poker thrown back into the fireplace from which it had been grabbed.

'I may as well leave this here,' said the Colonel, putting his pint down, 'I can't see this one taking very long. Rest of you, out of the way, I want this finished before the last one of you gets out to watch the carnage.'

'No point even going,' said Delaney addressing his empty tumbler. 'Another, Silas.'

Silas Martin watched the bar. Very few people had moved, and a worried murmur was rebounding off the walls.

'This ain't right,' he said to Delaney, 'you'd better go with him.'

'I'll go,' said Shallow.

'I'll go and see you stuffed!' cackled Enid who had rejoined the party. 'Stuffed like a turkey.'

'Bring whoever you like, these things always end the same,' concluded the Colonel who, at the head of a procession that comprised Enid, Shallow and Polly, followed Riddle out of the pub, a room of anxious eyes watching them as they went.

Outside the night was cold, vast and black, darkness falling in those hours lost in drink and talk. A frail half moon lay amongst a knot of stars, its wary light shining over the heads of the pugilists as they assumed positions at different ends of the fore-court.

'How did we end up here?' asked Polly.

'God knows,' muttered Shallow, 'how any of these things start. The Poles were probably asking themselves the same question in '39.'

'An end to all Norman tyranny!' sang the Colonel, as Polly helped him pull off his jacket, 'and death to all of good King Richard's foes!'

'Arsehole,' shouted Riddle, squinting in the dark, 'you'll be done with your love of talking by the time I'm through with you.'

'Can you feel the fear in your legs yet?' bellowed the Colonel. 'That's where it'll take hold of you the hardest.'

'Keep it route one, Thatcher,' ordered Shallow, 'you're far too drunk to try to have fun with it, just get the bugger within hitting distance and biff him until he can't get up.'

'He's right,' said Polly, his nerves troubled by the great outdoors silence they were breaking, 'be quick, it's not good to fight in the dark. And be careful of him; he hates you and that'll make him extra strong.'

The Colonel snorted dismissively. 'There won't be much fighting to be had. Right, let's have it then, Riddle my lad!'

Riddle, in the far corner, had pulled off his shirt revealing a bare freckled chest, and as the Colonel darted towards him, held his arm up, signalling for his opponent to wait.

'Pick your weapons!' Riddle shouted to the bemusement of the surprisingly small party that had come out to watch.

'What the devil?' the Colonel called out, halfway towards Riddle and too far from the comparative safety of Polly and Shallow to retreat.

'Weapons!' howled Enid. 'A fight to the death!'

'A gentleman fights with weapons,' Riddle announced triumphantly as a companion of his who had been waiting in the bushes thrust an overcoat into his arm, revealing the barrel of a sawn-off shotgun, 'it's about time you realised that, so-called Colonel. A game of gentlemen is to be fought with weapons, see?'

'You what, you lummox?'

'It's like a duel, Colonel, you choose your weapon and I choose mine. Stupid of you to leave yours at home! My advantage, I think!' Riddle grinned, his feud with the Colonel successfully ending on his terms, or so he hoped.

'You're one big piss-take, aren't you?' taunted the Colonel, assessing the distance left between him and Riddle, and bounding forward as fast as he could.

'Bollocks to you, Colonel,' shouted Riddle, and pointed the shotgun and fired. A woman screamed and a man started laughing. Enid rocked over on her back, her shoulder a pile of red mush.

Riddle squinted into the dark space ahead of him; it was the Colonel and he was on him. Both heads cracked together and a second shot fired off into the amalgamation of arms and legs that constituted their tussle.

'Hurry up and help him!' shouted Baxter, who had been relieving himself behind a tree. 'Someone could get murdered.'

Shallow and Polly sprinted up to the two men lying on top of one another and pulled the Colonel off Riddle.

'Sweet Jesus, it feels like I've danced with a forklift,' moaned the Colonel, rubbing his head. Beneath him Riddle lay showered in gravel, his face aghast at the twitching stump where his leg ought to have been, blood pumping out over his shattered boot.

'Missed, didn't you?' said Polly. 'Best get some antiseptic on that, if I were you, Riddle.'

In the distance the sound of a fire engine could be heard in the train yards, its siren the reminder of the laws of a world they had all forgotten. 'We'd best be making ourselves scarce, men,' said Shallow, the crisis reawakening his dormant desire to command, 'and as for you,' he said, turning to Riddle, who was gasping for the chance to scream through his pain, 'it's one of the great moral lessons to have inflicted on you what you were preparing to inflict on someone else. I hope you've learnt that now.'

'Well said, sir, well said,' agreed the Colonel, the slightest expression of concern leaving his face as he saw Riddle writhe in an agony that could only be the sign of one who would go on and live. Nestling up to Polly and Shallow in a psychic embrace that lasted a few seconds, the Colonel lit each man's cigarette, as he waited for the alcohol and shock to wash over him.

'Jesus,' shouted Silas Martin surveying the unconscious Enid, 'you comedians go from strength to strength, don't you?'

'We try,' replied Polly, picking up the Colonel's coat and cap.

'Right. Double time then, gents,' said Shallow. 'Best put a call in to the doctor, Silas, we're a couple of people down.'

Silas Martin, his hands on his hips as he looked down on Enid, whistled slowly in disbelief. 'Jesus, oh Jesus, where was God looking when he let me in for this?'

'Goodbye,' called Vivien Ross from the window of the Squirrel Skinner to the dark figures following one another out of the car park, Grumwood drawing in around them all like the tide.

7

VICTORY

Oliver Dawson looked forward to making a great show of coming home from work. Like many successful men he believed that he toiled harder than his wife, was employed in 'real' work (whereas she was not) and was therefore responsible for those items in their life they enjoyed the most. There were few things more likely to concentrate his wrath than walking over his threshold to find his wife unappreciative of his efforts or, worse, ready to claim that her errands were the equal of his industrial labours. Though Lou may have become prone to both responses of late, Dawson still expected her to glide down the landing to greet him at the sound of the front door closing, and her failure to do so was the first sign that there was something wrong in his house that night.

Dawson found his wife sobbing noiselessly over heaps of her old clothing, bagged up by the maid without her permission for philanthropic uses. This sort of scene, so familiar to him in the past few months, begat its own conclusion; that Oliver Dawson did not understand his wife, and never less so than when she cried.

Ownership of Lou's time and body had not meant the same thing as possession of the mysteries of her soul, a problem he had not had the foresight to anticipate and would have been helpless to prevent even if he had. Despite securing his investment at the altar, Dawson continually found himself running up against the limits of his knowledge, in regards to both Lou's true nature and his own. This was brought home painfully every time she departed from the personality of hers he felt most secure with: the good-time girl with the odd deep thought, that he hoped one day to understand. Convincing himself at the time of their marriage that an improved quality of life, buttressed by endless colourful distractions, would iron out any unforeseen difficulties they might encounter, Dawson had slipped into a life of cosy inertia, at least as far as matters relating to his wife were concerned. His awakening had been as swift as it was unexpected. Although he had kept them coming, Lou's enjoyment of the good times had quite inexplicably ended, and no manner of gifts, trips or chocolates had successfully brought them back. Worse still, once expressed, her deep thoughts which Dawson had intended to admire as one would artefacts in a museum, baffled him with their impenetrability, lack of self-interest and pessimism.

Pretending to understand Lou, when he palpably did not, was guaranteed to enrage her further so, filled with a feeling of intense uselessness, Dawson cleared his throat loudly and said, 'I'm home, my dear, in case you missed it.'

If he was expecting a positive response he did not receive one. Without turning from her dressing-table stool, Lou asked in a voice perilously close to a demand, 'What did you mean by trying to throw these away without asking me first?'

The anger and indignation that he had hidden with difficulty rose through his body so fast that Dawson could barely help himself. Picking up the bag of clothes nearest to him and flinging it at her head, he shouted, 'Here I am, working every hour of the day and night, coping with pressures that you couldn't possibly imagine, beset from all sides by every kind of rogue under the sun, and what the hell do I have to come home to? This! But do you find me crumpling up in a corner and having a bloody good cry about it? Do you hell! I bloody well roll my sleeves up and get on with it because if I didn't it'd be a tent on the floodplain you'd call home and not this sodding great mansion! And what do you have to cry about anyway, I ask you? That the maid's thrown a few of your old clothes away or that you don't get to see any of your old friends any more? Some bloody loss they are, they all hate you anyway. Good riddance to the jealous little toerags!'

Even before he had finished Dawson could sense the futility of his rebuke, as he had all those times in the past, since this speech had been delivered several times with slight variations depending on the perceived level of Lou's ingratitude. Though there was no doubting his words upset her afresh every time, they did not, in any meaningful sense, truly seem to reach her, forcing Dawson to throw his punches further below the belt than even he would have liked. 'You've run out of options, girl; you know and I know that if I finished with you, you'd be soiled goods round here, and through. And don't even bother giving me any of that jib about packing up and moving to London like you did last time . . .'

Lou had started to cry again in long dog-like sobs, her fists beating down on the table like small hammers.

Dawson flinched and undid the top button of his shirt. 'Don't give me that. You always give me that. You might cry the loudest but that doesn't make you right and . . . and . . . and besides, I love you, Lou, bloody love you and you know it, darling, but you're killing me! Bloody tearing my head apart! Haven't I given you everything you wanted, haven't I? What have I done wrong? Just tell me that. I mean, what's wrong with this?' He picked up a large china Dalmatian, a puppy tear wet in its eye. 'You liked this, didn't you? I mean, you helped me buy it for you, what's wrong with it, Lou?' he asked, holding the hapless dog in the air. 'You liked it, didn't you?'

'Of course I did!' answered Lou, virtually sweeping down on her vertically challenged husband. 'Oh of course I do!'

An immense sympathy for Dawson, as selfless as a great nation coming to the aid of a smaller neighbour, had always formed the strongest component of Lou's love for him whatever he may have thought to the contrary. Only she knew what a great need Dawson had to cry, and the extent to which his war with the town hurt him. With his face pressed against her breast, the two stood on the plush red carpet holding one another for dear life, Dawson's sobbing body wobbling in Lou's lithe arms.

Gradually, his crying subsided, and he drew away from Lou, rubbing off his remaining tears lest they sentimentalise his means of explaining them away. 'A damned hard day,' he muttered, 'a long damned hard day. It's left me tired. But no one can say that they didn't have it coming to them, though it cost me to do it.'

Lou let go of his arm, her tenderness abandoning her at the speed at which her husband had realised that it embarrassed him. It was typical of Dawson to swiftly change hats like this, his moments of vulnerability seamlessly paved over in his rush to portray himself in a more powerful light. Lou had ceased to wonder for whose benefit this was done, but her husband's monologues did at least have the effect of preventing her from having to talk, and with the memory of Shallow still too close, she prepared herself for the incoming torrent in the silent satisfaction of having a memory powerful enough to keep her going.

'You think you have it tough,' Dawson snorted, 'you ought to have seen what they've done to me! Oh, they had it coming all right, the work-shy bolshie bastards, that Terry Delaney of yours the worst of the whole bloody lot . . .' He paused in the hope that Lou would, on this occasion, rush to the defence of her former boyfriend so as to further justify his anger, but no such defence was forthcoming.

'I'm sure Terry can look after himself,' she said in full knowledge of what was expected of her.

'Ha! That's just the thing, isn't it? He can't any more, not him or any of those bloody monkeys. I've sacked the whole bloody lot.'

'Why?'

'Because, my dear, the weak live according to the will of the world and the strong live according to their own will. I don't have to explain myself to you or to them. I've the power to hire and fire and today I chose to fire. Simple as that.'

Dawson had spoken in this way several times before, and never made good on his threats, but this did not mean that he would never make good on them, and as Lou knew that he had already sacked Delaney she asked, 'Has something happened, did they all do something to you? What have they done today?'

Dawson laughed like one far above it all. '"done today"? It's not what they've done today but what they've been doing to me this past year, ever since I was damned fool enough to employ 'em.'

'I know you've all argued with each other before but—'

'Don't make it sound like a fifty-fifty! Half their fault and half mine! Jesus, woman, here we are, in a worse bloody state than Germany, and how do they thank me for putting the clothes on their backs? By trying to stick the fist into me every fucking day, fuck me with the fist, you understand? And bloody weak-hearted oaf that I am, I have stood by and let them, let them turn the tables on me, so it's me defending my actions as they get on with theirs!'

'Oliver, calm down and tell me what happened.'

'Their pièce de résistance is what bloody happened. This morning not one of them shows up for work, and after I'd already given them the day off for the funeral! So what do they do instead of work? They break in and rob the flaming factory, turn my office over and rip the number plates off my new Jag. Only the one I was going to surprise you with! What do they take me for? Do they think they can roll me over? No! From tomorrow there're going to be some big changes, you wait and bloody see!'

'You say they vandalised your office and robbed from the factory?'

'The tip of the bloody iceberg, woman! And worse!' For Dawson these exaggerations all still fell short of the pain inflicted on him, and so he could utter them with the same conviction an honest man would have spared for the truth. 'No use going to the police for help, they're useless to non-existent; no, the one thing that stands between stability and Bolshevist anarchy in this town is me, and from tomorrow they'll all know, because, believe me, the Bolshevists won't stand down quietly, and if there has to be one almighty battle then so be it . . .' Dawson smacked his fist into his palm. 'Their last it will be. They think they've seen war, but they haven't, not until they've seen what I have in store for them!'

After speeches like this her husband was as distasteful to Lou as he was when he would insist on calling her 'baby' in an American accent before trying to enter her in the middle of the night. Not only did he not understand her, but what Dawson lacked the wit to fathom was that she could understand him, however alien she considered his behaviour to be. Often she had been struck by premonitions that the same will to power that had created the Fox Brandy Chocolate plant would lead to its undoing, and finally this intuition seemed about to be borne out, 'But they have seen war, Olly! They have, and you haven't! A battle isn't like a good view or a play that can be summed up in a few pithy quotes once it's over! It's bloody horrible. They'll take you down with them, can't you see that?'

'What do you know about it anyway? You're the one who caused the trouble in the first place. If it wasn't for you and your bleeding-heart entreaties I wouldn't have hired any of that shower to begin with, but no, you—'

'Rubbish! You hired them because you wanted them to owe you like you want everyone to owe you! Have you forgotten all that talk you came out with about how you wanted to keep your enemies close so you could see what they were up to? Well now that you've turned them out they'll have nothing to lose . . .'

Dawson shook his head violently. 'You don't know what you're on about. That's your first problem, my girl. And your second is that you're the same as everyone else in this country.

You lot are terrified, aren't you? Terrified of stepping on a few toes and the social embarrassment that you're afraid will follow!'

'Oh Olly, how can you be so wrong, I'm not afraid for myself . . .'

'Then let me handle my own problems.'

'I want you to understand how you got here! Huge arguments can grow out of silly things and it's such a mistake to think they can't. The cause needn't be as big as the consequence, it need only be one tiny thing and then the mind does the rest. Your difficulties with the lads who went to war were never as big as you made them out to be, and nor were theirs with you . . .'

Dawson grabbed Lou and shook her. 'You're doing it again! Offering unqualified opinions on matters you know absolutely nothing about! You never take my side on anything, you always criticise me and see the good in everyone else; where a loyal woman would offer her support, you offer me your scorn. You don't see what they're really like; you misunderstand their true nature. They're animals, see? Like animals, pure products of their environment and no more; you can't expect to find anything human in them, they're pigs. You and the others—'

'What others? Why do you keep talking about "you lot" and "the others"?' interrupted Lou, pushing Dawson off her.

Not to be deterred he grabbed her with his other hand and continued, 'Because "you lot" is what you all are, all lined up to take me down! I wish I could make you realise what manner of thing your friends are. They're wild beasts. But none of you bleeding hearts know how to handle animals. The worst influence on animals is other animals; it's us humans that break and tame them. That's why where you see tame dogs I see the wolves that I've already broken! And I know how to handle 'em. It's why I split them up on different shifts, offered them the carrot with pensions and bonus initiatives, and was a fair and firm master to them. But they were wild, hated me for my kindness and rejected it. So now they've got to be put back into the wild again. The experiment's off, and don't think any one of them will think well of me for giving them the opportunity . . .'

'Of course not.'

'But why?' demanded Dawson, apparently unconvinced by his own arguments. 'What did I ever do to them except give them the chance to better their lots? You'd have to be evil to hate a man for that.'

Firmly, Lou moved Dawson's hand off her neck, and he allowed it to fall loosely to his side. 'You made too many men lose their pride, Olly, which is dangerous. Once you've done that to a grown man you don't have anything left to appeal to in him, only coercion. And as you said, they're not for coercing, are they?'

'Them, them, them!' yelled Dawson, picking up and emptying a plant pot. 'Always them! You'd think they're the whole workforce when you listen to you go on. All they are is the dregs. The others, the majority, they're the salt of the earth; they're the ones who know what I've done for them and love me. You should have seen the way they were singing my praises today when they saw my new motor.'

Lou stared at her husband with exaggerated patience. 'They sang your praises, you say?'

'You should have heard them! You'd think I was the king himself for all the noise they were making. "Look at Mr Dawson in his new motor," they were saying, "that's what you get when you graft as hard as he does," they went. I heard them with my own ears.'

Lou eyed him warily. 'How is it, Olly, that whenever it comes to you, you think flattery is sincere, whereas you're the first to spot it for the manure it is when you watch someone else being buttered up?'

'You're full of it, and why, are you jealous as well? Love was what I saw out there today and nothing you say could convince me different.'

Lou felt herself harden again. 'They don't love you any more than Delaney does, they've just the sense to realise they need you because, as you like to say, you're "the man of the moment".' The bitterness Lou managed to inject into this last phrase was so great that Dawson took a second pot plant, walked out of the room, and threw it off the landing.

'You can't help yourself, can you?' he yelled. 'Knocking me down when you should be building me up! Of course I know they need me, they're not stupid, they know that nowadays most people kick *with* the pricks and not against 'em. They won't mourn the sacking of a gang of scavenging scroungers like Delaney or Baxter. And anyway, who's to care if they do? I'm not going to be taking an opinion poll and if I did it'd only count if they gave a damn about their opinions, which they don't. Not where money's to be involved.'

'*Always!* Always money with you, Olly . . .'

'Says the wife of a rich man! Go on, give me that big speech about how life's more important than money, you know the one, the one you always trot out when you're feeling that you're better than me! Hypocrite! You know damn well that life isn't a value; only money is. There's no other way of measuring life and if you thought there was you wouldn't be here now, so let's stop kidding ourselves, shall we?' Dawson gestured round the room to confirm his point. 'You know the trouble with people like you, Lou? You make me enjoy my faults too much. I ought to have left you behind to darn your brother's socks for the rest of your life. Mark and you, the freak and the rich man's slop bucket! What a pair of jokes you are!'

'Is that what you think of me? And Mark isn't a freak, he's good-natured . . .'

'Ha! He needs to be, because he doesn't have anything else going for him.'

'He's honourable.'

'What, and I'm not? Honourable because he works in a poxy little garage and not for big bad me?'

'No, when he came back home he refused to wear his medals in public. I tried to get him to, but he said he didn't want to swank or show off, he's not the type of man who would.'

'Ha!' Dawson thrust his face up close to Lou's. 'No more than wounded masochistic pride, like the rest of them. But I grant you he's not as offensive as the other remedials who get under my skin, particularly that maggot Thatcher who calls himself the Colonel, for Christ's sake; he even tried to get Grundy to call him it too, the hopeless fantasist! Always skiving, when he isn't marching around telling anyone who'll listen what a fascist I am. What does he want, to be run by some Jew boy? And after what they're doing to our lads in Palestine? The way he carries on you'd think I was Hitler.'

'Aren't you?'

Dawson practically choked on his disbelief. 'What,' he said slowly and with emphasis, 'do you mean by that?'

'Well wasn't he motivated by a sense of social inferiority too?'

Dawson narrowed his eyes. 'Who have you been talking to? Tell me.'

'No one.'

'You don't sound like you, Lou. You sound like you used to in the very early days when you were trying to impress me with what a clever little sauce you were. All these arch remarks and dubious questions, they don't suit you any more, you've grown out of that. And these crying fits and what have you . . . has someone been talking to you, some silly bitch like Vivien Ross?' Dawson experienced an involuntary shudder, the horror of the previous evening's encounter with her revealing itself more clearly for being touched on by mistake. 'If I find out that she has—'

'It's me that thinks it, Olly, only me. I'm tired. Please leave me alone.'

'How dare you! You're tired? What about me! You're the one who started this. And now you expect me to stop when I haven't even had my say! I'm the one who has targets that need to be reached! What have you got to do in the morning?'

Lou sat down on the bed and disdainfully kicked off a shoe. 'There you go again. First you want to crush them, then you want to improve their lot and now you want them to reach your bloody targets for you. You like a bit of everything.'

Dawson steadied himself, his need to close an argument on his terms stronger than his desire to sleep through the next few days, or even break down and cry again. 'You think there's something funny about that, that there could be anything more important than me meeting my targets in my world? The very thing my good name and reputation rest on . . .'

'No, no, I'm sure you're right, Olly. There'll be plenty more talk about the targets you need to meet and the goods you need to buy before we're through. You'll meet your targets but you'll leave the people behind. And then you'll have to lie about the people, because the targets require you to.'

To his immense irritation, Dawson could hear a grim pattern emerging in his wife's attacks quite at odds with the hysterical outbursts he had managed to dismiss in the past. Moreover he was no longer as sure of what it was he was trying to defend: his pride, his business, their marriage? Tiredly, he lifted a stubby finger to her face, struggling to find a closing remark that would silence her, if just for tonight; 'Like I said to Grundy, the working class will always be shafted for as long as they think of themselves as the working class . . .'

'Oh for God's sake, Olly, I'm not Grundy and I've heard your crappy little speeches a thousand times. Why don't you tell me what it is you want for once . . . what it was you thought you wanted to be before you became the God almighty captain of industry you are . . .'

'No!' Dawson glared at her accusingly, the advantage, or so he perceived, having fallen in his lap. 'You started this, why don't you tell me what it is that you want, what you thought you'd become before hitching your star to my wagon, Miss

Polly? What was it you thought *you* could be, eh?'

Lou shrieked at the ceiling, clapping her hands against her sides like crashing cymbals. '*I can't believe that I was sixteen only ten years ago and only six ten years before that!*'

Dawson's shoulders dropped in a nervous release of laughter; it was obvious that his wife was mad and there was nothing for him to be scared of.

'Time, Olly, how quickly we pass through who we are into what we become, to end up as some person we don't even recognise as ourselves. Hours and days of wasted time . . .'

'You can stop right there. I thought we were meant to make each other happy, that's what you told me, you said I made you feel "alive". Jesus, you'd never even smelt perfume, let alone worn it before you met me. You need to get a grip, girl . . .'

'But what are you supposed to do when you're *alive*, you're meant to *live*, aren't you – aren't you? *Living*, Olly, it's the opposite of death, war, plotting and scheming and counting all your money, it's life, the opposite of all of that.'

Dawson stared at her bewildered, nearly wanting to understand the passion of this beautiful woman shaking her quilt in his face, but basically more convinced than ever that she was mad. 'You'd better be careful you don't go barmy, girl,' he said, 'and lose it and go crackers. I'm worried about you. I know we can't agree on everything but . . . it's got to you. They've broken you. But it'll be all right, I can help you—'

'I don't want help! I need you to . . . oh I don't know what I need you to do, but at least understand me, know me . . .'

'Of course I understand you, I love you, don't I?'

Lou looked at her husband as though he were much further away from her than his physical distance would indicate. 'I think you fell in love with something that I may have had, but I've left it behind, and you don't have it any more either and neither of us can go back and look for it because we've come to the end and we haven't found anything to replace it with.'

'Are you trying to tell me something? If you are, then spit it out, don't go on giving me all your open meaning rot; speak plain English.'

'I will, then. I want to leave you, Olly, but I don't know whether I'm brave enough.'

Dawson gawped at his wife open-mouthed, his thick tongue slithering out of his mouth like a third lip. What he had experienced in this room was suddenly very bad, like days that felt like they could last for the rest of his life when no one would play with him at school, or when he would become drunk and everyone disappeared. It was the reality he would never fully wake up from, and the nightmare that was ever present whenever he woke. He was what he was and he would never be anything else. He had lost his wife, but she was still here, near enough for him to hate her until his heart was avenged, however long that would take. 'You be careful with that kind of talk, there's a long way from a thought to a word, and even longer before you might do anything about it, so don't try anything funny, Miss Polly . . . I promise you it won't be worth your while . . . Are you listening?'

Lou was not listening. Ignoring Dawson, she walked to the window and pressed her face against the frosty glass. Gazing over the floodplain she watched the moon reflect onto it with an unusual compassion, her marriage to Dawson a vow ready to be broken.

The phone had been ringing intermittently in Les Mills's house for the past hour, causing him to sink deep into his covers. 'I thought I told you to tell them I was dead,' the hungover doctor shouted at his wife as she gave in to the persistent knocking at their front door, and let the unwelcome visitor into the house.

'There might be someone dead but it's not you, Doctor,' called Silas Martin from the bottom of the staircase. 'Thought it'd be the right thing to do to run the news past you. What with you being the doctor and all.'

Mills pulled the bandage that covered his head down over his eyes. 'I couldn't care the north end of a southward-facing badger who's dead. Getting up from this bed will kill me. Call the undertaker or the police if you want to run the bodies past anyone. I'm closed.'

'And there's another man who'll need you to patch him up, Doctor. He's not looking too good. Had his foot hurt real bad.'

'Martin, I wouldn't – no, couldn't get out of bed, even if you were to dangle the carrot of delivering your beautiful daughters' babies. I am not a doctor. I am a ship in distress. Now please unburden me of this horrible conversation and allow me to get well again.'

'Am I to take it that that's your final word on the matter, Doctor?'

There was no answer from upstairs. The doctor's wife shrugged her shoulders as she tried to stifle a yawn.

Martin laughed heartily and, apologising for the intrusion, made his way out onto the drive. Enid and Riddle could die of septicaemia for all he cared and, were it left to either him or Mills, they probably would.

Glenda kicked her bedding free and lifted her legs high in the air in a giant V, holding them there until the ice rolled down the beams of the low thatched ceiling, freezing the sweat on her thighs. Slowly she bent them back over her head, as if dismounting from an invisible bicycle, feathers and dust blowing sharply over her face, caught in a draught cold enough to hold.

She was surprised that her clitoris had been able to put up with such a hammering, for neither she nor it was prepared for the intimate path fate had picked them for. Tangled in her sheets lay the steaming bodies of Stanton and Venning, fixed expressions of contentment such as they had never known when awake, were cast over their sleeping faces. They had seen and caused many faces in Glenda that night, expressions worn as the only protection her body, shorn of clothing and devoted entirely to a single act, could afford her. First they had watched a 'can't believe what you've done to me' face she made whenever a man had gone past taking pleasure and forced her to climax, next her eyes had opened up in startled astonishment, as her nose scrunched in indignation, followed by an exhausted smile showing her attitude to be one of unrestrained and helpless approval.

They had fallen asleep immediately, eager to avoid a scolding for being cocky enough to transgress the taboo and pull the whole thing off. In their dreams each imagined Glenda as his girlfriend, but, as strong as this desire was, some part of their brains resisted the idea, conscious that she belonged to life and therefore to neither of them, the moon floating so close to the tops of the trees that it could still hear their sighs.

Tuesday morning

The Colonel woke, at once knowing what had to be done; whether this knowledge had come to him in his sleep, had been decided the night before or at the point of waking did not matter, the only thing that did was what he had to do next, the idea taking hold of him with such clarity that he gasped for breath. The chocolate factory needed to be destroyed, every rotten brick of it, so that by the time he was through there would be nothing left. Within seconds of this epiphany the Colonel was fast asleep again, a deeper sleep than he had known for months, populated by dreams of tanks, pots of honey, King Alfred and much beer.

It was mid-afternoon before he stirred again, a pigeon making itself comfortable over the heap of sacks that were his makeshift pillow and bed. He had come to in the railway carriage next to the Yank, his memory of the last time he had woken up under his own roof far away and vague. There was something wrong with waking up in this place, that much was already clear to him, as even by his own low standards the railway carriage was a hole best avoided, his presence there a sign that something had gone wrong.

Not wanting to rush himself he tried to exhale, doing so with the greatest difficulty. His throat felt sewn together, the effort of breathing separating the skin like razor blades. Why breathing should be connected with the question of where he was, puzzled him, but connected the two were; carefully the Colonel glanced at all four walls to see if he and the pigeons were alone.

The carriage was completely empty, which meant that his predicament was not one he could share, and was thus more awful than he at first thought. Fear lined the walls of his chest as he realised that this was not the weekend but midweek, and he was not at work . . . and never would be again. But how did he know that? Too much had happened for him to be able to perceive the difference between speculation and fact, several days' worth of alcohol scrambling those memories that had survived the binge, causing them to bleed into a more general paranoia. Pathetically he found that he wanted to call for help and answers.

'Polly,' he croaked, 'where the hell are you, Mark?'

Dimly, he could recollect the faces of Polly and Shallow – or was it Moat and Captain Sceptre? No, that was impossible as they were both dead – lifting him into the carriage, with worried expressions, but why? He knew he had fallen into a thorn bush but what had he done to make them so worried for him? Had he been any drunker than usual, or was there some awful thing he had deliberately put to the back of his mind to save himself further worry? Impossible. He never worried, left that to others . . . The Colonel grasped his stomach, a harsh burning burrowing deep into it like a flaming mole.

'. . . but isn't that the way with shock, Mr Baxter? Whoever heard of such things happening in Grumwood? I was *so* shocked that I found I was actually quite calm and resigned by the time the clearing up started this morning, and as Inspector Grundy says, shock can even take your fear by surprise, though who knows who he's going to blame for this mess, he really is a most gutless man.'

'Which in the circumstances we can all thank God for!'

The voices the Colonel could overhear belonged to Baxter and Mr Clubber Lang, the most unsuitably named inspector of train yards. What they were referring to was a mystery the Colonel had little inclination to discover the answer to, at least not at once, not until the burning stopped. 'Water,' he gasped, 'I need water.' His voice was barely audible, the fluttering of pigeon wings creating a wall over which the Colonel could not climb.

'You wretched feathered freaks . . .'

'Decadence is what I blame, Mr Baxter,' said Mr Lang. 'Do you know what I speak of when I say decadence, that's what I blame? Outright bloody dollops of the stuff. It's spreading like the plague.'

The Colonel rolled his eyes; only Baxter could have energy for this type of sport at a moment like this. 'Baxter,' he choked, his voice still a hoarse whisper, 'come here and help me, you bloody windbag.'

'Decadent, Mr Lang? You don't mean us, surely?' retorted Baxter, ignorant of his friend's plight. 'We're the least decadent people you could hope to meet, Mr Lang; for if your definition of decadence is enjoying the fruit of a culture without ploughing a bit back in or actively adding to it in any way, then we are its very opposite. That's what makes people decadent, all take and no give, leaves them with nothing to do except gorge.'

'Christ's eyes, the pair of you, help me!'

There was a pause in the conversation, that may have been either man wondering whether he heard anything, before it continued on similarly abstract lines.

'Tommy Atkins? No, I never met him, Mr Baxter; in my experience the British soldier at war was every bit as unpleasant as his German counterpart.'

In such pain that he briefly wondered whether he may actually have broken something in his body, the Colonel hauled himself to his knees and thrust his head out of the carriage door. His reaction to the sunlight that struck his face was positively vampiric. 'No, my eyes,' he groaned. 'Help me, you bastards, I've gone blind.'

No one moved and the Colonel opened his eyes again, the stinging still there but not as intense as when the sunlight had made contact. There, sat on a log, were the two conversationalists, bottles of Scotch in their hands. 'Oh my God,' the Colonel despaired, 'you're both high as kites.'

'What did you expect?' Baxter laughed, rubbing his stubble. 'A rescue party?'

'What's going on?' groaned the Colonel. 'I need someone to tell me what's going on, not this . . . mad-hatter's tea party . . . No, water, first water.'

The rail yard was scattered with the dazed bodies of men trying to do things – sleep, walk, drink – with faltering degrees of success, bottles of everything bar water changing hands.

'The water's yours if you can find it,' said Baxter as the Colonel clasped his stomach and, falling out of the carriage head first, vomited for a full minute.

'Where's everyone else?' asked the Colonel wiping his mouth on his sleeve, the smell of sponge cake baked in faeces wafting off him. 'What went on after I . . . dropped out? What happened to the others?'

'Our Terry Delaney's over there,' pointed Baxter, 'sat up there in that tree keeping watch. The Yank's lot have been arrested. We're lucky not to have been arrested ourselves, still might be depending on how stuff pans out.'

'Arrested? They broke up the centre of town yesterday, didn't they? We didn't, though, did we?'

'They certainly did,' butted in Mr Lang, 'but since I met your Mr Baxter an hour ago . . .'

'Was it that long?' asked Baxter.

'Long since when?'

'Since we started on the whisky. Did you bring it?'

'I'm a working man, what would I go to work with whisky—'

'Why aren't we at work?' interrupted the Colonel, suddenly aware that this question could hold the key to the others.

'Couldn't be there if we wanted to.'

'Why?'

'Dawson's posted pickets at the gates.'

'Pickets? What pickets?'

'Old Company men, which is the worst of it,' said Baxter sadly, 'posted at the gates with a list of people they're to shoot if they set foot on the site. Your name, you won't be surprised to learn, Colonel, features prominently.'

'Old Company men! God's balls, tell me you're lying, Baxter!'

'I wish I were, but I'm not. Though I grant you, it doesn't seem real to credit it. He's closed the whole place down for the day, and guarded it as he "re-organises"; but whatever that will involve, it won't include us, you can be sure of that.'

The Colonel felt as though he were about to fall over. For all his bravado, his tirades against Dawson, the general enmity towards all forms of working life and his promise to never set foot in the factory again, he had always believed the decision to leave the factory was his alone. Dawson's success at pre-empting him cast a very different light on matters, not least on the actual decision itself. The very idea of being *made* to leave the factory increased the place's appeal tenfold, transforming its status from a prison to an honourable place of employment.

It was obvious from Baxter's face that the same thought had occurred to him too. 'Funny, isn't it?' he said. 'Well not funny but mad. As much as I hated it, it was my job. And I never expected not to have it, much less be threatened at rifle point by men I'd gone toe to toe with for four years. Should have seen it coming, Colonel, but I can't help it, it sticks in your throat.'

'You can't fire me, I quit!' chuckled Lang. 'Bad as the bloody miners, you lot, always complaining about how dangerous your work is until they close a pit, and then all we hear is screams that your birthright's being taken away from you.'

'We should be running that place,' said Baxter, 'not being bloody thrown out of it.'

'That,' thundered the Colonel, in full possession of his voice again, 'is the greatest cunting understatement ever uttered, by Jupiter's bloody tusks, it is! "Sticks in your throat"? It makes mine burn! The man must be mad to think he can get away with this,' he continued. 'What does he take us for? Does he really think we'll take it lying down? Mad is what he is, abso-lutely clear off the page crazy.'

'I'm not so sure,' said Clubber Lang, this attack on the managerial classes reminding him of his place in Grumwood's hierarchy. 'I wouldn't be surprised if he had a fairly similar view of you. I've always thought of Mr Dawson as a canny operator who knows exactly what he's doing, so—'

'You keep out of it!' shouted the Colonel, pushing the small inspector of train yards over on his back, his boot catching Lang's head in a furious stamp. 'I'll have Dawson's guts for this! The shabby bastard – his guts!'

'Easy, Colonel, easy, it's not all bad news,' said Baxter raising his hands in a peaceful gesture. 'As it happens, we have some-thing we were saving for you. Terry!' Baxter called to Delaney, who had dismounted from his tree and was wearing his usual malevolent grin.

'Not all bad news, you say? Where's the good part in what I hear?'

'There's no good part in that; it's what you'll be able to see that should cheer you up. Take a look behind that carriage over there, next to the one you were kipping in. Here, come on, we'll take you round.'

The Colonel had no idea what to expect, but experience had taught him that 'surprises' usually fell flat if he was lucky, and were embarrassing when he was not. This applied particularly to those treats his friends assumed he would like, whether they were trips to army brothels or motorcycles, for the Colonel's range of interests was too narrow to hold up to the element of chance that came with any free gift. Death, in this sense, would have been the only surprise he would have welcomed, as it alone contained the certainty of asking nothing of him after its occurrence, or at least, that was his hope.

'I tell you, Baxter, waking up is a big enough surprise for me, without there being any need for this rigmarole.'

'Be calm and resist the urge to be yourself, Colonel, at least until you know what you're in for,' said Baxter, pushing him through the gap between the two carriages. 'I promise you you'll like this.'

'Games at a time like this, Baxter, you should know better . . .'

'Pick your head up and look, for Christ's sake!'

'At what? That . . . God . . . almighty . . .' It was the first welcome surprise of the Colonel's life; he tottered on his feet for a few seconds, before falling into Baxter's protective arms, his legs having given way under him.

'See! What did I tell you, you big girl!'

The sight that greeted the Colonel was one that had saved his life several times before in circumstances more dangerous than those he was currently in, and by virtue of its timely return, held the promise of doing so again. 'It's been a long time since I've seen anything so beautiful!' he exclaimed. 'What's it doing here? *What* is this wonderful machine doing here?' The Colonel shook his head and rubbed his eyes, quite unable to believe them. 'It's real. But it can't be. It must be Christmas; Christ's message couldn't be more gratefully received. How did you beautiful geniuses do it?' The youthful lift in the Colonel's voice spoke from the remains of his soul, as he bent down and picked Baxter up in a bear hug, the mannerisms and physical pain of a man much older than himself discarded in the face of his friend's unforeseen generosity.

'Don't let me take the credit, you great softie, it was all the diabolical Mr Delaney's idea, it shouldn't surprise you to learn!' joked Baxter as he wriggled out of the Colonel's grasp. 'I'm not mad enough to have come up with something this warped, couldn't be if I tried.'

Standing before them was a Crusader Mark I tank, the kind that had been used in the desert war, and the model all the men of T Squadron had trained in. Its condition, though not immaculate, was serviceable and, most tellingly, its ammunition racks were full.

'Yes, Delaney's the boy we need to praise or curse for this one . . .'

'There are two futures, Delaney my boy,' intoned the Colonel solemnly, a tear forming in his eye despite his best efforts at self-control, 'the predictable and the unpredictable and you belong to the unpredictable part. I asked you how, but sod how for the moment. Why?'

'I did it,' deadpanned Delaney, 'to show them what an Englishman can do.'

The Colonel was speechless. His one solitary tear was joined by others, and yet the Colonel did not cry, instead he allowed the water to collect in his eyes and make its own way down his face, the rest of his body unresponsive to the emotional pact between physical states and feeling. 'Of course you did, my boy,' he whispered, 'of course you did.'

He remembered now, waking in the night and knowing what had to be done. And he could not have been alone because Delaney had known too . . . they had all known . . . explanations were pointless, they were never alone because they were always a part of each other, always T Squadron, fearless and to the fore. 'By God, arrogance is only a problem when you're wrong,' the Colonel cried, thrusting his fist into the air with a flourish, 'and when were we ever wrong? Tell me the details, boys, the details!'

'Not a lot to be said about it, pinched it for the obvious

reasons, a good laugh and so easy to do, and because it had to be done,' said Delaney, seemingly unaffected by his friend's state of heightened emotion.

'But how did you get away with it, Terry my boy?'

'I had help . . .'

'Insiders?'

'Didn't need them. We are insiders. Marsh and Polly helped me, though, which is good of Marshy because he doesn't know the first thing about tanks. And anyway, he trucked us over to Bovington where they've been lining up for that big exercise the National Service boys are going to cut their teeth on. Neither me nor Polly had any real hope of getting hold of anything, there for the crack really, it was one of those ideas you follow through until you fail or are too tired to go further with, you know, like driving to Scotland or fishing in France. So it was a bit of a surprise for us too, all told. There they were, lines of these Crusaders sat outside the depot, all fuelled and ready to go for the exercise. Couldn't believe our luck, it was perfect. We took ours, armed her and brought her back here . . .'

'Wait a minute, are you telling me no one tried to stop you, that you rolled out of the place without a word?'

'The Scouse lad at the armoury wanted to know who we were, replacing blanks for live ammo and all, but I fobbed him off saying we're instructors; lads like that fear us anyway, can see we're veterans and that we know what we're doing. Absolute chaos there anyway, don't know their arses from their elbows, that lot.'

'And,' interjected Baxter, 'the sentries on the perimeter wanted to know why we were riding out on the thing twenty-four hours before the exercise was due to start . . .'

'Same thing again,' said Delaney, 'we're instructors. Delivered in my best square basher. Out on the road no one gave us any bother. With all the armour around here these past few years no civvy looks twice at a tank in a country lane.'

'So how did you get in?'

Delaney stared at the Colonel impatiently, the former's questions striking this man of action as pedantic. 'Hopped over the fence, of course, like we used to when we hit town and were confined to barracks. All old tricks, Colonel, nothing you wouldn't find in the manual, as prepared in 1066.'

'Unadulterated, lads, pure unadulterated, the best of the best, golden eggs all round. I didn't happen to give you the idea, did I?'

'Didn't need to. You remember what Moat said, that life would be a very different matter if it only lasted for one night? And all the things we would do if we didn't have to live with a tomorrow? I sort of got it from that place.'

The Colonel felt another surge of emotion accelerate through him, and to prevent a scene that would diminish him in Delaney's eyes for ever, quickly blurted out in regimental fashion, 'Mark and Marsh, where are they? You haven't lost any men, have you?'

'Marsh disappeared saying he had to help a lady fit a ladder into her shed, outstanding job apparently,' replied Baxter. 'Mark I don't know, can't remember really, one minute he was here and then I must have dropped off, though God knows where, and then he was gone . . . hope he didn't get himself picked up . . .'

'It's for the best,' said the Colonel gravely, his position and nickname aligned at last, 'I see this as essentially a three-man run, no sense in bringing any more of our own people into it than necessary.'

'That's what I was going to ask you about,' said Baxter, 'what we were going to do with it, because Terry . . .'

The Colonel raised his lower jaw in imitation of Churchill, or some less esteemed figure, and held a finger to his lips. Baxter stopped talking and turned to Delaney. They were all very excited.

'A simple question for you, gentlemen,' began the Colonel, staring into the middle distance. 'We have suffered at the hands

of an odious tyrant, of that there is no doubt. The question
is, does it make you angry or does it frighten you?'

'Angry,' Baxter answered, and made the motion of loading
a shell into a gun chamber.

'And you, Terry? What do you say?'

'Blow up the factory,' hissed Delaney, 'we blow up the factory.'

'Well done, man, spoken as a true soldier and friend.'

Baxter passed the whisky bottle to the Colonel; he was not
going to be the one to let his friends down at their moment of
need. 'To hell with them, the time-servers and clerks, let's blow
the shit right out of their arses. Clean through,' he said, intoxicated by camaraderie and Scotch.

'Then our path is clear, men,' said the Colonel, pointing the
bottle in the direction of the Fox Brandy plant. 'We attack at
once, we engage the enemy by surprise and we destroy him.
Any questions?'

No man made a sound, the afternoon sun sinking behind
the wall of pines that sheltered their tank from the town.

'Then, gentlemen, I give you glory,' cried the Colonel raising
the bottle in a toast. 'Glory, a fighting chance and the road
ahead!'

'Glory, a fighting chance and the road ahead!' they all
repeated. Delaney grimaced; the end was in sight and beyond
that nothing. He could not have wanted for more than that.

'Jesus,' smiled the Colonel wiping the spirit from his mouth,
'it's true what they say, isn't it?'

'What?'

'That there's nothing like a bit of a to-do to get your blood
going.'

'Always been that way for me.'

Nodding harmoniously all three men mounted the Crusader,
their war nearly over at last.

8

THE FINAL SOLUTION

'You look happy,' said Lord Ross to his daughter. The observation ought not to have been as unique as it was, but
Lord Ross could not recall a single occasion on which his
daughter, without prompting, had smiled at him since the end
of the war. 'Very happy,' he added, concerned that drawing
attention to the state might diminish it, 'and good for you, I
say.'

'I do?' Vivien asked in a tone verging on the coy. 'Look happy,
do I?' Her toast broke under the force of her knife as she smiled.
'Are you sure? I thought you said that I was in danger of looking
as old as the century itself.'

'You do. Look happy, I mean. Though Lord knows why you
shouldn't be. It's been all go in Grumwood, for once. I suppose
you've heard what happened in town last night, high drama if
the gardener is to be believed.'

'No, I've had a long lie-in.'

'Those men of Jack's, they went on the rampage, tore the
place up, that useless son of Grundy's had to be called from
Southcrawl; quite a performance by all accounts . . .' Lord Ross
paused. 'I heard that two of them, Jack's men, were here
yesterday afternoon . . .'

'They were, yes, they offered to gravel the drive.'

'What, again?'

'I know, we invited them in for tea instead.'

'Whatever for?'

'They knew Jack. I was feeling lonely and felt like talking
to them about him.'

'Of course.' Lord Ross rose from the kitchen table and walked over to the window. 'We were talking about him yesterday, weren't we?'

'And you were right.'

'Really? Remind me.'

'Yes, let the dead bury the dead. I need to see what happens next in my life. I'm glad you said so. Someone had to.'

'Do you mean to say that that . . . talk we had has actually persuaded you?'

'Let's say that I was ready to be persuaded.'

Lord Ross breathed in deeply and bent his head in what was meant to be a homage to Vivien's change of direction. 'That's splendid. I was afraid that I might have made a bit of a fool of myself. I'm glad you were able to see past that and . . . listen to what it was I was trying to convey.'

Vivien took a sip of her tea, without, to her father's surprise, removing the spoon.

'You do . . . seem different today, Vivien. The night's sleep's done you a world of good; you appear, how to put it, somewhat lighter than before.'

'Should I worry?'

'No, on the contrary, good for you!'

'You said the soldiers got into trouble last night,' said Vivien changing the subject back to one she felt a new-found interest in, 'not any serious trouble, I hope?'

'Oh yes, the soldiers. Nothing that great by the standards of a proper battle. I don't know all the ins and outs of it but Dawson's mixed up in it somewhere, I think, and some property was damaged . . . after he sacked some people.'

'Was anyone hurt?'

'Only the vicar, and then not badly, worse luck, though I think they did fight amongst themselves, which is typical of them, their trouble revolves precisely around that quality . . .'

'What trouble do you mean?'

'The underlying cause of it all.'

'Oh you've identified that, have you?' Vivien was amused,

the fate of Jack's men a personal concern to her now. 'This isn't a re-run of yesterday's speech, is it?'

'What are you alluding to?'

'How they're all noble savages who hate, and with whom you therefore feel a great affinity.'

'Did I really say that?'

'You did.'

'There's something to that, but it seems to me that a proper analysis of our problems would have to be a bit more far-reaching than . . . that sort of rant.'

'Really?'

'Of course, it's been obvious for years!' Lord Ross thrust his knife into the marmalade, his voice raised with passion. 'Obvious for years, Vivien. The rot didn't just start with Dawson and his ilk . . .'

'I rather thought we could blame him for most things.'

'It's true we can, but we've been preparing the way for his sort for years. Ever since the last war; that was when we lost our best, and the rest had their best knocked out of them.'

'I do hope this leads back to our miscreants . . . aren't they what we're talking about?'

'Of course, but not all at once! That war did for duty and trust, from then on it was rising living standards, better welfare and universal education all the way; suburbanisation in other words. The nation learnt how to read and write and with it came self-doubt. We got lost, so when war came again we were soft. The Germans should have won, they were better soldiers than us because soldiers is what they knew themselves to be, and we didn't . . . Think of all those cowards cheering Munich, that's where suburbanisation had taken us.'

'What were our men in uniform, then, if they weren't soldiers, Daddy?' asked Vivien her attention caught by some movement in the garden.

'Whatever they had been in civilian life, doctors, bus conductors, teachers, bank-tellers, soldiering being a rude interruption to their proper vocation, as far as they were concerned. That was the trouble with our citizen army, everyone still considering himself to be whatever he was in peace, and not what war demanded of him. But Jack and his boys, the men of *the elite formations*, they knew they were soldiers and that's why our "miscreants" are such trouble now.'

'I'm having trouble following you.'

'If war wasn't a wicked intrusion, but a true calling, then you're clear out of luck once your enemies are "beaten" . . . that's why they content themselves with meaningless little punch-ups, not because they're soft but because society is, soft and greedy.'

'You seem to be rather more sympathetic to them than usual,' said Vivien, her voice betraying that this attitude applied as much to her own feelings as to those of her father.

'Oh I'm not sympathetic as such, though you know I empathise between my predicament and theirs. My trouble is with our society that gets worse the further away it moves from what formed it.'

'Which is?'

'Killing and death,' Lord Ross responded cheerfully, cracking an egg open, 'what any society worth its salt is based on.'

'I think I'll leave you and society to it for the moment,' Vivien replied, pushing her plate to one side, a hope quite at variance with common sense suddenly taking hold of her.

'Will you be in for dinner? I feel quite up to it today.'

Vivien did not seem to hear her father, her attention the property of another, as she grabbed her coat and left the house through the servants' entrance.

Pleased that he had given a faithful account of his views, without the need for drink, Lord Ross helped himself to Vivien's uneaten eggs.

Scattered shadows had gathered round the men in the Crusader, disguising their faces to all but the most observant of watchers.

Shallow, who had been leaning out of his window smoking, was one of these, having already seen much that had puzzled, and then amused.

The wind had already dropped off when he heard a sound very like the engine of a Crusader tank propelling forward at top speed. Often haunted by the noises of shell fire or tanks, Shallow had ignored the evidence of his ears until the vehicle had come into view, riding round the corner as carelessly as the one he had trained in many years earlier, with Baxter and Delaney. To Shallow's amazement, Baxter was still the driver, his leering face sticking out of the hatch like a champagne cork ready to pop, as momentarily the two men made eye contact and, to their mutual incredulity, exchanged salutes.

Not one to miss out on protocol the Colonel had appeared from the commander's turret and bellowed, 'Ready and present for inspection, sir!' as though nothing could have been more common than this parody of normality, Shallow returning the salute as would a general reviewing a parade.

No sooner had the tank passed, than Shallow had noticed a figure in a demob suit running up the lane. It was unmistakably Mark Polly, who he had lost in the drunken fog of the night before, his collar up in what Shallow assumed was a bid to pass unnoticed. Like the others, Polly had looked up as Shallow looked down, and salutes were again, for no good reason, exchanged, Polly returning his rather nervously. Without stopping Polly had disappeared round the corner on a mission that appeared as urgent as the next drink would have normally been for Shallow. Uncharacteristically, however, Shallow did not feel like drinking at that moment, or even dwelling on his second favourite pursuit, the contemplation of wasted time. The wound in him had, if anything, closed, and whereas it would usually open in accordance with the amount of energy he was ready to spend on any worldly activity, today it was curiously unstimulated. For an hour he had leant there, smoking out of the window, expecting his troubles to slowly catch up with him, but they had not, a feeling of benign restfulness taking their place.

So this, thought Shallow, is how people get better, not through effort or improvement but through waking up to find a particular weight lifted because, for all one knows, God has willed it so. He chuckled and lit another cigarette off the butt of his last, seagulls swooping at the fallen ash in expectation of food. To his pained and not altogether unwelcome surprise, he was also ready to entertain a desire that even a day ago would have felt preposterous. He felt, in a vague way, eager to make love again, and eager to do so to Lou Dawson in a way that was highly specific.

The thoughts of the men on the Crusader, though less carnal, were similarly light and unburdened by the finality of their task. As in the approach to any battle, the terrible time of waiting was over and, with it, the fear of not knowing what was going to happen next. Here, together in a tank once more, the questions they had all failed so miserably to master no longer mattered to them, nor even the answers they held in low contempt. Truly, if the tank were to career off the road killing them all in an instant, none of its occupants would have minded, the last moments of their lives having been the most vital.

'Death' yelled the Colonel over the roar of the machine, 'was never as bad as having your legs blown off or catching shrapnel in your testicles.'

'No chance of that happening today,' growled Delaney thrusting a shell in the barrel of the gun.

'Certainly not, you need to be going up against equal opposition to incur that kind of injury. Dawson hadn't thought of that, had he? Pickets, my arse, he should have got his hands on a howitzer or anti-tank gun, the amateur. No, I'd be surprised if we weren't looking at zero casualties. Get your preparation done and go in with superior firepower, and that's half the battle won. Monty taught us that. No, there's no reason to fear death today, lads, no reason at all.'

Delaney, who unlike the Colonel had never lain awake at night agonising over his physical extinction, adjusted his sights and called back, 'A fast thing that makes a big difference, death.' It was as much as he had ever thought about the subject.

'But only to you,' chimed in Baxter. 'When you're dead the woods, towns and streets are still the same except for one thing – you're not there any more.'

'Remaining alive, eh?' shouted the Colonel, his towering presence in the commander's hatch the fulfilment of a life-long ambition. 'What's your excuse, eh? I'm clear out of them . . .' His words were a mordant inversion of what he truly thought, for at that moment he felt as though they would all live for ever, the battle between tank and chocolate factory ridiculously one-sided. 'Take her right to the front, Baxter, there's no better way to hit the place than by knocking the front door down . . . and then watching the whole filthy edifice collapse.'

Baxter slowed the tank down as the chocolate factory came into view, a thin line of cleaners sleepwalking their way home, the tank barely registering with them as it moved towards its objective.

'Up closer, Baxter, closer so we can have a clean shot at one of the chimneys!'

The guards Dawson had employed at the entrance glanced at one another and, without saying anything, laid down their arms and rushed through the open gates.

'Look at 'em go, pelting towards the rear; drew the line at dying for him, didn't they? Should machine gun them by rights, the traitors!'

'Didn't think of getting any ammo for that.'

'Less chat and more splat!'

Turning the tank at an angle, Baxter rolled through the gates into the main forecourt area, all his drunken tiredness evaporating through this effort of concentration.

'That's it, that's it. Beautiful. Now line her up, Terry, line her up and don't miss.'

'I never do.'

The first shell flew straight through the main chimney, slicing the top off it like a boiled egg.

Without waiting to admire his work, Delaney reloaded the gun and fired again, smoke pouring out into the cramped little cockpit.

The silhouette of a figure that may have been Dawson vanished from the gallery overlooking the yard as the second chimney collapsed, toppling down onto the factory and court-yard below; a vanquished symbol in the final battle between the stubborn and the wrong.

'Bingo,' said Baxter, 'two direct ones, two hits.'

'They always are hits,' said Delaney. 'We've done the body-work. We've done for the plant.'

'Beautiful,' muttered the Colonel, watching it burn, 'too beautiful . . . to know what to say.' The grim hypnotic effect of the fire had put an end to any thoughts of further action or, fatally, escape. 'Rest in peace, Moat, we're avenged,' he announced skywards, his words drowned by the whine of approaching sirens.

By the time Shallow reached the floodplain it had already begun to grow dark, red flashes and rings of smoke from Fox Brandy faintly visible behind the wall of trees that sepa-rated the scrub from the forest, though it would have taken lightning to deflect Shallow's attention away from the one he had come for.

'I knew you'd be here,' said Lou Polly, 'you must have known too.'

Shallow, unsure of how to reply in kind, but certain that asking Lou how long she had been waiting was too prosaic in the circumstances, asked, 'Why would I know you were here? No, I know, of course, it's why I am too . . . I should, well, we both wanted to see each other, didn't we?' Not for the first time in his life, Shallow's articulation of a situation was lagging hopelessly behind his grasp of it, and he frowned so Lou would at least realise that there was better to come.

Lou, again correctly perceiving Shallow's lack of experience in moments rife with romantic potential, took his hand and said, 'It feels, to me, like the decisions I've made in my life haven't had as much impact as the ones I should have made because of love.'

'You're lucky,' he replied. 'With most women it's the other way round, the decisions made in love govern all the others they make in life, it's probably where their freedom seems most obvious . . .'

'Well I haven't been like that,' said Lou, her eyes not straying from their target, 'but I feel like something, perhaps even God, is giving my life permission to go forward again. So far I've reaped what I've sown but I've never planted anything good before—'

'I – no, sorry, go on . . .'

'My husband, he's not really the monster he's allowed himself to be made out to be, though he is in a way, but not in the way people think. He's only a very, very weak man, and he won't change, it goes too deep in him. I know you have what you think are problems, but they're like mine; I mean, they can be solved, can't they?' She paused, hesitant of talking an opportunity away. 'Go on and lie to me if you want, but just for once can't the lies be the truth?'

Shallow pointed at a pony trying to drink from a pool of stagnant water. 'I don't need to, my problem is like his, I drink when I don't need to. I pretend my problems aren't alcoholic because I'm ashamed of how much I *like* alcohol. That's what I thought to begin with, anyway. It was because booze *was* the problem that I pretended it wasn't, then I figured that perhaps life was the problem, but now I realise that it's me. I'm the problem because I like alcohol and dislike life. But even that doesn't feel so bad now . . . it doesn't seem so important that I think anything now.'

Lou rubbed her hand against Shallow's cheek, her words at variance with this tender act: 'I don't want to be looked after by him any more. I don't want to feel sorry for him either. I'm not ruthless, but I've always been selfish when it comes to men; you see that, don't you? That I can't go on staying with him just because I feel sorry for him. You see things,' she said, pulling her chest into his, 'don't you? Because you've been so unhappy like me.'

'Yes,' said Shallow, happily unreconciled to his lover's misery, 'because none of us want all this,' he pointed at the sky above them, 'to just mean *that*.' Lou followed the line of Shallow's hand down to the pile of empty bottles and an old newspaper that he had left there the night before.

'Oh,' she said, 'I see.'

The pony had meanwhile moved from its puddle to the rubbish and, having sniffed at it curiously, had begun to lick the bark off the tree Shallow and Polly had leant against the night before, after having left the Colonel. 'They all look grey when it gets dark,' he said of the pony, 'I think I'll miss them after we go.'

Resisting the impulse to ask how or where, Lou replied simply, 'Yes. But not as much as me.'

Slowly they walked back towards Shallow's lodgings, both afraid that if they moved too quickly or turned the wrong way everything would be spoilt and they would fall off the hill they knew they had yet to climb, its summit still so far from hope.

Despite the noise, Delaney thought he could hear the Colonel muttering into his ear, 'Why does anyone do it, die in battle? They say there're social reasons, whatever they are; national reasons, I understand; and damn it, against Japs or spear-chuckers, reasons of race; perhaps perverts do it for a stiffy, war a useful cover and all that, though Moat, he killed because he just didn't give a fuck any more, same reason he killed himself . . .'

But this was a conversation that had occurred days ago. There were no more words. Only a courtyard covered in rubble, a discarded tank and pools of burning chocolate.

The Colonel had been lying a few inches away from him but a military policeman was now dragging him across the fore-court, handcuffed, his friend's last deranged words heard over the fire alarm and screaming sirens; 'I hear her beating, lads, I hear Drake's Drum beating . . .' And Baxter, only a few feet behind the Colonel, punch drunk and singing, 'What shall we do with the drunken sailor' the bruises on his face driven in like fresh tyre tracks on mud, 'earliiii in the morning . . .'

And then they came for the raging Delaney, brandishing their truncheons, knowing that he would not 'come quietly' and accept the inevitable any more than the last defenders of Berlin had thought of surrendering to the Russians. The repercussions were too terrible. Instead he would 'resist arrest', just as he had resisted everything else in a life many would have judged not worth living. All that remained, and would always remain, was to get even, even more even than he had already got, so that as the truncheons came down to smash his face he would welcome them, even *want* them; want them to smash the face that began the war, want them to smash Lou's face, to smash Dawson's face, to smash his own face and, ultimately, every fucking face in the world.

'Jesus, this one's smiling,' said an MP wiping his truncheon clean, 'lost bloody consciousness smiling.'

'Nutter,' answered his companion sympathetically, 'a bloody carrot-crunching nutter.'

Behind them the flames thundered on, their ghastly vapours filling the air like a gross presentiment of what they were designed to become, cheap chocolate biscuits, their owner's dreams of his New Forest Empire too great for his tired subjects' warrior souls.

Vivien Ross was not sure why Mark Polly was standing in her garden, but hoped it was because he had acknowledged the strength of their attraction for one another. A day ago this revelation would have surely embarrassed her, but today it did not arrive as a revelation. It had been hard ignoring her obvious feeling for Polly, and Vivien did not intend to be hard with herself any longer; for in a language Polly would have readily understood, she had wanted to get her hooks into him for some time.

In his hand he held what appeared to be a gas canister and, in a moment of blind panic, Vivien feared that it may have been a prop in a suicide attempt, the idea coming from her clear and intuited understanding of his unhappiness. As she strode towards him, the 'canister' transpired to be no more than a bottle of wine, unopened, 'A present,' he said, his expression of unmitigated terror requiring only a smile to become one of vast ease.

'For me?' said Vivien, allowing her long fingers to hold Polly's, as he brought the bottle towards her. 'Really, Mark, for a brave man you can quiver like the most awful coward.'

There was a warmth in Vivien's tone that rendered her hard words harmless, the same warmth Polly had detected the night before but had wanted to believe in too much to trust.

Glancing behind her, and then thinking better of discretion, Vivien appraised the situation long enough to gauge that she would have to make the next move, Polly's confused presence in her garden constituting the first.

'There's something you ought to know, Mark. I loved another man with all my heart and I think part of me always will. By that I hope you understand that I'm making a tacit admission that I'm ready to love again.'

'That's all right, Miss Ross; if you couldn't love someone else properly, you wouldn't be much good to me, would you? I mean, if you could love someone else that much it proves your love's worth it . . .'

'Call me Vivien now and yes, that really is a very wise way of looking at it,' said Vivien, trying hard not to laugh. Polly too was suppressing a testy smirk, neither of them troubling to speak until this feeling passed, if ever it would. They had mentioned love and it did not seem strange.

Vivien watched his shoulders relax, comfortable for once in her company, and saw him for what he was: naked in his lack of ambition, humble prospects and self-lacerating fear of the world. He could offer her nothing but a life in which she would be appreciated and in which nothing would ever change, and that this prospect secretly pleased her, and that she would marry him she already knew. She knew also that she would have to suggest this herself, for though she could cure him of fear, he would never be without his shyness.

'I think the past, if you don't mind me speaking of it, has weighed down heavily on us both,' she said. 'I've lived in it because I was afraid of feeling this powerfully again.'

'I think of it every day. Dream of it most nights.'

'Haven't you had enough of it, though?'

Polly nodded. 'More than.'

'I also . . . I've always been afraid of people finding out what I'm like, afraid that they wouldn't like me if they knew—'

'I thought people would think me strange if they knew me too well.'

'You interrupted me, Mark – a precedent! They say familiarity breeds contempt . . . I've never had the time or opportunity to test that before, but it seems to me a risk worth taking. I think risk was what I was missing, not my past, but not seeing you even though you were here, missing you for that strange reason that makes us all human . . .' Vivien's voice trailed off, Polly was eyeing her shamelessly, unencumbered by social restraint. 'What are you thinking about, Mark?'

'You.'

Without waiting to remember how, Vivien held Mark's face in her hands and kissed him. The first contact was small but warm, her cold lips feeling the long-awaited thaw; the second more assured, as they took one another's hands and stepped into the glorious reality of the present.

ACKNOWLEDGEMENTS

Thank you to my editor Jocasta Brownlee, my agent Eugenie Furniss, Peter Barnes, who advised me to make a mess this time round and whom I wish was still here, and to those friends and colleagues who, had they been born two generations earlier, would have probably populated the pages of this book.